The Engine What Runs the World

Quinn W. Buckland

The Engine What Runs the World

© May 18 2018 Quinn W Buckland

All rights reserved.

Cover by. Mnsartstudio

ISBN: 978-1-9993961-0-7

First Edition

For my late Grandpa, Wayne Hodges.

You've always supported your grandkids, no matter the endeavor. You were an inspiration to us and to me.

It's only right this first one is for you.

We miss you.

1

Her name was Blue.

Smoke Callahan closed the door behind the woman who had entered his home office and let out a sigh. Many times Smoke had been given jobs to track down and retrieve a missing person, typically a runaway slave or a kidnapped concubine, but rarely a free woman. Smoke didn't particularly care for such work, but a job was a job and bills needed to get paid.

He scratched his head lightly and sat in the plush chair behind his cluttered desk. His powder-blue typewriter sat front and center, while on either side papers waiting to be filed leaned from several haphazard piles. Near the right edge of the desk, a closeglass - a large piece of convex glass connected to a small bone handle - bore the impressive amount of grime that could only form after months of living underground. Next to it sat a pristine feather pen and inkwell. Other odds and ends of a private investigator lay strewn across a candlelit room.

Though usually dry, the air in his office had gained a low level of moisture, as if large amounts of water had recently evaporated. Not likely, as the only water that ever made its way to the underground came from the water pipes. One of the copper pipes serving the first level of the Underground had burst, letting large amounts of steam into the air. This moisture brought the smell of rot and mould alive. Though his small home of synthetic wood could never rot, the place still smelled as if something grew inside the walls.

As the woman entered she introduced herself as Marla Lang. She stood half a head shorter than Smoke, taller than most women. The scent she wore smelled of honey and flowers, a scent not normally found in the Underground. She gazed at Smoke with her large green eyes as he introduced himself; her eyes were red and puffy, clear signs of recent crying. She held her dark hair in a tight bun, a style more for convenience than fashion. The dress she wore was a dark blue and made from a fabric Smoke hadn't seen before. In her hand was a small hemp bag with what looked to be a few small objects he couldn't quite make out.

As Marla sat on the opposite end of the desk, Smoke marked her every move; the way her eyes narrowed at the sight of the clutter, though widening when she saw his revolving pistol or the bottles of mulch liquor. She lifted the side of her dress as she sat - Smoke assumed to allow for greater movement and comfortability.

Smoke opened the top drawer of his desk. Sliding a set of lock-picking tools aside, he pulled out a pair of lookers wrapped in a soft cloth. He wiped the lenses free of any dust that had settled from the air and placed them on his face. He then pulled out a large, faux-leather bound journal with onionskin paper. He opened the book to the blank page in front and slid a well-used pad behind it. All used pages had been carefully removed, leaving little evidence they had been there at all.

He stoically peered across the desk at Marla; he dipped his feather pen in the inkwell and patiently waited for her.

"Thank you for seeing me," Marla began. "My sister Blue is missing."

Smoke began to write, "How long has she been gone?"

"A week."

"Tell me about your sister," Smoke said without looking up.

"What do you need to know?"

Smoke looked up from his pad. "Anything you can tell me," he said softly. "Age, height, weight, who she hangs around with, what level you both hail from, her personality, if she has any enemies or friends. Anything like that."

Marla's eyes narrowed and her lips pressed tighter after Smoke mentioned needing to know the tower level. "She's sixteen, around nineteen hands tall, just under nine stone," Marla paused for a moment. "She wasn't the sort of girl who had many friends; she was more of a solo book person. We're from the second above, though she spent a lot of her time on the surface. I'm not entirely sure what I can tell you of her personality; she was a lone girl. That said; it's hard for her to have enemies when she spent so much time by herself."

Smoke sighed, "That's really not a lot to go on. Is it possible she'd have met someone on the surface or even in school?" Smoke paused for a moment. "People in tower still have schools right?"

Smoke's ignorance seemed to have amused Marla - a small curl of a smile formed on the edge of her lips as her eyes softened, "Yes Mister Callahan, we have schools."

Smoke matched her amused visage to keep her from becoming defensive, "It could be possible that she was approached by someone at that time."

"I'll be honest; I didn't know her well, at least not since she grew up," Marla confessed. "It is absolutely possible she met someone that took her," Marla slightly cocked her head to the right - she looked as if talking about it had given her a thought.

"She may have run away. She basically shunned the family business that brought us to the second above."

Smoke grinned, now they were getting somewhere. He scratched down the notes as quickly as he could, "Why would she shun the family business?"

Marla gave him a half shrug, "I don't know."

Smoke had to fight to stifle a small bit of laughter. Instead he raised an eyebrow, "You don't know?" Smoke inquired. "Miss Lang, I need to know everything you can tell me. Even the smallest detail could make finding her all that much easier."

Marla hung her head, "My family's business isn't exactly what some would call morally sound, I'm not going to get into what it is if it's all the same to you." Marla gave Smoke a pleading gaze before he waved her to continue, "Blue took issue with what we do. She looked like she'd come around though."

Smoke shrugged, "Sometimes people deceive you, especially when others are capable of doing bad things to get what they strive for?"

A poor choice of words. Marla's eyes narrowed again, her nostrils flared and she crossed her arms. "What do you know about my family or what they strive for?" she spat.

Smoke raised his hands in surrender, "Nothing, nor do I have intentions of asking. It's not my place to learn the inner workings of a family unless it's important to the case. If it does become important to the case however, I will have to start asking the questions you don't want asked."

Marla glared at Smoke for a moment before giving him an angry nod. "It is still possible she has been kidnapped; she left everything behind. She wouldn't have left without at least a book, some skins and some survival supplies. It's hard to say where she could have gone, but without skins she couldn't have gone up, so she'd have to be at least on the surface or lower."

Smoke smirked; it was always easiest when people came to the natural conclusion instead of wasting his time with conjecture. "Is it possible she won't want to come back?" Smoke asked.

Marla shook her head, "It doesn't matter, she needs to come back home."

Smoke gave Marla a scowl, "You should know - I don't like delivery jobs. Especially if the package is liable to fight back. This could cost you."

"We'll discuss price later."

Smoke shook his head, "We'll discuss price now, or I'm going to have to pass."

Marla glared at him from across the table. The small wrinkle above her nose gave her a look of dangerous attractiveness. If Smoke had been a younger man he may have tried wooing the woman. Her face soon softened and showed a look of lament as she hung her head, pressed her lips together and closed her eyes. "I don't have the authority to discuss price Mister Callahan," she said before opening her eyes. "My parents will discuss price with you."

Smoke resisted the urge to tell Marla that she was much too old to still be going through her parents. He dismissed the thought, leaving it to the sake that tower life was likely much different than the underground in more ways than just social status and luxury.

"Alright," Smoke said after a moment of thought, "how do I speak to them?"

The demeanor Marla had carried with her from the moment she walked through the door changed. She went from bereaved sister to stoic business woman in the blink of an eye. "They are currently working on getting you a one-time pass to the second above. It'll take a couple days to arrive, but you'll be able to talk to my parents."

"Excellent," Smoke said in the same calm manor he'd been using the whole time. He wasn't about to change how he held himself just because she did. "In the meantime, do you have anything of hers that I could look over and use to give myself a place to start?"

Marla nodded and raised the small help bag, "I have her diary, an image and a voice image."

Smoke scratched the back of his head, not out of itch but out of habit when he got less than what he needed. "Well, that should give me a start," he said trying to hide his disappointment. "If possible; once I'm in the second above I'd like to search through her belongings. In the event she did run away and was not kidnapped there may be something that could give me an idea as to where she might have gone."

A look of nervousness crossed Marla's face for a moment, Smoke made a mental note of that. "I'll run that by my parents," she said with a shaky voice. "I'm not guaranteeing anything though."

"Without seeing her personal space I may not be able to figure out where she's gone. You would be surprised what a person gives away with their room or their possessions."

The visage of Marla's face showed absent contemplation. She nodded slowly before standing, "That's all I have to say for now."

Smoke raised an eyebrow in suspicion, "All you have to say, or all you're permitted to say?"

Smoke expected a scowl; instead Marla gave him a soft smile before stepping toward the door. Smoke placed the feather pen back in the inkwell, stood and moved across the room. He opened the door for the young woman, "I'll find your sister," Smoke said in an attempt to reassure her. "There's never been a missing person I haven't found."

Marla stepped through the doorway. She turned toward Smoke and raised the corner of her lips, "I know," she said. "That's why I came to you."

She turned away from Smoke and walked down the dirt road toward the market and the lift. He closed the door after her and let out a long breath. "What am I getting myself into?" he asked out loud.

He walked toward the haphazard desk and sat behind the typewriter he used only to fill out his documentation. He scrolled a piece of onionskin paper through, then reached into the hemp bag and pulled out the small image of Blue.

Blue was pretty for a girl of sixteen. She appeared older than her age, though not wearied, a lifetime of good nutrition and a total lack of stress could have accounted for her appearance. In the background of the photo stood two trees in a field of green grass. Smoke believed both the grass and the trees to be artificial oxygen converters that pumped excess carbon to foundries to create manufacturing resources.

Grass was common on the surface, though there wasn't a tree to be seen. The only place a real tree could be seen was on the surface, and even then you'd have to go to one of the many great forests; not possible for anyone in his area. Even those in the towers would have to spend a great deal to see a real tree; a family from the second above would not have the skins.

Smoke opened the bottom drawer of his desk and pulled out a folder made from a thicker version of onionskin paper. He pulled his feather pen from the inkwell and wrote the job number as well as the missing girl's name on the top flap. He slipped the paper inside and left the desk

He tucked the image away in the folder and proceeded to pull out Blue's journal. It was an expensive notebook bound in real leather and filled with paper from trees. The cover alone would have cost a small fortune, nothing to someone in the tower, but inaccessible to someone from the surface and lower. "She's got expensive taste," Smoke whispered to himself.

The paper made from tree pulp felt smooth on his hands, it beat the translucency of the onionskin paper he was used to. He read each word slowly and carefully, making sure he didn't miss anything she had written. There had only been four short entries, the earliest entry showing him it had been recently bought.

Date: 25/05/4324/1594NE

I bought this journal today. I guess I can use it to write down my thoughts and shit like that.

Date: 01/06/4324/1594NE

I had a bit of a shock today, a woman came to me and offered me a job. She'd seen my report on how a healthy and sustaining underground could greater benefit the surface and the towers. I'm not sure if I want to know just how she got her hands on my report.

She said she knew I was only sixteen but it didn't seem to matter to her, she was very interested as to what I could bring to her business. I'm not sure exactly what her company does, but she did say she's not situated within the tower. That alone intrigues me, especially if she's able to come and go from the tower as she pleases.

I told her I would think about it and I promised never to speak or write any details, and I aim to keep my word. I don't think I'm going to take it though. It'd take me places I never thought I'd ever see, but I have to ask myself, are these the sights I actually WANT to see? Many of these areas are dangerous beyond all measure. I don't even know how I'd ever survive to get to the place of new employment.

I don't think I'm going to take it. When she meets up with me next week I'll let her know.

Date: 07/06/4324/1594NE

The woman convinced me to reconsider. I almost want to take it, especially after she explained what I'd be doing. It would certainly be easy on me to leave. I'm done with my family and I'm done with the second above. I want to see new worlds... It would be quite the adventure. Even if I don't take the job I think I'll still go see the underground. I'm actually excited for the first time for as long as I can remember.

I'm still going to think about it though. She gave me until the end of the month to come to a decision.

Date: 27/06/4324/1594NE

I've decided I'm not going anywhere. Too much has happened that I'll probably get into later. My parents dropped one fuck of a secret in my lap a few days ago... I can't even handle it. I'm blown away and astounded that I hadn't caught on before, everything points towards it. I can be such an idiot. I can't write it down, I can't even speak it. I guess it would make it too real. I can't stop the tears from falling; it's been this way for days now. They told me to take all the time I needed to come to grips with the secret and I intend on it.

I hope she understands. I hate to disappoint her, but I can't be allied with her.

Smoke flipped through the rest of the pages looking for anything else she may have written or any drawing or anything that could be on the pages; he soon put it down. A kidnapping seemed more like a possibility. Maybe the woman who had offered her the job wouldn't take no for an answer. He wished she'd have gone into more detail about the job or where it was located.

Smoke stretched his back and shoulders before returning to the journal. Something seemed off. The way she wrote about her family suggested that it was still possible for her to be a runaway. The clues pointed toward a kidnapping and he would treat the case as such, though he wasn't ruling out runaway just yet.

He placed the diary in the folder along with the image. The final item in the bag was a small voice image - a small vinyl disc, roughly the size of his thumbs, with several grooves within containing the voice imprint of Blue Lang. The disc was much too small for the voice imager he kept beside his desk. He needed the one he kept in his storage room, not a difficult task, just time consuming.

As Smoke entered the storage room he sneezed. A fine layer of dust covered the vast majority of the objects that lined the shelves and boxes. He placed a small-cloth over his face as he gazed over the contents before him. The shelf was a mismatched collection of random items he'd collected over the years. Some were still useful, though some were sentimental junk. The set of brass goggles, decorative short-blade and tall-hat would be useful once cleaned, though the set of broken lock picks, and collection of voice images from Glass had been kept because he couldn't bear to get rid of them.

He eventually came across the voice image player and picked it up. The small yellow box showed a speaker and a slot to enter the voice image as well as several buttons to play, stop or pause the recording.

He sat back at his desk, put the voice image in the device and pressed play.

A long stream of clicks and pops were heard as the voice

image waited for its user to start speaking. "My name is Blue Lang," the young woman's voice began. Smoke could hear a hint of panic within her voice. "If someone has found this and is listening to this, it means I am no longer home and I will have no intentions of returning. There could be several reasons to this; I could have left to pave my own way, distant from the pressure of being under my family's collective thumb. I could have been kidnapped either along my way after leaving... meaning she got to me..... Or... or I've decided to take the job offer. There's no way anyone would be able to find me."

Smoke could hear Blue's sense of urgency in her voice as she spoke her words. She was a young girl doing her best to keep her cool while frightened. Her voice gave everything away.

"Not that my death would give them pause anyway. I know I sound like some angst-riddled teenager, but I assure you this is not the case. My family has a secret that can't be repeated out loud. It'd shock the world to its very core. As dramatic as it may be, it is true and I will not speak it nor will I write it. It's too much to fall into the wrong hands. This is why I need to go, this is why I may get kidnapped, and this is why my time at home is coming to a close.... one way or another."

"Fuck," Smoke swore.

"In any case, I'm signing off now. This is Blue, bye."

Smoke massaged the area between his eyes, frustration was beginning to build. It was confirmed she had left home of her own free will. If she had been picked up along the way it could make things a little easier. Lift drivers were more observant if someone was being brought to the underground against their will. The problem was how far she could get before being picked up.

Through Marla, he knew she would have no skins, or at the very least a quite limited amount so she wouldn't be able to leave the immediate area; all she'd be able to do would be to go further down. He sighed in frustration as he ran his fingers through his thick black hair. He didn't want to have to go searching the lower levels. If he could avoid the Cartel leaders of the fourth below he'd be more than happy. Somehow he didn't think he'd be so lucky.

Smoke cracked his knuckles, and then placed his fingers on the keys of the typewriter.

From the desk of Private Detective Smoke Callahan

Month: 07 Day: 07   Year: 4324/1594 New Era

Name: Marla Lang Job Number: 0006543

Job: Missing girl, Blue Lang

Job Details: Blue Lang, missing for a week. Sister seems to believe Blue to be kidnapped, though upon reviewing the evidence presented it is clear that she had left home of her own free will.

Described to be age 16, 19 hands high and slightly under 9 stone. The image provided shows long black hair, narrow eyes and straight teeth. She doesn't seem to have any real distinguishing marks on her face.

Extra Notes: This case seems to be filled with red flags.

Starting with the fact that Marla was unable (unwilling?) to talk price and seemed to be close-lipped on a few matters, let alone angered by having to answer others gives me cause for concern. The lack of clues they'd given is also alarming. If the price is right I'll take the job, but if I continue to meet resistance I may have to turn it down out of principle. I'll have to wait and see.

Something that concerns me is the contents of the evidence presented. I would have a hard time believing the family didn't go over what they'd brought me. They would know Blue ran away. Why would Marla try to sell me Blue was kidnapped? There are a lot of questions that need answers.

Smoke cracked his knuckles and pulled the paper out of the typewriter. He placed it in the folder along with the evidence Marla had given him.

He grabbed a bottle of mulch liquor and took a large drink. The alcohol burned as it flowed down his throat and left his breath tasting like the mossy booze. He pulled the image of Blue from the folder and took one final look before slipping it into the inside pocket of his longcoat. It was possible this would be a difficult case that could take an awfully long time to complete, especially if she made her way to the lower levels in the underground.

He yawned as he left his desk and walked to his bookshelf. The books that lined his shelves contained secrets of the human body, practical information about lock picking, subterfuge and secrecy. He had a few books that explained the psychology of the human mind and how people think. There were books that outlined the history of the world reaching all the way back to the 21st century, aptly named the 'Age of Interest'.

He picked up *The Age of Interest* then continued to browse the titles. He soon found the book detailing a list of the major families of the tower. He grabbed the book and walked to his bedroom. He placed the books on the bedside table. He would need to research the Lang family, provided they were even mentioned in the book. It could wait until the morning however.

Smoke locked his front door and placed the heavy shutters over his windows, blew out the candles that lit his front room, and made his way back to the bedroom. He undressed and crawled onto his foam mattress.

He opened The Age of Interest and flipped through the pages detailing the history from two thousand years prior. He enjoyed looking at the pictures of the people of interest: the superhumans, the vampires and werewolves, all those creatures that no longer existed in the world. They fascinated him to the point that he wished he could have seen one, at least once in his lifetime. Yet he was thankful he hadn't. Those days were dangerous, and many people had lost their lives while the heroes fought the villains and the hunters stalked the creatures.

The only upside would have been the magic. While not accessible to the majority, it had been used quite prominently to shape the world and the cities within. While a small trickle of the original magic still existed, the users were very few. Smoke retained some of that magic, though his abilities were limited and weak.

He soon slept - the book still open on his chest.

2

The pass to the second above arrived two days after Marla had given him the case. He didn't waste any time after receiving the pass to getting everything ready to go to the surface.

A day later Smoke stood in the center of the tower on the surface floor. He could see everything was polished white and immaculate. The room lacked any distinguishing markers or scents, making Smoke uneasy.

He pressed the pass to the sensor and proceeded to push the button to the second floor. He smiled as the lift opened and he walked inside. Smoke marvelled at the advanced technology the tower had in comparison to the surface and the underground.

The underground allowed anyone to live on any floor provided they had the skins; though many lived on lower levels due to inescapable poverty. People were able to move freely between the floors, provided they had the skins to survive; no keys or passes required.

A bell chimed as the steam hydraulic lift came to a halt and the doors opened. He stepped out of the lift and walked forward into a perfectly white hallway, the only distinguishing marks being the red stripes where the walls met the floor and ceiling. Smoke had to wait for a moment for his eyes to adjust to the brightness of the light and the oddness of the hall.

Once Smoke started down the hallway he could see small black symbols on the walls. They were few and far between; the mansions in the tower were just as long as they were wide. He looked at the symbol on his card, six black crescent moons in the shape of a floral circle. He had yet to come across it, instead seeing arrows in the shape of a tree, a cylinder shape and what looked to be a man in a cowl.

He'd turned several corners before finally coming to the desired symbol. He pressed the card against the floral pattern and watched as the symbol lit up with a brilliant red hue. He could hear a chime ring throughout the residence through the hidden door.

Soon the ringing stopped and the door opened, revealing a male house servant. He was dressed in a black livery uniform with thin scarlet trim. He was a young man - couldn't have been more than twenty. "Can I help you?" he asked with a soft voice that told Smoke he had recently been taken from one of the lowest levels of the underground and had yet to feel any sense of superiority.

The boy looked nervous, the sweat beading from his forehead as he awaited Smoke's reply.

"Yes, I'm Smoke Callahan. I'm expected," he said, bringing his thumb to his chin. A hand sign for the servant to know he was under Smoke's protection while he was around.

The servant nodded as his demeanor eased and spoke, "Please wait here while I confirm this."

Smoke placed his hands in his jacket pockets as the door closed behind the servant. He let out a long drawn out sigh. He didn't like waiting, especially for people of the tower who he believed had nothing better to do.

Several minutes had passed before Marla c
He knew the servant would have informed Marl
of the household almost immediately. This was
he knew it. They'd make him wait and show hin
important they are than him. He'd play the
though he could see the power moves becoming
patience growing thin in the near future.

"Mister Callahan, please come in," Marla said with a false grin.

The male servant came to Smoke's side as he entered the household. "Your jacket and hat sir?" he said in his soft voice.

Smoke obliged the servant, for no other reason than to prevent the servant boy from a scolding or a beating after he'd left. People from the tower were reputable for getting rid of servants, even if the fault was with the guest.

The removal of his jacket and hat was to show to the servant Smoke had his interests in mind. He didn't want to be rid of his personal effects, but he could do without them as well. He pulled the closeglass, voice imager, and a small onionskin notebook from his pockets. Stealthily he watched Marla and her reactions to his items. Her demeanor was calm and remained unchanged to the untrained eye. He noticed the small and swift furrowing of her brow and the tips of her mouth move from a slight smile to a mild frown and back in a matter of moments. She didn't think much of him and seemed inwardly disappointed he hadn't caused any faux pas as of yet.

Marla smiled slightly as she asked, "Can I get you something to drink Mister Callahan?"

Smoke shook his head, "No thank you. I should start my investigation. If you could lead me to her room I-"

"That can wait," she said a little more forcibly. "Come, I want to speak with you first and foremost."

Smoke shrugged and followed Marla toward a study that rfed his entire house. She approached a wooden counter ...1owing several decanters filled with varying types of alcohol. He pressed his lips together and took in a deep breath from his nose. This was going to be a test of some sort. It wasn't one he was familiar with and as such wouldn't know what to do at any given moment. Marla poured a golden brown liquid into two tumbler glasses with two cubes of ice each. She handed him one and watched for his reaction.

He passed the glass under his nose and covertly sniffed the liquid for any noticeable traces of poisons or concoctions. All he could smell was the strong odor of the whiskey. He knew his suspicions towards a possible poisoning had been unfounded, but the test had been a force of habit from his early years.

He gave Marla a coy smile before taking a sip from the tumbler glass. The taste of the whiskey was exquisite, the best he'd ever had. He wasn't surprised a rich family had good whiskey, but instead that such a taste could even *exist* in a whiskey. He had the test figured.

Marla laughed as he purposely sighed in pleasure. "It is good," was all she said before taking a sip from her own glass.

"I apologize," Smoke said, making it seem as if he were trying to hide embarrassment. "I don't typically lose myself so quickly and easily."

Marla smiled softly at Smoke, "Do you know why I brought you in here Mister Callahan?"

Smoke shrugged, "I have my guesses, but I'm not thinking they're particularly correct, unless, perchance they are."

"There are three reasons. I've already seen two of them."

Smoke raised an eyebrow as he took another sip of the best whiskey he'd ever had.

"I wanted to see you make a faux pas so you'd relax. I knew you'd be on guard the whole time here and that just makes for dull company."

"Fair enough," Smoke replied, now hiding resentment.

"Besides," she continued, "If you're rigid, you could miss something. You'd be too busy trying to be composed and proper."

She wasn't entirely correct in her assumptions though; the alcohol could dull his senses and relaxation could result in his mind getting lazy. Being on edge could have the same result - she was right about that, but the overall mood he was in wouldn't have affected his job. He chose not to voice his opinion and instead asked, "What's the next reason?"

"I wanted to show you what you could have when you find my sister. The money we'll pay you could give you the finest of whiskeys, rums and spirits."

"And the third reason?" Smoke asked intrigued.

"To tell you I've looked you up. I know you're the kind of person who befriends hitmen and whores. You're the sort of man who knows slavers and members of the Cartel. To be fair, I did this before I hired you."

"If it makes you feel any better it's all on the level," he said. "As a private investigator there are many times I need to go into deep and dark locations and do some not—so-nice things. It pays to have friends and acquaintances that can help."

"That kind of help is never free though," Marla said as she leaned against a table that looked to be made of hard wood.

Whoever she had hired to investigate him must have done a poor job. There were parts of his life she didn't seem to know, including his abilities. If she wasn't aware of them, he wasn't going to give them up either. It was best if she believed he only knew people from the lower levels; even more so if she didn't know about what he could do.

"True, but the odd favour or small skin stipend I'd pay doesn't mean much to someone like you. You're looking for results - I can guess by any means necessary."

Marla began to laugh, "You're certainly not far off Mister Callahan,"

"Please, call me Smoke," he said looking to the doorway, wanting to get to his work.

"Your connections are exactly why I came to you. You've got people who know things, people who see things. You're not afraid to do what needs to be done no matter the cost. I need to know the man I hire is going to do whatever it takes to find my sister."

"It's good you came to me then," Smoke grinned. "Now, about my payment."

Marla gave Smoke a sly smile, "My parents will discuss that with you when they arrive. Until then, I'm sure you have questions you'd like answered."

"Very well," Smoke huffed as he opened his notebook. He pulled a feather pen out from his back pocket as well as a small wax-sealed inkwell. He broke the seal and dipped the feather pen inside. "Did you read Blue's diary and listen to the voice image before delivering them to me?"

"I did not," she said with a confused look. "My mother gave it to me to give to you. Was there something in there?"

"Oh there was something there alright," Smoke said as he scratched notes into his book.

"What was it?" Marla asked.

Smoke returned the same slyness Marla had given him

earlier, "I believe that should be something I discuss with the people who are actually paying me."

Marla scowled, "They don't care as much as I do about finding Blue."

"Nonsense darling," a woman's voice said from behind him.

Smoke turned to see an early middle-aged couple enter the study. The woman reminded Smoke of something from one of his books. She was dressed in a tight black dress with a long white fur coat. He couldn't tell if the fur was actually real but based on the odour, he assumed it to be genuine. She held a long black cigarette holder with a half-burned cigarette in the end of it.

The man was dressed in the way Smoke would have imagined, not to the same stereotype his wife portrayed, but close. He wore a black suit with a white shirt and black tie. "You must be Smoke Callahan," he said with a large, toothy grin, "I'm Row Lang and this is my wife Mullholland."

"It's an honour to meet you," Smoke said shaking Row's hand.

"You're here looking for clues as to what had happened to Blue?" Mullholland asked.

Smoke nodded, "I was just asking your daughter questions."

"I'm sure we can shed some light and give you an idea as to where to begin." Row said with a smile.

"Alright," Smoke began, "But, before we begin, there is the matter of my payment.

Row nodded, "Explain."

Smoke frowned, "I may have a long way to go, and I may have to pay a lot of people off to keep an eye out for her. So, there will be a payment upfront, and then the rest of the fee to be paid in full before I deliver her to your home."

Row nodded and looked to his wife, "Dear," he said, "what do you say to paying Mister Callahan six hundred upfront?"

Smoke almost choked when they mentioned the number. He'd never had a job that paid so much, much less that much upfront. Mulholland lowered her chin, "It's a good price. I'd say his full payment should be a million skins for finding her. Two for delivering her alive."

Smoke cocked his head, "I appreciate your offer, but that is much too much."

"Nonsense," Row chimed. "Two million if Blue is alive, a million if she's dead. If you can't find her, you just keep the six hundred."

"What's to stop me from taking the six hundred and running?"

"Your reputation," Mulholland replied.

Another power play. This was all posturing and no substance. Marla hadn't been far off when she had said they care less about Blue's safety than her. Although, she seemed to care more for her appearance than her sister as well. If they actually had any real concern he'd have investigated and been gone already. Row and Mulholland wouldn't have kept him waiting, Marla wouldn't have forced a drink on him. This case looked too strange and with the two million skins added into it, it was way too good to be true.

"No," Smoke said, "I will not take your case."

What do you mean you won't take the case?" Row said, his face growing red.

"What I'm saying is - there has been no part of this case that hasn't aroused suspicion, right from day one. This is way too obvious a parade, a show for the neighbors who will start asking questions. I won't take the case."

The Lang family stared at Smoke stunned. He doubted anyone had ever spoken to them in such a manner. Pride filled Smoke and gave him a sense of delight.

"Declining the offer is not really an option, Mister Callahan," Row snarled. "The moment you stepped into our home you agreed to take it. You just didn't know it. You come in here and fill our house with your filth; we never would have allowed such a thing to happen if there weren't conditions."

"What are you going to do? Ruin my reputation?"

"No, no," Row replied. "Something even worse."

Row and Mulholland both placed four fingers on their biceps. Panic filled Smoke as they made their actions. "We know your little underground hand signs," Row said. "We also know who you are and your past. You'll take the job, or we hand you to the Cartel."

Smoke snorted, nodded and grabbed for his feather pen. He dipped it in a nearby inkwell and began to write. "I understand you have had a chance to go over your daughter's possessions before they had been delivered to me."

"Of course Mister Callahan," Mullholland said as she poured herself a whiskey, seeming to forget the entire past conversation. "We needed to be sure nothing sensitive left the house."

"So you know of the job offer Blue had received?" Smoke asked as more of a statement.

"Yes we know," Row said as he hung his head. "We didn't know until we went through her stuff, but we know of it. We don't know what the job was though."

Smoke watched their reactions to his questions to see if they were hiding anything. There were excellent liars in the world; he imagined the Lang family among them. If they had been lying, they didn't show it. "She talked about a family secret."

Mullholland laughed slightly, "Honey, when you're an old family like ours there's always going to be secrets. It's inevitable."

"I hope you understand if we don't disclose what that secret is; it'd cause quite the embarrassment," Row said quickly.

Smoke nodded, his anger beginning to dissolve, though caution remained in his head. He didn't need to know some ancient secret to find their daughter, and it would be best if he didn't antagonize them further, despite the obvious flaws in certain things they'd said. "I'll take a look at her room now," he said quietly as he finished writing his notes.

Marla nodded, stood straight and led him out of the study and through several winding hallways, never once looking at him. He knew the tower had been wide, but he didn't expect it to be this expansive, especially on the inside. She eventually led him to a large empty room. The bed was large and looked comfortable; a few dressers and a bookshelf filled with teen romance books and other pieces of fiction lined the walls, the room was bare otherwise.

Smoke sighed and pinched the bridge of his nose. "I expected more," he removed his fingers and entered the room. "There's next to nothing here. I don't know what I'll find, but I'll try."

Smoke pulled out his closeglass and removed the cloth covering. He inspected the immaculately clean dresser and perfectly made bed, "Have the servants been in here cleaning?"

"Not since she'd disappeared."

"There's not a speck of dust on this dresser. She's been missing for what, a week now right? There should be dust here."

"The air filters remove the dust from the air. It prevents us from breathing it in and getting sick."

"It's a wonder you managed in the underground," Smoke

muttered under his breath. He didn't think she heard him. If she had, she showed no expression.

He looked around the room for anything out of place or odd and found nothing. Everything was immaculate; the bed was perfectly made and the floor showed no sign of dust or dirt. He sighed and shook his head, "Did she have any skins on her when she left?"

Marla shook her head, "Not a whole lot. She'd be able to live comfortably for a few days on some of the upper underground levels, but she'd be out of skins by now."

"Well that's a plus and it confirms what I'd thought before."

Marla gave him a confused look. "What do you mean?"

"She wouldn't be able to leave the area. I only have ten miles squared on each level to search. It seems like a lot, but when it comes down to looking through nine underground floors as well as the surface I'd rather search one area than the entirety of the planet. It just really narrows it down."

"So you have everything you need?"

"I think so yeah," Smoke said, placing everything back in his pockets.

The bedroom had been a bust. The tower's obsession with cleanliness had removed any possible chance he'd have had of finding a clue. A part of him even believed the room had been cleaned several times before he'd been in. A thought in the back of his head even told him several personal belongings had been removed from the room. If that were the case, the investigation may be as much a fool's errand as he believed. But, on the off chance everything they said was true; he couldn't turn the job down.

"Wonderful," Marla said showing a look of superiority.

She handed Smoke a small cloth sack. "What's this?" Smoke

asked, slightly confused.

"This," Marla said, "Is a holding sack. A relic of the old magic days. Basically you can put as much as you want in the sack and it will never fill. To get what you want, you just have to put your hand in and think of what you want. It'll come to your hand instantly."

"So my six hundred starting pay is in here?"

"Yes," Marla said, "Now that you've been paid, I must now ask you to please leave our home. Sport will be waiting by the door with your jacket and hat.

In a blur of moments Smoke had been shuffled out of Blue's room, down the hallways and out the door. He put his jacket on and placed his hat on his head. He put his hands in his pockets and angrily proceeded toward the elevator.

3

Smoke stepped out from the tower to the bright sunlight of the outside world. He had gotten used to having a dirt ceiling supported by a series of metal beams and a thick mesh over his head; he couldn't quite grasp the height of the sky. He looked up into the clear blueness of it and sighed in awe.

He took in a deep breath of the clear air that had not been first pushed through a series of filters. It had a sweet smell with the scent of plant life. He peered to the west and saw a small farm he assumed to be family run. It was large enough to feed a small family with enough effort and a good work ethic. He could see cattle in the distance grazing on the grass as well as sheep in a pen surrounded by wooden planks and chicken wire. He didn't know where a farmer would get chicken wire these days, but he chose not to dwell on it. It wasn't important.

He walked to the east back towards the lift. A tall shack stood beside the lift platform to protect the delicate equipment from the harsh weather conditions. He saw the old man who had brought him from the first below exit the shack holding a wrench. He was short and stalky with large shoulder and arm muscles. His face was covered by a long silver beard that Smoke admired.

Smoke shook his head slightly as he moved towards the elderly man.

"Hello again sir," the old man said with a smile. "Didn't think I'd be seeing you again today. Most who come to the surface tend to make a day of it."

"I still intend to, not that I'll have a choice," Smoke said with a friendly smile. "I'm just checking to see when you plan to make the trip downward."

"I'll be going first thing in the morning, just after sunrise."

"Alright," Smoke said happily. "I will see you then."

"I'd recommend getting yourself a place at the inn for tonight," the old man said as he stared off into the distance. "It's supposed to rain and you wouldn't want to get caught in the middle of that, especially this time of year."

"What time of year is this?" Smoke asked.

"It's autumn," the old man replied. "It's nice and warm in the day but cools off pretty well at night. Believe me when I say you don't want to be caught in the rain."

Smoke nodded his head, "Alright, I'll get a room. Where's the nearest town?"

"It's a small town about two klicks north of here, just behind the tower. You should be able to get a good meal and a place for the night."

Smoke nodded and began to turn away, "Sounds good. I'll see you in the morning."

The old man nodded while looking at the lift and he continued to work on the contraption.

Smoke turned and walked the short distance to the farmhouse. He'd talk to them first to see if Blue had holed up there for a night. From there he'd walk to the town and rent a room. He didn't want to sleep outside no matter the weather. A soft bed or even a bed with a slightly higher comfortability than the ground would certainly be ideal.

The farm was quaint and cozy for a small family. A two story house made of what appeared to be real wood and a metal Smoke believed to be tin. The windows looked to be made of glass instead of the clear plastic the underground often used. The front door had a happy vibe with the words 'A Happy Family' painted across the door.

Smoke knocked on the door three times and waited. He didn't know if anyone would be home, but it was worth a shot. It didn't take long before he heard movement from within the house. He could hear someone walking up a set of stairs before the door opened; on the other side stood a young woman with black hair and large green eyes. She gave Smoke a look of utter confusion, "Hello?" she said as she opened the door fully.

"Greetings madam," Smoke said as he removed his hat in politeness. "My name is Smoke Callahan. Would I be able to ask you some questions?"

The woman nodded, "What's this about?"

"I'm a private investigator," Smoke said sincerely as he pulled out his badge. "I'm looking for a young woman and I'm checking everywhere I can for any leads and information."

The woman gave him a nervous glance, "Is this girl in trouble?" she asked, her eyes giving away more than she knew.

Smoke smiled softly and shook his head, "No," he said trying to calm the woman. "Her family just wants her to come home."

She looked around for a quick moment before motioning Smoke to come inside. The place was quite tidy, better than he had expected. He didn't know much about people on the surface, but he had always believed them to be a little disorganized. He was pleased to see he had been wrong.

He looked to a small toy chest in the corner of the room before looking back at the woman, "You have kids?"

The woman looked back toward Smoke, "Two of them, a boy and a girl."

"How old?"

"I don't see what this has to do with your investigation," The woman replied with a slight hint of annoyance.

"I'm just asking questions," Smoke said. "I am letting myself know the person I'm questioning. It's a common practice; at least in the underground."

"You're from the underground? What level?"

"First," Smoke said as he searched for any alarm or distrust dissolving from her face. He didn't feel it pertinent to flash the hand sign for indication. Not being from the underground she wouldn't have understood anyway. He could have told her about how he grew up on the fourth below, though she wouldn't have understood that either.

"So you're not too different than us," she said showing the beginning of a smile.

"The only real difference is the lack of sky for me," he said with a slight laugh. "I've been up to the surface a few times and I still can't get over how high the sky really is."

"I'm sure you'll get used to it in time," she said as she grabbed two glasses from a cupboard.

"I'm sure I will," Smoke replied quietly. "Is your husband out working?"

The woman poured herself and him a glass of water, "Yes, though he should be back anytime now. It's pushing dinner time."

"In that case I won't keep you long," Smoke said with haste as he pulled out his notebook. "Was there a young woman who stayed with you for any amount of time?"

He already knew the answer since he'd been invited into the house, but he wanted to be sure she'd comply. The woman handed him the glass of water and sat down at the kitchen table. Smoke joined her as she said, "Yeah, there was. She said someone would probably be coming after her. We expected the tower officers or someone like that."

"I can assure you I mean her no harm," Smoke said softly. "I really just need to find her to bring her home."

"How much are they paying you?" The woman asked with a sly smile.

"I'm afraid that is not up for discussion," Smoke said matching her smile. "Could I get your name for the records?"

"Season Weaver," she said with a smile. "My husband's name is Paul and my kids are Harrison and Kitten."

Smoke wrote all the names down. He didn't need all the names, but if she was willing to tell him, he'd write them down. "Did the girl happen to give you her name?"

Season nodded, "She said her name was Blue. Nice girl; didn't say much but was very polite."

"Did she say where she was going?"

Season shook her head, "Not directly. We knew she was staying only the night so she was more than likely going to the underground, but that's about all I know."

Smoke took a drink of the water. It had a sweet taste to it with a slight tinge of metallic. The water had copper traces in it from what he could taste, but had been more or less covered by a mixture of sugar and soaked fruit. It tasted good regardless of the copper; it was better than the water below. "That's alright,"

Smoke said, "I have a direction now. I will get out of your hair."

Season smiled, "It's no bother at all. I'll assume you're going to want to go back to the underground tomorrow?"

"That I am. First thing in the morning."

"You're welcome to stay here. We have a spare room we allow people to stay in if they are going down. Provided they actually look like good people."

Smoke finished his glass of water and stood, "No thank you," he said calmly. "I am going into town to see what I can learn from there. There's a good chance Blue had gone there to get supplies after staying here."

Season nodded slightly, "Alright," she said, standing. "I hope you find her. She's a good girl and I don't think she's fully prepared for the underground."

"She struck me as a smart girl; I don't think she'd go too deep. So long as she's on the first three floors she should be okay if she keeps her head down."

Season didn't reply as she followed Smoke to the front door. He reached for the handle just as the door opened. He stood face to face with a large muscular man who stood at least a foot taller than Smoke. "I didn't know we were expecting company," the man Smoke assumed to be Paul said with a massive grin.

"I was just leaving," Smoke said as he moved to allow Paul through the door.

"You sure you wouldn't want to stay for dinner?" Paul asked. "Season is an excellent cook."

"I don't doubt that," Smoke said with a grin as he looked Paul up and down. "I really should be going though."

"This is Smoke Callahan," Season said to her husband. "He's investigating that girl Blue who stayed here last week."

A look of surprise flashed across Paul's face. "Is she alright?" he asked, showing concern.

"As far as I know she's alright," Smoke said as his smile disappeared. "Though I am just trying to confirm, and bring her home."

"Would you at least like to take a look at her room?" Paul asked.

"Your wife said you allow people to hold up for a night all the time. I don't think I'd be able to find anything. Besides, I already know where she was headed."

"Nobody's been here since she left." Paul said as he removed his boots. "Please, feel free to check the place out, you might find something anyway."

Smoke shrugged as he moved from the doorway to the kitchen. He followed Paul to Blue's room. He didn't think to ask if anyone else had stayed, *though why would he?* The admittance that people stay here often had already told him he'd not find anything concrete, even if nobody had stayed since they would have cleaned the room and prepared it for another lodger.

The room Blue had slept in for a night was pretty bare. The bed had been made and everything looked clean. "Have either of you been here since her departure?" Smoke asked casually.

Paul shook his head, "No, she made the bed and did all the cleaning herself. She was probably one of the best who've ever stayed here."

Smoke nodded, lacking any sort of surprise. He scratched the back of his head and brushed his fingers through his hair as he walked from the room. "There was nothing in there," Smoke said.

"I guess this was a waste of your time then," Paul said hanging his head. "I'm sorry."

"Nothing to be sorry for," Smoke said with a smile as he tried to reassure the man. "It was worth a look."

"Well, okay then," Paul said with a smile.

Smoke liked the hulking man who stood before him. He and his wife were simple farming folk who did what they could to get by. He respected that and he didn't want to hold them up any longer than he had to. "I should get going."

Paul nodded, "Alright. It was great to meet you Mister...."

"Callahan," Smoke reminded him.

"Callahan. Please come back again. You are always welcome."

Smoke smiled as he nodded his head. He shook Paul's hand before leaving the farmhouse.

The sky had begun to darken by the time he made it to town. He took in a deep breath as he watched the clouds form and darken. The old man had been right. It was going to rain.

He could see a large wooden sign with the words TOWER'S SHADOW scrawled across it with black paint. He laughed to himself slightly as he thought about how many towns out there shared the same name. It wasn't an especially clever name but an apt one all the same. The tower stood next to it casting a shadow across the town.

He walked through the town, seeing nobody on the streets. He passed several buildings that seemed abandoned, including the shop that would have sold supplies. Smoke frowned as he realized he'd missed his chance to see if she had been there.

It wasn't until he reached the inn that he began to hear signs of life. To the side of the inn he could see another small shop; this one however looked to have had people in and out in the last few days. He'd have to hunt down the shopkeep to see if Blue had come this way before descending into the underground.

He opened the doors and stepped into a barrage of beer, cards and people. The smell of alcohol and sex filled the air as he heard people laughing and grunting as they played cards. He could hear the slightly muffled screams of a woman in the middle of an intimate ordeal and wanted the man to feel he was doing a good job.

A small band played on a makeshift stage. The singer was a heavy set man with a gravelly voice that paired well with the slender redheaded woman beside him. The rest of the band played a wide plethora of instruments including a violin played by a tall man with a neatly trimmed black beard, kettle drum played by a short tough looking man, a piano played by a woman with short blonde hair and a guitar played by a short fat man. Smoke smiled as he listened to the music, they were talented at their craft.

He sat himself down at one of the very few vacant tables and flagged down the serving girl. She was tall and slender with a sense of power about her. It explained why the place seemed to be in such good shape and everyone seemed to be obeying order. Her hair was long and golden brown; it had been tied back to prevent it from swinging into people's food and drink. "What can I get you?" she asked without a smile.

"I'd like a drink of ale, something good, whatever your cooks are making and a room for the night. If possible I'd also like to speak to the shopkeep if he's available. "

The woman nodded, "Alright, that'll be thirty skins. If you have it."

Thirty skins was a lot for a meal, a drink and a room. At least it was in the underground. Smoke nodded and produced three small pieces of purple tanned hide from his pocket. The woman gave him a smile and took the skins. "The shopkeep is at that table over there. I don't know why you'd want to talk to him; his store's closed and he aims to keep in that way until morning."

"I'm not looking for supplies," Smoke said as he eyed the shopkeep.

"Figured I'd let you know," the woman said. "Just in case."

She then turned and left to fetch his drink and meal. As she walked away he could see her in his peripherals look back and give him a smile. She didn't realize he had been looking.

Smoke looked to the shopkeep again, this time taking in a better look. He was a large burley man with a thick black beard and long, well-kept hair. He reminded Smoke of a man who should be more of a smith than a shopkeep.

Smoke gave the serving girl a look and showed her to hold his ale until he returned to his table. He would be speaking to the shopkeep. She gave Smoke an understanding nod in response before he stood and walked toward the large man. He took a seat and looked the shopkeep in the eyes. "You the shopkeep?" he asked, already knowing the answer.

"Shop's closed for the night," the shopkeep said softly.

"I'm sure it is," Smoke said as he felt the corners of his mouth give away his slight amusement. "I'm actually here to ask you a few questions."

"What sort of questions?"

Smoke reached into his longcoat and pulled out the picture of Blue. "I'm looking for this girl. I'm wondering if she has been through your shop in the past week or so."

The shopkeep took the picture and stared at it for a moment. "I haven't seen her," he said softly.

"Is yours the only shop in the town?"

"The only functioning shop," the shopkeep said. "Old man Cavers had the shop down the road, but nobody took it over when he died and mine came to be the only one running."

coming to the first below. The serving girl did the same as she did last time, showing him her cleavage; this time when she stood straight she gave him a wink and placed a small folded piece of real paper beside his plate.

He unfolded the paper and read the note. 'Your room is #5, talk to the barkeep and he'll give you your key. He already knows your face, you shouldn't have any trouble. I will be there after I'm done work. If you want me, take the note with you. Show me you took it. If not, leave the paper on the table and I'll leave you alone. I don't need to know your name, nor do I plan to give you mine. Anonymous is more fun anyway.'

Smoke smirked and read the note a couple more times before placing it back on the table. He hadn't decided as of yet if he would take the company. It had been a while since he'd known the touch of a woman, but at the same time he couldn't afford to get distracted. He mentally applauded the woman for her brazen attempt at silent seduction. She knew what she wanted and she wasn't going to be asking herself 'what if' later.

He took the iron knife and fork and cut the sausages into small bitesize pieces. He popped one into his mouth and felt as the hot meat juices erupted on his tongue and flowed down his throat. It was a taste he wasn't familiar with. It had a bit of a salty flavour along with the taste of being a domesticated animal. He eventually narrowed it down to pig as he finished the last of the sausages. He didn't think pigs existed anymore, but here was his proof.

He poked his fork into one of the slices of carrot and ate it. He smiled as the buttered carrot rolled around his mouth as he chewed and filled his taste buds. He didn't know who cooked the food, and frankly he didn't want to know. All he cared about was whoever they may be; they were excellent at their craft. The ale may have been better in the underground, but the food was not even close to being comparable.

Once he'd finished his plate he pushed it away. Once the serving girl came to retrieve the plate he showed her the piece of

Smoke smiled and stood, "Thank you for your time. I apologize for interrupting your meal."

"Wish I could have been more help."

He took another look around the room. Nobody but the shopkeep seemed to have noticed him; if they had, they didn't seem to care. He was just another face of many in the inn's tavern. He walked back to his table and sat.

The serving girl noticed and walked toward him. She placed a large mug of dark ale in front of him. As she set the mug down she bent over, giving Smoke a good look at the space between her sizeable breasts. This was intentional on her part; she could have placed the mug without bending over quite easily, but the woman wanted to be seduced and Smoke was a man she hadn't met before. He was alone and non-threatening, an ideal mate for a night…. at least so he assumed.

He thanked the woman and pretended not to notice. If she did something similar when she brought the food he'd consider taking her up on the nonverbal offer. Provided he didn't decide to just eat and go to sleep.

He took a drink from the mug of ale. It was bitter, not near as good as the ale he'd come to love in the underground. It hit the spot though and gave him the desired effect of mild intoxication. As he continued drinking he could feel the effects becoming more prominent; this was a good thing since it made the ale taste better. The mug was large, big enough to be considered a stein. If it had been made of stone or had been ornamental he would have called it as such. The mug was made of synthetic plaster; it was cheap and suited for a place like this. Cheap mugs meant the place didn't lose many skins when people got drunk and rowdy and broke things.

When the serving girl returned she brought him a big plate of potatoes, carrots and two large sausages on an iron plate with iron cutlery. Smoke hadn't seen that much food on his plate in years, not since his time in the fourth below, not since before paper. He smiled as he placed it his pocket. He could see the woman get red as she noticeably tried to suppress a smile. She took his plate and cutlery and brought it back to the kitchen in the back.

He took another drink of his ale and grimaced at the taste. The heavy food had absorbed a great deal of the alcohol and sobered him up. He cursed lightly and took another drink and frowned as he noticed the bottom of the large mug showing the drink was coming to an end.

He finished his ale and stood from the table. The rush of what was left of the alcohol in his system rushed to his head as short lasting light-headedness. He smiled to himself as he collected the key from the barkeep and wandered to find his room.

The inn had been constructed of spare lumber a long time ago. Smoke entered the hallway, he could tell from the smell of musty wood and the departure of the scent of booze he had exited the tavern and entered the inn. He could see the above floor through the gaps in a few of the floorboards above him. The inn was two stories tall, something Smoke couldn't help but think as a safety hazard. All buildings in the underground were single level with the possibility of a basement if an owner was lucky.

His room happened to be on the first floor, something Smoke felt thankful for. He pulled the steel key from his pocket and put it in the keyhole. He heard the kind click of the lock as the door opened. The room was small, holding a small desk with a chair as well as a bed he could only imagine over a thousand people had slept in before him and a thousand more would after. Across the room a small bath sat with a tap overtop; a bar of soap and a folded towel sat on a small stand beside the tub. Smoke smiled to himself. A nice bath to clean him up would be in order, especially if a woman was coming to him later.

He walked into the small room not bothering to remove his boots. He sat down on the bed and let out a sigh. The mattress was soft and filled with down, real or not, he didn't care. He smiled as he thought about the sound sleep he'd get; though he'd have to be careful to not sleep too long. He stood and moved to the wash bath. He turned on the tap and watched as the hot water began to fill the tub. He walked to the front door and removed his boots before going back to the bed and removing his clothes.

A large mirror hung over the tub, Smoke looked at his naked body. He ran his hand down his abs and chest, after looking at the men from the surface he saw people who had been living comfortable lives and had the stomachs to show it. It was a rarity for someone to have any sort of wideness in the underground.

As he descended into the tub he saw the scars on his legs and scoffed at them in disgust. They had been from a long time ago, and while the skin had reattached itself to his muscles, the scars remained. He tried to take his mind off the scars, but every time he saw them he went back to his days on the forth below; the dark days of his childhood and teenage years. If he hadn't met her... he shook off the thought and did what he could to enjoy the hot water.

Plumbing was something accessible along all the floors and classes. It didn't matter where a person was located, they'd be able to access a bath or a functioning toilet. The ocean water that pumped through the pipes to the underground told Smoke the water was clean and good for bathing. So long as the pipes were regularly cleaned it wouldn't matter how much salt went through them. Bathing was a very important part of living in the underground, if a person was able to keep themselves clean their odds of getting sick decreased exponentially.

He found a small bar of soap on a ledge beside the tub. He ran it along his body and watched as the dirt and grime from the surface and the underground stained the water a brownish grey. When he had finally cleaned himself of the sweat and dirt, he climbed out of the tub and dried himself with a towel that sat beside the soap. He pulled the plug and watched as the water emptied from the tub.

He dressed and sat at the desk and opened his journal to go over his findings for the day.

It was still dark when Smoke awoke. He looked to the naked woman sleeping beside him. She had come in promptly after her shift had ended. They made a good night for themselves and had fallen asleep without saying a word to each other. He watched as her naked breasts ascended and descended as she calmly slept. He left the bed and began the search for his clothing. He dressed himself and gathered his equipment.

"Where are you going?" she asked as she woke.

"The underground," he said as he put his boots on. "I have a job to do and I can't stay."

He looked back to her. She had a smile on her face as she exited the bed, "Would you like some company?" she asked. "I'd like to go down to the underground, I think it'd be a great adventure."

Smoke shook his head, "I'm not on an adventure," he said as she dressed. "I'm looking for a young woman. I can't just bring someone along; I'm not expecting things to be safe."

"Then you're definitely going to need me," she said with a smile.

"What makes you say that?" Smoke asked coldly.

"You saw how people down there behaved with me around. If I can keep a tavern in line while it's filled with drunks I can keep you safe as well."

"Be that as it may," Smoke said as he draped the longcoat over himself. "The tavern has had you long enough for the people to know not to mess with you. Believe me, I don't doubt your abilities, I doubt the usefulness of those abilities in a different surrounding."

"You can't stop me from coming with you," she said as she climbed out of the bed.

Smoke was beginning to feel annoyed with the woman. He closed his eyes and took a deep breath and felt a primal energy fill him. "You're not coming with me," he said as a command.

"Give me a chance," she said as she began to dress herself.

Smoke's eyes grew wide. It was rare for someone to ignore his command. He began to go through the entire conversation in his head; everything that had been said and everything that could be said. There was no possible way for him to convince her otherwise. He didn't have time for an argument and there would be no way for him to stop her from following him, with the exception of physical violence, "Why do you want to go?" he asked.

She gave him an uncomfortable look, "I have my reasons. I know it'd make things easier if I told you, but I just can't right now."

"Alright," Smoke said with a sign of regret in his voice. "I'm only doing this because I know I'm not going to talk you out of this. However, just so you're aware, when or if you do decide to tell me what's going on, I am not going to be able to help you. I'll give you what you need to survive down there, but that's all. I am busy with my own job and that's just how it is."

She gave him a look of understanding as she walked towards him now fully clothed. "Sounds fair to me," she said. holding out her hand, "I'm Constance Ibot."

Smoke shook her hand, "Smoke Callahan. We should be off. We have a lot of ground to make before the sun rises."

Constance giggled, "So much for the anonymous tryst."

"We're on a timeline," Smoke said coldly.

Constance nodded, "I'll be back in a moment. I just need to

grab a few things. Meet me outside."

Smoke nodded as she left. As she left he looked up and down her shapely body. She'd fit in well in the underground. She had a toughness about her that said she'd be able to handle the majority of whatever came her way. It wouldn't be easy for her, but there was a chance she'd survive. He hoped they wouldn't have to go too deep; it would be a whole new world for her, not something she'd be able to gauge and react to as well as she expected.

He made one final look for his equipment, making sure he didn't leave anything behind. He didn't expect to be back, at least not any time soon, if ever. Once he was sure he had everything he exited the room and walked down the hallway towards the tavern. He gave the barkeep back the key and exited the tavern without stopping. He could have sworn the barkeep had given him a dirty look as he passed. He found a small bench and sat and waited for Constance to exit.

He didn't have to wait long before she emerged the tavern with a small sack across her shoulder. "Okay, let's go," she said with a grin.

Smoke looked at Constance as she walked up to him. She had changed from her tavern outfit made up of a tight cotton shirt and tight slacks; a tactic to get drunk men to give her more money. She now wore a loose fitting shirt with comfortable pants. This would go well with the underground. People never dressed to impress, but for comfort. "You ever been to the underground?" he asked promptly.

"A couple times," she said as she let the bag across her shoulder hang in her hand. "Why do you ask?"

"Your attire," he said with a smile, "It's suiting."

"That's good," she said as her grin became wider. "Let's go. We don't have long before we miss the lift."

Smoke nodded, "Indeed."

They saw the old man as they crowned the hill above the lift. He gave Smoke a smile, "I wondered if you were going to make it."

"I don't really have much of a choice," he said as he shook the old man's hand.

The old man looked over to Constance, "Hello madam, you weren't with the mister yesterday."

"I'm a new addition," she said with an excited grin.

"Let's get down to the first floor sir," Smoke said with a professional look. "Are you expecting anyone else?"

The old man shook his head, "Not that I know of. You're still going to have to wait. The sun hasn't begun to rise as of yet."

Smoke nodded and turned to Constance, "We're going to have to wait a bit."

Perfect," Constance said happily, "I have a question about the underground."

"Alright."

"I know the people in the underground have a sign language that's universal to all levels. I've seen a few of the signs, but I have no idea what they mean. If I'm to fit in I'm going to at least know the basics."

"Alright," Smoke said with a straight face. He put his forearms together in the shape of an X. "The forearms are a sign of respect, but how you use them means different things. This means good fight," he slapped his forearms together once. "This is a salute to a commander. You probably won't need it, but it's best so you don't accidently salute someone," he slapped his forearms together twice, "this is a sign of respect for someone. I'd recommend using them when I do it."

Constance slapped her forearms together twice, "Okay, I think I get it."

Smoke put his hand over Constance's right ear, "Do the same," he said calmly. She obeyed, "This means well met. It's a must and the one you'll probably use most often."

"Well met?" Constance asked confused.

"It basically means hello."

"Well met," she repeated. "This is good."

"Okay, now put both your fists on your biceps," he instructed.

She gave him a look of confusion as she obeyed.

"This will tell people you're from the surface," he said.

"Why would I want people to know that?" she asked. "Don't I want to fit in?"

"Yes you do," Smoke replied. "But you're not going to know the lay of the land, nor the general history of the levels. You may pass easily in the first two levels, but you will be spotted pretty easily from the third and lower. This is important because it'll show everyone you're from the surface but you care enough to learn our sign language. They will respect you for it."

Constance nodded, "Alright. Anything else?"

"This is all you will need for now. I'll answer questions if you have them, but a lot of the underground is pretty secretive. We don't share everything with anybody off the hop. You get me?"

Constance nodded, "I get you."

"Besides," Smoke said with a slight smile. "You'll pick things up pretty quickly. I have no doubt that by the time my job is done you'll be able to live comfortably in the first two levels."

"I don't think I'm going to want to do that," Constance said with a chuckle.

"Good," Smoke said looking toward the old man and the rising sun. "I think our ride is getting ready to leave. We should get going."

Constance nodded as she followed Smoke to the lift.

4

Smoke watched as the old man turned the crank to allow the lift platform to descend down the quarter mile shaft. The distances between the floors had to be sizeable to prevent cave-ins from large amounts of people in one place as well as the weight of the tower, though they varied in depth it was the distance between the first below and the surface that remained the longest. He looked over to Constance, who watched the massive chain that ran through the lift contraption allowing their descent.

The old man carefully continued to do his job in silence. A lift platform could typically carry a dozen people at a time, and in all the time Smoke had ridden lifts, not one person had ever spoken a word the entire time. The fear that the lift driver would lose focus or become distracted and send all riders to their deaths frightened everyone. Though there were safety precautions in place to prevent the platform from crashing down on the lower floor, nobody wanted to take the chance something could fail.

He looked back to the old man as he concentrated on his job and then back to Constance again. She had a look of amazement and wonder as she watched the rocks and dirt blocked in by closely knit wire mesh pass by.

It had taken an hour and a half for the old man to bring them down to the first floor. Smoke thanked the old man and walked away. Constance followed with a concerned look of confusion on her face. "Aren't you going to pay the man?" she asked.

"He doesn't get paid for his service, at least not in skins," he replied without looking at her. "When the drivers are down here they get their food and housing for free. Their lifts are also well guarded when they're getting food or rest, not that anyone would dare touch it to begin with."

"Why do they get so much for free?" she asked. "It looks like they get one hell of a deal for only a few hours of work."

Smoke supressed a laugh, "You really are from the surface. It is rare for someone to have the commitment to be a lift driver. It's a lifetime contract that cannot be subverted without great reason. They get treated as kings in the underground because they are our ticket to the other levels. If they all quit everyone would be trapped."

"Nobody would take it up?"

Smoke shook his head as he continued walking, "Some might try, some would succeed. Ultimately it would result in a few being able to move around and the rest being trapped. Did you notice we went at a constant pace the whole way? It was a safe and hazard-free descent. All because he knew what he was doing, he trained for it and built his stamina and endurance to be able to turn that crank no matter the weight on the platform. I thought you'd been to the underground before."

"I have," Constance said as she looked toward the floor. "It's just been a while and I always paid the lift driver during my trips up and down."

"Okay," Smoke said as if he were only half paying attention. "Just follow me and do as I say, alright?"

Constance nodded and followed. Smoke continued through

the well-lit market place of the first floor. The smell of freshly baked goods filled the air as he looked towards the bakers and underfarmers - people who had figured out a way to grow edible vegetables and fruits without sunlight or artificial light, all of which were aptly named darkplants. The darkplants typically had a bitter taste, but were filled with all of the nutrients the body needed. Smoke didn't know how they did it, nor did he really care. It didn't matter anyway; so long as he and everyone from the nine levels had something to eat he was happy.

The first two levels were known as the market places of the underground. The first level typically got some of the food from the surface, which was then mixed with the darkplants. Smoke had been surprised when no surface vegetation had been on the lift downward this time around, an oddity to be sure. It didn't bode well for the shoppers who would be looking for surface vegetables; though darkplant was a more than suitable alternative.

"Where are we going?" Constance asked above the sound of the crowd.

"My place."

Constance stopped in her tracks, "Why? I thought you were on a case."

Smoke stopped and turned to face the defiant woman. "I need to get some supplies. I don't think Blue is here on the first level. Regardless, I plan to take a look around, but I'm not holding my breath. That said, I'm going to need to pack a bag. Much like the one you've got there," he finished, pointing at Constance's pack.

"Okay," she said with a frown.

"What crawled up your ass all of a sudden?"

"The fact that I hardly know you and you're already taking me to your place."

"You chose to follow me," Smoke said dismissively. "You didn't have to do that. You knew me even less then."

"The personal home is more intimate," she finally said with a small voice. "Besides, you said to follow you."

"Is this because we sex'd?" Smoke asked, shocked, "Woman, get this clear. What we did last night was fun and a great release, but that's all it was. I'm not going to get possessive nor am I going to go domestic on you. You're free to come along if you want; you're free to sex if you want, you're free to leave if you want. I'm not going to ask or force it on you. I have a job to do and I don't have time to be going rounds with you."

He could see her face darken and Smoke could see the idea of leaving enter her mind. Suddenly the beginning of a smile appeared on her face as she lightened up a little. "Good," she said as she continued walking.

"Fucking women," Smoke muttered silently.

They'd been at Smoke's home for about twenty minutes before he finally told Constance to stay put. This would be the last chance for a real rest she'd get so it would be wise for her to get it while she could. Constance didn't fight back or try to argue. Smoke was thankful she didn't, about as thankful as he was she continued to stay. The more he thought about it, the more he knew having someone like Constance around could be an asset. A second set of eyes, and a self-proclaimed skilled fighter could always be utilized.

He made his way to the lift between the first and second floors. He chatted with the lift driver for a little while asking when he'd be able to go the second floor. Once he had his answers he thanked the man and left as quickly as he had arrived.

He'd considered asking the lift driver if he had seen Blue, but decided it wouldn't be worth the time. Lift drivers saw over a dozen to two dozen faces in a day. Unless she stood out, which Smoke highly doubted she would, the odds were fairly low she'd be remembered by any of the drivers above the seventh below.

Smoke also believed it to be a waste of his time to ask around the first floor if anyone had housed Blue for a night or to check the inns. There'd be no way she'd still be here in the first floor; without a doubt she'd be lower. Second floor or lower.

Still, he'd have to check and make sure; to see if he could find anyone who knew where she'd be going. Anything he could find would be worthwhile. He just didn't think he'd find it here. Blue wouldn't want to be near to the surface; it'd be too easy to find her. He sighed in anguish when he knew he'd have to piss his day away asking pointless questions just in case.

His first stop was a small inn named THE MOLE'S HIDEAWAY. He shuddered as he entered. The place was dingy and poorly lit. If Blue had been looking for a place to avoid detection this would be the place. Nobody would expect a high class girl from the second above to stay in a place like that.

He approached the innkeeper, a tall lanky man with a rat like face. The tufts of black hair made him look like a mangy rodent. The sheer look of him told Smoke he could fall over and die at any moment. "What can I do for you?" the inn keeper asked.

"I'm looking for someone," Smoke said casually.

"You'll want the third below for whores. You a surfacer?"

Smoke glared at the man and put four fingers on his bicep. Smoke had to stop himself from letting out a loud laugh at the man's frightened look. "Look, I don't want any trouble. Especially from your sort," the innkeeper stammered.

"I'm not with them anymore," he said with a frown. "Don't think that doesn't mean I don't remember every little thing I did." A bluff, but a good bluff none the less, one shrouded with truth. He looked to be buying it. "I don't think anyone would miss a little worm den like this."

The man began to shake, "I'm sorry," he said six times before Smoke told him to shut up.

"Now, let's start this again," Smoke began. "I'm looking for a girl. Roughly sixteen, maybe seventeen. She'd look highborn, maybe looked like she tried a little too hard to look like she belongs here, but would still stand out."

The rat man nodded, "I saw someone like that. Only she didn't try to stand out. She was looking for a man. What was his name... Smoke?"

"Smoke Callahan?"

"That's the one!" he said with a grin.

Smoke couldn't help but be insulted. Marla had done research on him and she still believed him to be the sort of man who frequented places like THE MOLE'S HIDEAWAY. "Did you know where to send her?"

He shook his head, "No, I'd never heard of the man. Figured he'd be some first floor pansy P.I. and never gave him another thought."

Smoke's reaction didn't change at the insult. He didn't feel anything towards the man's suppositions towards him, they didn't know each other and it would be foolish to get worked up by this man's opinions. "Did you see anyone like her before?"

He shook his head, "No, She was the first I'd seen. Obviously from above the surface. Don't know why she'd have been down here. Not my place to guess, I guess."

He was telling the truth, not that there had been any reason for the rat man to lie. He slipped the rat man five skins and promptly left the inn. He got more information than he had intended, but not in the right direction. Now he resented his employers even more than he had before.

His next stop took him to a more high class place named UNDER INN. The place was decorated with expensive tapestries and lights. If Blue hadn't been in the dirtiest place in town there would be a possibility of her having been in the cleanest. He walked to the inn keeper and placed his hands on the front desk. The inn keeper wrinkled his nose at Smoke, "Hello good sir, you can't afford to stay here. Please leave." The inn keeper said.

Smoke looked down to his clothes. He had changed when he had returned home from the dusty clothes he had been wearing before into the clean red plaid button shirt he wore now. His trousers were held up with grey suspenders, though they were hidden under a fabric longcoat. He knew he didn't look high class by any means though the rudeness from the inn keeper was uncalled for.

Smoke flashed the fourth below symbol, hoping that would get a response. He hated doing it, but he didn't have time to fuck around. The inn keeper didn't seem phased anyway. "That doesn't frighten me," he said with a straight face. "You think I haven't fought your type before?"

It was a fair point; the Cartel had tried to take down and intimidate the high class places of the first floor before and failed.

"Look," Smoke said, "I'm looking for a young girl. It's a job of mine from the second above. I'm pretty sure if I gave them a call they wouldn't be too pleased you've impeded my investigation."

"You're a private dick?" the inn keeper asked with a look of shock.

"You didn't think I was here for a room did you?" Smoke asked smugly. "Now, are you going to comply with what I want or am I going to have to tear you down? I know the Cartel couldn't do it, but let's see what someone from the above can do."

Panic began to flash all over the inn keeper's face. "No, don't do that!" he said almost in a falsetto shriek.

Another bluff. There would be no way for him to get the message to them with his communicator and have Marla or someone else from the Lang family come down to do something about it. Even if he did, it would be days before they made it down, every day counted and needed to be used finding Blue.

"Tell me what I want to hear," Smoke demanded.

The innkeeper swallowed hard and spoke, "I don't know who you're looking for. If I had a family name I could look through the register and see if anyone had stayed."

"Her name is Blue Lang," Smoke said, slipping the image across the counter.

The inn keeper's eyes shot wide open, "You're dealing with the Lang family? Fuck! Fuck fuck fuck fuck fuck!"

"What's wrong?"

The inn keeper shook his head wildly, "That is not the sort of family you want to fuck with. What are they doing getting a fourth floor roughian?"

Smoke gave the inn keeper a look of suspicion, "What do you know about the Lang family?"

"Nothing I can repeat," he said as his body began to shake. "I know where Blue is though, or at least I know where she was going from here."

"Where?" Smoke asked a little too forcefully for his own comfort.

The inn keeper shook his head, "I can't tell you that either. I'm sorry I said anything."

Rage began to build in Smoke's head. He grabbed the inn keeper from across the counter and pulled him across. He picked up the little man and pushed him against the wall. "Look," Smoke said trying his best not to shout. "I don't have all day. Fuck, I don't have much for time as it is, if you know something, I highly suggest you tell me. I really don't have time for you to tell me you have information and then beat around the bush or straight up refuse to tell me what I need to know."

"I can't," the inn keeper said with bulging eyes filled with fear. Tears began to run as he spoke again. "You can kill me, beat me to a pulp or worse but there's no way I can tell you. What they'd do to me..."

Smoke could feel his power beginning to rise as he looked into the inn keeper's eyes, "Tell me what you know," Smoke said firmly.

The inn keeper began to relax under Smoke's control. "This goes way deeper than just a missing girl," he said in a voice much calmer than before.

"How do you know this?"

The inn keeper managed a warbled smile as he said, "Walls have ears. Nothing said in an inn is ever a secret. It can be kept for a price, that's all."

Smoke took in a deep breath as he let the man down. "So that's what you do? You listen in and blackmail their secrets?"

"More or less," the inn keeper said. "It's tough having a high-priced inn in the first underground. People from the upper levels do tend to come down here for dirty deals. Sometimes what they pay for a room isn't enough to cover the extravagance. Not to mention the rarity of seeing someone from the above levels coming down here. On top of that I do have people from other levels trying to tear my place down."

Smoke gave the inn keeper a disapproving look. People from the upper levels had secrets; he knew this from the Lang family, but dirty dealings... while not surprising, would be something to look into at a later date. What he cared about was where Blue was going.

"You're not going to turn me into the authorities are you?" the inn keeper asked.

The authorities would have congratulated the man on his way of saying 'fuck you' to the upper levels. The authorities in the upper levels would probably have an idea of what was going on, though Smoke doubted it would make any difference. The families wouldn't go to the authorities unless they didn't mind their secret being revealed. Not to mention the lack of authority the officers in the upper levels had down in the underground. They'd be killed by an unnamed person before they'd have found who they were looking for. A death nobody would ever investigate.

"No," Smoke said in response. "However, you are going to shut down your blackmail scheme. Charge more for the rooms, you'll get more that way"

The inn keeper nodded, "Yes sir."

Smoke nodded his head once, "Wonderful. I'm still going to need to know where Blue was headed though."

The inn keeper sighed, his fear was still present. "Alright, all I can tell you is that she was headed below. Can't tell you what floor because I really just don't know, it's a secret even I don't have. The people after her though, they would know. If they've caught up anyway."

It was times like that when Smoke felt thankful for the abilities he'd been gifted. Being able to make people obey his commands or tell him the truth had been extremely helpful in his profession.

Smoke removed his hat and scratched his head, "Alright, that'll have to do."

The inn keeper audibly sighed in relief as Smoke approached the exit.

Smoke paced the market place up and down several times trying to clear his head. The fear of the Lang family had shaken the inn keeper to his core, which interested Smoke. He wanted to know the secret more than ever now. The only way he'd ever find out would be to track down Blue and ask her, if she were still alive.

The more he thought about Blue going below filled him with a sense of dread that he didn't think he'd feel. The fact that people were after her made the feeling even worse. Who were they? Why would they want her? It was clear the Lang family didn't care about her disappearance much farther than their public standing. His job was a farce, a farce that paid quite well. The digging in Smoke's gut didn't subside.

As he walked home the shops began to close. The noise from the market had been mildly successful at distracting him and keeping the depressing thoughts from entering his head; now that it was silent he was alone again with his thoughts. The lights began to dim as the shop keepers extinguished the candles and torches which kept their booths lit. All that remained were the dimming florescent bulbs that hung from the ceiling.

His thoughts turned to Constance. He had left her at his house while he asked around. That had been hours ago. He didn't know what he'd find when he returned. Would she have gone with his stuff? Would she still be there waiting?

When he finally arrived back at his place he was delighted to see Constance nose deep in one of his books. As he entered she looked up at him and smiled, "You get what you were after?"

Smoke nodded, "Yeah, it was a bit of a pain in the ass and I had to do some things I'm not happy about, but I got some information."

"Well," she said as she closed the book, "that's something at least."

Her smile as she stood and walked towards him made him

feel better. He didn't know why; there had been no real emotion towards her other than a passing carnal attraction. Even then, it wasn't something he spent a lot of time thinking about. He soon narrowed it down to the fact that she had been genuinely pleased to see him and she had a bit more of an optimistic outlook than he had.

"When do we leave?" she asked.

"I talked to the lift driver to take us down to the second level. He's already made his trip down so we will have to wait until tomorrow. We've got some time to kill so we can do whatever you want to do for the next little bit."

He saw her face light up at the prospect of doing what she wanted but then fade back into a straight face. "I don't actually know," she said in a flat tone. "I don't know what there is to do. I don't even know what's on this floor that the others don't have."

Smoke thought for a moment, "I don't really know what we could do either. I typically just read so I couldn't say if there's anything a woman would enjoy doing. The underground is not really that type of place I guess."

"Didn't think that one through did you," she said with a sly smile.

"Nope, I sure didn't," Smoke said as his face flushed slightly.

"It's alright," she said as she turned back towards the table. "The gesture was nice. Though I could go for some food, you have anything here?"

Smoke shook his head, "Not unless you consider mulch liquor as food."

They both laughed a little at the thought and agreed they should get something to eat. They found a small bistro serving what Smoke assumed to be synthetic meat with several darkplants swimming in a bowl of hot flavoured water. This was what the underground passed off as soup.

Smoke took a spoonful of the soup with a piece of darkplant and synthetic meat and ate it. The flavour didn't hit him like the food had days before. He lamented for a quick moment at his new high standards and continued to eat.

He looked to Constance who was devouring the soup. She didn't seem to be stopping for anything; either she found the soup delicious or she had been hungrier than he anticipated. The man behind the counter of the bistro, who Smoke knew to be the owner, grinned as he watched her. Smoke believed the owner hadn't seen someone eat his cooking so quickly. "Is good?" he asked with a hopeful expression.

Constance looked up from her soup. She gave a quick look of embarrassment and smiled, "Yeah, it's really good. I'd never had darkplant before; I didn't think it'd be this good."

The owner smiled deeply and asked if she would like another bowl on the house. Constance's eyes lit up as she had to restrain herself from excitement. "Yes," she said in a voice that was forcibly calm.

Smoke grinned as he watched the women gobble down the contents of the second bowl. He had finished his bowl roughly halfway through her second. They thanked the owner as Smoke paid for the two bowls.

"You don't have to keep paying for me," Constance said when they had been out of earshot of the bistro.

"To be honest I didn't give it much thought," Smoke said in a satisfied tone, the kind that only came after a hearty meal. "If you want to start paying for yourself you are more than welcome to."

Constance laughed, "So long as you're not doing it because you don't think I have the skins. I have enough to get me by for a while, especially in the underground."

Smoke logged that bit of information away in the back of his mind. It wasn't something he needed to remember, but he would just I case. It was almost habit for him at this point.

"How far down do you think we'll have to go?" Constance asked as they walked down the corridors of the first floor.

Smoke let out a short breath. "I don't know," he said vacantly. "I'm hoping not too far. I'm really hoping for the next floor only."

"All hopes aside though?"

Smoke closed his eyes for a moment, "All the way down. All the way down to the ninth below."

"Why do you think that?" She asked.

"This is a girl who wanted to get away from her family. She learned the family secret and chose to leave instead of dealing with it. All I know is she came this far alone and that someone is after her," Smoke stopped to take a breath. "Plus, that's just my luck."

"At least you have a direction," Constance said warily.

"All I know is downward," Smoke said. "The intel I got down here today confirmed it. He didn't tell me exactly where she was going but it was down. And before you ask if I'm sure he was being truthful I am an expert and deciphering lies from truths," Constance didn't need to know about his abilities.

"Really?" Constance asked as he watched an idea rush through her head. "Try it on me. Two out of three."

Smoke smiled a half smile, "Alright, Want to put a wager on it as well?"

Constance snorted in amusement, "Yeah sure, why not. You get two out of the three statements right and I'll do whatever you ask for the duration of my time down here."

"And if I get two of them wrong, I will pay your way all through your time down here. Deal?"

"Deal," Constance said shaking Smoke's hand.

Shaking hands was an odd expression of deal making for Smoke; he knew it to be a common custom on the surface, but physical contact from a person you were making deals with typically meant dirty dealing or intent to get close enough to kill. He knew Constance wasn't that type of girl so he obliged her surfacer ways. In the underground people would give a slight upward head tilt to seal a deal.

"Alright," Constance said as she searched for a statement. "I am not originally from the surface," she said trying not to give anything away.

Smoke watched her expression as she spoke. "True," he said in a matter of fact tone.

"Yup, you're right," she said with a smile. "I ran away from home when I was a teenager."

Smoke knew instantly it was. "True," he said without skipping a beat.

"Wrong, it was a lie," she said smugly. "My parents were from the first above. They went broke and had to move to the surface."

"You're a good liar," he said with a grin.

"No," she said softly. "You just spoke too fast, you didn't' think about it and you got one wrong. This is the winner takes all statement. Think before you speak."

She wasn't wrong. He had been overconfident and missed some of the lesser telltale signs. The fact that he wasn't using his abilities gave her the slight advantage. Not that he really needed them to win. "Alright," he said. "Let's do this."

Constance thought for a moment. "I've got the perfect one," she said with a devilish grin. "My real name is not really Constance."

Smoke watched her face closely for any sign of lies or truths. He had seen mixed signals, the telltale eye movement of a lie but the steady breathing of a truth, the steady voice of a truth and the personal grooming of a lie in the shape of her hand playing with her hair. Pieces began to fall in place within his mind and a picture began to show itself.

"It's a trick statement," he said confidently. "Your real name is Constance, but it wasn't your birth name, thus making your name both Constance, and *not* Constance."

She looked confused, "You really are good. Well, a deal is a deal."

Smoke grinned triumphantly, "Wonderful. You're paying for breakfast tomorrow."

The look of humoured shock that crossed Constance's face amused Smoke further, though he chose to not comment or react to it. "Alright," she said with a grin. "I could go for soup in the morning as well."

5

Constance had kept her word when she said they'd be having soup for breakfast. The owner, who still stood behind his counter like a soldier on eternal sentry duty watched as Constance ate with delight. Smoke smiled internally as he slowly finished his bowl. The darkplants mixed with the synthetic meat tasted better than they had the day before, but still weren't great by any means. He believed it would take some time before his taste buds reverted back to what they once were and forgot about the dish he'd had on the surface. He had forgone the mulch liquor in fear the whiskey he'd had on the second above had spoiled his drink for him as well.

Constance ate much slower this time, taking time to enjoy every bite and taste. Once she had finished her bowl she paid the owner and they left. "Is the food as good on the lower floors?" she asked in an obvious attempt to make conversation.

"I guess it depends on your taste," Smoke said as he looked and walked forward. "Personally I don't think so, but you seemed to enjoy the food here more than I did. I guess you'll have to see for yourself."

Before leaving the house Smoke had been sure to collect as

many supplies he believed they'd need. Food would be available to them wherever they went. It's not like people were starving in the lower levels, not with everyone having the availability and ability to grow darkplants. New clothes were not a needed item either, though he'd be on the move for several days to a couple weeks, but there'd be places to wash himself as well as his clothes. He only grabbed the essentials. He knew what the lower levels had in store and he'd be prepared; nothing would hinder his progress.

They walked toward the lift driver for the first and second below. He was a stout man with dark skin and no hair. He grinned at Smoke as he approached. He gave Smoke a friendly nod.

Smoke said casually, "Are you good to take us to the lower floor?"

The driver smiled in a friendly manner, "I am."

Smoke and Constance walked on top of the platform as the lift driver began to turn his crank. Smoke looked at the driver as he did his job. Speaking to him the day before he had learned he had been from the sixth floor. He was a former Nagara slave trader and now a lift driver doing his best to go straight and learning the common language as he went along. The Nagara had a specific slaver language that took a lot of time and effort to learn. It wasn't really a proper language; it was more of a shattered form of Common.

People often became frustrated at the Nagara language as well as at the humour of the Naraga when people couldn't understand them. Some Nagara knew the language of the upper levels, those were the people sent to make the deals. Those were the slavers a person had to be careful around. They'd mastered the art of lies and deceit; they'd learned the ways of the upper levels and knew how to speak to anyone looking for a slave.

Smoke decided the slave thoughts were not the best to be having at this time. They were nowhere close to the sixth floor or much less the seventh where people were kidnapped or stolen to become slaves.

Constance had slid down the wall of the lift and now lay on the floor with her eyes closed in a satisfied food sleep. He'd let her remain until they reached the bottom. Her chest moved up and down in a steady rhythm playing up her comfort and dreamless state.

He watched as the former slave trader turned the crank, his shirtless muscles gleaming with sweat in the dim light of the tunnel. He didn't feel any level of envy or empathy for the man who was doing his best to do what he could to be an aid to society, though he couldn't help but feel a little scorn for the fact that he was able to get such a job where he'd only have to do a little work every day and get everything else handed to him for free. It was not an easy life as a lift driver, but there were worse occupations out there.

His mind soon shifted to the lifts of the upper levels. The steam powered hydraulics could get people up and down all day and there would be no need for lift drivers anymore. If they could find a way to implement them into the underground, things could be much easier and people could potentially get what they've always needed, a way out. Provided they had the skins to survive.

In the ancient days the majority of the human race had gone underground to escape the Apocalypse War that had been going on for decades. After the war had ended people remained underground due to disfigurements or other afflictions that were deemed unsightly for the surface. People had only begun resurfacing once the ancient technologies had failed and crashed. This sent the populace into a feudal state where everything reverted back to an age of monarchs and hand held weapons.

After the age of feudalism ended an age of magic followed behind it ushering in the New Era. Those days were short lived, a few hundred years in length before the majority of the world's magic had been used and humanity had to revert back to their old ways and reintegrate technology into their lives. Magic had become almost an unheard of commodity.

Things hadn't got much better since. Revolving pistols existed again - that was a down side. Smoke placed his hand on the revolving pistol he'd grabbed before leaving his home for the second time in as many days. Six shots sat in wait to be shot while a dozen more sat in the inside pocket of his longcoat. He sighed at the fact that he would probably need it; for years it had sat on his desk unused and gathering dust. He never bothered to clean it before because it had been a reminder that the first floor was safe and he didn't really need it.

It sat in its holster, clean and polished, waiting for the first shot in decades.

The lift's platform sank smoothly to the soft ground of the second floor. The lights that hung from the ceiling were dimmed by a collection of dust nobody had ever bothered to clean off. As they came to a halt, Smoke shook Constance awake and they were off without even a goodbye to the lift driver.

Constance yawned and said, "That was a short trip."

"You slept the whole way. Sleeping always makes time shorter."

"You seem grumpy," she said after another yawn.

Smoke shook his head, "No, I'm just in thought."

"You'll have to tell me about it sometime."

Smoke nodded in agreement and continued forward. The second floor was another market place, this one shadier than the first below. Clerks shouted from their many booths offering weapons, narcotics and several other miscellaneous items to protect oneself or avoid their responsibilities. Smoke had always hated this floor. Bad memories came flooding back of his time when he used to supply for people like these. He didn't want to break that story to Constance, at least not yet.

Smoke began to look around the crowd for the lift driver to

the next lower floor. He didn't think he'd need him, at least he hoped he wouldn't, but it would be wise to keep his bases covered. If it happened Blue wasn't on this floor he would need to be on the next lift downward.

"So where are we looking this time?" Constance asked.

"Local tavern. I'll see if anyone had seen her and then we'll get a drink."

"You don't think she's here?"

Smoke continued to look forward while he spoke, "I'm hoping she is."

They walked around through the crowd and out the other side of the town before coming across the lift driver. Smoke could hear Constance exhale sharply as she saw the man's brutish size and height. Smoke approached the giant and said, "You gone down already?"

The lift driver looked down at Smoke; he was about two feet taller and had about a hundred pounds of muscle over Smoke. Smoke looked up at him and hoped he knew how to speak. "Been down already," the lift driver said with a kind tone. "I'll be going back-"

"First thing in the morning," Smoke said before the man had a chance to reply.

The lift driver shook his head. "No sir, I'm going back down tonight. Six hours from now. Be here if you want to go down."

Smoke nodded his head in agreement before walking away.

"He was a bit of a softy," Constance said as she trailed behind him.

"I expected as much," Smoke said while he looked around for a tavern. "Lift drivers don't have anything to worry about. There'd be no reason for him to be aggressive."

"Do you think this trip will be faster?" she asked in a hopeful tone.

"Yes, it's a shorter distance."

Constance didn't respond. He figured she didn't think she'd have to with a statement like that. He turned the corner back towards the town and to the market. He wasn't in the shopping mood, but he'd look at the weapons. He decided to bring it to her attention, "Since we're down here and probably going to go lower you should probably get yourself a good weapon."

Constance looked at him with a look of surprise. He didn't think she expected him to say she should arm herself. He knew she was strong, but he didn't think that strength would come in handy if someone pulled a blade or a revolving pistol on her. "You serious?" she finally said after her brain had been given time to process his words.

"I am," he said bluntly. "That's an order too. Choose a weapon and I'll get it for you."

He had half expected Constance's face to light up like it typically did when he made suggestions. She seemed to enjoy the adventure and followed his every command with the bright eyes of a child. Now she looked at him suspiciously. "I'll take a blade. I know revolving pistols are good and all, but I think I can do more with a blade."

"You certain?" he asked before taking her to a weapons booth.

She nodded without a smile or any look of humour or happiness, "Yes, I'm certain."

The closest weapons booth was filled with different sized blades and several revolving pistols. It made Smoke uncomfortable to be in the vicinity of these weapons. While he didn't supply these exact weapons he had delivered several like them once upon a time.

Constance looked over the weapons before deciding on a hidden shortblade encased in a hard metal casing, shaped to be a walking stick with a rounded head. The booth keeper smiled at her choice. He quickly pulled the shortblade away from her to show her how everything worked. "So as you can see here," he said with a rehearsed and over-excited tone that told Smoke he had given this speech to a few customers already today, "the rounded hand rest for this walking stick has spring loaded pommel and cross guards so you can get a good grip on your blade while you swing it."

The booth keeper pressed a button on the metal circle and just as he said the pommel and cross guard ejected out. He then pulled the blade out of the walking stick and held it in the air. The short blade was longer than Smoke had anticipated; over two feet long.

The booth owner handed the blade to Constance who gave the shortblade a couple swings and placed it back in its metal walking stick sheath. "I'll take it," she said still without any sign of happiness, but without any sorrow or unhappiness as well. Her face remained blank.

"Wonderful," the booth keeper said with a wide, toothy grin. "That'll be fifty skins."

Constance's jaw dropped at the price. Smoke was un-phased at the mention of fifty skins; blades were expensive, almost more so than revolving pistols. While pistols took more time to make, short blades took more metal, and metal had been a rarity since the construction of the underground. Smoke placed five purple stained skins on the booth and walked away with Constance trailing behind. "Thank you," she said sheepishly.

Smoke supressed his smile knowing Constance at the very least would be armed in the event they got separated or if he had been taken out. He didn't reply to her thanks or even acknowledge it. The only thing he wanted was to get off this floor as soon as he could. Too many bad memories, too much of a chance of being recognized.

The first tavern they found had a painting of a mole on the side with the words 'UNDERGROUND HAVEN' painted across the top of the door. Smoke looked to Constance who gave him a slight shrug before opening the door. He looked around the silent tavern in the same way a hawk scans for its prey.

He approached the barkeep and ordered two large ales for himself and Constance. She didn't seem to care that he insisted on paying for the drinks; they were his idea after all. The barkeep handed him two large mugs, bigger than those on the surface. Smoke took them graciously and returned to his table. Constance gave Smoke a look while he placed the ale on the table. "Time to try what good ale tastes like," he said with a smile.

The two of them took sips from their giant mugs. When Constance pulled back with a sour expression on her face he had to refrain from laughing. She had been used to the bitterness of the surface ale and couldn't quite handle the sweetness of the underground. "It's good," she said maintaining the expression. "A little sweet though."

"Holy shit!" a familiar voice shouted from behind him. "Smoke fucking Callahan!"

Smoke knew the voice and swallowed hard as he looked around the room. He looked to the dark skinned, short skinny man who had called out his name. A flood of memories came back to him all the way from his childhood. "Fulcrum?" he asked in amazement.

Smoke couldn't help but grin as his childhood friend slapped him on the back and joined his table. "How the fuck are you?" Fulcrum asked in a voice much louder than his body would have suggested.

The slap on the back was all Smoke needed to know Fulcrum was putting on a show for the patrons and for Constance. Smoke knew his game.

"On a case," Smoke said flatly.

"Ooh, look at mister serious over here," Fulcrum laughed while speaking to Constance. "By the way, I'm Fulcrum, Fulcrum Brown."

"Pleased to meet you Mister Brown," Constance said with a forced smile, "I'm Constance."

"Shit Smoke, you married now? I never took you for the type. At least when it came to anyone but Glass."

Smoke was beginning to remember why he stopped liking Fulcrum all those years ago. The man didn't know when to stop talking. "We're not married," he said. "She's travelling with me. Two sets of eyes are better than one."

"Bullshit!" Fulcrum said before taking a swig from his ale. "You've got to be at least fucking her."

Smoke shot Constance a look telling her to not answer that. He knew that was all the response Fulcrum would need, but it was better left unsaid.

"What are you doing on the second below?" Smoke asked trying his best to not sound like an inquisitor.

"Just up here to get a good weapon. The fourth floor is great for a lot of things but if you want a good revolving pistol or a sharp blade you've gotta come here. Shit, even the drink is better."

"It's better here?" Constance slipped up and said in shock. She immediately shut her mouth trying to look like the accidental speaking was intentional.

"So tell me about this case," Fulcrum said stopping his laughter immediately.

Smoke should have known better than to tell Fulcrum about him being on a case. There was no turning back; he knew Fulcrum wouldn't be satisfied if he didn't know every detail.

"I'm looking for a highborn girl," he began.

"Really? You're working for them now? I thought I knew you better."

"Money was too good to pass up," he said ignoring Fulcrum's obvious bigotry. "Anyway, she's supposedly down in the underground somewhere. I'm trying to find her."

"Not trying too hard," Fulcrum said with a straight face. "I didn't even know you were here until I saw you. Had you been asking around I'd have known much sooner. You're not trying, you're pissing time away."

"She's not on the second floor," Smoke said with a matter of fact tone. "She'd be lower."

"What makes you say that?"

"I'm just so goddamn lucky that way," Smoke said with a sarcastic grin.

Fulcrum paused for a second before bursting into a fit of loud, overblown laughter. "Got an image of her?" Fulcrum asked after he'd calmed down.

Smoke hesitated at showing his old friend the picture. He knew too much as it was, but at this point Fulcrum wouldn't do anything but help. If Fulcrum hadn't seen her it'd be possible for him to keep an eye out. He had people all over the place, if Fulcrum didn't know at that time, he would soon.

Smoke pulled out the image and slid it across the table. Fulcrum looked the image up and down and at several angles; he was doing it to hold for time, not because he wanted to further inspect it. "Yeah I'd seen her, she was on the sixth below," he said finally as he placed the image back on the table, sliding it back toward Smoke. "Last I seen her though she was headed to the seventh below."

"Shit," Smoke said a little too loudly.

"Don't I know it," Fulcrum said matching his volume. Eyes had begun to peer their way. "Pretty thing like her is bound to get picked up by the Nagara."

Smoke looked at Constance and back at Fulcrum, "Can I speak to you outside?"

Fulcrum finished his ale and nodded. "Yeah," he said before letting out a loud belch.

Fulcrum followed Smoke outside and behind the building. Smoke turned and looked at the man a foot shorter than himself; Fulcrum had already drawn his revolving pistol.

Smoke nodded and said, "I need a favour from you."

"You need a favour from me?" Fulcrum parroted as his demeanor turned into one of hostility. "That's rich. That's just fucking rich."

"I know I don't deserve it," Smoke admitted.

"What you deserve is a fucking shot between your goddamn eyes," Fulcrum spat.

"And I'll let you do it; just this one favour and you can do as you wish."

Smoke did his best to refrain from sounding panicked or frightened. The truth was he had deserved the bullet for a great many years, almost a decade. He was amazed Fulcrum hadn't come out of the darkness at any given night and done the deed.

"I'm listening," Fulcrum said, "but make it quick."

"Half a million skins," was all Smoke said. It was all he had to say.

He could see Fulcrum think about it for a quick moment, letting his guard down for a quick moment before raising the revolving pistol again. "I don't believe you."

"The girl I'm looking for is worth that much to this family. They've agreed to pay me half a million skins to bring her to them."

"Could have held out for more when you made the deal," Fulcrum snarled.

"I could have also lost the job," Smoke replied.

"What's to stop me from fetching her myself?"

"Honestly, nothing. I just can't guarantee the family would pay you. Their deal is with me and I think they'd see someone else bringing her as a breach of contract. Don't think you can bring them down to get your pay either, you couldn't even take down a high class place on the first below."

One of Smoke's biggest assets was his brain; he had been a bright boy for a long time, which made the team up of him and Fulcrum dangerous back in the day. Fulcrum was the silent knife while Smoke was the planner. Fulcrum wasn't especially bright. He knew enough on how to keep himself from being seen in any situation and how to survive the lower floors, but that was about all.

He could now see the thoughts going through Fulcrum's brain trying to figure out a way to get his vengeance and get the half million skins. Smoke decided to expedite the process, "You let me live and protect me through the underground and I will let you shoot me in the face and take the half million skins."

"How do I know you won't pull a fast one on me?" Fulcrum asked. "And don't even think of using your abilities on me. They won't work."

"I figured knowing about what I can do would help protect you from my abilities," Smoke said gravely. "Keep eyes on me; watch the entrance to the tower. I have to deliver the girl to their front door so all you'd have to do is wait for me to exit."

"Half a million skins and my revenge; I think I can do that."

Smoke nodded, "All you need is a little patience. That's all."

Fulcrum lowered his revolving pistol and placed it back in the holster. "Alright you have a deal. I'll keep you safe in the underground for the half million skins and your death."

Smoke silently thanked whatever gods he thought may still be there and said, "Thank you. If it means anything, I'm sorry about how things went down."

Fulcrum managed a smile, "It means a lot my old friend. It doesn't change anything, but it means a lot."

Smoke nodded and waited for Fulcrum to leave, "Good bye, old friend."

Fulcrum nodded, "I'm not protecting you on the fourth or fifth floors. I hope you understand."

Smoke nodded again, "Don't want to burn bridges. I get it."

Fulcrum nodded before turning away and disappeared into the shadows. The thought to shoot Fulcrum in the back had crossed Smoke's mind as he watched him disappear. Any normal man in the underground would have tried. Smoke, however knew Fulcrum well enough to know the folly of the idea. Not due to some honour code or moral ethics. It was because Fulcrum was a much better shot and several times quicker than most men in the underground. He'd hear the revolving pistol leave the holster and Smoke would be dead before he'd have a chance to get his finger to the trigger.

He allowed a tear to fall down his face in the knowledge his death was imminent and there would be very little he could do about it; he knew he deserved death, though it didn't make him feel any better about it. He slowly walked back inside where Constance waited patiently. A man lay sprawled across the floor by her chair, "What happened here?" Smoke asked, trying to lift his spirits. This was sure to amuse him.

"Someone decided to get a little grabby so I knocked his head in. He's not dead, but he'll be feeling it for a long time."

Smoke chuckled at the story, he didn't know how else to try and take his mind off his and Fulcrum's deal.

"What happened to your friend?" Constance asked.

"He had to go. Business."

He watched Constance read the look on his face before nodding and taking another sip of her ale. She made the same sour face with every sip. That amused him less and less as the night went on. He kept waiting for her to ask about his past with Fulcrum, if she did he'd answer. He would owe her that much at some point.

"So what did you guys talk about?" Constance asked finally.

"About the past mostly," Smoke said trying to half hide the truth. She didn't need to know he was going to die. Not yet at least. "He's also agreed to keep us safe while we go down the floors."

"Well that's good," Constance said with a smile.

"Yeah, it is," Smoke said trying to not meet her glance.

He could tell she knew something was wrong, something he'd have to remedy as soon as he could. If he walked around acting gloomy, she'd start asking questions. After a second thought he decided he didn't want her to start asking anything. He'd just tell her, at least when the time was right. Potentially before the fourth floor.

Smoke had been silent for the majority of the night. This put Constance on edge, not because she thought of him as a chatterbox by any means. What aroused her suspicions was the fact that he typically talked to himself in a low mutter. That night there had been nothing. Something had happened outside with Fulcrum that had set him off and she wasn't going to press the issue. It wasn't her business, at least not until it would start affecting Smoke's abilities. Until then she'd let him deal with his problems on his own.

As the minutes ticked down to when they would have to be at the lift, Constance could feel her heart racing with excitement and dread. She had heard some horrible things about the lower levels. Though the third level wasn't that low she didn't expect to see anything good.

As they walked down the road she couldn't help but think about the reason she had come along with Smoke; it sure wasn't for his winning personality. There was something down here there that she needed. Something she wanted for herself that she couldn't get on the surface. The image flickered in her mind before she mentally shooed it all away.

She could hear a man shouting before they saw a crowd of people surrounding him. "It's been too long for us to be stuck down here."

"What's going on there?" Constance asked.

She watched as Smoke looked to the man on a small box made from false wood, shouting about the oppression of the underground."

"People are never satisfied with what they have. They're willing to take it from those they believe don't deserve it."

"People like me?" she asked in a worried tone.

"No," Smoke said as he stared towards where they needed to go. "People of the underground have no problem with surfacers. They're an oddity down here, but they know surfacers have been dealt the same shitty hand, they just get a sky for their troubles."

"That's what they want? A sky?"

"Not quite, but it would sate their blood lust for a time. At least until they began to believe that the people in the towers need to be taken down."

"When that happens?"

Smoke let out a long drawn-out sigh. She didn't know if it was for dramatic effect or if the truth was too much to think about. "Let's just say with nine levels of people who have had to do nothing but work for a living, compared to the minority of those in the towers who've done nothing but make business deals, but at the same time can afford their own personal army," Smoke gave her a grave look that made her step back. "It'd be a blood bath for both sides. I don't even know who'd come out on top."

"Look at us down here!" The man on the box continued to scream. "Yeah we've got food with our darkplants and our synthetic meat. Sure we've got baths and the like. Sure we have everything we could ever need to stay alive. But you know what? That's not enough for me. I want real sunlight vegetables, real meat from an animal that wasn't a mole. I want to be able to see the sky and let the rain dance on my face…. Consistently! The longest any of us ever get at any given time is a day, and even that could bring any one of us to financial ruin. I say it's time we put a stop to it!"

Constance could hear the cheering and applauding from the crowd. Dread began to fill her as she recalled what Smoke had just finned relaying.

"I wouldn't worry though," Smoke said as if picking up on her fear. "People have been in that man's place screaming and preaching almost the exact same words since before I was born. You don't see many people from the underground on the surface and you don't see any of them taking up housing in the towers.

It's because the whole lot of them are all talk. They're big bags of wind that need to get their emotions off their chests. Makes living here more bearable. When you feel you're working toward a task everything seems easier, even if the goal is nearly impossible."

Constance looked back to the crowd and saw the fear and anger in their eyes. She didn't know if this was a common thing in the underground but the looks on all their faces made her uneasy. She almost believed they would start marching at any moment towards the lift to the first floor and then finally to the surface.

She didn't know how many people it would take to fill the small town of Tower's Shadow and she didn't want to know. She didn't know how many it would take before they invaded the small family farm not far from the small town she once called home. Again, something she really didn't want to know.

Smoke looked at his pocket watch and over to the lift in the distance. "Shit," he said in a voice so low she almost didn't hear him. "We're still early. How the fuck does that keep happening?"

"Maybe we're just walking fast," Constance said, trying to give answers.

"Maybe," Smoke said as he removed his hat and ran his fingers through his hair. "I guess it doesn't really matter now, we may as well go there and wait. We can't go back into town, we'd risk missing it."

Constance took in a deep breath as she resisted the urge to slap Smoke and yell at him to cheer the fuck up. To give her the smile she enjoyed. A lot of it may have been the lack of sleep he'd been getting since leaving the surface. She knew he didn't sleep much the day before on the first below. He was too busy making sure he had everything he needed.

He didn't sleep like she had during the ride down the lift and he hadn't slept during the entire time on the second below. He was going to collapse soon if he didn't. Fulcrum also didn't help with his mood. The moment Smoke saw the small man she could see Smoke get tense and seemingly wishing he'd go away. Fulcrum had helped with the investigation, but that's about all.

She watched as Smoke stepped lightly and languidly towards the lift and the huge lift driver. He didn't get far before Constance began to follow. She didn't know what was ahead; all she knew was the moment they knew when the next lift was leaving she would make sure Smoke went to sleep and she wasn't hearing another word about it.

6

The desire to continue descending the floors had begun to wane for Constance. The spirit of adventure and the joys of traveling alongside Smoke had been short lived, especially since the man seemed to get more irritable and quiet as they went along. Instead of paying attention to the man slowly becoming more and more exhausted on his feet, she decided to watch the large muscle-bound man turn the crank to the lift that allowed them to go to the third below.

She didn't expect it to happen but watching the muscular man was oddly arousing for her. She didn't know why; she had never been attracted to guys so heavily set. Once she realized what had been going on she turned her head away and chose to sit on the floor of the lift and think.

She thought about her parents, long dead and burned. The image of their funeral pyre brought tears to her eyes as she remembered watching their ashes float away into the distance as she tried to distinguish their ashes from the wood they had been burned with. The pyre had been illegal; the burning of a precious commodity such as wood could have landed her in jail for a long time. When the officers had come to investigate a large number of the town's people had come to her rescue. They told them they would rather die than let her go to prison for honoring her parents. The officers quickly relinquished the case and allowed her to go on with a warning. She wouldn't require a second warning.

Her parents were good people, even when they had lived on the first above they did what they could to help those on the surface and even some in the underground. It wasn't until some family from a higher level wanted them out of the tower and did what they had to in order to force them to leave. It succeeded pretty easily; her parents could no longer afford to live on the first above and promptly took up housing on the surface. The majority of the town's folk remembered them and aided them as best they could. Her parents had been thankful and soon became productive members to the town of Tower's Shadow.

Her father took the job as the town's physician while her mother became a teacher for the children. They were well loved within the community and Constance loved them for it. They had her change her name to Constance before they moved; a name like Constantinople Ibot would have sounded nothing short of pretentious. She liked her new name more. A tear fell from her eye as she thought about her parents and their tragically bloody deaths.

As the platform safely came to rest on the third below she picked herself up and dried her eyes. It was time to put on her game face. She didn't know what to expect from the third below, but she would be waiting for danger.

The third below was better lit than the first two floors. The red and white lights were almost blinding after the dimness of the lift shaft. She held her hand in front of her face to protect her eyes until they adjusted. Once she had been able to look upon the third floor she was surprised to see a bustling market of fresh darkplants along with several buildings advertising sex and pleasures beyond any wild fantasy. People were everywhere as they picked up the street women and food in their down times.

Smoke snorted in disgust, "I've never liked this floor. The

faster we're out of here the better."

Constance looked at Smoke. She could see his discomfort and agitation. "Aren't you going to ask any questions while you're here?" she asked, trying to slow the man down.

"Fulcrum said he saw Blue going to the seventh below. There's no reason for him to lie, I made sure of that. We'll go see when the next lift is leaving and go from there."

She could see the exhaustion behind his eyes. "When we get there I command you to sleep. I don't care if it's by the lift or in an inn," Constance said sternly. "You're not going to be any good to anyone if you can't focus." She hoped the lift would take some time before the next departure. The two of them desperately needed some rest - Smoke more than she.

Smoke nodded at her demand, "You're right," he said almost vacantly. "I just have a lot on my mind and sleep has not been easy. I tried on the lift, but it just wasn't happening."

Constance nodded, "So long as you get some sleep, that's what's important."

As they walked through the red lights, Smoke kept quiet about everything. He didn't even seem to know where he was or where he was going. His eyes were glazed over and his attention seemed to be on whatever he was thinking of. Constance felt she could have said almost anything and he wouldn't have heard it.

The lift had been exceptionally easy to find. It was placed right in the center of the town. The woman at the lift held a wrench in her hand. A bag of tools lay strewn around the ground as the lift driver twisted a bolt free from the contraption, allowing a noticeably cracked cog to fall free to the dirt. "Hello there," Smoke said, lacking any emotion.

The woman looked up at Smoke. "Hi," she said as she wiped several beads of sweat from her forehead. "I'm sorry but the lift is broken. I'm doing what I can to fix it but it may be a little while."

"What happened to it?" Constance asked trying to sound as if she weren't thankful for her luck.

"Same thing that happens to any contraption when it gets used a lot. After a while it just breaks down. Parts wear away and things break. It shouldn't take more than a couple days to get everything replaced though."

Smoke swore louder than he should have. Just more proof he needed sleep. "Don't mind him." Constance said trying to maintain the damage Smoke's little outburst may have caused. She didn't think it'd be much, but from what she understood it was wise to stay on the lift driver's good side. "He's just in a hurry. The cursing was uncalled for."

"It's better than him trying to kiss my ass like everyone else does. Let me know where you two are staying and I'll come collect you personally before I go down. Deal?"

She saw Smoke try to hide a look of surprise. "Yeah, Thank you," Smoke said with wide eyes.

"Anyway, I have to get back to work," the lift driver said with a smile.

Constance and Smoke waved to the woman and walked away. The shops and brothels shined in her eyes as they walked past. She couldn't help but look towards each building. Topless women danced behind windows showing what prospective men and women could potentially get. Constance shook her head and continued forward as Smoke continued. "We should get a room for the next couple days," she said with a straight face.

Smoke looked down to her, "Yeah, you're right. I haven't really slept since the surface. I'm feeling it."

"It's really showing," Constance said trying her best to not seem callous.

Smoke gave her an amused huff as they began to look around. "One of the biggest problems about this floor is that the majority of the inns here are also brothels. You can't really get a room without buying a girl for a night."

"That's not really good for us," Constance said with concern. She wasn't against sleeping with another woman, but it wasn't her first choice and she didn't want to have to buy a human's company just for the use of a bed. "I just want to get some sleep."

"Smoke? Is that you?" a woman's voice chimed from behind them.

Both Smoke and Constance turned to see a woman looking to be in her early forties, a little younger than Smoke. She wore her age well with a sort of calm and wise dignity. She was a slender woman with shoulder length vibrant red hair. Her green eyes grew soft as she saw Smoke's face. Constance looked to her companion and saw a look of desire and terror. She didn't know this woman but there was a history there.

"Glass?" he whispered. "How did you find me?"

"A friend in the second below saw you on the second floor and said you were coming down here. I knew you'd be looking for a room."

"I've been down to this floor a number of times and you've never sought me out before," Smoke said, the surprised expression never leaving his face.

"Nor did you," she said with a shrewd grin. "We're a part of each other's past. We're busy people. There's any number of reasons we wouldn't have looked for each other. Besides, I know you live on the first below. I could have come to you if I so desired."

Constance watched the back and forth as Smoke and Glass tried to get a one-up on the other. "It's nice to meet you,"

Constance said trying to cut off the pointless dialogue that had been taking place.

Glass took her eyes from Smoke and looked Constance over. "Your women keep getting younger," she said with a slight laugh.

Constance had failed at hiding her flushed cheeks but managed to hide her disdain for the comment and decided to play nice. "I'm Constance, a friend of Smoke's, just a friend though; I'm travelling through the floors with him."

"You're giving tours now?" Glass asked.

"I'm on a case," Smoke said as his eyes softened and became the inquisitive and scanning eyes Constance knew. "She's tagging along to help and so she can see the underground. I don't know why she wants to be here, but I'm happy for the company."

Glass gave Smoke a look of interest before breaking into a fit of laughter. "Oh shit, I thought you two were fucking. Here I was about to get jealous."

Constance gave Smoke a look before turning back to the laughing woman. "I don't know what the fuck you think is so funny but what Smoke and I do is none of your business."

Glass calmed her laughing as she noticeably ignored Constance and spoke again. "You two have a room yet?"

Smoke shook his head, "We don't; we just left the lift."

"Come stay at my place. I can give you both separate rooms so you can have your own space. Rooms all come with private baths and a wash basin for clothes."

Constance wasn't sure what to make of this woman. She could see Smoke wanted to go. She really was just there for the experience and to get what she came for. Smoke looked at Constance as if he needed her consent to accept. She knew he was gauging for her comfortability but it was all a show. She gave Smoke a slight nod before looking forward at Glass.

"Yeah, we'll take the rooms. How much for a couple nights?"

Glass pressed her lips together into a tight smile. "For you and your companion, it's on the house. All I'll ask is for a chance to catch up over a drink."

Smoke smiled, "I think that can be arranged. Though I think a chance to sleep is paramount."

Glass walked in to close the distance. Her and Smoke both placed both hands over each other's ears and smiled as they brought their foreheads together. Constance didn't know that gesture though she had a pretty good idea that it was a sign of affection. Constance's eyes grew wide when she saw Smoke and Glass close in for a long kiss.

"Of course," Glass said once the kiss had ended. "Just follow me," Glass said as she separated from Smoke and walked past him and Constance, she walked down the street without looking back. Smoke followed the woman almost instantly while Constance waited a few moments before taking up the rear.

Smoke breathed in the scent of incense as he walked into the brothel run by Glass. The place had a sweet floral smell to it that he found pleasant. The women within tried to grab his attention with every step he took. Once they noticed he was with Glass they backed off and went about their duties of cleaning the place or looking at any of the other men who had walked in.

Glass walked to the front desk and grabbed two keys from the wall behind. He watched her smile gently as she paused to look at the keys. He didn't know what had gone through her head, but he knew it was something nice. She handed both him and Constance a key. "Your rooms are side by side. That way you can find each other when need be."

Smoke thanked Glass and proceeded towards his room. He couldn't tell if Constance had been behind him at all the whole way to his room on the upper floor. The place was an oddity of sorts to have a second floor to it. He unlocked the door and stepped inside. The place was better furnished than his home on the first below.

The bed had a double mattress covered in a large loom woven duvet. The typical wooden desk and chair sat in a corner. It was nicer than the ones on the first floor or on the surface. The desk and chair had been carved to depict naked women in the legs and back of the chair. He wasn't surprised by any of this; the place was a brothel after all. The rooms were designed to get both men and women into the mood.

The room split off to another room complete with a wash basin with a washboard and a small mangle for his clothes. A clothes line hung above the wash tub. Smoke grinned as he removed his clothes and placed them neatly folded on the chair beside the desk. Once he woke he'd have a bath and dress himself again. He'd clean his clothes before going back to sleep. It was a possibility they could be here longer than anticipated and some clean clothes would be a good idea.

He removed the duvet and crawled under the smaller blanket and was asleep before his head hit the pillow.

The tavern within the brothel was filled with men and half naked women. Smoke ignored them all for the woman sitting alone in the back wearing a scarlet dress and black corset, attire suited for the owner of such a place. She smiled as she saw him emerge through the crowd. A small glass of wine awaited him as he sat down. "Hello Glass," he said with a soft voice.

"It's good to see you Smoke," she said before taking a sip of her wine.

Wine in the underground was a rarity. Finding the proper fruits to make a wine drinkable was almost impossible. People at one point had tried to make wine from darkplant but failed horribly. There had been a small distillery that made wine from surface fruits on the first floor at one time, but had burned down when they couldn't meet the demand.

Smoke brought the wine to his lips and absorbed the fruity taste. He let out a breath of pleasure and placed the glass back on the table. It was easy to let his guard down around Glass. In the entire world in all the levels the only place he felt any sort of safety to let down his guard in any way was when he was with her.

"So you're a private investigator now," Glass said, breaking the comfortable silence.

Smoke smiled, "Yeah, I didn't think it'd be a good idea to go be a full officer with my past."

"You'd likely be arrested on the spot," she said with a giggle. Smoke joined her in the laughter.

"Look at you though; you've got your own place. I'm happy for you," Smoke said happily.

"I was good at what I did, this really was an inevitability," Glass said as she shifted her eyes to the side.

Glass supposedly had always been ashamed of being a prostitute. She had always believed she had been made to do bigger and better things. Things she never got to do. She believed she had been trapped here on the third below perpetually stuck in an endless loop of selling her body to men and the need to survive. In all reality she could have left the third floor at any time and been free of the lifestyle. Smoke believed deep down she secretly loved it and that was why she never left. She made a lot of money at it, enough to own her own place.

"Why not leave this place? Sell it to one of your girls and come live with me," Smoke said giving her an easy way out.

Glass gave him a soft smile. He knew she'd refuse before he

had said a word. "I'm flattered," she said as she took a sip of her wine, "I really am. Too many years have passed between us though. I don't know if I could handle it. I have become accustomed to this floor, this lifestyle. I don't think I could leave it after this many years."

"It's not too late to start a new life," he said, making it look as if he were actually trying to convince her.

"I think I'm going to pass. It's really appreciated though," she said with a smile. "So you're on a case," she said changing the subject right on cue.

"I am," Smoke said calmly. He had no intentions of relaying all the information on her all at once. If she asked he'd answer truthfully. There'd be no real reason not to. Glass was the safest person he'd known.

"What are you able to tell me about it?" Glass asked.

Smoke gave her a wide smile and cocked his head slightly to the side, "I guess it depends on the questions you ask."

The silent stand off as Glass decided which questions to ask would have been hilariously tense to observe. The crowd around them paid no attention to the two; though there may as well have not been a crowd making a cacophonous noise around them for all they cared or noticed. They were busy staring each other down.

"Who's the target?" Glass finally asked.

"Her name's Blue. She's a girl from the second above."

"Classy," Glass said with a whistle. "Didn't think you'd ever get a job like that on the first below."

"Me neither," Smoke admitted. "Though this could be my ticket out of the underground."

Glass nodded, "How much are they paying you? If I may ask."

"Two million skins, though... I don't think I'm going to get to enjoy it for any amount of time."

A look of worry crossed her face as Smoke took in a deep breath. She ran her finger around the brim of the wineglass. She took in a deep breath as well before sighing deeply, "What did you do?"

Smoke looked at his glass of wine. Almost untouched with the exception of the initial sip. "I escaped the fourth floor."

"Fulcrum?" she asked with a concerned look, knowing exactly to what Smoke was referring.

"Fulcrum," he confirmed.

"Hide here," she said. "He can't get you here. None of his men would dare get themselves blacklisted by all the women on the third floor, not even Fulcrum would be so bold."

"You have that sort of power?" Smoke asked surprised.

"Like I said, I'm good at what I do," Glass said with a slight hint of a smug expression. "Very good at what I do; and I've been doing it for a long time."

Smoke smiled internally as he maintained his straight face. She had learned the politics of the third floor and had become a major player without him knowing. He really could live the rest of his days on the third floor and be safe from Fulcrum's guns. His thoughts immediately shifted to Blue.

He smiled, leaned across the table, took Glass by the face and planted a small kiss on her lips. "You have no idea how much I want that. I would stay here but I need to finish this job. If anything for my own integrity, I'm not having you take care of me while I grow fat living off you. If I abandon this case I'd never get another job again."

"What if you can't find her anyway? She could very well not even be in this area," Glass asked.

"Then I tell the family they will have to get more eyes out there. I am only one man and while two million skins is a lot, I can only do so much before then."

"The money is not worth your life," Glass said as he watched a tear begin to well in her eyes. She had been trying to talk him out of it and was failing.

He couldn't tell if they were crocodile tears or genuine. He didn't want to risk getting it wrong. "It's not the money," he said softly placing his fingers beneath her chin. "It's a matter of my credibility as a detective."

She nodded as she pulled her face away from his fingers. She looked away from him as she closed her eyes, "When you find her, get your ass back here then."

Smoke nodded and smiled softly, "I will."

"Good, I don't want anything to happen to you. You're kind of important to me."

Smoke let out a sharp breath as he took a second sip of his wine. "One last case and then I'll do my detective work here. I may have to give Fulcrum all the skins anyway if I happen to run into him. It may buy my safety."

"I will personally make sure Fulcrum doesn't do anything to you," Glass said sharply.

"I don't doubt that," Smoke said with a mild laugh. "I think I can deal with him though. He's not expecting two million skins."

"Whatever you have to do. Just get back here to me."

Smoke couldn't blame her for wanting him to come down to the third below instead of her going to the first below. She had built a name for herself here, she had skins and influence. What did he have? A small home and a slowly failing detective agency doing jobs he didn't want to do. While he wasn't especially keen on moving to the third below, considering it was a little too close to the fourth, he would move to keep himself safe and to be near the woman he'd loved for so many years.

He thought to why the two of them had parted ways. She didn't want to leave her career no matter how she hated it, and he wanted to reach for the unobtainable goal of living on the surface to get away from the Cartel. Now here they were a decade later, ready to move in together at the drop of a hat.

"Do you remember how we met?" Smoke asked suddenly.

The question seemed to have shocked Glass because she almost dropped her wine glass. A small dribble of wine fell to the floor from what had escaped. "I remember," she said bluntly. "I don't want to remember those days though."

"I understand," Smoke said with a smile.

It had been three days since Glass had taken them into her brothel. Constance had begun to wonder if they would ever be getting off the floor. The morning of the third day Constance had taken a walk to see the lift driver. The lift driver had apologized profusely before going into a lengthy explanation as to what was wrong. Constance didn't understand much of it, but she got the gist that something was wrong with the pulley system and she had to wait for a part from the first floor. There was a possibility it would be done that day, but odds were it would be finished the day after.

Smoke had spent the majority of the past three days with Glass. They seemed to be catching up, though there looked to be some long pauses in their talking as they stared at each other with dreamy gazes. They were adorable.

There were times though when Smoke would leave the brothel and begin asking questions around the third below. Constance didn't go with him on any of his interrogations; she felt she wouldn't be needed. Besides, a bit of time off was nice.

THE ENGINE WHAT RUNS THE WORLD

She sat in the tub soaking the hot water into her skin. She loved the feeling of a good long bath. The feeling of cleanliness was something of a luxury traveling with Smoke in the underground, as she had learned. She leaned back and allowed the water to envelop her entire body leaving only her mouth and nose clear from the water.

Glass had been a pleasure to visit with. It was the happiest she had ever seen Smoke in the short time she had known him. She could see how much the two of them cared for each other and she wondered if or why he would ever leave the third below. She wasn't going to mention it to Smoke or try to force him into something he may or may not have wanted to do. It wasn't her business what he did. If he chose to continue after Blue she would follow. If he chose to stay she would eventually have to make her departure. It would upset her to do so, but she wouldn't find what she needed if she stayed.

At least the odds were quite slim that she'd find it if she stayed.

She knew Smoke was a good detective. He was skilled at noticing things she hadn't even thought to look for. However, the man got really cocky and believed he had the ability to notice everything. She had shown him on occasions he was not as great as he believed. Though, if anyone could find Blue by themselves it would be Smoke Callahan.

She carefully took in a deep breath as she ran her hands down her body. The feeling of flesh on flesh contact within the hot water was titillating; even if it was just her hands on her own body. She had been given offers from the male prostitutes from the third floor. She had refused them; the repulsion of buying another person's body persisted even through the loneliness of having her own room and being virtually ignored by Smoke. She found she'd rather be alone over spending a night of meaningless sex that she had to pay for. It wasn't worth it in the long run.

The thought of what she'd done with Smoke crossed her mind, though she shook it off. Sex with Smoke was a tactic to better convince him to bring her along. Men were often more agreeable after a night with a woman.

She didn't know how long she had spent in the tub but the water had almost gone ice cold by the time she pulled herself from the murky water. She dried herself with a woolly towel and collapsed onto her bed. She stared at the ceiling as she felt her bare chest continue to move up and down with every breath. She didn't know how much longer she'd be able to handle being here. She wanted to get out, but anywhere she went she was met by nothing more than bare breasted women and males who either wanted her to buy their time or by men who wanted to buy hers.

Eventually she sat back up and dressed herself. She'd realized she had gotten hungry in the time between going to see the lift driver and finishing her bath. Her traveling clothes had been clean from the day before. She didn't really go anywhere to soil the clothes so they had remained clean through the rest of the day and all night.

Constance opened her door to see Smoke's door closed. A slightly muffled sound of moaning could be heard from the other side. She was reminded of her days back on the surface working in the tavern. It had been her duty to keep the peace as well as keep the tavern girls safe from the over drunk and aroused patrons. She had been good at her job.

Constance chuckled under her breath and shook her head in amusement. At least the old boy was having a good time. He'd need it as a bit of relief for where he was going. Though Constance had sex'd with him the one night she didn't seem to have any real desire to sex him again. He had been a hapless stranger who was only staying at the inn until the lift could take him down. Her desire to travel with him had been on a whim and the ability to go where she needed to go with a bit of protection. Even the anonymous tryst line had been a ploy to better ensure she got her way.

She thought to the hidden shortblade she kept in her room. She had been thankful for Smoke buying it for her. She had more than enough skins to buy the shortblade herself, but Smoke had insisted. Who was she to argue with a free weapon, especially a weapon as fancy and expertly crafted as the hidden shortblade? It had understandably been forbidden for her to carry it around the brothel. Her room was a safe enough place for it.

The tavern had a familiar smell to it. She ordered a small cup of ale to wake her up and a plate of synthetic venison and darkplant on the side. She didn't know what it was about the taste of darkplant, but she loved it. She had seen Smoke almost keel over trying not to laugh as she ate the vegetable.

The food was pretty good. She didn't care for the synthetic venison as much as she thought she'd might. She'd had real venison on the surface and the two tasted nothing alike. She ate it regardless, Glass was paying for it.

As she left the tavern she came face to face with the lift driver. The two of them almost colliding as she exited. "It's ready to take the two of you down to the fourth floor." She said quickly and with a smile.

"Fantastic!" Constance said with a massive grin. "I'll go get Smoke. You'll wait for us right?"

The lift driver nodded her head, "Of course I will. You just get your friend and I'll be waiting."

Constance's spirits lifted. She didn't expect her luck to hold out and have the lift repaired that very day. She didn't want to jinx anything and leapt up the stairs to Smoke's room. She could no longer hear any moaning from the other side of the door. Any sex that had been going on was over. She breathed a sigh of relief and knocked on the door. It took a moment before she heard a muffled, "Yeah!"

"Lift driver stopped by," she said as loud as she could without being disruptive to the other men who were behind some of the other doors. "She said the lift is ready to take us down to the fourth below."

She didn't have to wait long before she heard Smoke shout, "Alright, I'll be right out. Just give me a bit."

Constance didn't think she needed to respond to it. The thought of Smoke being naked behind the door was not exactly a flattering thought, especially since he'd be naked behind that door with a naked Glass. She shook her head in amusement again and proceeded to get her stuff packed up.

"I've got to go now," Smoke said softly between kissing Glass's face and neck.

"I know, you have a job to do," she said with a gasp.

She soon tossed him to the other side of the bed. He laughed genuinely before standing. She watched as he dressed. He grinned as he saw her eying his crotch and backside. "Do you ever wonder what the world would have been like had magic never faded?"

"That was out of nowhere," Glass said with a chuckle.

"It's just something I've been pondering for the last couple days. Just something to amuse myself," he said with amusement.

"Wishing abilities like yours were not so uncommon?" Glass asked as she sat up in the bed.

"No, not really," Smoke said casually. "It's just been a fun thought. I've had some of the best days I can remember since coming here and if I'm being honest, I really don't want them to end. Once I walk out that door I'll have a job to do and any level of enjoyment will have to wait until my return."

"However long that takes," Glass pouted.

"I promise to come back as fast as I can," he said with a gentle smile.

"You'd better," she said as she covered herself with the blankets.

Smoke let out a small amused huff of a chuckle as he strapped his suspenders up and placed his hat on his head. As he walked towards the door he looked back at Glass. She looked more beautiful than she had when he had first met her back in their youth.

Her eyes said everything he needed to hear and wanted her to say as he left the room.

7

The days spent with Glass had refreshed Smoke in ways he didn't know he'd needed. It wasn't the days off the case; he hadn't had many days working the case to begin with so he wasn't over-exhausted from that, it was life in general. If he could find a way to bring Blue home safely and alive and if he found a way past Fulcrum he'd finally be able to live an easy life. He'd be able to live out the rest of his days in comfort. Glass could live as a major political figure for the third floor, maybe going as far as to cut supplies off from the fourth floor until the Cartel got choked out completely. A plan was brewing in his head.

The urge to stay on the third floor with Glass had been difficult to resist. He knew he had a lot of work to do and that he needed to get this case finished. There was something pulling him forward that he couldn't explain. It bothered him that he had to leave, but he knew he would be happier once he returned - if he returned.

The lift driver was nice, not very talkative before the trip downward, but nice. Smoke doubted he'd so much as remember her face a half an hour after they'd left. She seemed to have struck a chord with Constance however. He didn't think the two of them would ever be friends; he had a hard time imagining

Constance staying on the third floor.

The ride down to the fourth below took longer than it had with the other lift drivers. He wasn't angry or upset by any means over this; the longer it took to get to the fourth below the better. Once there he'd probably try camping out by the lift to the fifth floor just so he could be there as quickly as possible. If it were possible he would pay off the lift driver to get below sooner.

During their time on the third floor he had neglected to tell Constance of his history. He hoped it wouldn't have to come up at all. She may see his secrecy as a breach of trust and may decide to part ways with him. The thought of Constance leaving upset him, though it wouldn't bother him so much to have her away from him; it was that he would worry more about her personal safety in the underground. He doubted he'd be able to forgive himself if something were to happen to her while they were separated. She was a tough woman who had managed to keep the peace in an inn on the surface through her physical strength, but the fourth below was a dangerous place and the lower floors would only get more so.

As they left the ceiling for the fourth below he could see the massive lights that illuminated the entirety of the floor. He could see nearly the entire town; he even managed to mentally point out the places where he had once hung out and gotten into trouble. He could see the warehouses where weapons and narcotics were made and those where bloody interrogations happened. A feeling of anxiety began to flow through him. He did his best to keep a straight face and do what he could to pretend that being back where he had been born and raised didn't bother him. The feeling only grew as he and Constance stepped off the lift platform.

A plan began to take form in his head. If everything went perfectly, both he and Constance would be on their way to the fifth below before anyone knew they were there. If they did get noticed though, the plan would have to adapt.

Constance looked over to him with a straight face. She could sense this floor was bad news and that they needed to get out as quickly as they could. "What is this place?" Constance asked once they were off the lift. "It feels wrong."

"That's because it is," Smoke said, taking a look around. "This is the floor where the Cartel takes up shop. It's beyond the reach of standard officers and those who do come down here are more corrupt than anything else. A Cartel member could shoot an officer in front of an officer and they'd say they weren't even on the fourth floor that day. They are just around for show. This place is more dangerous than you know. We need to get out of here as fast as we can."

"Hold it," a voice said from one of the few shadows the floor had to offer.

"Oh for fuck sake!" Smoke screamed. "Does everyone know where I'm going?"

A short, stalky man stepped from the shadows holding two revolving pistols. Smoke knew that firing those pistols even once would create one hell of a kick back; Reggae's muscular arms would have been able to take the kick easily. "You know who we are. You know we have eyes everywhere. We know what you're going to do before you do it."

"Reggae, I can't believe they have you picking up an old bastard like myself."

Reggae narrowed his eyes, "We're not taking any chances with you Smoke. We remember you. We remember what you're capable of."

"I bet you do," Smoke said with a clear frown. "Let her go though. She has no part of this."

"She seems valuable to you," Reggae said, now showing his half-smile. "We'll take her as well. Let's call it insurance so we know you're not going to do anything stupid."

Smoke looked to Constance who had her hands on her hidden short blade, ready to draw and attack. She looked back at him, ready for him to give the order. If he did, he knew she'd cut through Reggae before he'd have a chance to react; his attention was focused on Smoke. Reggae also knew Smoke would have a revolving pistol of his own. Pistols were always the bigger threat than a blade.

The problem was what would happen after. If she cut Reggae to bits she'd have a mark on her head and she'd be dead before the next lift ride off the floor. He thought of several escape attempts before finally coming up with something great. It was a shot in the dark and relied heavily on everything falling into place and people acting as he expected. It wasn't much, but it was something. He looked back to Constance. "Surrender," Smoke said flatly.

"What?" Constance asked, dumbfounded.

"Surrender."

Constance gave him a defiant look. "I can take him," she whispered.

"I know you can. That's the problem. Trust me, I have a plan."

He could see the conflict in Constance's eyes as she threw the blade to the ground. Smoke carefully pulled out his revolving pistol and placed it softly on the ground. "We'll come without a fight," Smoke said hanging his head.

"Good," Reggae said with a relieved grin.

Something hit Smoke in the back of the head. He heard Constance scream and everything went black.

Smoke awoke in darkness. The back of his head ached where he had been hit. He could feel the fabric over his face preventing him from seeing what was going on around him. The ropes that bound his wrists and ankles dug into his flesh as he tried to move. He knew exactly where he was.

The room was hot, very hot. The coolant in this part of town had been tampered with just enough to make the natural heat nearly uncomfortable, though not so hot as to kill a person. Beads of sweat poured from Smoke's forehead, soaking the bag. Every breath he took brought in his salty sweat into his mouth and into his lungs.

He sat in silence for a few long minutes before he heard Constance awake with a frightened gasp from right behind him. He felt some relief in knowing he wasn't in the room alone, though Constance would be used as a sort of bargaining chip. He felt bad for what the men would end up doing to her if he didn't comply with their demands. Her terrified gasps seemed to echo through the room.

He tried to visualize the room within his head. It was a place he had been in many times. It was the room they took people to interrogate them. The floors were made of a metal that prevented blood and any viscera that may get spread around from being absorbed, and they allowed for a quick cleanup.

"Constance," he said trying to remain calm. It was true that her breathing had begun to send shivers down his spine and forced him to ask the question - if they would survive an escape. "It's okay, I'm here."

He could hear her swallow loudly, "Smoke, who are those men?"

"They're members of the Cartel," he said without hesitation. Now was the time. He had to tell her everything. "I have some confessions to make," he said with a depressed tone.

"If you're going to say that you grew up down here I already pieced that together," she said without anger, but she maintained her panic. "I've known since the second below."

"Well, that's good," he said trying to hide the smile from himself more than anyone else. "I've done some horrible things though."

"Whatever you've done you can tell me later. I already figured you'd been a part of this lot. The way you looked at the narcs and weapons booths showed me all I needed to know about you. You despise this life and you're ashamed of your past. You don't have to tell me how you smuggled narcotics and weapons. You don't have to tell me how you tortured and killed people who double-crossed you. You don't have to tell me anything."

"There is still one thing I have to tell you - though I agree – it can wait until we're out of here. But I do have to ask, what tipped you off."

"Fulcrum," she said with a smug voice, "the way he carried himself and the way you tried to shoo him off. It said a lot. My suspicions were confirmed when you said he agreed to keep us safe as we traveled downward. I don't think you're going to see the reward money for long dealing with him."

Smoke let out a sharp singular, "heh," and remained silent as the sweat began to run down his face.

"How long are they going to keep us like this?" Constance asked.

"Until we break," Smoke replied after a moment of silence. "They know I'm not going to break quickly. They think it'll be you. They'll keep us here with these dark bags over our faces without any food or water until we break down and beg. That's when they'll begin the torture until we tell them what they want to hear."

"What do they want from us?"

Smoke hung his head in shame, "From you, nothing. You just happened to be in the wrong place at the wrong time and showed you were too much of a threat to leave out in the street. They want me. I'm the one who left."

"So they want you just for leaving?" Constance asked, surprised.

"This is supposed to be a lifetime job. I just got stuck with the rotten luck of being born into it."

Smoke waited to hear any other signs of life. He listened for a second set of lungs, a slight scuff of a boot across the floor, voices in the distance, anything. He knew there would be someone watching though he couldn't place them in the room. This was something he was familiar with, someone would sit and wait for the prisoners to begin talking and listen to anything they said.

"You may as well take the bags off our heads, the mind tactics won't work on us," Smoke shouted loudly.

He could hear the faint sound of a pair of boots hit the floor and slowly move towards him. As the body moved closer he began to hear his breath. He heard the sound of the man shuffling in his pockets and pulled something out. He heard more shuffling before the sound of an igniting match filled the room. Constance's breathing became more rapid. The sound of small flecks of dried plant burning could be heard as well as the sucking motions of a man lighting a pipe. The smell of burning tobacco cascaded over the two of them as Constance coughed a little.

The bag was suddenly ripped from off his head. The man who had grabbed it had not taken care to avoid grabbing Smoke's hair and took more than a few with his fist. Smoke managed to avoid yelping in pain but couldn't hide the pained expression as he tried to let his eyes adjust to the light of the room, making his captor laugh.

Smoke focused and saw Conrad Toomie standing before him. The short man standing just under four feet high continued to laugh at Smoke's surprised expression. "Conrad?" Smoke asked,

THE ENGINE WHAT RUNS THE WORLD

"You're a part of this now?"

Conrad had been a nothing more than a kid when Smoke had left the fourth floor. Now here stood a strapping young man with a heavily pronounced jaw and a grin that could have won over any woman above the third floor. "That's right Smoke," he said in a deep voice that had formed while Smoke had been away. "I'm the prime inquisitor. Master of interrogation and the-"

"Patron of bullshit," Smoke said with a grin. "Tell me, did you practice this little speech when you heard I'd been caught or do you try this little fear tactic on everyone you guard?"

Conrad gave a look of anger and surprise. Smoke had hit the mark in his assertion and it showed all over the kids face. Smoke looked over to Conrad as he tried to think of something to say back and he was taken back to the kid who used to tag alongside him when he'd be out and about shaking down small businesses for protection money. Conrad had never been permitted to go inside the building or touch any of the money. He had been too young and much too innocent. Smoke thought back to his last words to the kid, telling him to get out before his soul became as tainted as his own.

"Smoke, you taught me a lot during your best days here," Conrad said.

"I didn't teach you shit," Smoke snapped back. "You were never permitted to take part in any of the dealings, you weren't allowed to be where interrogations took place. You didn't get to see or hear anything. The best you got was my presence, and that's because I thought you'd be useful if anyone tried to shake me down."

He knew Constance was listening and more than likely silently judging him through her black bag. He began to stare down Conrad, whose grin never left. This concerned Smoke. "Oh I know you didn't let me in on anything. That doesn't mean I didn't find ways. Small holes in the wall to watch you interrogate someone, thin glass and walls to listen to what you said when you took money from people. I wanted to join you Smoke. I would have followed you anywhere and done anything you said."

"You didn't do the last thing I said for you to do," Smoke said coldly, channeling his abilities.

Smoke's words seemed to hit Conrad like a fist in the face. He gave Smoke an angry look before his features softened. "You're right - I didn't. But I couldn't listen to someone who wanted to be weak. I couldn't," Conrad looked apologetic with those words.

"It's not weakness to leave something toxic. It's strength. Besides, last I saw of you, you were going to leave. What happened?"

"Cobble," Conrad said with his head hung.

"He talked you into staying," Smoke said as the pieces fell into place.

"He convinced me to hate you. I did a good job of hating you for leaving for such a long time. But now that I see you here, tied up to the chair, I can't hate you either. I understand your leaving. It was-"

"Let's not get into it," Smoke said with a slight half smile.

Conrad nodded his head, "Okay," he whispered.

"What I want you to do now is to take the black bag off Constance's head and get the Boss. Tell him I want to talk to him."

A wide toothy grin that almost seemed childish spread across Conrad's face. He immediately took the bag off Constance's head and ran off to get the man Smoke wanted to see least in this world, but needed to see if he had any intentions of progressing.

"That was easy," Constance said in amazement.

"So, I'm sure you listened to all of that," Smoke said trying to get a view of Constance.

"I did," Constance said blankly. "I can't say I'm surprised or disappointed. Remember, I knew you were from down here. I didn't think you were giving money to the poor while you grew up. I knew you did some dark and deplorable things. Stop feeling sorry for yourself and face your past so you can accept it. You'll live longer."

Smoke hung his head. She was right, he had spent so long running from his past and trying to atone for actions no man could ever atone for - he had lost who he could have been. Even as a private detective he had been unable to do as much good as he wanted. People didn't come to him for missing family members as often as he needed. They didn't come to him hoping to find an unfaithful husband or to investigate an unscrupulous business. Instead they called on him to follow people for information, to track down concubines and slaves - the dirty work that nobody else would do and work he had no choice but to do.

They sat in silence for the remainder of the wait. Smoke heard the sound of the steel door creak as three men entered. The man on the left was someone Smoke only knew as Metal Jaw. He had a suit of metal armour he'd had welded around him to make himself a powerful bodyguard. He often smelled bad from the sweat and waste that would get caught in the metal, but he did his best to bathe regularly. The man on the right was Cobble Raw, the right-hand man of the Cartel's boss; he was the only man Smoke considered smarter than himself. The only problem with Cobble was his ambition and his desire to be the Boss and he'd do it any way he could.

The man in the center stood over Smoke. He was an elderly man made from sinew and muscle. His face was covered in scars and cuts. Each one from a well fought battle against a rival leading to his eventual rule over the entire fourth below in that area. Each scar told a story that could never be spoken. Despite his age and scars, the old man held a level of handsomeness most men could only hope to maintain. He looked at Smoke tied to the chair and gave him a warm smile, "I didn't think you'd still be here," he said softly.

"Where's Conrad?" Smoke asked in a way that said he demanded an answer.

"He's asleep in my office. He had to be punished for leaving a prisoner unguarded; especially you. You must have really wanted to speak with me."

"What makes you say that?" Smoke asked with a grin.

The Boss smiled, "We both know if you wanted you could have escaped from that chair a long time ago. After all, I've yet to see a prison that could hold the great Smoke Callahan."

"It's true," Smoke said with a grin. "I also would have gotten away completely if I didn't have Constance with me. One person could escape without being seen. Two, not so much and I'm not leaving without her."

The Boss grinned, "So you care for this woman."

"She's in my care. Be assured, if anything happens to her I will rain hellfire upon you. You know I can and you know I will."

The Boss showed a look of shocked amazement before bursting into a fit of laughter. "I know you could have back then. I don't think you could these days. You have no skins as well as no influence down here."

"No, but what I do have is the ability to be unnoticeable even when people are looking for me. That's why I was such a great narc. That's why I'm a great detective. Visibility and prisons mean nothing to me."

"That is why I named you Smoke," the Boss said with a grin.

"I know it is, and where there's smoke there's bound to be fire. If not at the moment there will be eventually."

The Boss took a couple steps backward; his grin never left his face. "Look, I don't want to hurt you. In fact I plan to hire you. One last job and I'll let you and your bonnie lass move freely through the fourth below as often as you like."

"Take the job," Constance said before Smoke had been given a chance to respond.

"Take it?" Smoke asked. "You don't even know what it is?"

"I think someone's desperate to get out of here," the Boss said with a snide smile.

"Of course I am," Constance said. Smoke couldn't see her though he assumed she had a massive grin on her face, "but that's not why."

"I like her," the Boss said with a grin. "She's ballsy. Tell me, why should Smoke take the job?"

"Because it's probably something simple like a drop job," Constance said. "Just dropping off a package whose contents we'll never know. It'll be quick and simple."

"How can you be so sure?" the Boss asked.

"Because you would know enough to know Smoke wouldn't do anything like an interrogation or an assassination. He would rather die and take me with him than kill someone else or torture them. Trust me, it's not a fact I'm especially pleased about, but you and I and Smoke know it to be true."

The Boss frowned in amusement, "seriously ballsy. Also right. Smoke, I want you to take a package to the fifth below and leave it in the waste basket beside the statue of Pedro Argos."

Pedro Argos. That was a name Smoke hadn't heard in a very long time.

"I'll do it," Smoke said, knowing he'd regret it later.

"Wonderful," the Boss said happily. "I do have to note that your woman will have to stay here in our custody until we know you've dropped off the package."

"How am I to prove that?" Smoke asked.

The Boss grinned, "I have an imager in my office you could use. Bring us back an image of the package in the bin with the statue of Pedro Argos and we'll let her go. You'll be free to come and go as you please and we'll be square."

"Should I ask what's in the package?"

"I wouldn't," the Boss said somberly.

Smoke nodded in agreement. He didn't really want to know what was in the package. "Well, are you going to let me out of this chair?" he asked impatiently.

The Boss nodded to Metal Jaw and signaled to allow Smoke to go free. He pulled out a knife and cut the ropes binding his wrists and legs. They had been good knots. The kind Smoke would have had difficulty getting out of. It wouldn't have been impossible; in fact he would have been out of the ropes long before the Boss have arrived. The feeling of the ropes going slack and falling to the floor as Metal Jaw cut them felt incredible. He felt the rush of blood return to his fingertips; they had gone numb off and on while he had been tied up.

He stood and brushed off his jacket. There had not been any dirt or dust on it, but the compulsory action was almost automatic. He looked at the Boss and grinned, "Well, you going to take me to the package?"

The Boss nodded, "Someone is eager to get things done. For tonight though... we drink."

"Constance comes too," he demanded.

"Of course," the Boss said with a grin. "Metal Jaw, cut her free."

As the ropes that bound her to the chair fell free she rubbed her wrists where they had been. She sneered and raised her middle fingers on both her hands. The gesture meant nothing to any of the men from the underground. Smoke assumed it was intended to be a rude gesture, but he could tell the Boss, Metal Jaw and Cobble took no notice of it.

"Come," the Boss said with a grin, "It's been too long."

Smoke and Constance followed the Boss and his henchmen with Metal Jaw holding the rear to be sure nobody tried to run. They were led through the center of the floor until they came to a small dilapidated looking place that appeared as if it should have been condemned several generations before.

Hey," Constance said "What's a narc? We don't have that word on the surface."

Smoke had hoped she wouldn't have openly stated she was from the surface within earshot of these people. The damage was done though. "A narcotic trafficker. It's just faster and easier to say narc."

Constance nodded her head and kept quiet.

Metal Jaw opened the door and waited as the party let themselves through. The inside didn't look any better. The living room that had been viewable from the main entrance was furnished with rotten couches and gas lamps that had been broken since before Smoke had been born. The smell of mould filled the air around them as The Boss opened the door to the basement. A flood of memories came back to Smoke as he reminisced about his days coming to this house and taking a load off with several glasses of mulch liquor.

The basement was almost like stepping into another building. Bright lights filled the room allowing for maximum visibility while still maintaining an atmosphere fitting for a drinking hole. Several faces Smoke recognized stopped and stared as he slowly walked past and entered the Boss's personal booth.

Metal Jaw and Cobble both stood at attention outside the booth as the Boss ordered three glasses of the finest booze they had in the joint.

The barkeep leapt at the opportunity to serve the Boss, as he probably did every time the Boss entered the establishment. "So," the Boss said over the sound of the band's music, "you're a private detective on the first below. I gotta say - I expected much worse to come of you when you left. I'm pleased to see you've exceeded my expectations."

He peered over to Constance, who was gazing over at the band. They were a heavy set group dressed in waist coats and slacks fitting for the scene in the fourth floor. The singer had a monocle hanging from his lapel that swung back and forth as he sang. Each man wore top hats that had been heavily soiled by many years of wear and use in the underground. They sang a song about a battle between metal workers.

Smoke didn't want to appear as if he had been distracted or hesitating at a loss for words. Nevertheless he planned his words carefully, suspecting the Boss believing him to be at a loss anyway. "It wasn't easy getting a foothold up there," Smoke finally said. The worst thing he could do was to seem boastful of his supposed success. "The worst part was securing the skins to get started and make sure I could survive until I got a job. Luckily the first below is the sort of place where people go missing and others actually care. I think I'd have starved to death if I'd have set up shop on a lower floor."

The Boss burst into a fit of laughter. This is what Smoke had anticipated him to do. He had known the man all his life and knew what pushed his buttons to activate anger, happiness or laughter. Laughter was the best reaction he could have hoped for in his predicament.

"You'll kill me Smoke if you continue to make me laugh like this," the Boss said between hiccoughs brought on by the laughter.

Smoke smirked as he tried to not give away his plans. Everything hinged on the Boss' complete and total ignorance from as to what laid hidden behind Smoke's eyes. The barkeep finally arrived with the glasses of liquor. Smoke brought the cool brown liquid to his nose and took in the scent. He watched as Constance mimicked his movements, doing her best to not appear rude. He smiled visibly at the smell before taking a small sip. He didn't know if the alcohol would be drugged or not. If it was he would only take as much as his body would be able to combat. A small sip would suffice. Constance took a large drink and placed her glass in front of her.

"That's really good," Constance said. He could see the alcohol take a mild effect on her as she smiled. If the drinks were drugged he would find out soon.

"What is this?" he asked with genuine curiosity as he took a sip of the liquor. The alcohol had reminded him of the whiskey he had drunk on the second above, only it wasn't whiskey.

"Would you believe we've finally found a way to make an alcohol out of darkplant that's actually okay to drink?" the Boss said with a ham-fisted sense of pride.

Smoke knew the Boss had nothing to do with the creation of this alcohol; he'd have left that to the chemists who typically designed his narcotics that the narcs would deliver to the various floors. "Really?" he said trying his best to sound surprised, "I didn't think that was possible."

"Neither did anyone else, but I put my best guys on it and now we're going to be selling everywhere, maybe even up to the towers. My contacts have yet to get back to me on that."

Smoke continued to eye the Boss and pretend to listen to what he was saying. During the walk he had seen the revolving pistol sitting in the holster on Cobble's hip. If he was careful and maintained the same sleight of hand he had learned in his days he should be able to grab the revolving pistol without him noticing and get the drop on the Boss. That's only if he were lucky, and the Boss would most certainly have been prepared for such an eventuality. Smoke looked to the revolving pistol again through his peripherals and saw the latch on the holster was specifically designed to prevent a sleight of hand theft. That was good for him, which meant it would take that much longer for Cobble to pull his revolving pistol out.

He would have been stripped of any and all weapons when he was knocked out so he wouldn't have had any way of defending himself in a fight. What they didn't expect was Smoke's hidden blades built into his boots. They weren't very long, but they were spring loaded and could poke a lot of holes in a person as fast as he could move his foot. He clicked his heel on the floor in a manner that would have made walking harder, a design to prevent the blade from extending during regular travel. He felt with his other foot to be sure the eight inch blade had extended. He avoided making a sigh of relief when his foot felt the long sharp piece of metal. He slowly moved his foot to the Boss while he took another sip of the alcohol. Constance seemed to be okay and had even sobered up a little.

He could see the Boss's face twist as he brought the blade to his belly. "It's that time then," the Boss said calmly. "I guess I should have known you'd have an ace up your sleeve that my men would have overlooked. Bunch of fucking idiots."

Metal Jaw and Cobble had turned by this point and had pulled their revolving pistols. Smoke had been impressed Cobble had managed to release the anti-theft device from his pistol as quickly as he did. The Boss looked to his men and scowled. "Back up," he screamed loud enough the entire drinking hole had turned to see the commotion. "Back the fuck up!"

"So," Smoke said as he maintained his calm expression, "still surprised?"

The Boss smiled, "Not in the least. If it has to be anyone, I'm actually pleased it's you. I was afraid I'd have to die of old age."

Smoke felt a wave of unwanted pride fill him as he quickly

moved the blade upward, stopping at the ribcage. He pulled the blade away and watched as his father's insides spill out. The smell of blood mixed with the smell of alcohol gave the air a bitter sweet scent. Smoke repressed a memory and exited the booth. He moved over to the Boss and took him in his arms. Cobble and Metal Jaw kept their eyes on Smoke, unsure as to what they should do. They knew the rules and they knew they had failed their duties as body guards.

Smoke could almost feel Cobble's eyes burn into the back of his skull and he rested the Boss's head in his palm. "Just let it happen," Cobble said reluctantly.

Blood poured from the Boss's mouth and spattered forward as he spoke. "It's yours now," he said as he closed his eyes. "It's all yours."

The Boss died in Smoke's arms, leaving him with a mixture of sorrow, relief, happiness and disappointment. "Goodbye father," he said quietly.

Smoke stood to face Metal Jaw and Cobble. He knew they were smart men and they would obey his commands. When they didn't put down their revolving pistols he felt panic mix with the emotions he had already been battling. "What now?" Metal Jaw asked Cobble. Smoke wouldn't let the snake get a chance to reply.

"As blood heir to the position of Boss of the Cartels, won by both blood rite and the death of the former boss, I will be taking charge of the fourth below Cartel in this area," Smoke said in a voice he wasn't entirely sure was his. He did his best to not look at Constance, who would either be keeping a straight face or have a look of utmost horror. He decided he didn't want to know at this time. "That said, you two and all who were under my father's command will now answer to me and obey my orders to the letter. Understood?"

Both Cobble and Metal Jaw stood straight and simultaneously chirped, "Yes sir."

"Good," Smoke said to the two men. "First things first. I want you to take Constance and I to the lift to the fifth below. I have every intention of returning here to give you all your orders and to take control. Until then I have a couple jobs to do. First job will be to take the package to the statue as agreed upon."

"You plan to carry out the mission?" Cobble asked in shock.

"I took the job and as the Boss I now have a duty to remain honour bound to my brethren. After that I have my own mission that must be dealt with."

The lift had been held for him. The driver had been informed the Boss was coming and he was sending a package to the fifth below. Smoke had always found it fascinating how the Boss could hold and command a lift while people from the towers couldn't do a thing about the lift times in the odd moments they came to the underground. He believed it came from a mutual respect and the free protection that came with it. Smoke saw the look of confusion on the lift driver's face when Smoke came walking up with Cobble, Metal Jaw and Constance. "Where's the Boss?" the driver asked.

"I'm the Boss now," Smoke said without missing a moment.

The driver took a moment for the new information to register. He nodded his head and prepared to take Smoke to the next floor. "Ready when you are, Sir."

"One last thing before I go," Smoke said as he turned around. "Constance, you are going to hold my place as the Boss of the Cartel until I return."

"Smoke no," she started.

"That's an order," he said sternly. "Remember our deal; you'll do as I say until we both go back to the surface. Besides, they need someone strong to keep them all in line."

Constance grimaced. She looked as if she wanted to argue. In a flash her face softened and she nodded, "Alright," Constance said sadly. "Just don't take too long."

"I promise to be back as soon as I can," he said with a smile. He turned to the lift driver, "Alright, let's go."

8

Constance was going to be livid with him. Smoke held no illusions to her being angry at him for forcing her to stay within the den of murderers and thieves. The Cartel was no child's game but he knew Constance would be able to take care of herself and bring a sort of purity to the Cartel. Even short lived purity would be an improvement.

Things in the tavern had happened quickly and he hadn't been given a lot of time to deal with the consequences and how he was going to get out of there. He made a call and he would have to live with it. He knew men like Cobble and Metal Jaw were men of loyalty and honour towards the Cartel boss, but Smoke's sudden return and spontaneous take over didn't seem to fill them with glee. They seemed more shocked and angry for what had happened to what was now their previous boss. That being said, they hadn't gunned him down; this was something he was grateful for and had counted on.

He had wanted to place Cobble in charge of the Cartel. He would have made an excellent leader who wouldn't have had the level of ruthlessness his father had shown and would have given back to the economy of the fourth below as well as the lower floors, possibly bringing together the gangs of the fifth and the slavers of the sixth. That had to wait though.

Smoke had been correct when he said that he alone could slip through the floors with a higher likelihood of not being noticed. He had been up and down the floors countless times without being detected. Having Constance with him on the lower floors would have been great, but with the package job, he had to make detours. The risk of being spotted and gunned down became a high risk; Constance undoubtedly would have gotten hurt or killed. While he had no doubt towards her abilities to take care of herself, the reality that he had been noticed by people from the second, third and fourth below gave him a great cause for concern.

He shook his head and thought about the fifth below. This was by far the most dangerous floor so far and they'd only get more dangerous as he descended. This was the floor of the Worms. The Worms were a gang that ran the fifth below. While being akin to the Cartel they were less organized, had much less skins and even less influence. Though what they lacked in skins and influence they made up for in sheer brutality with the shoot first and not bother with the questions mentality. They were people Smoke had dealt with before though had no intentions of dealing with again any time soon.

He looked to the package he had agreed to deliver. It was small, only eight inches long and six inches wide, the package wasn't thick by any means, perhaps nothing more than a few papers or maybe a small narcotic delivery. It couldn't have been anything substantial, though if they needed someone like Smoke to deliver the package, they must be expecting Worm activity in the area. This concerned Smoke heavily. He didn't want to be caught in the middle of a group of Worms or in some sort of feud between the Worms and the Cartel.

The Worms had a habit of killing Cartel members with extreme prejudice if they ventured to the fifth floor. Though Smoke was no longer a part of the fourth below, some of the Worms may recognize his face and take him out. Some may just see him as an intruder and take him out anyway. He'd have to be on high alert until he'd be able to make it down to the sixth below. That was a whole other problem he'd deal with once he got there. For now he'd have to deal with what was directly ahead of him.

If he had planned on making a direct route to the lift to the sixth below the Worms would leave him alone. As far as they were concerned, if a person is going any lower, there's nothing they can do that's worse than what they could experience down on the lower floors. It was when a person wandered or strayed from the path - that was when a person's life was in danger. Smoke had traveled through the fifth below many times, but always the road to the lift and nowhere else.

As the platform of the lift landed softly on the ground of the fifth below, Smoke gave the lift driver a quick fleeting good-bye and continued along his way. The floor was dark, darker than any of the floors before it. The place made him feel uneasy and forced him to keep his guard up. He had always hated the fifth floor for what it was.

The buildings surrounding him were dilapidated with boards and bars over the windows and doors. The tin siding that had once been attached to the outside of each house had crumbled and fallen off; most of the siding pieces lay strewn across the front yards. In the spaces in front of the houses before the sidewalk and dirt roads were several darkplant gardens.

Smoke did his best to keep his head down and stay out of the lights. If he managed to stay in the shadows he'd be able to make it to the statue of Pedro Argos and plant the package unseen. At least that's what he hoped. He'd do his best to be gone and down to the sixth floor as quickly as he could. A part of Smoke told him to walk along the sidewalk and do his best to not bring attention to himself - an idea he considered for a moment before dismissing it and remaining hidden in the darkness.

He could feel eyes on him as he moved. He wasn't quite sure if the eyes he felt were real or imaginary - he assumed the former but hoped for the latter. He almost seemed too conspicuous staying in the shadows and for a moment regretted not listening to his inner voice. He couldn't afford to be seen however so within the shadows he'd have to stay. He'd be much less conspicuous staying in the shadows than if he were to suddenly emerge from them.

As he moved he did his best to control his breathing. If he took a breath too sharp or let too much air out at one time there would be the possibility he'd be noticed. He had known it wasn't going to be easy getting to the statue without being seen, but it wasn't an option.

"Out of the shadows!" a voice bellowed from across the dirt road. The voice sounded equal parts annoyed and amused.

Smoke sighed as quietly as he could. He knew he had been spotted and knew the eyes he had felt were as real as he'd feared. This was not looking good for him. "Come on, out with you!" another voice shouted as several hammers belonging to a dozen revolving pistols cocked back.

Smoke shook his head in his own form of self-pity and the knowledge that he would die. "I'm coming out!" he said loud enough for them to hear.

He stepped out to see twelve young men wearing softcloths around their faces, which hid their identities from their noses down. Each of them held a shiny revolving pistol in his direction. He could see from their eyes they had no idea who he was and what he was doing there. He took in a deep breath. He did his best to hide the shock that they didn't just open fire; they actually gave him a chance to show himself.

The man Smoke assumed to be their leader stepped forward, "Alright, I want a name, I want your reason for being here and I want a damn good reason to not shoot you."

Smoke furrowed his brow at the mention of a reason to not shoot. That was odd behaviour for a Worm. "My name is Smoke

Callahan and I'm looking for a young girl who was last seen on the seventh below."

"Lift's the other way numb-nuts!" one of the Worms said, which caused a short bout of laughter. "Besides, nobody is going down anymore, haven't you heard-".

Without looking the leader had shot the talking man in the head. The answers part was a difference, but their ruthlessness to their own had remained the same.

"I'm on a job from the fourth floor," Smoke said knowing it had the high probability of getting him shot. It was best if he told the truth though; if they caught him in a lie it'd be a guaranteed death sentence. If he had been caught in a lie he'd suffer more than a few bullet wounds. "They wanted me to drop off a package in the garbage beside the statue of Pedro Argos."

The mention of their saint's name caused half of them to lower their revolving pistols. Their leader didn't seem phased. "Prove it!" he said loudly. "We are expecting a package from the fourth floor. We were on our way to look and see if it had arrived when we found you. Throw it to us and if we see what we expect to be inside you will be let go. You will be able to go to the statue of Pedro Argos to pay your respects and then to the lift. No other detours and no other stops. We will be watching you."

Smoke could feel sweat begin to bead from his forehead and under his hat. He didn't know what was in the package nor did he trust these men were the intended recipients. He didn't really have a choice in the matter. He reached into the inside pocket of his longcoat and threw the package to the leader. The leader caught the package; Smoke noticed a grin could be made out from the leader's cheek movements. He pulled out a small blade from his pocket and cut the package open.

Smoke didn't know what to expect from the package. A small shipment of narcotics had been his first guess. He wasn't fond of the prospect of being a narc again, but the lack of product floating into the air or falling to the ground when the Worm caught it set his mind at ease a little. His second guess had been a bomb set to blow at the time of opening. This obviously was not the case when he saw the man grin again. Smoke didn't quite know what to think when all he saw in the package was a bunch of small papers. He couldn't even begin to guess what had been written on them. "What's on the papers?" he asked as an attempt at finding out.

"None of your goddamn business!" the leader shot back. "If they didn't tell you above we will not tell you here. This is exactly what we wanted, in a way a little more. As promised you are to go to the statue and pay your respects to Pedro Argos and then straight to the lift. We will tell her to wait for you. She has not yet gone today and she will not go without you aboard."

Smoke nodded politely and continued towards the park. There was no more need for him to remain in the shadows. He may have screwed up his mission and given the package to the wrong people, but it was what he had to do to get out of there safely. After all, he accepted the job to keep him going through the underground, not through any sort of duty. Thoughts began to run through his head about what could possibly be on the papers. Curiosity began to engulf him as he walked. He did his best to force the need to know from his head, but to no avail. He knew he'd never find out, at least not until he made it back to the fourth below and forced the information out of Cobble... or Metal Jaw... or Conrad... or Reggae. Someone would talk and he was going to find out. Knowing he would find out later soothed the itch of not knowing - a little. He knew as he continued forward it would get pushed to the back of his head as necessity persisted, but it was still a heavy annoyance for the time being.

The statue of Pedro Argos stood in the center of the only park the fifth below had. Of everything on this level the statue was the only thing that was immaculately clean. People from all around must come up on a daily basis and clean all the dust from the crevices. The brass shone within the dim lighting of the floor making it a shining monument to the man who had freed the fifth floor from the Nagara.

The statue had been erected shortly after the man's death fifty years prior. Smoke remembered hearing the stories as a kid about the man who single handily fought off dozens of Nagara in the name of the fifth below. Smoke had always thought of the man as a bit of a folk hero and that his story had been exaggerated to an extent. He didn't doubt he played a major part in the forced exodus of the Nagara, but to be one man fighting such odds didn't seem likely to him.

Smoke looked to the ten foot statue showing the stoic face of Pedro Argos as he held two revolving pistols aimed and ready to fire. No detail had been left out of the statue, including the scar across his left forearm. He could see the bullet holes the artist had carved into Pedro's chest and back indicating this had been his final stand against the Nagara. The battle of the lift where Pedro shot until no Nagara had been left standing. The story had depicted Pedro collapsing shortly after the battle had ended and he had died all alone. He had been found after all the smoke had cleared and someone had been able to get to him.

It was a nice story, one Smoke enjoyed even as he got older, but it was nothing more than a story.

"Pedro Argos," Smoke said in a low prayer like voice, "saviour of the fifth below. I wish for you to continue to protect this floor and prevent any Nagara from poking their heads from their corner of filth again."

He didn't mean the words. If the Worms had been wiped out the next day he wouldn't shed a tear for any of them. He may not like the deaths of the children, but it'd be a better fate than what they had ahead of them.

He turned to leave the park towards the lift as the leader of the Worms stepped forward with a similar package to what he had given them. "Before you leave," he said, pulling down his softcloth, "we require you to take this and give it to one of the Nagara slavers."

"You're working with the Nagara?" Smoke asked in shock.

"Desperate times," the leader said.

Smoke nodded and he decided to not ask any more questions, "So you want me to take this? Will I have to take another one from that person to the floor below?"

The leader shrugged, "Don't know. Not my place to guess. But you must give this to a man named Blaze Pox."

Smoke's eyes shot open. It was a name he knew very well and a face he thought about with great glee. "I know Blaze," he said stoically.

This time it was the leader's eyes that widened, "You know the Pox? I'm not sure if you're a fortunate man or the most unlucky one I've ever met."

"Some days it's hard to tell," Smoke said in agreement.

"You must be Smoke Callahan, I've heard of you," he said with a short nod. "I'm Homer Thatcher."

Smoke returned the nod and took the package from Homer. "Odd name Homer, does it mean anything?"

"My father said a man named Homer was a great storyteller from thousands of years ago. He'd tell them to me before I'd go to sleep as a little boy - stories of a great wooden horse and the sea voyage that happened after. They were always my favorites as a kid. It was a bit of a shaming later though when my namesake was considered a sign of weakness. I fought to the top of the Worms and here I will stay."

Smoke cocked his head slightly, "Why are you telling me all this?"

Homer gave him a devilish grin and said, "Because I can and because you have to listen."

Smoke gave no sign of interest, anger or apathy, though he did give the leader of the Worms a look of respect. He wanted to be on his way though, he knew the lift driver would be there waiting for him. "Well, I don't know any of those stories and I don't know if Homer was a real person, but what I do know is that I have a lost girl that needs to be found. If I may, I will go deliver your package and continue on my way."

"Perhaps I'll regale you in one of the stories my father told the next time I see you." Homer said with a grin.

"Until that day."

Homer nodded and made a slight hand gesture to show that he was permitted to pass. Smoke took the opportunity and began his walk to the lift that would take him to the sixth floor.

Blaze Pox.

The name rang through his head like a bell that wouldn't stop. He hadn't seen the man in many years and didn't know what sort of ground the two of them stood on. He wouldn't be as hostile as Fulcrum had been, but he doubted they'd be drinking together upon their meeting.

He allowed those thoughts to go to the backburner of this mind alongside the curiosity of what was in the packages. He would cross those bridges when he got to them, but for the time being he had a girl to track down as well as thinking of a way to prevent his death at the hands of Fulcrum. While the honour of keeping his word would translate well to the other floors below, Glass would much rather he be with her than maintain some pointless honour among criminals. If he were being honest with himself, he had the same preference.

He couldn't help but grin to himself as he walked towards the lift, which had finally come into view. The thought of Glass grounded him and gave him a reason to get things done as quickly as he could.

9

Rage bubbled through Constance as she watched Smoke depart the fourth below. Once Smoke disappeared from view she stormed off back toward to the basement tavern. He had left her in the fourth below and she couldn't help but hate him for it. It wasn't that she was an essential part of his mission and he wasn't an essential part of her plan. What had caused the rage was the sake he put her in charge of the Cartel. She had no interest in being their leader, even if it was only a temporary position.

    She had been impressed with herself for remembering where the tavern had been. She opened the door and quickly walked downstairs. As she entered the tavern she scanned the room. The majority of the people had cleared out by this time, including the body of the former boss. One of the serving girls was on her hands and knees scrubbing the now-congealed blood from the synthetic wood floor. There would be no way all the blood would ever come out. Constance thought to the near future where the blood that had been on the floor would leave left a tell-tale stain that would only ever disappear after several years of foot traffic and replaced boards.

    She gritted her teeth and sat in the seat where the Boss had made them sit only a few hours prior. She raised her index and middle fingers in the air to summon a serving girl. The one that approached her was a young woman with long golden hair with sparkling green eyes. She gave Constance a nervous smile and asked, "What can I get for you?"

"Darkplant liquor. Bring the bottle."

The woman nodded, "Right away. I should tell you though Miss, you should probably find another place to sit, that's where the new boss sits and I doubt he'd like anyone at his table."

Anger began to bubble higher within Constance, "And what if I don't move?"

She could see the instantaneous fear in the woman's eyes, "Bad things for both of us Miss."

Constance swallowed the anger she had within her. She wasn't going to bite this woman's head off for trying to protect her own job and possibly her life on top of Constance's. She looked back up to the serving girl and said, "I'm the Boss for right now. Smoke decided to go down to the fifth below and probably going deeper. He's left me in charge while he's gone."

The serving woman gave Constance a suspicious look. "Alright," she finally said, "I'm going to need proof."

"Talk to Cobble or Metal Jaw," she said as she began to lose her patience.

At the mention of the names the serving girl moved aside and quickly moved toward the bar. Constance watched as she grabbed a bottle of the darkplant liquor and a small glass. She immediately brought it to Constance's table and placed them down gently. "Here you are ma'am, and I would like to apologize for my rudeness."

She could see the genuine look of apology in her eyes and it sated a lot of Constance's anger. "It's alright," she said calmly, "I can't expect everyone on this floor to know every little bit that goes on as soon as it happens. I also know you are just protecting yourself. I would though, like you to send out a message to Cobble. I'd like to speak with him."

The woman nodded and moved to speak with her boss. She pointed to Constance as she spoke. The woman said a few words to the man behind the bar and soon left the tavern. Constance poured a small bit of the dark liquid into her glass and swallowed it in one gulp. The alcohol burned down her throat but it still had the taste of the darkplant she loved so dearly. She poured herself another glass and proceeded to take sips from it at a much slower pace. She didn't intend on getting drunk, only calm her nerves enough she could think straight.

The tavern was nearly deathly silent. The band had left while they were gone, leaving the place with nothing more than the sounds of moving glasses and footsteps. She took in a deep breath and let it out slowly. Smoke had left her; there had to be a good reason for this. She didn't think he had any interest in coming back to stay. He'd probably put her in charge to hold the fort while he thought of something. He couldn't stop his investigation; not for her or anyone else. Not even for himself; not even for Glass.

Then it hit her. Something he had said while they had been tied to their chairs. He had said he could move around without getting noticed if he were alone. Another person was one more the enemy could spot. She had stayed to keep Smoke safe from the dangers of the lower floors - this wasn't about her or her capabilities - it was about making sure he made it down each floor safely.

She smiled and finished her glass of the darkplant liquor. She poured another glass and continued to think. The major concern of hers now was what she was going to do while she remained here. She had been told to hold the fort down in a world she knew nothing about. Smoke must have known she wouldn't have the first clue as to what to do or how to lead these men. Fear and worry began to creep into her brain, replacing the anger and rage that had recently vacated.

She took another sip and placed the glass down. She was already beginning to feel a slight buzz from the alcohol and it was pleasant. Constance never really enjoyed the feeling of being drunk, but this time it was quite nice. It allowed her to put away her feelings.

She heard a small noise come from the entrance as Cobble walked through the door. She couldn't tell if he had been angry with this outcome or if he had been relieved. She didn't really want to know. He met her eyes and she gave him a slight head nod, the way Smoke had taught her, and he approached her and sat down across the table. They sat in silence for a minute before he asked, "How much of that have you drank?"

She looked down at the glass again as a sense of shame passed through her and had disappeared as soon as it had arrived. "This is my third glass. I'm only filling them half full though."

Cobble contorted his face and nodded his head absent mindedly. He raised his thumb and put his index finger to it. This was a hand signal she didn't recognize. He must have been able to tell her ignorance towards the more intricate hand signs and laughed, "I'm asking if I may share the bottle with you."

Constance remained stunned for a moment before she furrowed her brow and nodded, "By all means."

Cobble raised his index and middle fingers in the air once he caught the barkeeps attention. He nodded to Cobble and brought him a glass. Cobble silently took the bottle and filled his glass. He placed the bottle back on the table between them and said, "Well, this is quite the turn of events. I don't think I'd have ever guessed Smoke would take the reigns as boss, and then to put a surfacer in charge after leaving. That's just blowing me away."

Constance gave a single chuckle, "I know. I didn't see that coming at all. I don't know what goes on in that man's head, but sometimes I swear he's not thinking things through fully."

Cobble's face straightened as he took a small drink from his glass, "In all honesty, I am really at odds with myself. I want to be the boss of the underground. I'd have taken it years ago, but Smoke would have to verbally renounce his right as heir to the Cartel. He took off for ten fucking years and that wasn't a true renouncing, even if he thought of it that way. If his father had died, one of us - probably me - would have had to go to the first below to fetch him. He'd have to come down to the fourth below and do his verbal renouncing in front of the entire Cartel."

"You're at odds because I'm in charge," she said, feeling the fear return.

"I am," Cobble agreed. "Though you can rest easy. We have rules and laws we all abide to. It keeps things from falling into disorder and chaos. Our heir system is even there to prevent power vacuums between those who hold ranks within the Cartel. So because Smoke is now the boss and he placed you in charge you are officially the Boss and under our protection until he returns."

Constance did what she could to avoid breathing a sigh of relief. The last thing she needed was to look weak in front of the second in command. "That's a good thing to know," she said trying to seem as if his explanations didn't matter to her. She didn't think she was doing a good job of it though.

"Besides," Cobble said as he took another drink from his glass, "killing you wouldn't get me any closer to the position of boss."

"Are you planning on killing Smoke?" she asked.

"Not if I don't have to," Cobble said as he hung his head. "As long as Smoke renounces his position upon arrival he will be permitted to leave the fourth below alive and will even have free access to our supplies and men as needed. He'll be an honorary guest, just not a member."

"How do you plan to convince him to give it all up?" she asked knowing the answer before the last word left her lips.

Cobble gave her an evil grin as he finished his glass. "Through you," he said. "We're going to keep you here hostage until he comes back. You'll still be able to give orders, or at least mimic the orders I give you until he returns. The lesser people of the Cartel won't know that you're not in charge, just the two of us."

"There is one thing you may be wrong about though?" she said trying desperately to get the upper hand.

"What's that," he asked with a cocky grin.

"There is still the possibility he wouldn't stop you from killing me to keep his position. Then you'd have a dead body on your hands and a very angry leader of the Cartel. I think you'd be lucky to get a quick death. I know Smoke doesn't want the position, but if you threaten to hurt his friend I think he may be stubborn enough to dig in his heels and see if you're bluffing. Either way you're not going to win."

The look on Cobble's face was almost priceless. He had a look of utter bewilderment on his face. She could see him racking his brain to try and get the one up on her. She wasn't going to allow it. "So," she began, "here's how things are going to work. I am going to keep you in second in command and you will give me the best council you can muster. You are going to show me you are able to handle this rabble and that you're capable of leading. When Smoke gets back I will convince him that keeping the role of boss of the Cartel is not what he wants and that he should hand the reigns to you and your future children. This way everyone gets what they want. You get to lead the fourth below, Smoke gets to leave his past behind and I get to continue going after what I'm after. Nobody has to die or get hurt. It'll all be in accordance to the Cartel's laws and nobody will have room to argue. Deal?"

Cobble contorted his face again. He thought for a moment

before giving her a smile and said, "Deal. I don't want to kill Smoke or you anyway."

"Wonderful," Constance said with a drunken grin.

"What are you after anyway?" Cobble asked. He must have believed the question being asked so directly to be rude. He made an apologetic face and said, "If I may ask."

Constance took a sip from her previously forgotten glass and said, "I'll tell you when it's time. I've no doubt you would be able to help me. For now I have some questions."

"Ask away," Cobble said seemingly more relaxed.

"Smoke didn't ask what was in that package. I don't think he wanted to know. His own father said he didn't want to know."

"But you want to know," Cobble said before she could.

"Exactly, I want to know what is going on here."

Cobble made the same asking gesture again. Constance nodded and he poured himself another glass of the darkplant liquor. He took another drink before saying, "You're not going to believe this, but things are changing and a lot of people are very likely going to die."

Rest was an impossibility. The words Cobble had said rang through her head and left her feeling disoriented, confused and very frightened. She wasn't quite sure just how to cope with the knowledge she'd been given.

The alcohol had gone to her head and made the room spin whenever she closed her eyes. That was just insult to injury. She needed the alcohol to try and cope with the horrible day she'd had, but the alcohol would only punish her further. She had already vomited on her way back to the Boss' house.

Cobble had been very gentlemanly and escorted her there, not that she had known where to go to begin with. She honestly thought Cobble was going to do everything he could to get into her good books for the sake of a peaceful negotiation with Smoke; or at the very least do his best to get in her pants. She didn't think he wanted violence in any way. That put her mind at ease a little, but Smoke's willing ignorance towards what had been in the package he had carried irritated her immensely. She had no doubt he had already dropped it off and would be on his way to the sixth below. She didn't know what was down that far, but she didn't think it was anything good. She had always heard stories of people going missing in the lowest floors never to be seen again by their family or friends. It wasn't a thought she wanted to think about.

Thoughts continued to bombard her with horrifying thoughts about the future, what Smoke was going through and what lied in wait for her. She closed her eyes again and when the alcohol decided it was going to play nicely she finally drifted off to sleep.

10

When Smoke took on the case to find Blue he had expected to go all the way to the bottom. He had hoped it wouldn't have to come to that. He had hoped he'd have caught up with her well before he had gotten this far and he'd be on the fast track to the tower. However, this was not the case. He couldn't help but feel a little discouraged about this; he didn't want to have to go all the way down to the ninth below.

As the lift driver continued to turn the crank that moved the gears that allowed the platform to move downward, Smoke pulled out the package he'd received from Homer and looked it over. It was wrapped in a brown paper that felt as if it had actually come from a real tree. Smoke didn't think it was the case, he'd just found a thick form of onionskin that didn't have the typical transparency and a different feel. He'd have to be as careful as he could with the package, just in case the paper was real.

Curiosity began to take hold as to what was in the package. It looked and felt as if it was filled with papers just as the package before had been. Were they the same papers? He had no intentions of opening it though. If he gave Blaze an opened package he'd assume it had been tampered with and wouldn't accept it. He'd just have to ask after he had handed the package over.

The trip to the sixth below seemed much longer than the others. He wasn't sure if it was general impatience brought on by boredom or if the platform had been moving at a much slower pace. Either way, all he wanted was to get off the platform and get moving.

The young woman who drove the lift was strikingly fetching. Her golden hair had been cut short and the muscles she hid beneath her shirt showed with every turn. She had an attractive face that was locked in a state of concentration. He didn't know why, but the look made her seem even more comely than she may have been otherwise. He'd never seen her before, he didn't know how long she'd been driving the lift, but since he hadn't been down this way for quite some time, she could have come in at any point.

The lift's platform touched down on the sixth below and Smoke took in a deep breath. This was a place he knew would be safe for him. People knew him here and while he didn't exactly like the company, he was willing to make things easier by being nice.

"You planning on staying on this floor long?" the lift driver asked.

"No," Smoke said turning back towards her, "I'm going to take the next lift to the seventh below. If I have to I'm probably going to be going all the way to the ninth."

The driver gave him a seductive look, "Well, if you don't happen to catch the next lift down today let me know. I'd like to have a drink with you."

Smoke furrowed his brow, an action he'd found himself doing a lot lately. "Why's that?" he asked.

"The majority of people I see coming down to this floor are

slavers or people looking to buy slaves. It'd be great to have a conversation with someone who wasn't a part of the slave trade."

"How do you know I'm not in the slave trade?" Smoke asked with coy amusement.

"You don't look like it," she said with a grin. "Anyone looking to buy slaves typically either try to hide their faces as best they can or they are a little boastful about the benefits of slavery."

"I take it you don't agree with slavery then," Smoke said as he placed his hands in his pockets.

"I don't," she said. "I can't get behind the barbaric treatment of people nor can I stand behind a system that allows for the removal of someone's freedoms. Look at the two of us - we are locked into our jobs, but we had the freedom to choose our jobs. We were able to do what we wanted. You could also potentially leave your job as well. I guess I could, though it would cause a lot of people to be trapped for a long time, thus resulting in my eventual and tortuous death. But, the fact of the matter is, I chose my life; I knew what I was getting into when I got into it and I have no intention of leaving."

Something was off about the way she spoke to him and finished her speech. Something seemed less than truthful. Smoke nodded his head. "I agree," he said, "though I can't see anything changing until the slaves themselves rise up and say no. The Nagara have weapons sure, but they are outnumbered by the slaves almost tenfold."

"This is why I want the conversation," the lift driver said with a smile.

"What if I get to the lift in time?" Smoke asked.

"I'll call it bad luck and catch you before you go back up," she said coyly. "After all, I can stop the lift until I get my way. And if the lift stops guess who they'll be angry with - it won't be me."

Smoke had to stifle his laughter. The woman had managed to discover the perks of being a lift driver. They always got their way. "Alright," Smoke said with a grin, "If I don't catch the lift to the seventh below I will for sure let you know and we can go for a drink. Shit, even if it's going to be a while I'll come get you."

The woman smiled and placed her hand over his ear. "I'm Zombie," she said happily.

"Smoke Callahan," he replied.

She gave him a slight nod and he turned away from her. The floor was very well lit, allowing for very few shadows to be seen. This was intentional to prevent any escaped slaves from hiding in places where they otherwise wouldn't be seen. He looked to the buildings with all their boarded-up windows. A product of the floor, with lights being on at all hours they required their rooms to not allow any light in. This would allow for sleep.

As he stepped toward the town he could hear the hustle and bustle of the slaver's market. It was the sort of place Smoke detested. He had been honest with Zombie earlier when he said he didn't agree with slavery. It was a detestable trade that had been a staple of human culture for many centuries. A long time ago slavery had been abolished and everyone had begun to work towards a sense of true equality. It wasn't until the feudal times when slavery had made a comeback. It was a common thing these days. People from the upper undergrounds and even some on the surface and the lower floors of the tower made use of slaves. They were cheaper in the long run than servants and could be abused without any reprimand.

The conversation he'd had with Zombie would have been less of a surprise to Smoke had it been on any other floor. The Nagara slave trade and whether or not an individual agreed with it had been a point of topic for several years amongst the underground. Those who agreed saw their purchase as helping a poor person from the seventh below gain a better standard of living, even if the only things the slave ever received from its owner were a home and food. Those who disagreed saw it as the forced removal of a person's human rights.

There had been talk of shutting down the slave trade by the upper floors and even by a few of the center floors. Ultimately it was up to the slaves to free themselves. When they decided to be free, there would be no force that could stop them. While Smoke heavily disagreed with slavery, he agreed with that notion.

The moment Smoke stepped into the town he was bombarded with slavers looking to sell their products. Men and women and children sat behind metal bars. Many of them thin and losing hair from malnourishment. Their nearly naked bodies were covered in dirt and filth from head to toe, with greasy hair and missing teeth. Smoke felt remorse for them in the deepest parts of his being. But a slave will always be a slave until they set themselves free.

"Smoke?" a man behind him said.

Smoke didn't sigh or feel any feeling of anger or anguish. This was one of the only times he had intended to be seen. He wanted to get noticed. He turned to see a man roughly as tall as him though much more heavily built. Roark Taggart stood before him with a massive grin on his face. Roark had been the lift driver the last time he had come down to the sixth below. "Roark!" Smoke said as he approached his old friend. "How the fuck are you?"

They placed their hands over the other's ears and grinned. "I'm good," Roark said with a massive toothy grin. "I guess you can see I'm not the lift driver anymore."

"I did. What happened there?"

"Got tired of the ups and downs," Roark said with a laugh.

Roark had always been the kind of person to make bad jokes and be the only person to laugh at them. Roark had also been one of those rare lift drivers where a person could hold a conversation with them and not have to worry about falling. Smoke forced himself to laugh at the awful joke and said, "In all seriousness though. What happened?"

Roark's face lost all the humour. This concerned Smoke. "I can't tell you," he said with a loud breathy sigh. "I want to, fuck I really do. I just can't."

"Why not?"

Roark sucked his lips in and said, "I just can't tell you. All I can say is that I found a replacement and she's doing a great job."

He could tell it pained Roark to not tell Smoke what was bothering him. He wouldn't press the issue further. "Alright," he said with a nod.

"What are you doing down here anyway?" Roark finally asked.

"I'm looking for Blaze," Smoke said without hesitation.

"You're in the market?" Roark asked with more surprise than anything.

"Not even close," Smoke said

"Then what are you looking for him for?"

"I can't tell you," Smoke said. He hadn't intended on parroting what Roark had said to him but it was true.

Roark nodded without any sign of a smile or frown. He just accepted it for what it was, "If I see him I'll send him your way," Roark said with a nod. "Where can I say you will be?"

"I'll be in that tavern there," Smoke said pointing to a place across the street.

Roark nodded, "Alright, I'll let him know."

Smoke raised his eyebrows, nodded in acceptance and turned away. "I'll see you later Roark," he said without turning, "and we'll grab a drink."

"I'll make sure that happens," Roark said with a more joyous tone.

Ten square miles always seemed like a lot of space until it was filled with people. The town within the sixth below had always been a consistent crowd of buyers and sellers and slaves. A crowd to the point that it made Smoke seem uncomfortable. A loner by choice - though not averse to having people around him or near him, but at any given moment there was a point at which Smoke could no longer handle the people. The sixth below seemed more crowded than usual. Smoke had to push his way through the crowd - each person showing a face of discomfort and longing. He didn't think anyone he saw would be wealthy enough to purchase a slave, but he didn't care about that. He had a job to do and a means to be on with his journey.

Smoke entered the tavern he had pointed out to Roark to get away from the crowd. The inside wasn't clear of any crowding, but it had been better than outside. He sat himself at the bar and ordered a drink. Sixth below mulch liquor always had a better flavour than the majority of the underground floors. It was to keep the high paying customers happy and gave them the incentive to come back.

Smoke thought about the slave trade, and though he hated it and thought very little good came from it, he also knew that it had been the majority of his business to track down the runaways. He took a drink of the mulch liquor that had just been placed in front of him as he thought about all the good that came from the bad and vice versa.

The door opened and a large dark skinned Nagara man waked through the door. He had grey hair and white dots tattooed along his face. The white dots signified the man's standing among other slavers. Blaze Pox was a Nagara of high repute.

Blaze Pox looked towards the bar and grinned when he

spotted Smoke, "Sm'k m' ma," he said gleefully as he approached the bar, "Hw y' b'n?"

Smoke had taken a lot of time learning to understand the Nagara's use of a shattered version of the Common Tongue that passed for a language in these parts. It was not something easy to learn, especially since they had a tendency to leave no spaces between the broken words which left most people thinking the Nagara had said nothing more than a long stream of gibberish. Smoke didn't care enough to learn how to speak the Nagara language though, his tongue didn't move in quite the right way. It was okay; the majority of the Nagara understood the much slower proper Common Tongue that had been spoken.

"I'm alright Blaze. How's business?"

"Sld a fw slvs tdy. Slwn dow tow."

Smoke nodded in understanding, "Any idea as to why things are slowing down?"

Blaze gave Smoke a wide grin, "Ya, inten. Ting chan rnd 'ere. Ned t' redu stk."

"Why though, what would make you need to reduce stock?" Smoke asked before taking another sip of the mulch liquor.

Blaze held two fingers in the air and the barkeep approached him. He ordered a full bottle of the mulch liquor and had it placed between the two men. "Thr's mr y' d'n no," Blaze said as he poured himself a glass of the mulch liquor.

"Really?" Smoke said in disbelief. "I'm a smart guy. I'm sure I can figure it out."

"Na," Blaze said taking a drink. "F y' havn figr towt ye, you prob won."

"Tell me then," Smoke said. "What's going on?"

"Na," was all Blaze said.

The two men sat in silence for a short while. They both took turns drinking from their glasses until Smoke's was empty. Blaze made a gesture showing Smoke he could help himself to the bottle. Smoke proceeded to fill his glass again. "I hrd y' bn lkn fr m," Blaze finally said.

"I was," Smoke said pulling the stack of paper sized package. "I got this from the Worms. They wanted me to bring this down to you."

Blaze took the package from Smoke and began to inspect it. He soon opened the corner and looked at the corners to several dozen sheets of paper. Blaze finished his drink, opened the package and pulled the first sheet of paper out. He cocked his head to one side as Smoke watched him silently read. He was almost disappointed when Blaze didn't mouth along to the words as some people did. A smile began to spread along Blaze's lips as he placed the papers face down in front of himself. "What's that all about?" Smoke asked.

Blaze gave Smoke a single amused huff, "Nothn y' cn d abou tit."

"Seriously?" Smoke said as he began to feel annoyed and a little angry. "I get a package from the fourth below to the fifth and then a package from the fifth to here and nobody wants to tell me a single fucking thing. Come on Blaze, I think I'm owed that much."

Blaze shook his head, "Ne Sm'k, y' me bra bu I cnnt t'll y'."

"Why though?" Smoke demanded.

Blaze hung his head, "Y' wount lk tit. Y'd tr 't sta tit."

"That doesn't fill me full of any sort comfort Blaze," Smoke said as he took another drink from his glass. "What's to stop me from taking this over and doing everything I can to stop it?"

"I'd sht y'," Blaze said with an upset face, "R smbdy'd sht y'."

"Really," Smoke said in disbelief. "I have a hard time believing you of all people would shoot me."

"Tings ave gn 't fr. Thrs na stpn tit."

Smoke couldn't imagine what had started to go through so many motions that it couldn't be stopped. What surprised him even more so was the fact that he hadn't seen it. It would have to be one of those things under his nose that he didn't think anything of. He began to rack his brain and wonder what it could be. When nothing came to him he sank back into his stool and took another sip of the mulch liquor.

"If there's no stopping it, then it shouldn't make a difference if you tell me," Smoke said.

"Dn tk tit s hrd," Blaze said as he slapped Smoke on the shoulder, obviously trying to calm him. "I mk shr y' na lef dow her."

"I appreciate that buddy," Smoke said with a frown. "Still; I can't believe nobody is going to fill me in on wha-... What do you mean by get left down here?"

"Wn sy," Blaze said.

Smoke gave Blaze a sour look, "Tell me what's going on!"

"y'll-"

"Try and stop it, I know," Smoke said with a huff, cutting off Blaze.

The two continued to sit in silence. Smoke was getting irritated at the fact that everyone seemed to know something he didn't, and worse yet they were actively keeping it from him. If it was something so big he knew there would be no way he could stop it. He trusted Blaze though, at least enough to know he wasn't lying; he knew the man would be straight with him. If he thought it would be something Smoke would be adverse to so far as to sacrifice his own life to stop he'd have to trust him. Besides, he already had something of great importance to deal with.

"S' wha bro y' t' th six b'low?"

Smoke battled with himself for a moment, he was giving too much away to too many people. Though, Blaze could easily help him in the case Blue had been captured by a slaver. He reached into his pocket and brought out the image of Blue. "I'm on a missing person's case. I'm trying to track down this girl here."

"Prett," Blaze said. "Cld ge a goo pri fro hr,"

"She's not for selling," Smoke said angrily.

"I no Smk," Blaze said apologetically. It was obvious the Nagara meant it as a joke, but Smoke wasn't in the mood for slaver jokes.

"I know it's a longshot," Smoke said as he put the image away, "but have you seen her by any chance?"

Blaze shook his head, "Na."

"If you do see her by any chance, especially in one of those slave cages could you get her for me? She was last seen going to the seventh below and I'm concerned."

Blaze gave Smoke a suspicious look. He didn't seem to believe that things were from the goodness of his heart, "I wan haft th skns."

Smoke hadn't told him how much he'd be receiving before, "Alright," Smoke agreed, "It'll only be a few hundred. I think half is a fair."

The two men gave each other a slight nod to seal the deal and Smoke took another drink from his glass, finishing it off. He looked within the glass and wanted more of the good tasting mulch liquor. His taste buds must have forgotten the second above whiskey, underground liquor tasted good again.

"I'll see you later Blaze," Smoke said as he stood from his seat and feeling thankful he had been wrong before. He had been able to have a drink with his old friend.

Blaze slapped Smoke on the back and smiled, "Stll goo?"

Smoke nodded with a forced smile, "Yeah buddy, still good."

He went to place a few skins on the bar to pay for his drink when Blaze stopped him. "Son m'," he said with a grin.

Smoke placed his hand on the Nagara's shoulder and thanked him before walking out the door. As he walked out he was once again met by the busy crowd mixed with the smells of sweat and high emotions. He took in a deep breath and proceeded to fight his way through the crowd to find the lift to the seventh below. That was where Fulcrum said Blue had been going.

As he passed the slave carts he kept an open eye to see if Blue had been in any of them. With each cage he passed he felt more and more relieved. If she wasn't in any of the cages it was possible she may be in the lower levels as he suspected. There was still the possibility she had been bought by someone, though that didn't seem as likely.

When a potential slave was taken they would be put through a series of tortuous situations causing them to become meek and bringing them to accept slavery as the better option. He highly doubted Blue had been in that sort of situation. The training took months, sometimes years to fully wash a person of their former lives. Blaze would have seen her if she had been in the program. The few hundred he'd be getting paid also ensured Blaze would spring her just in case he had been lying. It'd be more than he'd get if he sold her.

Smoke considered staying an extra day on the sixth below. Just to give Blaze a chance to bring her out. He decided against it though. It would give Blaze the impression Smoke didn't trust him. That wasn't something conducive to his trade as an investigator. He needed people to trust him and to know that he trusted them. That's how things worked, a mutual shared trust and respect which allowed for favours and information to be shared quickly and easily.

The lift was set up just on the outskirts of the town. The man who stood with the lift was a large man with a massive bushy beard. His long hair hung down half way down his back. As Smoke approached him he gave him a welcoming and friendly smile with kind eyes. "Hello there," he said cheerfully.

"Hi," Smoke said absently, his mind still wandering and wondering.

"Looking to go down to the seventh below?" he asked. It was a rhetorical question.

"Just wondering when you're going next," Smoke said, deciding to give the big friendly man some of his attention.

"I'm headed down in a few hours. Is there anything you would like to do in the meantime?"

Smoke didn't have to think on this one, "Yeah," he said with an almost smile, "I can make sure to be back here before you decide to go down. I've just got to make sure I have a ride back when I'm ready to come back up."

The lift driver gave him a confused look but then shrugged and went back to his work, "Come back when you're ready. I'll wait for you."

"It's appreciated," Smoke said before turning back towards the town. This time he'd try and avoid the town all together until he made it back to the lift to the fifth below. He'd hoped Zombie hadn't left quite yet. If she had he'd have to wait until he made his way back up. That wouldn't be the best idea with Blue tagging alongside.

As he approached he could see Zombie working on the lift.

Her shirt, arms, hair and face covered in grease. The look was oddly attractive on top of her look of concentration, something about a woman capable of working on machinery with her hands was something he hadn't thought he'd find expressly attractive. He had been wrong.

When Zombie had noticed him she gave him a wide joyous smile, "I figured you'd be back sooner than later. Get what you came here for?"

"I've got to go lower still," Smoke said. "Figured I'd take you up on that drink. I have a few hours to kill."

She gave him a pleasant smile, "Alright, just let me get cleaned up and we'll head to the town."

Smoke shrugged, "Alright."

She moved to the back of the lift and began dunking her hands into a large washbasin and splashing her face with the water. He couldn't help watching as the streams of water poured from her face and down her neck to between her breasts. The entire washing ritual was a little arousing, that may have been her plan all along. He'd have to do what he could to prevent anything but drinks from happening. He could see himself being swayed by her seduction and being dragged away into a series of sexual mistakes. He had committed himself to Glass once again. This was not going to change. Not this time.

She had removed her shirt in front of him. He turned away as soon as she gripped the bottom edge of her shirt. "Oh come on, they're just breasts, nothing to be embarrassed over," Zombie said with a little bit of playfulness in her voice.

"It's not that," Smoke said scrambling to think of something to say. "It would have just been rude to watch on." A poor excuse, but it was the best he had.

Zombie didn't seem to mind his embarrassment and continued cleaning herself. Once she had changed into the clean shirt she had saved by the washbasin she said he could turn around. She was clean of all grease now with the exception of a few streaks on her pants.

"Let's go get a drink," Smoke said trying to keep a straight face.

Zombie followed alongside him as they went back into the town. Smoke continued through the crowd while doing his best to not lose the woman. It would take a long time to re-find her again with all the people. Zombie somehow managed to keep up with him and entered the tavern just after him.

This was a different tavern than before. It was set up as a very low-brow place. The tables and chairs were covered in a fine layer of dust. The barkeep was a tall, greasy looking man much like the tavern owner he shook down on the first below. Smoke almost laughed, though only a little longer than a week had passed since the days on the first below it seemed like he had been on the trail for over a month.

He and Zombie took a chair at the table that seemed to have the least amount of dust. "So I have to ask," Smoke said. "When you were cleaning, did you just happen to have that shirt and washbasin just lying there?"

Zombie snickered, "I did. I put them there before I started working on the lift. I'm not going to go into town covered in grease from head to toe. I may be new to the lift driver job but I know what I'm doing."

The barkeep came to the table and placed two large mugs of ale before they had even ordered. "Thanks," Smoke said in a tone between the lines of sarcasm and gratefulness.

He took a sip of the ale and placed the mug back down. "Not your first drink today I take it," Zombie said, the smile never leaving her face.

"What makes you say that?" Smoke asked with a raised

eyebrow.

"You didn't grimace at the taste of the awful ale they have here," she said with a laugh. "Only someone with alcohol in their system already can handle the taste."

"I met with one of the Nagara earlier," he said.

"Why's that?" she asked. "I thought you didn't like the slave trade."

"It wasn't as a buyer," Smoke admitted. "I was as a delivery boy. It's not my chosen profession but it was what I had to do in order to make it to your lift."

Zombie nodded knowingly and took a drink from her mug. She wiped away some of the liquid from her top lip and said, "Yeah I get that. The Worms can be a bit of a pain to deal with. It's really just a matter of doing what they say when they say it and they won't try looking for someone to replace you."

"They do seem to think they're more powerful than they actually are."

Zombie agreed and said, "But they did drive the Nagara out of their floor."

"They did," Smoke said in response, "but that said, if the Cartel wanted the fifth below, the Worms wouldn't have anywhere to go. They'd be dead before any of them had been given a chance to make it to your lift."

"You know the Cartel?" Zombie asked in surprise.

Smoke took another long drink from his mug of ale before saying, "Technically I'm the new boss of the Cartel."

Zombie's eyes widened. This was the first time he had seen her smile disappear as it transformed into a look of absolute fear. "What do you mean you're the new boss?"

Smoke took in a deep breath and sighed loudly, "I killed the last boss. Since I was his son I was automatically given the reigns and now I'm the new boss. I don't want the title but I had to leave a friend of mine with them… it was the best way to keep her safe while I continued down the levels. I need to remain as hidden as I can while I continue downward and I can't do that with another person with me."

"Wouldn't leaving her up there just mean you're leaving her with a collection of thieves and killers?"

"I had the same thought," Smoke admitted, "but the second in command and the bodyguard are loyalists. They adhere to the code and laws of the Cartel, that's why my father had managed to stay alive as long as he did. Cobble may be a greedy, money-hungry bastard who wants nothing more than to lead the Cartel, and once I get back I'm going to give it to him, but for now he's going to obey the laws."

"What do you do?"

"I'm a private investigator. I'm on a case I doubt you'd be able to help with. You see too many faces for her to stand out."

"Fair," Zombie said. "Not like it's my business anyway. I mean, you're only here to make sure you can get back up to the fifth."

"That's mostly true yeah," Smoke said honestly. "Though if I'm being honest I do actually enjoy talking to you."

"Bullshit."

"Truth," Smoke said trying to be reassuring. "Just like you're only here because you're looking to get sex'd."

"So what if I am?" Zombie asked in a standoffish manor.

"There's nothing wrong with it. Lift drivers can get almost any human they want for sex."

"And I want you," Zombie said without her kind smile.

Smoke nodded knowingly, she had tried the meek and mild tactic to try and seduce him. It had almost worked, but when she saw that it wouldn't get her anywhere now she'd refuse him passage until she got her way.

"Look," Smoke said trying to play damage control, "It's not that I don't think you're attractive. In fact under different circumstances I'd be all over you at the drop of a hat. This time though I have a woman waiting for me and I don't want this hanging over my head."

Zombie's face soured before it lightened up a little. "Monogamy, who needs it," she said trying to supress a little laugh. "Alright Smoke, I understand. Who am I to ruin something just for my own meager satisfaction? When you get back I'll take you."

Smoke nodded gratefully and finished his mug of ale, "I'll have someone with me when I get back. She's my mark."

"I'll do my best to not get jealous," Zombie said, this time not hiding her amusement.

Smoke laughed to be polite. He didn't think it was humorous in any way but it was the least he could do to make sure he had guaranteed passage. They gave each other a farewell nod and Smoke continued his way towards the lift to the seventh below.

11

Constance followed Cobble through the streets of the forth below towards a large meeting hall. She had expected a large group of people to be arriving and was shocked when Cobble had told her only two others would be among them within the hall. The building which had been chosen was nothing more than to make the meeting seem more official to the others than anything else.

The inside of the meeting hall was well decorated with a large chandelier above a large round table looking to be made of real lumber though she highly doubted it. Over a dozen metal chairs with cushions attached to the seat and backrest circled the table with plenty of space between them. Constance figured she could have put another four or five chairs and still be given enough room for comfort.

At the back of the hall a table sat with a spread of food and drink that made Constance's mouth water upon noticing. She hadn't been hard up on food or drink since being in the fourth below, but the thought of food enticed her. It wasn't hunger; it was the fact that food was laid out on the table for anyone to have.

Cobble rounded the table and placed sheets of onionskin

paper in front of four of the chairs; those were the itineraries for the meeting as well as the plan. In the days since learning of the plan she had come to grips with what was happening. It wasn't exactly hard to deal with. It had been the thought of her whole world changing, the world changing for everyone that had shaken her enough to require time to think.

"So, when will the other two be joining us?" Constance asked.

Cobble had been a great help in making sure things went according to plan. She didn't have any say as to what was going on as of yet due to coming in so late in the game, though he had explained everything to her and explained her role in everything. She assumed Smoke would have been in the same position; maybe would have tried to stop it, but being from the underground it was hard to say just how Smoke would handle things.

Cobble had told her that though she was the acting leader of the fourth below Cartel she would be the acting representative of the surface. The surface was a place of high importance to the underground and Cobble must have felt the surface deserved a representative; even if it had been last minute. The surface was a place the underground had no qualms with and they'd do their best to leave the surfacers out of the bloodshed.

"They should be here today," Cobble said as he sat down in one of the chairs. "Probably quite soon."

This surprised Constance, It hadn't been long enough for Smoke to have handed the packages over and still give the people enough time to get up the lifts, especially if the lifts had already made a passage upward. "What about the lifts?" She asked.

Cobble let out a little sigh, showing her that he was getting mildly annoyed with all the questions. If she had been anyone else he probably would have lost his temper by now, but since she was technically his boss he could only sigh and explain, "The Nagara and the Worms as well as the Cartel have the power to control the lift drivers," he said, not looking up from his papers. "We decide when they come and go. They'd have been on strict orders to wait for the representatives and go up when instructed. I wouldn't be surprised if the Worm and Nagara representatives took the same lift from the fifth below."

Constance didn't think anything more needed to be said or asked so she took a seat beside Cobble and began reading the documents. They were very detailed outlines of both the meeting and the plan. She read and made sure everything was going to work for her and not harm anyone from the surface as Cobble had promised. When she saw everything was alright she placed the papers back on the table and walked to the food table.

She grabbed one of the sweet cakes and put it in her mouth. She didn't know what they sweetened it with but the taste was exquisite. The cooks down on the fourth below were some of the best she'd ever seen. They were able to make her meals that reminded her of home and sent her on a taste adventure as they used ingredients she'd never heard of.

She moved to a giant metal container. The words COFFEE was written along the side. "What's coffee?" Constance asked.

"It's a dark bitter liquid that is served hot," Cobble replied as he continued to read the documents for what Constance could only assume as the fifth time, It's a rarity in these parts, but we have a supplier that comes by once a year and drops off a few decent sized bags of it. It's not something everyone enjoys, but it keeps people awake and full of energy."

Constance shrugged and grabbed one of the four plaster mugs from the table. She poured herself a cup of the hot black liquid. The steam rose as she brought it to her nose. It didn't smell awful by any means, though she wasn't quite sure just what to make of the odor. She placed the cup to her lips and took a drink. The hot brew almost scalded her tongue as it filled her mouth. She swallowed quickly feeling the heat pass down her throat and into her stomach.

She blew on the beverage to cool it and took another sip hoping to get more of the flavour and less of the heat. Cobble was correct when he had said coffee was bitter. She didn't typically enjoy bitter things, with the exception of surface ale. Coffee was good though. She couldn't explain the taste or as to why she thought it was good - all she knew was that she enjoyed it.

She took the mug and sat back down at the table. She sipped her coffee in silence until the door opened and two men walked into the room. One of the men was dressed in faux leather attire with his hair cut in a strange manor, while the other man was large and dark skinned with several white dots running down his face. They each grabbed a mug of the coffee and took seats in front of their papers and waited for Cobble to look up. When he finally did he grinned and said, "Let's get this meeting in order," he stood and gestured towards the dark skinned man. "From the sixth below I present Mister Blaze Pox of the Nagara slave trade," he then gestured towards the leather wearing man, "This is Mister Homer Thatcher, leader of the Worms of the fifth below. I am Cobble Raw, current representative of the fourth below Cartel after the tragic death of our previous leader and the absence of our current boss. And this is Miss Constance Ibot of the surface."

Each of the men as well as Constance exchanged greetings towards one another. The Nagara and the Worm gave her a strange look as they made their greetings. She could tell the two new men didn't see as to why she was there, though they didn't question it. "Alright," Cobble said as he flipped through his papers, "Just so everyone is clear as to what the plan is and to prevent any cockups, we will go through the plan. The first step is to properly evacuate the entire underground. The surface will be a bit more crowded than what any of us are used to, but there's less than a thousand people in all the underground and the surface.

"Next, we go after the tower. We gain access to their lift and place boomers around. We will be met with a considerable resistance and thus we will have to be ready to fight. Hell, it may be a fight just getting to the lift."

"There is another problem," Constance said, when she saw all eyes on her she continued, "The lift in the tower is controlled by access cards on the surface. They only allow you to go as high as the access card allows. Those who live in the tower are capable of going anywhere; they have what they need implanted in their arms."

"How is that possible?" Homer asked, stunned.

"The tower is home to a lot of people who invent things. They had found a way to make their home one of the safest places imaginable and it's going to be very difficult to get inside. There is another way to get the lift to open, but someone on the inside would have to be running the control panel beside the lift. I can teach someone how to do it."

"Is there another way inside?" Cobble asked.

"Potentially," Constance said. "I have to take a look. Once I'm there I'll know for sure, but I don't want to say any more until I know. You three I'm sure can find other ways to get in if this doesn't work."

The three men seemed satisfied with her explanation. Cobble continued, "First order of business is the assurance that the seventh, eighth and ninth bellows are filled in of our plan. They have to be on the same page before anything goes underway."

The Nagara man, Blaze, spoke up, "My people have already emptied out the seventh below and lower already. They are making their way to the fifth below and up as we speak. You can expect them to be here any time now; a half dozen came up with Homer and I. We've also halted the slave trade for the time being until we've achieved our objective, provided that we actually reopen the trade afterwards. I had to tell Smoke a few lies, but all is well."

Constance looked the man up and down, "Excuse me Mister Blaze," she said quietly, "I'm from the surface so excuse my ignorance, but I had been told that the Nagara spoke in their own language. I just didn't expect you to speak so... clearly."

Blaze seemed to have taken no offence to her comment, "You're not mistaken," he said with a grin, "Even our closest friends think we only speak with our language. They are under the impression that only a handful of us actually learned the Common language and that's only to be liaisons to the upper floors and the towers."

"Also," Constance continued, "Why would destroying the lower floors help in taking out the tower?"

"It's simple," Cobble said before Blaze had been given the opportunity to answer. "When we destroy the lower floors, or the whole underground for that matter, it gives us nowhere else to go but the surface. That means the prices on the surface will change to accommodate the massive expansion of the population. From there we can use our combined power to destroy the tower once and for all."

Constance nodded as he spoke, "Alright, sorry for the interruption."

"Not at all," the Nagara man said.

"Moving on," Cobble said with what Constance assumed was his best attempt at hiding his irritation, "with the mass migration it is inevitable the lift drivers are going to be going non-stop for quite some time to get everyone topside. That said - have we trained several lift drivers, enough to last for an entire day?"

"Yeah," Homer said as he leaned back in his chair. "The Worms have been training people non-stop. We've made sure all the lift drivers know what's going on and that they're not going to be replaced... At least not until the boomers are set to go off."

"Have all the boomers been placed?" Cobble asked Blaze.

"Yeah," he said almost as if he hadn't been listening. "We've made sure everything from the ninth to the sixth will collapse. All the floors above will be spared, only the opening to the first below will be affected. We ran the math and if we collapsed every floor we'd be left with a sizeable crater that'd kill us all."

"What about Smoke?" Constance asked as she thought of Smoke being trapped in the underground forever, slowly suffocating to death if the weight of the earth didn't kill him first in the event he were caught within the lower floors.

Blaze gave her a friendly grin while Homer continued to look uninterested in anything she had to say. Cobble shot her a scowl, though it may have been for interrupting the meeting again. "The lift drivers know to watch for Smoke, they also know to not let him in on what is going on. They are to give him false information so he will continue on his mission. Smoke's mission is important to our plan for reasons you don't need to know. I almost think it's hilarious that of all the people in the underground, at least in our area, he's the one man I know who would do his damndest to prevent us from tearing down the fucking towers. It's hard to know for sure, but it's better safe than sorry," Blaze said with the friendly smile plastered across his face.

"But he's going to be alright?" Constance asked pointedly at Blaze.

Blaze nodded, "We're going to be behind from the rest of the areas, and they may think we've failed in our mission, but yeah, he's going to be alright."

"That said," Cobble said purposely interrupting Blaze and Constance's back and forth, "waiting for this one man could cost us dearly. We can still get the tower down, but our waiting until Smoke returns could cost us a lot in the way of respect from the other Worms, Nagara and Cartel."

"And that's bad?" Constance asked.

"Bad? No it's not bad," Cobble said sarcastically. "Why don't we just scream out at the sky until someone puts a bullet in our heads. Respect is everything for us, without it we have nothing."

Blaze and Homer gave each other knowingly worried expressions. "He's right," Homer finally said. "I've run the Worms for a long time through wit and smarts. Even going as far as using brutality when necessary. I can't afford to look weak when the rest of the Worms are looking on."

"Same goes for the Cartel and the Nagara," Cobble said with a sly though nervous grin.

"Still," Constance said with a sneer, "Smoke is your leader. You could easily say you were waiting for your boss. That would give you credibility from the rest of the Cartel. The rest of you could say that you held on out of respect. For the first time, I'm assuming, the three floors are finally working together towards a common goal. This should not be something that is thrown away by something as irrelevant as a deadline.

You outnumber the tower and their guards a hundred to one. I've been there, I know. Plus you'll have the advantage of not being closed in and over a hundred feet in the air. That's where the first above begins. You could easily hold them off and prevent them from escaping while we wait.

So, when people start asking questions as to why you haven't blown the tower, because we're not doing either until Smoke gets back because he's your leader and you can't go forward without your boss, you can tell them that your boss was on an errand of great importance and they should leave you alone."

Homer, Blaze and Cobble looked at Constance with a look showing mixtures of confusion and admiration. "Since when did you become a tactician?" Cobble asked. His face said he wasn't quite sure if he should be angry or pleased.

"I'm not, I just know enough from watching the politics of the tower as a kid. They taught me to think outside the box and to know when to hold your ground. I am holding my ground on this because I know we have a way to get away with waiting."

"Alright," Cobble said showing his anger once again. "The boomers will destroy the underground, only once Smoke has returned." The last part he said while shifting his glance towards Constance. "After that we will be able to disband or continue on with the Cartel criminal organization, the Worm's gang and the Nagara slave trade. Undoubtedly there will be other crime syndicates but we will be able to police and impose law and order upon those who would disrupt our new government. The three factions will be the most powerful of all."

"Do we have a leader in mind?" Homer asked.

"Someone from a different area," Cobble responded. "He should be around before the rest of the areas blow their towers."

"Alright," Homer said, sounding as if he weren't too impressed with the decision.

"So," Cobble continued, "The deadline is in one month from today. I don't think Smoke will make us late; he must be just leaving the seventh below by now, but just in case something is delaying him we can also only wait so long. I want to make a motion that if he's a week later than the deadline we collapse the underground. There's a chance he may be dead and we can't wait forever for a dead man."

"All in favour," Homer said making the vote official. "We wait only a week after the deadline for Smoke to contact us. Otherwise we blow the whole place up regardless if Smoke is still alive or not."

She watched as Homer, Cobble and Blaze put their hands in the air. It was a common way of voting, finally an action she recognized. She as well raised her hand. It wasn't out of fear of being the odd man out or dismay at being the only person who thought otherwise. Constance had raised her hand to make sure they all agreed to wait. If she needed to halt the boomers longer she'd cross that bridge when she got there. She didn't think it'd come to that, but she didn't want to take the chance.

"Let it show the voting was unanimous for us waiting a week after the deadline to hear anything from Smoke. The lift drivers will be told to wait for him until such a time. From there we will begin."

"Back to the subject of lift drivers," Cobble said, "I need to know that we will have a maintenance crew ready to repair the lift as they go. The last thing we need is everyone trapped between levels with no way to fix anything."

Blaze lifted his chin, "I have a maintenance crew ready after every fifth trip to do the necessary repairs and to do a full inspection. If anything and I do mean anything looks suspicious we will halt the lifts until it's been fixed. Once the time has come the lift drivers have instructions to come up to the surface so we can boom the place."

Cobble nodded in glee as Blaze told him exactly what he wanted to be told. The meeting continued on for hours. After the three hour mark Constance could feel herself getting bored of all the tactical talk and the ways they were going to tear down the towers without jeopardizing the town that sat almost directly beneath it.

"I guess this meeting is adjourned," Cobble finally said after five hours of the three men talking.

Constance hadn't said much after the first little bit, she didn't think she really needed to. The talks about Smoke and how they would go about his mission had been what concerned her most, when it was made clear he wouldn't be left down there unless necessary her worries had eased. Anything else she had to say was virtually moot - by the time she had thought it, it had already come up in their conversation. She'd made some points about the town that the men agreed with for the most part.

As the three men stood to leave the large Nagara man

looked at Constance and said, "I'd like to speak with you in private."

Constance said, "Okay." She proceeded to follow the man out of the meeting hall. An agreement only because she really needed to stretch her legs and the fact that the Nagara man fascinated her.

As soon as they were out of any possible earshot of Homer or Cobble he asked, "So how did you come to be the representative of the surface? From my understanding they were unable to send a representative down in time for the meeting."

"It's a really long story as to how I got to become the representative," Constance said. "One that I do not really want to tell, if it's all the same to you."

Blaze shook his hand, "No problem. So what's your connection to Smoke? You seemed really eager to make sure he came out of this alive. Don't get me wrong, he's a long-time friend, but he's still on Nagara language terms with me. I've never spoken actual Common to him. I'm certainly not willing to sacrifice everything I've worked so hard for."

"He's the man who brought me down to the underground. I'm on... a mission of my own, one could say," Constance said trying her best to not give too much away. She expected the question the moment Blaze had asked to meet with her. "I owe him a lot for what he's done for me. It may not seem like a lot, but it means the world to me."

"I can understand," Blaze said after taking a moment's silence to think.

"I do have to ask though," Constance said, "why is it so important that Smoke doesn't know anything about the plans? I mean, he's only one guy. There's really not much he can do against the greater scheme. Especially as far along as you are now."

"Smoke's a talker," Blaze said with a straight face.

"Bullshit,' Constance said with a grin, "I've hardly been able to get him to say anything in the time I'd been with him."

"He's gotten quieter with age; though there was a time we couldn't get the asshole to shut up. Anyway, that's not really what I meant. What I mean is he has a way with words that can change a person's mind. He could be the one person who could just as easily tear this whole operation down just by talking to people. After that his message would spread and we really will have failed. He has abilities that are not very common in this day and age."

"Do you really think Smoke would abandon his mission to find Blue if he knew?"

Blaze hung his head, "I don't know for sure, but I'm not willing to take the chance. Smoke is a man of his own convictions and moral authority that he made himself. If he decides something is more important he will change his mind and go after it."

"Smoke didn't strike me as that kind of person," Constance said as she thought about her interactions with Smoke.

"Thing is," Blaze continued, "Smoke really is a wild card. We don't actually know what his thoughts would be about our plan. He could very well be all for it, but since we don't know we are not going to be taking any chances. We keep Smoke from knowing and that will inevitably lead to our victory. There is always the possibility that I'm wrong and I'd owe him a decent bottle of whiskey for it, but I'd rather be wrong about him and take the chance he'd ruin it than be right and do nothing."

"Interesting," Constance said.

"Do you love him?" Blaze asked with a raised eyebrow.

It was a question Constance hadn't really considered. The

fact that it had been completely out of the blue, the mere asking of it had taken her aback. It didn't take her long though to regain her composure and answer. "No," she said with utmost certainty. "He's a great man and a good friend... I guess. But his heart belongs to another, and mine certainly does not belong to him or to anyone else. He helped me into the underground and I owe him for it. My choice to be down in the underground is not as selfless as you may think."

"Your mission," Blaze said with a grin, "I'd like to hear about it if you're willing to tell it."

Constance gave him a look, "I don't know," she said with hesitation in her voice.

"There's a good chance I may be able to help you," Blaze said with a slight smirk.

Constance looked up at the Nagara. He'd be ruggedly handsome, gorgeous even if he were a couple decades younger. He looked to have more age on him than Smoke, though he wore it much better than Smoke ever would. His skin was darker than any that she had ever seen and it was interesting to see just how well the man blended in with the rest of the underground. The fourth below wasn't dark by any means, but when the two of them walked beneath a shadow the man seemed to almost disappear. She could see why the Nagara were excellent slavers, the potential slaves would never see them coming.

She ran her fingers through her hair and scratched an itch she didn't know she had until doing so, "I'm looking for the man who killed my parents. He's someone from the underground and I don't know who he is. That's been the whole problem. Nobody on the surface got a good look at him. All they saw was a shadowy figure running away and that was it. Nobody saw who it was and I have been trying ever since to avenge their deaths."

"A noble cause," the Nagara said, emotionless.

"My only cause," she replied.

"What's your plan for after you find him? Or better yet, after you've killed the man. Providing you do kill this man."

"Honestly? I think my world will open up. I may try to save up enough to get to Red City. I hear there's a lot there in the way of opportunity that I could never find here."

"And once you're in Red City?" Blaze asked.

"Who knows?" Constance said.

The truth was she already had enough skins to make it to Red City and continue to live a slightly comfortable life, if she could get herself a menial job. If she got something that paid she'd be able to do as she pleased. Letting the Nagara know she had the skins was not an option under any circumstance though. That was just a fact.

"What did you say your family name was?" Blaze asked.

Constance narrowed her eyes and gave Blaze a dirty look, "Why?"

"I'll be honest," the Nagara said, "my memory is not what it used to be, but I do remember quite a lot. It's one of the many reasons how I came to be a great slaver. I am one of the few who have the most white dots on his face. It's a sign of pride and dignity - what was I talking about again? Oh yes, my memory may not be what it used to be, but I have spent a lot of time studying people of the tower - you said you used to live in the tower - don't give me that look. There are not many families who live within the tower in our area. I'm actually amazed any live here at all. I guess they have to live spread apart to protect their own pompousness.

Anyway, I remember the majority of the families and some of the dealings they've had. Get a few drinks into many of them and they open up like a woman... Woops, sorry. So, if I had your family name, I may be able to help determine who killed your folks."

Constance had to think for a second to weigh the pros and cons of telling the man. She soon shook her head and said, "You should know. You have such a great memory. It was mentioned at the meeting during the introductions."

The Nagara man named Blaze grinned a wide toothy grin. His teeth were all perfectly white, something Constance found oddly unsettling, "I knew you were smart Miss Ibot," Blaze said, "But I didn't think you'd actually catch on."

"Sometimes I amaze myself," Constance said doing her best to hide her unease.

"Well I have some good news for you," he said as his face changed from a wide grin to a perfectly straight face devoid of any emotion or feeling. "I know who killed your parents... Better yet, I know who hired them."

12

Once the lift made contact with the seventh below Smoke looked around the dark floor. To his surprise the place was empty. Not a soul or building could be seen as far as his eyes could see, not that he could see very far with the light so low. The smell of smoke filled the air.

"You'll be wanting to get off this floor as quick as you can," the lift driver said.

"Why's that?" Smoke asked as he continued to look around.

You wouldn't want the Nagara to find you. They'd think they missed someone. You know how they hide in the dark for someone."

"And you help them bring people back," Smoke shot back.

"Jobs a job," the lift driver said looking offended at the insinuation.

Smoke nodded, "Yeah, it is."

Sometimes Smoke forgot he had been the kind of person, not all that long ago, to track down and return slaves to their owners. A job was a job. He slapped the lift driver on the back and apologized for the venom he had spit. The lift driver didn't show any sign of amusement or happiness, though he didn't have the same offended look as before.

"So what happened here?" Smoke asked, "Did the Nagara really take everyone away?"

"Some fled below," the lift driver said with a raised chin. "Though yeah, the majority of the people were taken by the Nagara. Shitty deal for them, can't say as I envy them at all."

"Well," Smoke said with a look of serious annoyance, "I'm not sure what to make of that. I never thought the slavers would ever take everyone away. It didn't look that way when I was up there. It was crowded sure, but the cages weren't any fuller than they'd ever have been."

"A lot of them are probably still in training," The lift driver said, "damn shame."

"I should be off," Smoke said as he began to walk away, "I'll see you soon."

"Looking forward to it."

Smoke continued through the seventh below looking for the town. As he approached he could see the ruins of what had once been the homes of several hundred people. They had been burnt down and smashed to pieces, likely killing any who had escaped the Nagara. His heart dropped as he remembered having his drink with Blaze. He had fraternized with a man who trapped, tortured, indoctrinated and sold living humans.

His thoughts soon shifted to Blue. She had last been seen going down to this floor. It was hard to say just how long the place had been like this, though he hoped beyond all hope she had missed this forced exodus. If she had been captured there'd be no finding her. He tried to calm his mind. Blaze had said he hadn't seen her which means she hadn't been in the training camps. He had no reason to not trust Blaze and that was how he would continue thinking until he knew differently.

Smoke let out a depressed sigh and continued on. He wanted to get to the lift before he had the chance to see more of this floor. It was not the sort of place he ever wanted to be again. The dim lighting made the place seem more of a graveyard than a place any living person had once lived. He could see the smashed bulbs that had once illuminated the place enough for people to see and to prevent the Nagara from taking everyone in the streets.

Something clicked in his brain. The Nagara would typically nab people when they ventured out of the town. It was the best way to prevent being seen. On top of that the town was defended against the Nagara. Smoke had been to this town a few times and had seen the sentry towers where men with revolving pistols would shoot any approaching Nagara on sight. They wouldn't even give them a chance to speak before shooting. That said, if the lights had started going out around the town suspicions would rise and everyone would bring out their weapons. There'd be dead bodies everywhere. Since arriving on the seventh he hadn't seen one body.

Things looked exactly as if the Nagara had rushed the town and stolen everyone. It was all perfect... too perfect. He entered one of the burnt houses and looked around. Heavily charred furniture was seen as well as several charred petty personal effects. There had been something missing though. Something he couldn't quite place, something that should have been there.

He entered another burnt house and saw the exact same thing and the same sense that something was missing. He did the same with several other houses before it finally hit him. Memorables. Images, toys, anything a family or a person would want to keep had been missing from the blaze. It had been true that the majority of those effects would have burned away without a trace, but in every house? No traces at all? It seemed a little too odd for his liking.

There was something that was being kept from him. Did this have anything to do with it? He knew how to find out.

He made his way to the lift and looked at the young woman. She didn't look as if she was a capable lift driver. She had olive coloured skin, black curled hair and dark eyes. "What happened here?" Smoke asked.

"The Nagara came and took everything away," she said casually.

"You're a terrible liar," he said with a grin.

The more he thought about it the more he realized all the lift drivers had been horrible liars. He didn't see a reason to look into anything due to his dedication towards his own mission and the fact that he just hadn't been looking for lies. The only one who had gotten away without any notice had been Zombie because she had tried to use sex as a distraction. Clever.

"Excuse me?" the lift driver asked angrily.

"Lying, you're bad at it. Look at this floor; did anyone think this would fool me? It's all too perfect. How things look to have happened don't make any sense and the sake there's no bodies anywhere was a major red flag.

And on top of all of that, why would the Nagara want to take everyone? They'd need their 'breeding stock'. It doesn't make any sense, at least no more than there being no dead bodies. So I'll ask you again," Smoke said, pulling out his revolving pistol and pointing it at her head. "What happened here?"

The lift driver gave him a sudden look of shock which quickly changed to a look of sheer annoyance. "Put that away before you get yourself hurt. I'll tell you, but come on, resorting to violence almost immediately?"

Smoke couldn't help but feel bad as the woman scolded him. He could have shot her at any minute and attempt to lower himself to the eighth below; it wasn't something he wanted to do. "First off," the lift driver continued, "we should be introduced; I'm Penelope."

Smoke blinked absently for a moment as her words sunk into his brain. He couldn't get over how brazen she was or how plucky she acted while staring down the barrel of a revolving pistol. "Smoke. I'm Smoke Callahan."

"A pleasure to meet you," Penelope said with a sly smile. "Hop on, I'll tell you everything as we go deeper. But first, you have to tell me why you're going down."

Smoke didn't want to waste any more time. He opened up and told her about his mission to collect Blue as well as showing her the image of her.

"I've seen her," Penelope said. "I don't see many people going to the eighth below so I tend to remember a bunch of them. She was with some woman. Couldn't tell you her name or anything though."

"She went to the eighth?"

"Hop on," Penelope said with a nod. "It's a long ride down, and I'm not afraid to talk while I work."

13

Smoke's head was reeling from the information Penelope had given him. "So why don't they want me to know about what's going on?" Smoke asked as Penelope continued to turn the crank that allowed the lift to travel to the eighth below.

She took a moment to look at him, "They don't want to have to shoot you. They fear you'll get in their way and try and stop the towers from coming down."

"But that's stupid," Smoke said feeling mildly offended. "I'm not in support of the system we have; if people are wanting to band together and take down the towers I'm all for it. We'd have to evacuate them first, or at least make an honest attempt at it, but I do agree the towers should come down."

Smoke took a moment to realize what he was saying. If he managed to live long enough to get the two million skins he'd have been able to live in the tower. He'd have a lavish life of luxury the likes he could have only dreamed about. If the towers were to come down he wouldn't be able to live there and he'd have to spend the majority of the skins to build any sort of life for himself, at least one where he could continue to live well.

It hit him; it could be possible they were unsure due to his job... But how did they know? He knew news travelled fast in the underground. Much faster than a person could move. It would have taken only a few days for news to reach as far as the ninth below. The question still remained though, how did anyone know how much he stood to make? It was information he kept pretty close to his chest. The only person he'd told since coming to the underground that had any sort of influence had been Fulcrum, and even then the amount was a lie.

Fulcrum.

Smoke placed his face in his palm and shook his head. Fulcrum had a mouth on him; he should have known the man would have been the type to brag to others about what he stood to make. Fulcrum would have also known Smoke would try and tell him a lower number than what he truly stood to make.

No, this would have been going on too long for his job to have had any bearing on whether or not they disclosed any information to him. No, they kept the plan from him intentionally. He'd have found out sooner than later, the job would have been what had kept them from saying anything before everyone began exiting the underground.

"I get it," Smoke said lightly. "So what's your story? You don't look like a lift driver. Shit, you don't even look like someone from the underground, surface or the towers. You don't really look like you're from anywhere."

Penelope smiled, "What makes you say that?"

"It's in the way you carry yourself," Smoke said. "You don't look like you're having any trouble with that crank, but it doesn't seem natural to you. You don't hold yourself like a person from the underground, you don't have that look of worry that seems to be branded to everyone's face from the point they realize how bad off we really have it. You look like you've seen a lot, but you don't have the underground look."

"People from the towers look down on everyone from the underground, even if they lose everything and have to come down here. It's just the way they are. And people from the surface are somewhere in-between. Honestly, I can't quite place you."

"My story is pretty long," Penelope said as she watched for a depth marker. "Honestly, we could sit here for a week and you still wouldn't have gotten half of it."

"Really?" Smoke said with a sceptical amazement. "Forgive me, but I find it difficult to believe anyone has a story that expansive."

"I try to stay away from excitement if I can," Penelope said with a sigh, "but The Writer seems to enjoy throwing me in those situations."

"The Writer?" Smoke asked in disbelief.

Penelope nodded, "It's a faith from-"

"I know what The Writer is?" Smoke asked. "I thought that old religion died a long time ago."

"To many it did," she said with a frown, "but with everything I've seen and the way history panned out I can't help but believe it's out there."

"Do you think other gods are out there as well?"

Penelope cocked her head to the side as a means of shrugging while continuing to descend the lift platform. "It's possible, but they'd be constructs of The Writer as well."

Smoke shook his head, "Your entire religion is just loopy."

The two of them continued their journey downward in silence. Something about the crazy woman with the outdated religion didn't sit right with him. He had been truthful when he said he hadn't been able to place her. She looked as if she had spent her entire life in the underground while also spending it on the surface.

It was her eyes that really threw him off. He had seen inside the eyes of killers, victims, average people and psychopaths. He had never seen a gaze like hers before. Her eyes looked timeless, as if she had seen things he couldn't begin to imagine. It was possible she had been from another area originally, possibly Red City.

"So why'd you become a private investigator?" Penelope asked.

Smoke leaned back and sat down on the platform, "Pardon?" he said, pretending he hadn't heard her question.

"Why'd you become a private investigator?"

"It's a long story," Smoke said, trying not to grin as he threw her excuse back at her.

She didn't look as phased as he had expected. In fact she gave him a mischievous grin and stopped the turn crank. Fear and panic rushed through Smoke. He had the vivid image of Penelope letting go of the crank, the safeties failing and the two of them falling to their inevitable doom. He immediately leapt to his feet. Penelope began to laugh, "I'm not moving this thing until I hear the story."

"You could seize this thing!" Smoke shouted, "We could be stuck here until we die!"

"Calm yourself," Penelope said with furrowed brows and a look of utter annoyance. "Stress is bad for the blood."

"Then get this fucking thing moving!"

"I'll start it once you start telling me the story. You stop telling it and I stop the lift. Nobody's looking to come up or down. They haven't for days now. I have nothing but time. And don't even think of pulling out that revolving pistol. If you do I'll flip the switch and send us both down faster than you've ever experienced."

"We'll die if you do that."

"I'd die if you shoot me as well. Looks like you're the only one with something to lose here."

Smoke couldn't stop his scowl from poking through. He pressed his lips together and muttered, "Fine." He sat back down in an attempt at relaxing, "So," he began, "I'm from the fourth below originally. I'm the son of the previous Cartel boss; that said I had an expectation to do right by the Cartel. I was raised to be this cruel and brutal machine that cared only for skins and business. I did some horrific things; I actually made my way to chief interrogator. There was nothing any given person wouldn't tell me.

There had been so many people who had disappeared because of me, my family and our organization. And you know, I didn't feel a single damn thing about it. At least not for a long, long time. About ten years ago something clicked in my head and the blood and the death and the crime and the drugs and the Cartel started making me sick. I couldn't handle it. I got my friend, Fulcrum, and we agreed to leave the fourth below and start new lives."

"What happened to Fulcrum?" Penelope asked, interrupting Smoke's story.

He gave her a look telling her not to ask any more questions and continued, "The day we were set to leave he got caught. My father was livid. I managed to escape and left Fulcrum behind. He stayed in the fourth below. He's now the Cartel's best assassin.

I managed to make my way to the first below after a long retreat to the third."

Penelope nodded her head knowingly, "Had to blow some money huh," she said with a judgemental tone.

"Not at all," Smoke said with angrily, "I have a woman there. Someone who's been very close to me for a lot of years. Her and I are well beyond a sex relationship. Anyway, I'm getting off topic. I soon made my way to the first below and decided the best way to make up for what I had done would be to become an investigator. I'd be able to track down people who had gone missing and at the very least give them closure if the missing person died. It was more than what the people had been given all those years ago. There, that's my story in a nutshell."

"What makes you a good investigator though? It takes more than a few abilities to be able to push people around for answers. It takes a keen eye and the like."

"Well," Smoke said, a little more relaxed than he had been minutes ago, "being the chief interrogator I got to know when someone was lying to me. I knew what to look for and what to listen for. As for my keen eyes, it took a long time to train myself to be able to see the unnoticeable. This was before the first below. You'd be amazed at the skills I had to learn in the fourth. It wasn't a pleasant place."

Penelope nodded slowly. She had remained silent for the remainder of the trip. Her silence had been more unnerving than her persistent urge to bring up the long buried past. It seemed it had been a long time coming though; the past always had a way of resurfacing and coming to light. First he had run into Fulcrum, then Glass and the Cartel and Blaze Pox. It had been one big unwelcome reunion. The only one he had been happy to see was Glass and he didn't know if he would actually see her again. He was glad he had been given the chance, though the reminder of her made his heart ache for her. The thought he could very well die after the job was done or even before gave him a sizeable lump in his throat.

Once the platform touched the ground Smoke stepped off and walked in the direction of the next lift. He turned to say his farewells to Penelope and saw she had followed him off the lift. "What are you doing?" he asked.

"I'm coming with you," she said with a straight face.

"The hell you are!" Smoke said with a little more force than he had intended. It seemed to work though; his words had caused her to take a step back.

"I'm coming with you," Penelope repeated. "Look around this place. There's nobody here. There's nobody going to come up to the seventh below, nor will there be anybody going to the eighth below. I will literally be here all by myself. Tell me, would you really be okay leaving me here with nobody to talk to or keep me company? Would you really be okay with that?"

Smoke sighed loudly, making sure she could hear his dismay at the choice he'd have to make. If nobody remained in the lower floors it would be cruel to force her to stay by her lift until he came back. He didn't know when that would be. "What about the other lift driver?" Smoke asked, "Am I supposed to bring him with me as well?"

"Not unless you want to," Penelope said with an assertive tone, "I can drive the lift to the ninth below and send him up to the surface. I can then bring us back when we find Blue."

"How do we get back if the lift driver has taken the lift up?"

The look Penelope gave him irked Smoke. "The lift has a mechanism, right along with the safety that would bring the lift down slow enough to safely land it on the lower floor."

"Why don't lift drivers use that instead of using the crank? It'd be much easier."

"It's not built for that. If any extra weight gets added to it the mechanism would fail and bring the lift down to the floor at a speed that would destroy it. Even a lift driver would be doomed."

"Why do you want to come with me?" Smoke asked, knowing there had to be more to the story than what she let on. "There has to be a reason beyond that you'll get a little lonely in the few days I'd be gone."

Penelope rubbed her arm, "There is a reason. A few reasons if I'm being truly honest. You're not going to like any of them."

Smoke leered at her, "Tell me."

"Well, the first reason is the fact that this place is going to be coming down in a month. Time is seriously of the essence. I got thinking on the way down and there is no way you can find Blue either on this floor or the next without help. Face it; you need a second set of eyes here.

The second reason really is the sake that I really just don't want to be left alone. This place is so far from the surface and freedom. It's tolerable when there are people around to take one's mind off it, but now - now it's nothing more than an echo of what it used to be. It's creepy and I just don't want to be left alone here.

The third and final reason is The Writer. It has taken an interest in me, actually has for pretty much my entire life. It's the only explanation for everything that's happened and everything I've gone through. I wish I could go into more description with that, but I really can't. You wouldn't believe me even if I did."

Smoke nodded his head with each reason she listed off. She had been somewhat correct in her assumption of his disapproval of the reasons. The first reason was a pretty sound reason. He had to admit she had been right that he would need help finding Blue, if she were anywhere down in the eighth or ninth bellows. It'd be easier now that nobody remained on the floor, but there would still be too many places a girl could hide. There'd be no way he could check them all on both floors and still make it up to the surface within a month.

The second reason was understandable. She didn't want to be left alone on a floor. Smoke thought about it and the place did seem eerie in a way that made him uncomfortable, almost as if something was watching him while nothing had really been there.

He could see himself yearning for company in the silence of the empty floor. He had never experienced silence like this before. Even on the surface when he had been by himself there had been the sound of the wind rustling through the grass and the trees. The birds, at least those which remained after the Apocalypse War had chirped and flew through the air. The underground was always filled with people going about their lives, with no real night or day things continued at all times this place was unnaturally still.

The final reason had rubbed him the wrong way. The religion of The Writer dated back thousands of years ago to a man who had claimed to have spoken to the creator of the universe. He couldn't remember the name of the man who had presented the religion to the population but it had spread like wildfire among the masses. It took a major foot hold after the fall of the ancient gods and it filled a void for those who felt as if they needed something to believe. With everything that had happened through history the stories of The Writer and the sick and twisted game he played with people's lives had caused many to renounce their faith and leave the religion behind. Still it had persisted in those few that wanted to be the people included in his supposed stories. Only a few believers in The Writer wanted nothing to do with what he wrote.

Smoke scratched the back of his head, almost knocking his hat down. "Alright," Smoke said with a mild sigh, "you can come with. Your first two points are valid, I can't ignore them. But your Writer reasoning is faulty at best. I pray to whatever gods may be out there, but I have a hard time believing a writer created them all."

Penelope shrugged, "That's your faith. Fair enough. Odds are I'll eventually have to explain my reasoning, but we really don't have time right now to waste on my stories."

The walk to the town on the eighth below was a quiet one. Neither of them spoke, only the sounds of their boots on the flat rough ground broke the silence of the floor.

The town was deserted as Penelope had claimed. "How did you manage to evacuate two whole floors in only a matter of days?" Smoke asked once the question entered his head.

"By going non-stop," Penelope said as she rolled her shoulders. "It was really tough. By the last load I could have sworn my arms were going to fall off. There were some who relieved me as well for hours on end, though by the end we were all done with it. I chose to stay behind and wait for you. You must have noticed a massive crowd somewhere along the way."

He had on the sixth below. He had assumed the majority of them were slave buyers and didn't take a second look at them, though in retrospect many of them did seem to be less than capable of buying slaves. The people who surrounded him looked as if they had been from lower floors. The people in cages, they could have easily been from the ninth below. Everything was making more sense to him.

His mind had been on Blue a lot lately, doing his best to make sure he would be able track her down and bring her home. The thought of her slipping past him and making her way back up towards the surface had crossed his mind several times. If that were the case he'd be going in the direct opposite direction, but he wouldn't know until he made his way down to the bottom.

Besides, if she had made her way upwards he believed he'd know. There wasn't a doubt in his mind Fulcrum would be watching him from a few steps behind. He'd have seen Blue get on a lift upwards and somehow he'd let Smoke know. The only thing greater for Fulcrum than killing Smoke would be getting the half million skins and then killing Smoke; he would be doing everything in his power to be sure that happened. If anyone would know, it would be Fulcrum.

The town was abandoned as Penelope had said. It still had the same drab look the seventh below had, but the buildings hadn't been burned. Smoke opened the door to one of the houses to find the place had been left in a condition of makeshift cleanliness. Smoke looked through the rooms searching for any signs it had been stayed in since the home's abandonment. It looked as if the people of the eighth below had just picked up and left with nothing but the clothes on their backs and maybe a small keepsake. Everything looked almost pristine. Beds were made, dishes were clean; it looked as if people had planned on returning to their homes at the end of it all.

As he left the first house he watched as Penelope exited the house adjacent to it. She gave him a shrug and shook her head as she ventured towards the next home. He watched as she rammed her shoulder into the door thus breaking it open. Somebody must have locked the door out of habit. Smoke watched her enter the single story home and continued to enter into the next one.

The contents of the house were similar to the last. The biggest difference had been these people hadn't taken the time to clean anything before they had left. He then proceeded to check the rooms for any sign of Blue.

House after house the results were always the same. They'd check a house and Blue hadn't been anywhere in sight. Smoke could feel himself getting tired as the search continued. He tried to think back to the last time he'd slept and found he couldn't quite remember. This had become an ever increasing habit of his. It wasn't healthy; he needed to get some sleep before he continued any farther. Blue wasn't on the eighth below.

He watched as Penelope rounded a corner and gave him another shrug. "No sign of her anywhere," she said with an apologetic tone.

"We'll continue tomorrow," Smoke said, "I need to sleep. I don't really know how many days it's been since."

Penelope looked around, "Yeah alright. I'll keep looking. I'm not tired right now anyway. When you wake I'll let you know where all I've looked."

Smoke rubbed his chin. His face had grown sizeable stubble in the time since the third below. He didn't know how long it would be before he'd have a chance to shave. He hadn't brought his straight razor so shaving for the time being was right out of the question. Not that it really mattered anymore; by the time he'd make it to Blue and back to his home, everyone would already be on the surface. There'd be nobody to look professional for.

Penelope had helped him build a fire from the remains of one of the abandoned homes. She had found a pair of wrecking bars and they had demolished one of the walls for the fire. As soon as the fire had been lit he curled up beside the heat and closed his eyes in preparation for sleep. Penelope would continue searching. In a matter of days they'd have checked the whole floor and know for sure if Blue would be on the ninth below.

The days seemed to string together as Smoke and Penelope searched for Blue. Things would have been much easier if there had been anyone to ask. Or if at the very least he could manage to actually fall asleep. He slapped himself on the forehead, "Fuck sake!" he screamed.

"What?" Penelope asked almost immediately.

"I can be so fucking dense sometimes," he said as he shook his head in shame. "I kept thinking I'd know for sure where Blue is if there had been someone in the town to point me in a direction. I'd find her anyway, but a person's confirmation would make it so much easier."

"Yes it would, but there's nobody in the town," Penelope said.

"You don't get it," Smoke said, "There's nobody in the town, but the floor's not deserted. There's still the lift driver to the ninth below. He could tell me if he brought Blue down there. If you remembered her it's possible he could remember her as well."

"I've already asked him," Penelope said. "The first time you made an attempt at sleeping I asked him. He said he did remember her going down there, but in the mad rush to get everyone up from the ninth below he couldn't tell me if she had come back up. I figured it was safer to check the place out before going down.

"Also, it's no wonder you didn't think of the fucking lift driver until now, do you seriously not know how long it's been since you've slept?"

Smoke thought for a second, "I think I've slept a few hours at least."

"Accumulatively," Penelope said as she pointed an accusing finger at him. "You're sleeping, even if I have to knock you out to get there."

"I'll sleep once we've found Blue. I think that's what's been keeping me up, knowing there's a time limit and having not found Blue."

"I don't care," Penelope said frowning. "You'll be no good to her if you pass out, especially if she's in crisis."

"I want to sleep, I really do, but something is keeping me awake. This is my best guess. I don't think I'll get much more until we find her."

Smoke hung his head hoping to evoke some sort of emotional response within Penelope, at least something that would make her stop yelling at him. Every word she spoke was correct, he knew this and she knew he knew it. But shouting at him for something he had no control over wouldn't help in any way. He would have been able to sleep had he not known about the time limit, but the plan to collapse the underground changed everything. Maybe that was the real reason nobody wanted him to know. There would be a hundred stories as to why they wouldn't want Smoke to know, but him losing sleep due to a time crunch would be his main guess. Blaze and Cobble knew him well enough to know he would, especially if there was a job underfoot.

He rubbed his eyes with his thumb and index finger and led the way towards the lift to the ninth below. The floor outside the town looked like every other floor. The flat landscape was illuminated by the overhanging bulbs that seemed to never go out. Those that did were replaced almost instantly by people unknown to him or anyone else. Not that anyone actually cared, so long as the bulbs continued to be replaced and the air ventilation continued to spew oxygen to the underground, nobody ever cared who the people were.

Smoke's mind couldn't help but wonder in his sleep deprived state. The floor's flatness allowed anyone to see where the lift and the lift driver stood so long as no obstructions stood in the way. It had often been said the towns were built with the lifts in mind; people who wanted to make it to the lifts to go above or below didn't have to travel far. It would always be unsure as to what people would be bringing with them and nobody wanted to be dragging a hundred kilo trunk several miles to the lifts. The only real exception to this was on the seventh below; they purposely put their town at a distance to deter and defend against slavers.

The lift driver smiled and waved at the two of them as he saw them approach. He was a large burly bald man who looked as if he had taken the lift up and down his entire life. His body rippled with muscle with every move. "Hello," he said with a grin, "I wasn't sure when you'd be coming to see me. I had orders to wait for you."

"Orders from who?" Smoke asked much too quickly for the lift driver's comfort, he could see it in the man's eyes.

"Man from the sixth. He said to wait for a man in a longcoat and a silly hat."

"My hat's not silly," Smoke grumbled under his breath.

"He said to wait for you," the lift driver said, "Now you're here, we can go now."

"You're not going," Penelope said without any sense of humour in her voice, "I'm taking this lift to the ninth below. You're going to get to safety on the surface. Though, when you take each lift up with the other lift drivers use the slow descent mechanism. That way Smoke and I will be able to get out of here safely."

The lift driver nodded his head with every word Penelope spoke. Smoke couldn't tell if he understood the words coming out of Penelope's mouth, but he'd make sure. "Could you repeat that for us?"

The lift driver scowled at Smoke. "I'm not an idiot," he said angrily.

Smoke raised his hands in surrender. He didn't want to take a hit from the big man if he didn't have to. It'd likely kill him with that amount of muscle. "Didn't mean to offend," Smoke said apologetically. "I only want to be sure so when we try to go up we won't have to do something drastic to get back up. No offence intended, just covering my ass. I hope you understand."

Penelope shot him a look that he didn't know exactly what it meant. It either said he made a nice save or that he was an idiot in this sleep deprived state and would say anything to anger someone. He hoped for the former. The lift driver gave Smoke a wary look and said, "I'm to take the lifts back to the surface with the other lift drivers and use the slow descent mechanism to send it back down to you. You are obviously someone important and doing something important otherwise you'd already be going back to the surface."

Smoke nodded accordingly, "Yes, that's exactly what I wanted to hear. Have a safe trip; we should hopefully be back up only a few days after you."

The lift driver nodded and turned towards the lift on the

opposite side of the town. He'd soon take it up and be safe. At least safer than Penelope and himself which really wasn't saying much. "Well," Penelope said as she moved towards the crank to the lift, "final floor. Do you think we'll find Blue down there?"

Smoke shrugged, "I sure hope so."

As Smoke stepped onto the platform he could see Penelope looking into the distance. Her eyes squinted as she attempted to see farther. "Holy shit," she said with surprise.

"What is it?" Smoke asked.

"It's Blue."

"Bullshit."

"It's true," Penelope said with a grin. "Look!"

Smoke looked in the direction Penelope had been staring. He couldn't see anything, "What are you talking about? There's nobody there."

"I'm sorry Smoke," she said quietly.

Pain erupted in the back of his head as everything went black.

14

The pain in his head eventually woke him, though he couldn't quite open his eyes. He concentrated on what he could in the way of his surroundings; he could feel he wasn't moving up or downward. He didn't know how long he'd been out. He groaned and touched the back of his head where Penelope had hit him. He managed to open his eyes a bit and look upward at the ceiling of what he assumed, or at least hoped to be the ninth below.

He managed to roll over to his side and looked up at Penelope who'd been sitting on the lift, "It's about time you woke up," she said with a hint of humour.

"Where are we?" Smoke asked with a groan.

"Ninth below," she said with her grin never leaving her face. "I did a bit of a look around, no sign of Blue anywhere yet, but we've still got some time."

"How long was I out?" he finally asked.

Penelope said something under her breath and Smoke demanded to know again. She shrugged and said, "About three days. You really needed the sleep Smoke; I figured the best way to make sure your body didn't continue to keep you awake was to knock you out. Essentially I turned you off and then back on again."

"What?" Smoke asked not recognizing the saying.

Penelope gave a lazy wave of her hand and said, "Don't worry about it. It's an old saying, you wouldn't understand."

"I can't believe you hit me," he said, ignoring the comment and rubbing the hurt spot again.

"It worked didn't it?" Penelope said with a sense of pride.

Smoke shook his head and managed to get to his feet. He looked around the ninth below and marveled at how much it looked like the eighth. He had been here a few times in his younger years and the floor had always seemed darker than the others. Some of that may have had something to do with the people who had lived down there. They were just as likely to kill you where you stood, for no reason at all, than to help you along your way. It was hard to tell which people were which, considering the odds were great they all were savage killers.

Since the creation of the ninth below it had been used as a prison for those too dangerous to live amongst the rest of the underground. It had made sense that the lift driver for the eighth and ninth belows had been a hulking man; he'd need to be in order to bring prisoners down and to check in and make sure everything was alright. Normally things were not the best for the prisoners; it was uncommon for someone new to survive a week. Those that did tended to do alright until such a time when they could be released back into the rest of the underground. Prisoner releasings however, were very rare; almost unheard of.

The killings were not needless though, the people of the ninth below had a tendency to starve. Darkplant was rarely grown this far down, typically because the seeds didn't usually make it. The last of the seeds would be taken by the eighth below which left very little or nothing for the ninth. Killing a person meant a fresh supply of meat. Not good meat that was safe for human consumption, but it was something to put in a person's belly regardless.

Without the prisoners, the floor seemed brighter and ironically more full of life. He took a step and found his legs trembled. His head hurt and that would be a problem. He doubted any serious or permanent damage had been done, though the fact that his legs wobbled concerned him. As he took more steps towards the abandoned town he found his legs getting more and more stable. He sighed in relief.

"We have any food?" Smoke asked eagerly.

"I was able to find a few small rations," Penelope said with hurry. "They won't last long, but it'd keep us fed, or at least fed enough for a couple days at least."

She handed him a small chunk of protein wafer wrapped in a small piece of onionskin paper. He took a small bite from the morsel and began walking. The wafer didn't have much of a taste to it, but it filled his belly with only a few bites.

A question then crossed Smoke's mind. Why would they bring anyone who is a savage killer to the surface? He looked around and saw countless bones and the left over carnage from the level, but nothing recent. Nobody had come down and slaughtered the whole place, thus meaning everyone from the ninth who had been alive would be going to the surface with everyone else.

It was possible they would be used as cannon fodder for what Smoke hoped would be an army. Skilled fighters with a taste for blood could be something of an asset to a fighting force. They'd eat well, better than they had in a long time, and get to sleep on real beds, not the cots supplied for them or the ground. Basically they would earn their freedom if they help in the destruction of the towers. A great deal, one Smoke couldn't imagine any of them would have turned down.

The town was smaller than Smoke remembered. A dozen small single story houses stood in two rows of six. It was less of a town than a tiny homestead. A shame with all the open space the ninth level had to spare. Smoke would check out the tiny town and would then continue searching the open areas in hopes he'd find a place Blue could be hiding. If nothing came up he'd have to turn around and hope he came across Blue on the surface. Though he believed the lift driver would have told Smoke if she had come back up. It wasn't like he was the driver for the second below; he'd only see maybe a few faces weekly, not a dozen or more in a day.

The houses were drab and falling apart; the decades of ill repair had taken their toll and Smoke couldn't believe a person could live in such a way. The holes in the walls gave anyone from the outside a way in to kill the person residing inside. He doubted there would be locks on any of the doors; they would have been pointless anyway. As he passed each house he looked inside to see if Blue would be in the rooms. When Blue wasn't present in any of the visible rooms he walked back to the first house and opened the door. Penelope went to the house across the road and entered.

The house was a depressing image of poverty and despair. No furniture or personal effects were present anywhere. It didn't look as if anything of the sort had ever been present in the home. He walked through each room inspecting it thoroughly. When he couldn't find anything he promptly left the house and entered the next.

Each place was a copy of the last. Smoke couldn't help but feel remorse for the people of the ninth below. More so than for the people from the seventh or the eighth. The people on the seventh may run the risk of being captured, re-educated and sold into slavery, but if they acted properly and accepted their role, their lives actually turned out fairly decent.

People from the eighth were certainly worse off in their ways of living, but their desperation brought the opportunity of servitude. They were more willing to sell their freedom or the freedom of their children to a tower family. It gave them the ability to live life to its fullest, the only drawback was they had to cook and clean for the families. Almost seemed a fair trade once a person thought about it.

For the people of the ninth there was no respite. They lived and died in perpetual fear of being killed and eaten every moment of their lives. Smoke had never heard of an elder from the ninth. There was a reason behind that. The ninth below was the most dangerous of all places, you fought to survive and if a person couldn't fight they died thus becoming the food for others.

The people of the ninth were dying quickly though. Smoke suspected it had been due to the cannibalism. He'd read many years ago from an ancient text that the consuming of human flesh was detrimental to the body. Something called a prion and something called Kuru had to do with it. He couldn't remember the exact wording or what the prion and kuru had to do with any of it, but he knew it was deadly.

After each home had been checked Penelope met back with Smoke. She gave him a look of grave confusion and said, "She's not in the town. There are a few houses… or I guess what I'm assuming are barns would be more accurate, farther out that I could see. We could go check them out."

Smoke nodded. The exhaustion of the case had begun to catch up with him, not in a physical or mental way that the lack of sleep had caused; this was taking more of an emotional toll. He was beginning to get frustrated that it didn't matter where he looked, Blue wasn't there. "Yeah, let's go check them out. I counted five of them surrounding the town."

"Which one first?"

Smoke sighed and scratched his head. He knocked the hat off and watched as it fell to the ground. He picked it back up and shook the dust off. "I don't know," he said feeling more disheartened than he knew he should have. "That one."

He pointed to a small barn in the distance. It was a three mile walk, nothing terrible, but far enough out of town that a person could scream and nobody would ever know, not that anyone would have cared regardless. The barn was in better repair than the homes in the town, though it looked as if it could be knocked over with enough effort. As they approached the smell of rotten flesh filled their noses. Smoke slid the door open and looked inside. A body sat strung to a chair. The smell of death and rotted flesh was putrid and pungent.

Smoke's immediate thought was the body was Blue and she had died a horrid death. The face had been peeled off as well as suffering several stab wounds to the torso. As Smoke examined the body further from the doorway he could see the body was male. He didn't know who the man was or what he had done to warrant such brutality; he didn't really want to know either. It was more than possible this man was intended for a future meal.

He looked to Penelope. He expected her to have a look of horror or for her to have left the door to retch. Instead she stood beside him with a hardened stoic expression. She had been examining the body alongside him. She looked less phased by the horror in front of her than him.

"What do you think?" Smoke asked.

Penelope rubbed her nose and said, "We should burn this place down. It's a travesty that he was just left here to rot and be buried by the boomers. We'll burn it down and continue on. Give this poor guy a bit of a funeral. Same as any of the others that may have bodies within. They may be criminals and killers, but they are still human."

Smoke nodded, "Do we have anything to start the fire with?"

Penelope entered the barn and began searching. Smoke followed suit almost immediately. The barn had been pretty bare, nothing that Smoke could see that would start a fire with any sort of efficiency.

"Eureka," Penelope said finally.

Smoke turned as she produced three kerosene lamps. "These should work just fine," she said with a grin, "Do you have any matches?"

Smoke shrugged and began searching the pockets of his longcoat and his trousers. He shook his head and pulled his hands from his pockets. "Nothing," he said sadly. "We may have to leave this poor guy here. He'll be buried soon enough."

Time of death had always been a tricky thing to pinpoint this far down in the underground. There were no insects to eat away the dead flesh or spores from plants to bring along fungi. The best a person had would be the state of decay that took place from their natural microbes. This man looked to have been dead for quite some time though not enough to have left the bloating stage however.

Smoke rubbed the back of his neck and left the barn with Penelope quickly, leaving the dead man behind. He could see the look of disgust on her face mixed with the despair of not having the matches to give the man a proper send off. Smoke thought back to the town and if he had seen any matches anywhere. If any had been there he didn't recall, it was not something he wanted to go back for only to leave empty handed anyway.

"Let's try the next place," Penelope said, "and hope to hell there's no bodies in that one."

"I don't think there will be," Smoke lied.

Penelope raised her chin a little in agreement and continued following him. "Should we split up?" she asked. "We could cover more ground that way."

Smoke shook his head, "No, the barns are dangerous places that could be trapped or still have a person inside. If Blue had been kidnapped I'd be expecting to see her kidnappers with revolving pistols. I'd need backup if that happened. She might be alone, but if that's the case she's dead already and I'll need help with her."

The rest of the walk to the barn was in silence. That was one thing he enjoyed about Penelope, she knew when to stop talking. He liked traveling with Constance, but she did enjoy talking and letting him know what was going on inside her head. She was a sweet girl who forgave a lot, more than she probably should have, but Penelope was better traveling and inspecting company. The sound of their boots on the ground had been the only noise present along with their breathing and the sounds of the ventilation shafts.

Smoke looked up to the vents that shot out oxygen from the surface to allow the people of the ninth below to breathe. He didn't know if anyone would be brave enough to come down to this level to do any repairs if anything went wrong. Someone must have been brave enough; otherwise this place would have been a graveyard as far back as a century.

When Smoke had been nothing more than a young boy he had heard of all the killing that happened on the ninth below and he couldn't help but picture mounds of dead bodies reaching all the way to the ceilings. He'd picture the lift drivers taking the corpses of other floors as well to add to the piles. He'd been an imaginative child; he sometimes wondered what had happened to his imagination as he got older.

The first time coming to the ninth below had been a bit of a shock for him. He had expected things to be a horror show of carnage and terror. Instead he had been met with dozens of people who eyed each other warily and avoiding coming into any sort of close proximity with one another. He couldn't remember why he had gone down to the ninth below for the first time. It was an uncomfortable place to be then, and now that nobody remained it was still unpleasant, though only a fraction less. Before ever going he had done his best to avoid the place as best he could. If he didn't have to go past the sixth below he was happy.

The next barn was much larger than the previous. Smoke took a second to smell the air. If anyone had been dead inside he couldn't smell it. Penelope opened the door and peered inside. She turned back to him and shook her head, "There's nobody inside. It looks like this place hasn't seen a soul in several years."

Smoke nodded, "We should move on then. We've got a few more to check out."

Penelope closed the door and looked towards the barn near the edge of the area. "I think we should check over there. We've looked at this place, and the one closer to town, but we should get the places near the edges done. We can then spiral our way around checking all the places."

Smoke shrugged and began walking towards the barn at the edge. It was a place that hadn't been checked. Though he didn't exactly agree with Penelope's reasoning, he realized he didn't really care which barn they checked next. It was very likely they'd all have to be checked before they made their way back to the surface. He hoped against all reason that Blue had been trapped in one of the barns. He hoped against all reason she was still alive.

The more he thought about bringing Blue back safe the more he believed the act of bringing her to safety before the underground collapsed was a possibility. He found he cared less and less about the skins. He wouldn't be able to do anything with the skins if he died down in the underground anyway.

The walls to the next area were coated with a form of steel that prevented the walls from collapsing if something big hit it, to carry the weight of the upper levels of the underground as well as to prevent people from tunnelling into the other areas.

He couldn't imagine anything big enough to tear down the walls to the next areas being in the ninth below. If they happened to find a way to get all the required materials they would still have needed people with the intellect to build the contraption. Smoke highly doubted that would ever be a possibility.

The biggest risk was the people of the ninth tunnelling to the other side. The walls were almost a quarter of a mile thick to give the proper stability to the ceiling and the other underground floors. It was the thickest wall between of all the floors. If the tunnel happened to collapse while a person was half way through it would be enough to kill a person. It may not bring down the wall, but it certainly had the possibility. The steel that coated the walls were more a necessity than anything else.

The two approached the next barn until Smoke halted Penelope in her tracks. He placed his finger to his lips signaling her to be quiet as he listened. He could hear movement coming from within the barn. He motioned for Penelope to come close and whispered, "You don't have a revolving pistol do you?"

Penelope shook her head, "I don't. Don't really need it though."

Smoke resisted the urge to curse and pulled his revolving pistol from its holster. He slowly inched towards the barn. Penelope reached the door first and gripped the handle. Smoke motioned her to hold until he gave the signal.

He took in a deep breath as quietly as he could and gave her a nod. She opened the door and without thinking or hesitation Smoke came through the door with his revolving pistol cocked and ready to fire. The man inside stared at Smoke with wide and frightened eyes. His hands were up and he looked as if he were ready to speak. Smoke wouldn't give him the chance. "Where's Blue?" he asked forcefully, "You have three seconds to tell me something I want to hear before I put a hole in your fucking face."

It was a bluff. Smoke wouldn't have pulled the trigger on an unarmed man, at least not one who didn't have his weapon in his hand. "I know where Blue is!" the man said almost too quickly to actually be words.

Smoke slowly moved towards the man, his revolving pistol ready to fire if he tried anything, "Say that again, slowly this time."

The man took a loud deep breath and said, "I know where Blue is. I can take you to her. Just put down the revolving pistol and we can go."

Smoke shook his head, "How do I know I can trust you?"

The man shot Smoke a smile, an action Smoke did not expect from the man; he didn't know if it was nerves that were misfiring in the man's brain or if he somehow found a small shred of bravery. "I've been waiting here for a long time Mister Callahan. I've been waiting for you. You've come a long way, but I'm afraid Blue is not here on the ninth below."

This time Smoke did curse... loudly. All the time he had spent on the eighth and ninth below could have been spent going back up towards the surface to find Blue. She could be anywhere now. There was still the chance the man could be lying to him, Smoke decided he would hear him out first. "That's still not a reason as to why I should trust you," Smoke said loosening his grip on the revolving pistol, though not so much it would be noticeable to the man staring down the barrel. "You could have sought me out, could have sent someone to fetch me, could have done literally anything other than what you've done. You just expected me to stop by? This barn above all?"

"I knew you'd be checking all the barns. This is the ninth below, Blue could have been in any of them. Instead I chose a barn at random, set myself up for a few months and waited for you. When the exodus of the ninth below happened I resisted the urge to emerge from my place and here I stayed until this point. I'm glad you found me when you did. I was almost out of water. I'd have had to venture out to get more and I may have missed you."

"So where is Blue? Which level is she on?"

"She's not on a level Mister Callahan."

"So she's dead?"

"Not in the slightest," the man said as his grin got bigger.

Smoke tightened his grip on the revolving pistol again; this man was pissing him off, "You better start speaking straight. Tell me where Blue is or I swear to whatever gods may still be out there that I will shoot you down where you stand."

"You wouldn't shoot an unarmed man Mister Callahan," the man said as his grin disappeared, "That's not who you are, at least not anymore. Blue isn't on the ninth below or any other level of the underground. She is below the ninth level."

"There is no tenth below," Smoke said as he began to debate shooting the man.

"You're right, there is no tenth below, if there were that would mean the public had access to it. No, where I come from is a place secret only kept by those worthy enough to see it. If you follow me I can show you."

"Penelope, what do you think?"

He couldn't see Penelope's reaction to any of this. His eyes were locked onto the man's every movement.

"I don't know," Penelope said with almost a coy tone, almost like a cat getting ready to play with a mouse. "It's hard to trust a man when you don't even know his name."

The man nodded, "Of course, how rude of me. My name is Robert Hardy. I'm here to take Mister Callahan to Blue."

"Should we let him take us to where he wants us to go?"

He could hear Penelope get closer to Smoke, "You know, I actually do. There is a chance he actually knows where to find Blue. This could be a good thing for you."

Smoke's eyes went back to Robert. "Alright we'll go with you," Smoke said with a steady pace. "First though, I want you to take your revolving pistol out of its holster and slowly place it on the ground. You try anything, and I do mean anything and I will shoot you down where you stand and wait for whatever power wants me to come find Blue to send another representative."

"What makes you think they'd send another?" Robert asked as he furrowed his brow.

"They sent you to wait for me. They knew I'd make my way down here and what do you know, here I am. That means they want me to find Blue, they want me to go down to your secret tenth below. You however, may as well be expendable. So, place your revolving pistol on the ground slowly and Penelope will pick it up. Then, you are going to lead us to whatever masters you serve and then I am going to leave with Blue. You get me?"

Robert nodded, "Yeah Mister Callahan, I get you."

Robert slowly brought his hand down to the revolving pistol and removed it from its holster using two fingers. He slowly knelt down and placed it on the ground. Penelope quickly rushed in and picked it up and pointed it at Robert.

"Alright," Smoke said, "Move. Show us where you want us to go."

Robert nodded and shuffled his way to the doorway and began walking towards the wall. Smoke still didn't trust the man, he didn't believe there to be a level below the ninth. If there had, someone would have found it after all this time. Someone trying to escape from the ninth would have found it. Smoke himself had been all over the ninth a time or two and had never seen a lift that went any lower. This was as far down as it got. This man seemed to believe his own story though; Smoke chose to give him the benefit of the doubt. It was more than likely he was leading them to a gang who had been well hidden. The only reason he could think that could be true is if they were hiding Blue. His journey downward had been made common knowledge and the kidnappers would have known he'd find them eventually. On the plus side, this man would lead Smoke to Blue, and that was all he wanted, he could figure out the shooting part later.

He looked to Penelope who held her revolving pistol as if it were an extension of her own arm. The weapon looked natural to her and that made him feel more secure. It didn't matter what went down or where this man took them - Penelope would be there to back him up and she wouldn't be the sort of person to cower at the sign of danger.

As they approached the wall Smoke continued to expect people to jump out at them. Smoke looked the wall up and down and then down both sides and couldn't see anywhere a person could hide. All he saw was a small combination spin lock fitted into the wall. A small lock easily missed by anyone not paying attention.

"What's going on here?" Smoke asked.

"I'm taking you to the last place you'd ever expect to exist Mister Callahan. Though I'm afraid your compatriot is going to have to wait here."

Smoke shook his head, "No, she's coming with me. I don't know where I'm going or what's going to happen. The last thing I need is for there to be dozens of you against just me."

"With the two of us we can feel safe," Penelope said in agreement.

Robert shrugged and turned to the combination lock. He spun the wheel several times, more than what seemed right for a lock of that style and soon stood back. Steam poured from the wall as two large doors opened revealing a similar lift Smoke had seen in the tower. "Is that a hydraulic lift?" Smoke asked as soon as the awe of the spectacle wore off.

Robert nodded and took a step back. "After you two," he said with a grin.

Smoke's hairs on the back of his neck stood on end; he didn't know if it was from his nerves reacting from the unknown or if it came from his growing distrust of Robert whose demeanor seemed to be becoming more and more relaxed no matter how many shots were ready to enter him. That alone was more off-putting than the unknown.

Smoke gestured for Robert to come in with him. He obeyed and entered the lift with them. The doors closed and Smoke could hear the steam fill the pipes and push the lift cart downward. "This thing go all the way to the surface?" Smoke asked.

"Do you recall seeing any other locks on any of the floors? No, this thing only goes to the ninth below."

"You don't have to be an ass about it," Penelope grumbled.

As the lift moved downward Smoke relaxed his grip on his revolving pistol; he could see Penelope was still on edge, rightfully so. Once they got closer to their destination Smoke would get ready to start shooting again until such a time he felt safe.

He heard Robert take in a deep breath and let it out even louder, "You know Mister Callahan," Robert said, cracking his knuckles, "you really should have listened to me when I said your friend should have stayed behind."

Robert was fast. Faster than Smoke had ever seen a man move. He could feel Robert's grip on his wrist, pain shot through his arm to his brain causing him to let go of his revolving pistol allowing it to fall to the floor. Smoke let out a sigh of relief when it didn't go off. Robert then turned to Penelope, twisting her wrist into an unnatural shape. Penelope screamed in the moment, and gave Robert a vicious gaze after.

"Think about this carefully Robert," Penelope said as she nursed her damaged wrist. "Think about this very carefully."

Robert shot her an evil grin as he said, "I already did."

The sound of the revolving pistol being fired went off like a sonic boom in the small quarters. Smoke could hear ringing that he knew was hearing damage. Several splotches of chunky red bits coated the side of the wall where Penelope's head had been, a trail of red led downward. At the floor her lifeless body lay slumped into a folded mess. A small red hole just above her left eye seemed small in comparison to the crater in the back of her skull as the shot had erupted out the other side.

Her mouth hung open and her eyes were stuck in the look of angry surprise. A look she would carry on until the flesh from her face rotted or had been burned away. Smoke felt a tear fall down his face and rage build within him.

"You son of a bitch!" Smoke screamed.

Robert pointed the revolving pistol at Smoke and said, "Stand up, you'll get blood on yourself and the person you're about to meet will not want blood on you if possible. Your boots are fine, they'll clean, but your clothes, I don't think we could get that out."

"You didn't have to shoot her!" he screamed again, completely ignoring anything Robert had to say. Robert appeared to ignore Smoke's words.

The lift stopped and Robert grinned, "Come Mister Callahan, it's about time you met Blue. But first, you get the grand tour."

The lights that poured into the lift were blinding, "The grand tour to what?" he asked in confusion, still feeling the effects of shock.

As his eyes adjusted he saw the contraption that spanned as far as his eyes could see. Platforms upon platforms filled with people spanned across his vision. Robert stood beside him and grinned, "The Engine What Runs the World."

15

Smoke had never seen anything so vast or expansive. The cogs which spun in a synchronised pattern spanned as far as he could see. Hundreds of boilers sat on interconnected platforms manned by no less than three people at any given time. The pipes that brought water in and let out steam came from the ceiling. Copper wires were spread in every direction, giving the look of a chaotic, though intricate web. Several sprockets attached to the walls and platforms spun massive columns of chain that looked to be what rotated the gears.

Robert grinned at him and slapped Smoke on the shoulder. "Come with me. I have to bring you to my boss."

Smoke could hardly hear him. It wasn't that the noise had been deafening. The place was loud; it would have been neigh impossible for a machine this large to have been silent. He could have heard Robert perfectly if his mind hadn't still been preoccupied with the machine. He tried to piece together everything that he could see to figure out what the machine did. To his dismay he couldn't think of anything.

He turned towards Robert, "Did you say something?"

Robert grinned; this hadn't been the first time he'd had to repeat himself to a person recently introduced to 'The Engine What Runs the World'. He gave Smoke a slight chuckle and shook his head. "Every time," he said before taking a long pause to chuckle to himself. "Everyone needs me to repeat this part. I always try to give enough time to adjust at least to a point but it never works. I said we should get going. I need to take you to see my boss. She will give you the grand tour."

Smoke nodded, he wasn't quite sure just what to say to that. He followed Robert through several narrow paths over the spinning gears and sprockets. One false move or even the lightest shove and a person could fall over into the gears. The body would never be found or reconstructed; the cogs would tear a body to shreds, leaving unrecognizable red goo. That hadn't been a thought Smoke wanted, but it had been where his brain went and he was stuck with the mental image of himself being turned into the red goo on the floor beneath, the only distinguishing feature being the tattered remains of his longcoat and hat.

He didn't trust Robert to not push him off the ledge. If he tried anything, he'd be taking the psychopath along with him. "How far is your boss?" Smoke asked, trying to break the silence between them, filled only by the sound of metal on metal.

"Not much farther," he said, pointing towards a cliff standing several hundred feet upward. "We're going there. It's an easy walk, lesser men have made it, and so will you."

Smoke gave a half smile and continued forward. He wondered what kind of person could run this sort of place. He wondered what sort of person could build such a place and keep it secret. He didn't know just how long this engine had been running, but he believed it to be older than he could reasonably believe. Probably spanning centuries back.

He shook his head to remove the speculation and wonder to continue concentrating on putting his feet in the right places. The pathway had been made from closely-knit steel mesh that was melted together with intense heat.

As they stepped off the pathway onto the rocky island where the office sat on a small mountain, Smoke took a deep breath in relief. He was safe for now from the gears and sprockets. Robert continued on without looking to see if Smoke followed. He must have been sure the detective would follow; he was right in his assumption, though the urge to explore the engine was an alluring one.

Robert showed Smoke the steep stairway which spiralled around to the top of the small mountain. "This is where I have to leave you Mister Callahan. I am not permitted to enter the office. After this one meeting neither will you. You'll be able to go anywhere you want, just not there. You get me?"

Smoke nodded, "Yeah I get you. I'm also going to be sure you're punished for what you did to Penelope. You get me?"

Robert's grin pissed him off more than he wanted. It was a look of a man who believed there would be no repercussions for his actions. "Best of luck to you," he said before turning and going back the way he had come. Smoke sneered and made an obscene gesture with his hands before ascending the stairway.

As he climbed the stairs his mind continued to think of Penelope. Her face as she told him her fears of being stuck in the eighth below alone while she waited for his return. He thought of her stern look as she demanded he sleep. He rubbed the back of his head as he remembered waking from the sleep she had forced on him. Finally he remembered the look on her face as her body lay lifeless on the steam hydraulic lift floor. "I'm sorry I allowed you to come with me," he said without realizing it.

His mind soon went to Constance whom he had left in the fourth below. He didn't know what had happened to her as he continued his journey. If she had come with she surely would have died along with Penelope.

His mind then went to Blue. It felt like time had slowed down during his time in the underground. He couldn't believe it had only been a little less than two weeks of wandering and searching. He couldn't imagine what Blue would be doing down here. Perhaps this had been the job she had spoken of in her voice image.

As the thoughts drifted from his head he continued the climb up the small mountain. Smoke chuckled slightly; he called this a small mountain though he had never actually seen a mountain, neither in the distance nor up close. He had no real frame of reference to know if this really was a small mountain or nothing more than just a large hill. It sure felt like a mountain to him. He had been used to flat ground everywhere. If there had been any deviations in the ground they had been manmade and never lasted long before they'd get filled back in or levelled off.

The office house looked closer as he rounded the small mountain. He could begin to see the faux-wood textures of the siding and the plastic glass that allowed the light from within to illuminate the surrounding area. He couldn't quite see inside the office house but he knew it wouldn't be long before he could.

It took him much longer than anticipated to reach the top. By the time he reached the flattened patch he had begun to breathe heavy. Sweat beaded from his forehead and rolled down his face. He growled as he collapsed to his knees as he caught his breath. He wasn't out of shape by any means, for a person in the underground at his age he could be considered pretty fit. Elevated land had just never been a part of his life unless he made his way to the surface.

He staggered back up to his feet. He could feel the pain in his legs screaming as he took a step forward. He approached the door; it looked to be made of the same faux-wood the rest of the building had been made from. The words 'Portia Lincoln: Manager to The Engine, Section #12846' had been carved into the door. Smoke wondered if they had to change doors whenever a manager had to be replaced. He then wondered how often they changed managers. Odds are it was a lifelong position. If they didn't give him Blue they may be changing the door sooner than later.

He knocked and waited for a response. If he could get Blue out and be on their way without any bloodshed, he'd take that option. The texture his knuckles felt told him the door had been made of real wood. He could hear rustling on the other side of the door

He knocked again. Once again he could hear someone inside moving around. His knocks were being heard. This could be a test, a test to see how many knocks it would take before he'd come in. It was possible. He didn't care either way. As he knocked again he could feel the surge of wonder shift through him. What was on the other end of that door? Would how he entered matter? Was the door even locked?

He didn't hear any more shuffling - that didn't matter. He grabbed the wooden handle and twisted. He could hear the sound of the mechanism as the door opened. The interior of the office house was brightly lit with electric bulbs. Papers were scattered around in a form of organized chaos on the several desks that lined the walls. In the center of the room, a woman sat behind a desk with a bright red typewriter. She sat and continued typing as he entered. "Three knocks… interesting," she said with a voice that soothed his nerves. "Welcome Mister Callahan, and forgive me for not greeting you. I am just finishing up this report."

"What report?" Smoke asked. He felt a genuine curiosity enter him as he asked the question.

She finally looked up from the typewriter. It had been difficult to see the details of her face with her bright blonde hair covering the majority of it as she looked down. Now he could see the kind, green eyes that hid behind them. Her face had been nothing fancy, not exactly a homely woman but certainly not fetching by any means. Her smile revealed the wrinkles around her eyes and mouth – a sign of many years of laughter. "The goings on in this office is of nobodies concern than my own. You'd do well to remember that Mister Callahan," she said as she stood from the chair.

She had a slender body with high breasts. She looked to be

fit, thin from a high metabolism. Her arms were long and ended with claw like fingers. She stepped towards Smoke with a smile that seemed too sincere for his comfort. Something about it made him uneasy. "Portia Lincoln I assume," he said with a sour look and attitude.

She nodded, "I am, and you're Smoke Callahan. The pleasure is all mine."

"You're not wrong there," Smoke said too low for her to hear.

Portia's nonchalant demeanor angered Smoke. She had been dancing around what he wanted to know and she knew he knew it.

"I was told I'd be able to find Blue here," Smoke said as he straightened himself up.

"Yes," Portia said. "Blue Lang, a stubborn girl, but will make a great manager someday."

"Look, I don't have time for this," Smoke sneered, "I came a long way and lost a friend to one of your men for this. Bring me to her."

He did his best to prevent his voice from wavering. It was all for naught though. The woman, though having a thin frame that Smoke likely could break with his bare hands, intimidated him. It wasn't a shock either. It took a person of immeasurable strength to run an engine like this, even if she was only one of many. She approached him and placed her hand over his ear. Not wanting to be rude he mimicked her motion and they both smiled. As they brought their hands away she said, "In due time Mister Callahan. In the meantime you can be rest assured she is safe."

"Let me guess, you're going to take me on this grand tour Robert mentioned."

She nodded with the same smile she had on before, "That is

correct Mister Callahan. I'm going to show you everything you need to know about this engine. Then I'll take you to Blue. If you have any questions pertaining to the engine feel free to ask. If the questions are not relevant please keep them to yourself. Understood?"

Portia was much more intelligent than Robert. Smoke had assumed as much, though he didn't expect her to know he'd try and derail the entire tour before it had begun. He took a deep breath and began to think. He could see Portia watching him and studying his every move, learning how he moved in every moment. It wouldn't matter what he tried, it wouldn't be enough to get the upper hand on this woman. He knew it, she knew it. Smoke finally nodded.

Portia grinned and grabbed her scarf that had been hanging on the coatrack hidden behind the door. "Wonderful," she said as she wrapped the scarf around her neck. "Let's begin." The two of them stepped out of the office house and Smoke could see farther than he'd seen before of the engine. Even at this height it looked as if the engine never ended, "This, as Robert probably said, is the Engine What Runs the World."

"How does an engine run the world?" Smoke asked. He knew he'd get a lengthy explanation, but he'd wanted to know more about the engine since the first moment he'd laid eyes on it.

Portia's eyes flared as he asked the question. He could tell it'd been a question she'd been asked many times before. "It doesn't necessarily run the world. It's just a catchy name for what we have. But it does play a major part in how the world is run and the survivability of the people in the underground."

"Care to explain?" Smoke asked feeling a little more perturbed than before. His sense of wonder had not left, but the growing annoyance with this woman was beginning to make him feel increasingly petulant.

"It's a really long story," she said, "Follow me and I'll explain everything as we go."

"Lead the way," Smoke said trying to calm himself down.

The two began to walk down the stairs of the small mountain. Smoke watched as she walked down the steps with grace and ease, something he couldn't muster. "It all began with The Apocalypse War," she said. "The world was in chaos and people were dying all around. People had begun to tunnel under the ground and make living places there. It was as safe as a person could be from the ravages of violence. About twenty-five years into the war, some people decided to build a device that could render the technology of the war useless. The world would be safe; people would still die, but not in droves as before. In some sort of miracle they managed to find the only spot where the war had yet to really do any real damage.

However, the war had ended before any part of the engine could be built. There were no winners, countries dissolved and everyone began to live in a dog-eat-dog sort of world. Construction began regardless. It would be ready just in case the world began fighting again."

"Why did it take so long to dig? If the engine hadn't even been started by the time the war ended that means it took them over twenty five years to dig... what... twelve miles under the ground?"

"Nice try Mister Callahan," Portia said looking back at him with a grin. "I am not at liberty to discuss just how far down we are. Nice try though. Anyway, that is a good question. It took a long time to get this far down mainly because they were trying to keep everything a secret and the heat of the earth, the farther down they dug, was a killer; quite literally. All it would take was news of the tunnel to have fallen on the wrong ears and the whole project would have been compromised. It also took some time because the workers needed places to stay so they built the beginnings of what would eventually be the underground. That, Mister Callahan, takes time. They also got seriously held up trying to find a way to keep the underground cool enough to support life. By all rights everyone down here should be dead. Hell, by all rights anyone under the third below should be dead from the earth's natural heat.

Anyway, work on the engine began and roughly a hundred and fifty years later they finally completed it - an engine capable of supporting life as well as disposing of it. Majestic in its own way while also terrifying to those whose minds are unable to grasp the sheer size and function."

Smoke followed along her every word. He didn't want to miss anything, "So they turned it on after it was built?"

"Not necessarily," she said. "The records are a little fuzzy and scattered since the engine's genesis. I do know however that it did eventually get turned on after the acts of one man took hold and threatened to turn the world into a war zone once again. A man who went by the name Alex Cooper. We don't know if that was immediately after the engine was completed or if it was years after."

Smoke racked his brain for a moment. He knew the name from his encyclopedias. "The last of the frozen men," he finally said.

Portia smiled again, "You know your history. I'm impressed. Well, one thing they don't tell you in the history books is how he led an attack on the oxygen suppliers, claiming the air was perfectly breathable. He was right, but that started a domino effect. Do you know what a lynch pin is?"

Smoke didn't want to seem rude so he avoided the scoff at the question, "It's something that holds various parts of a structure together. If someone would take out the lynch pin it could be catastrophic if the structure is big enough."

"Now let's take the man Alex Cooper and ponder what he did, taking out the oxygen suppliers. He showed the people how the government had been lying to them their entire lives. That brought the whole of the enterprises on top of him as well as the government.

Several battles and skirmishes that began to bleed into other parts of the world eventually turned it into a full on war. People from all over were picking sides, freedom from a benevolent tyrant or a good, clean and safe life. People were once again willing to fight and die for nothing more than an ideal in which they didn't or couldn't know how it would end. Not just the people on the surface fought either, the underground as well as a group we don't really know much about began to fight as well.

They started up the engine but it took too long and the fighting had stopped before the engine had a chance to do anything. In fact, it had to power up. That took a lot longer than the original designers had intended. In fact, it took two hundred years for the engine to build up the energy it needed to stop the fighting and the wars. It only takes a year now, but at this size it just took time to get all the gears moving."

"What did it do?"

Portia hung her head, "They didn't know what it would lead to. They wanted their utopia, a place to which they could bring freedom as well as peace and harmony."

"What did the engine do?" Smoke asked again.

"What it was designed to do. It released a massive electromagnetic pulse through the earth. It shut down anything that contained microchips or computers. I know a lot of this doesn't mean much to you, considering you'd have gone your whole life never seeing a computer, knowing its function or anything of the sort. So when I say it sent an electromagnetic pulse, I want to help you realize just what it did to the world."

"I've read the history books," Smoke said with a sneer, "That was the new Dark Age, the end of the Common Era and what paved the way for the Magic Era and the New Era."

Portia nodded, "That's right. The people of the engine didn't know what it would do though, there was no way to know the sort of impact it would have on the world. They sought to end the violence - they failed in that endeavour. They just forced the people to kill each other in more primitive ways."

"Okay, so that's the history of the engine," Smoke said, wanting to move on, "What does it do now?"

Portia pointed to the ceiling, "See all those pipes and vents that go through the roof?"

"Yeah," Smoke said not sure where she was going with this.

"Now, see all those sprockets spinning those chains?"

"Yes," Smoke said sounding more annoyed with Portia than he had intended, "What's your point?"

Portia's smile faded as they left the small mountain and continued towards the path Smoke had previously taken with Robert, "When people started migrating to the underground and as the population boomed, they needed air, more than what the engine had been designed to handle. We fixed it so the underground was not only livable, but comfortable.

These pipes and vents pull air from the surface and vent it to the various levels. Same as with water. I'm sure you've noticed at some point in your life that water is always readily available in any level, even in the gulags of the ninth below."

"Gulags?" Smoke asked. It was a term he hadn't heard before.

"It's an old term; I read it in our library and found the similarities comical. I now refer to the ninth below as the gulags."

Smoke shrugged, he still didn't get what gulags were. He didn't feel it to be important at this time so he motioned for Portia to continue. "We keep the underground alive," she said with a sign of pride in her voice. "We weren't quite sure just how humanity would do it, staying alive in the dark. We helped in any way we could. The boilers provide the electricity needed to light the bulbs that illuminate the floors," she paused for a moment.

He wasn't sure if it had been for pointless dramatic effect or if she had been trying to find the right words to use. "We who run the engine also decided that we would use the engine to halt the progress of technology as best we could."

"That doesn't sound promising for humanity," Smoke said with an accusatory tone. "People need to progress to evolve. You're trying to halt our evolution. What happens when someone smart comes along and tries to change things? Do you use the engine to stop them before they even have a chance to begin?"

"We haven't used an electromagnetic pulse for probably a hundred and seventy years now," Portia said ignoring every word Smoke said. "Good thing too, we found the power the electromagnetic pulse the engine emits was enough to fry the light filaments in the bulbs that light the underground. More people would die and it would be on our hands. Regardless, we don't need to, we have a different alternative."

Smoke knew what she would say before she said it, "You bring them down here to work the engine."

Portia nodded, "That's right. We have a large number of people who work for us outside the engine who fill us in on the goings on of the above worlds. When they find someone who has a talent or a way to create a scientific breakthrough that could revolutionize the world we send our scouts to bring them down here. They then work on the engine and for the engine. If they come willingly and can accept what the engine does and that their contribution will be remembered for all eternity, they are permitted to do what they need to do for the engine.

Those who refuse to come of their own free will are taken down here by force and thus are re-educated to accept the engine and all it does. It's a harsh truth, but one people always eventually come around to. One way or another."

Those last words hit Smoke in the chest like a mallet. "Which one was Blue?" he asked. He believed he knew the answer but didn't want to guess it either. It could be the precursor as to how easy or difficult it would be to bring Blue from the underground.

"Blue was a difficult child," Portia said sorrowfully. "She's a smart girl. She knew the best thing for her to do in order to escape was to leave the tower as quickly as she could. When our scout came to get her she wasn't there. From there on Blue continued down to the underground looking to get lost within the masses. She managed to make her way to the ninth below before we caught her. Considering she'd never descend alone, she always had someone with her, either waiting for someone to join or finding a friend to go down with."

"Why would that make a difference?" Smoke asked.

"We don't kill. The people of the engine are not killers. We are permitted to defend ourselves and can cause as much pain to another as we so choose. But we do not kill. That is our strict rule."

"Your man Robert killed someone - a friend of mine in the lift on the way down here. He shot Penelope, my fucking friend - in the face!" Smoke seethed at her.

Portia raised an eyebrow, "Really? Well, we will certainly get to the bottom of this."

She reached into her pocket and pulled out a small communicator. It was different than those Smoke had come to know in the more recent years. It slid open at the top and bottom to reveal two speakers. One a person spoke into and the other where the voices came out. She pressed several buttons with symbols Smoke didn't recognize and lifted it to her ear. "Hello? Robert? Where are you right now?"

She paused to let him talk. The volume coming out of the speaker was loud enough Smoke could hear every word Robert said. He didn't know how the voice wasn't deafening so close to her ear.

"I'm just about to head back to the ninth to get my next

target. Why?"

"I'm speaking with Mister Callahan and he just told me you killed one of his friends. Shot her in the head - that ring any bells?"

"It's a lie," Robert hissed into the communicator.

"You sure that's the story you're going with?" Portia asked, knowing his guilt.

"You're going to take his word for it?" Robert hollered through the communicator.

"I am," Portia said coldly, "Think of it this way - he wasn't abducted. He came down with a specific task in mind. If you hadn't actually killed someone there would be no reason for him to want to see you reprimanded. If anything, you've aided him in his journey, he'd have been thanking you. So yes Robert, I believe him when he says you killed his friend, because it's the only logical reason to do so."

The silence on the other end of the communicator was as much of an admission as if he had actually said it aloud. Smoke finally heard a small voice come from the other end. He couldn't make out what it said but the shame in the voice told Smoke Robert was admitting to his crime.

"Where's the body now?" she asked, "The incident supposedly happened in the lift while you were coming down here. The body must be somewhere."

"We tossed it into the machine," Robert said, sounding as if he were crying, "We cleaned up the mess."

"So you have witnesses to your crime as well," Portia said with a slight smirk, "Not a very well thought-out lie."

Sorrow and rage filled Smoke. He had brought a friend down to the engine and she hadn't even been given the option to get a proper funeral. Many didn't in his world, but Penelope had deserved better than to be the cause of a little rust on the gears and wheels of the engine. Robert didn't even have enough humility to refer to Penelope's body as a she. The word 'It' rung through his mind and repeated until the anger began to boil over. "She deserved so much better," he grumbled.

Portia told him to shush and continued with her communication, "Robert, I'm really sorry to do this, but you know our rules. You know the vow you made; it's something you have to do yourself. If you don't do it, you know what happens next."

The sobs increased before saying, "Alright. I'm sorry ma'am and I wish I'd have thought about what I was doing before doing it. I was caught up in the heat of the moment and things got out of hand. There was two revolving pistols pointed at me and I acted. I only hope you can forgive me."

"The girl meant nothing to me," Portia said. "It's hard for me to get too angry over her death. What hurts me was the blatant disregard for our rules, in front of our guest no less, and then to attempt lying to me. Regardless, I will forgive you after you fulfill your duty. I can't speak for Mister Callahan however; he doesn't look to be in the forgiving mood."

"Don't speak as if I'm not right here!" Smoke said angrily, "You're right, I'm not forgiving him. Not because he killed her. I've done so much worse in my time, but for the reason that he refused to feel anything afterwards. The reality in which he seemed to take pleasure in it, he grinned when I said I'd tell you about what had happened, as if he would get away with it. The fact that after everything he still had the audacity to throw her body into the engine and not even refer to her as a woman or a human afterward, just an 'it'. Even the Cartel, the Worms or the Nagara are not as cold as him!"

Portia snorted in amusement, "Well, aren't we the paragon." She went back to the communicator, "You know what to do Robert."

"So..." Robert whimpered.

"You know what to do," Portia said more forcefully.

He could hear Robert sobbing loudly, then the sounds became farther away. Soon all Smoke could hear from the communicator was screaming. Blood curdling, painful screaming that could only have come from a quickly dying man. "What the fuck did you do?" Smoke asked, mortified.

"Reminded him about our zero death policy and the vow he made when it comes down to breaking our rules. He jumped into the engine. There'll be nothing left of him by now. I'll send a cleaning person down to the floor in a few hours. Give it time to stop dripping."

Smoke's jaw dropped. "You people are cruel. You're sadistic and sociopathic!"

Portia's frown turned back into a smile, "I'm sorry you feel that way Mister Callahan, after all, the anger you feel toward Robert or me is actually quite hypocritical."

Smoke nodded, he knew where she was going, "My time on the fourth below?"

"Exactly," Portia said, "You killed a lot of people and you seemed to enjoy it as well. Maybe it was an act, maybe the pleasure was genuine. Only you know the answer to that. But, due to your abilities we have quite the proposition for you."

"Proposition?" Smoke parroted.

"We want you to be one of our finders and one of our trainers, one of our people who finds suitable candidates for the engine, and educates them in our ways. You have a way with words that can convince people to do as you wish. You have some of that old magic Mister Callahan, you know you have it. We would have actually collected you a long time ago, but we wanted to see you develop your abilities more. But, it doesn't seem like that's happening on your own. We can train you Mister Callahan, we can teach you to use your abilities in ways you'd have never thought imaginable."

"I know what I can do, and I know the extent of it," Smoke said, already knowing where this was going.

"You mean your abilities not working on stronger minds or those who possess a certain sort of cunning. We can teach you to make it more powerful, you're not the first we've seen and you won't be the last. Do you agree to join us?"

"No, but now that I've seen this place I'm not going to have a choice. You're going to force me to stay," Smoke said with a grimace on his face.

"That's right," Portia said with a grin, "Since I know you won't be playing nice through this whole thing, I'm afraid you'll have to go through the re-education program. Don't worry; it won't leave any visible marks... with your clothes on that is."

He expected her to laugh maniacally; instead she just stood before him smiling the same cool smile she held for the majority of their conversation. It had occurred to Smoke that through the tour he hadn't really payed much attention to the engine. He was standing in a field of spinning gears and cogs, only the small grated path keeping him from the grinding death. He had no idea where he was or how to get back. The story had been too enticing; he had been too busy trying to know more and more about the engine before he figured out his escape plan. Now it was too late and there was nothing he could do.

He let out a heart breaking sigh as he let his shoulders go loose and hang at his sides. "Fuck," was all he said.

16

Pain greeted Smoke as he awoke.

Every part of his body screamed in pain. They had put him away in a small cell without any sort of bed or coverings, just the cold hard stone of the floor and a small bucket for him to relieve himself. The bars that lined his cell on all four sides gave him a sense of mild claustrophobia he didn't think possible. Life in the underground had been full of small spaces, many only large enough to move a person's arms with a little wiggling involved. The cage was larger than many of those holes, the difference being he could get out of those holes as he wished, he couldn't escape the cage.

The room which surrounded the cage was much larger and empty. A locked steel door separated him from the rest of the engine. The grey stone walls showed an irregular pattern of brick and mortar. He passed whatever time he could by counting the stones in the walls. After a while due to exhaustion and the pain in his body he always found he'd lose track of the stones and would have to start again. Something he considered to be almost a mercy in his own mind. If he'd counted the bricks too quickly he'd soon run out of things to keep his mind occupied.... Not that it mattered, it was only a matter of time before the boomers would bring the underground down and he'd suffocate in his cell. At least the engine would die with him. There'd be nobody left alive to maintain it. After that it'd take only one malfunction before the whole thing would come to a screeching halt. Maybe a decade? Maybe a century before the engine finally ceased to function.

He had been stripped down to nothing. The cold stone of the floor felt good on his bruised naked flesh, though the irregular patterns of stone and the several bumps and dips disallowed for anything close to a comfortable sleep. Humiliation and a general disruption of dignity - that was what the nakedness was for. It would be easy for most to show bravery while clothed. Now naked, everything out for the captors to see, bravery was not something that would be on many people's minds. Smoke didn't mind his nakedness; his dignity was not so easily taken.

He looked at his arms to the bruises where the masked man had placed his hands. Smoke hadn't any idea what the torturer had been planning until he began to press and squeeze on the pressure points. Many of the spots erupted into immense pain immediately. The masked man whose name had been etched into his breastplate reading 'Officer Tak' paid no attention to Smoke's screaming as he continued on the pressure points of his body and soon pressed harder. The bruises up his arms and along his body held the shape of fingertips and knuckles.

He closed his eyes, just for a moment.

He didn't know how long it had been since the officers had thrown him back in his cage. When they opened the door, this time he felt a slight surge of joy to see them. Torture was horrific, but it beat boredom and loneliness. The men wore the same steel breastplates with their names across their chests as Officer Tak wore. These two were officers 'Laramie' and 'Poe'.

Their entire bodies were covered in a stretched fabric that covered every inch of their bodies, including their faces. The masks they wore over the fabric contained blue-glass goggles intended to protect from melter flares, now to aid in concealing identities. Small respirators covered their noses and mouths giving their voices a soft hollow sound. Smoke didn't believe they could get a proper seal with the fabric over their faces, meaning it was unlikely the masks were to protect from any dangerous gasses. The gloves and boots were coated with a metal that could only be designed for offensive use against unruly captives. They'd be used in case a prisoner fought back. Smoke wasn't about to fight back. They'd expect it, possibly even hoped for it.

He closed his eyes again and waited for his next round. He could feel his feet drag along the ground. The stone was rough and uneven. He almost scoffed at the fact that the ninth below was more level than these passageways.

He faked weariness; he needed to maintain the charade of weakness so he could navigate the place around him. While they believed him to be passed out he'd be memorizing the way to the torture chamber from his cell. When the time was right he'd be able to navigate his way to wherever he needed to go. The places he didn't know, he'd find in short time.

The officers threw him into a metal chair affixed to the floor. His spine hit the back of the chair with enough force to knock the wind out of him. As he slowed his breathing to bring the air back into his lungs he could feel his arms and legs being strapped to the chair. The leather straps gave him no wiggle room. Even flexing, a great tactic to use in the event of being tied by rope, didn't give him any leeway.

Officers Laramie and Poe left the room. It didn't give Smoke any feelings of hope. As he awaited the inevitable pain he studied the room. Shiny steel coated the walls. It was a place built for easy cleanup after bloodshed. The table across the room from him held several instruments designed to deal as much pain as possible without causing debilitating injury. Several soft mallets with varying lengths of handles sat beside miniature hooks and small blades. A person could be cut for hours with those blades and wouldn't bleed to death, provided the cuts were placed in the right place and shallow enough.

To his left sat a large engine. Several copper tubes wormed their way in and out of the rusted steel. Two tubes in particular made their way to the chair he sat in. He didn't want to know what they were for, though he could only guess it was meant to shoot steam into the chair thus heating it. He'd receive several burns to his body before being thrown back into his cell. The burns would never heal fully leaving behind a perfect chair outline of disgusting scar tissue. He doubted he'd be able to sit properly for a long time.

He pulled at the straps that gripped him at the wrists and forearms. He then tested the straps that bound his legs. There was no possibility of movement. He could feel the false faux leather coverings of the chair arms and legs on his skin. He didn't know what could be hidden beneath the coverings, but he knew he didn't want to find out.

He could hear footsteps down the hall. Someone was coming. He listened and could hear two other steps following behind - one with boots and the other barefoot. *Another prisoner?* It was possible they would try to get to him through his humanity. Try and break him by watching another get tortured. But who? His eyes shot wide when he realized who they would be bringing. Blue. A sound of dragging accompanied them, an object Smoke couldn't quite place.

The first officer entered the room. He could hear him whisper to the people outside before closing the door. The torturer wore the same generic uniform as the other officers. Smoke made a mental note of this and peered towards the name. The words 'Officer Raven' were etched into the breastplate.

"So, Mister Callahan," Officer Raven began, "How did you enjoy stage one of our re-education?"

Smoke let out a long breath before replying, "To be honest, I thought it to be a little weak. Your man has some great skill with his hands; I'm going to be sore for a while. Though I do have to say, torture is probably not the best way to change a person's mind. At best all it's going to do is cause me to resent you all."

He couldn't see any facial expressions from behind Officer Raven's mask. Though he could only assume he was smiling when he said, "You have no idea how many people I've heard say that. Let me guess, you also plan to get out of here and you will tear this entire place down with your bare hands."

This time it was Smoke's turn to grin. He looked into the officer's goggles and said, "I don't have to. In a matter of probably days by now, the entire place will be dead. The boomers will go off and the underground will collapse. I don't have to tear you down; the underground will do it for me."

"You greatly underestimate us Mister Callahan," a woman's voice said from behind him.

Portia stepped from behind the torture chair. She couldn't have been there the whole time. Could she? He hadn't been fading in and out of consciousness. He'd been alert enough to hear the officers coming in with someone he assumed to be Blue by the bare feet. He should have heard her breathing. It was possible she'd be standing there as he'd been dragged in. His eyes had been closed and he hadn't been listening for anyone else in the room. The thought of Portia being behind him the whole time made his skin crawl.

"How long have you been there?" Smoke asked.

"Long enough," she said showing she had no intention of giving a straight answer. "As for the boomers, we already knew about them. We've already gathered them and dismantled them. You see, there's an informant among their ranks. Someone in the top echelon."

"Who?" Smoke asked, "You might as well tell me, it's not like I'm leaving here without succumbing to your ham-fisted brainwashing techniques."

Portia chuckled and grabbed Smoke's chin, "You amuse me Smoke. I enjoy seeing bravado in people before they succumb to the power of the engine. You see, the engine is not just the collection of gears and wheels and sprockets and boilers that you see. The engine is also all of us. Everyone down here. It depends on us to keep it moving. To make repairs when necessary. It requires care. We all are the engine and you will become another unquestioning cog in the machine as well."

She ran a hand over his face before strapping his throat and head to the chair. "What's the plan?" Officer Raven asked. It was probably a customary question, not one he really needed to ask, but did out of respect.

"Do what you need to do," Portia said. "Take it up to level three, if that doesn't work, level five will do nicely. He will submit after that. They all do." Portia then turned back to Smoke, "Goodbye Smoke. I doubt we will ever see each other again."

Officer Raven nodded dutifully as Portia left the room. He watched as best he could as Officer Raven walked to the machine. He switched on a lever and the engine sprang to life. He could hear the pumps pull water into the machine while the flame that heated the boiler ignited. "How does the flame work?" Smoke asked. The last thing he needed was to become curious at the inner workings of the machine, but none the less, curiosity gripped him.

"What?" Office Raven asked once he realized Smoke had asked a question.

"The flame that heats the water in the boiler, how does it work?"

Smoke wished he could see the utter look of confusion on Officer Raven's face as he asked the question. The officer cleared his throat, "It all started back at the first buildings of the underground, just as the engine was being conceived. The people would come across methane and other natural gasses which were deadly to breathe in, but could hold a flame. They managed to capture the gasses and send them downward towards the engine when they required it. Now we use alchemists to change the carbon in carbon dioxide into methane and other forms of fuel for the flames. It's really useful."

"Do you know how the alchemists do what they do? I tried inquiring a few times on the surface, but I've never actually been given an answer."

The officer shrugged, "The secrets of the alchemists are theirs alone to keep. I have no interest in their magic."

Smoke rolled his eyes. "Lazy answers," he said under his breath.

Officer Raven approached the chair and pulled the false coverings off the chair. They were designed in a way to allow for removal while a person had been strapped down. A quick pull from the sides and the coverings came off in three separate pieces for each limb. Smoke could now feel a soft, heavily perforated rubber under his arms.

"Mister Callahan," Officer Raven said softly, "I just want you to know I really don't like this chair. I've sat in it myself. It's not a great place to be and it still makes me uncomfortable to see anyone else in it, but this is my job. I just want to assure you beforehand that you don't have to worry about any infections or anything of the sort. We properly sanitize every day."

"Properly sanitize what?" Smoke asked knowing he'd find out very soon.

"I'm sure you noticed the arms and legs were a little wider than necessary," Officer Raven continued, "That's because there are hundreds of little steam powered pistons under there. Each piston has a set of needles attached to them. At the lowest speed they won't even break the skin. You'll feel them, but they aren't horrible. Once I reach full power though those needles start going at super speed and can actually puncture the skin. We don't do full speed for very long, we still want you to be able to use your arms and legs sooner than later. Just, don't expect you'll be without any scars after today."

"I'm no stranger to scars," Smoke said, his bravest face beginning to fail him.

He could hear Officer Raven sigh from behind his mask as he pressed one button out of six. A shot of pain went from his wrist to his elbow and to his shoulder. He wasn't sure if it was the shock of the first of the needles hitting his skin or if they had gone a little deeper than intended. Then another a little farther down his arm. Soon he was feeling little pin pricks all over his arm. "This is one arm at our lowest speed. This will bring you discomfort. Almost like an itch that you just can't scratch. Nothing serious."

Officer Raven pressed the second button. His second arm began to feel the sensation of the little needles as they pricked his skin. The irritation was unbearable. He wanted to pull his arm away but was unable. Officer Raven pressed the third button and the needles began on his left leg. Smoke pressed his lips together as he tried not to scream in frustration. He concentrated on his breathing. He concentrated on anything he could to keep from shouting out in discomfort.

Officer Raven pressed the fourth button thus agitating his right leg. His skin crawled with discomfort and pain. He tried to lift his arms and he tried to kick, both were impossible.

Officer Raven pressed the fifth button. Smoke's eyes shot open as the needles rapidly punctured his flesh. He let out a loud groan of pain as he tried to maintain his composure. He wouldn't give in so easily. He wanted to cry out for the needles to stop. He would beg and cry to whatever gods are out there to make the pain stop. Seize the motor, cause a clog in the water pipes, make the gas to the flame run out. He prayed in his head for it to stop. He wouldn't give them the satisfaction of hearing him give.

He shot Officer Raven a hellish glance. The Officer could tell Smoke was in a lot of pain. Smoke didn't try to hide the pain as the skin in his arms and legs felt as if they were being ripped off. Officer Raven looked to Smoke and let out a sigh. "I'm sorry Mister Callahan," he said sorrowfully.

He pressed the sixth button and all hell broke loose on Smoke. The needles were puncturing his skin at an alarming rate. He couldn't help himself. The scream that escaped from his lips was deafening. At least in his own mind it seemed that way. He could see Officer Raven hold his head in his hands. Smoke could see the memory of the needle chair was still alive within the officer. It wasn't enough for him to stop the chair from turning Smoke's arms and legs into ground meat however.

Smoke could feel his blood pooling around his feet. If not for his screams of pain he believed he could hear the blood dripping from the chair arms. That's what the rubber was for, to keep as little blood from getting into the chair as possible. The chair would be thoroughly cleaned afterwards, somehow the thought didn't give Smoke any comfort.

As the needles tore his arms and legs to shreds something snapped in his head. Smoke stopped screaming and began laughing devilishly.

"Why are you laughing?" Officer Raven asked more confused than angry.

Smoke coughed from the pain and said, "I-I wish I'd h-have thought of th-th-this back when I was in the fourth b-below. Fucking brilliant! J-just imagine th-the confessions I c-could have gotten with th-this thing."

"You're stubborn," Officer Raven said, "I hate it when they're stubborn."

He did something with the machine Smoke couldn't see and the needles retracted into the chair and stopped. He could still feel the thin pieces of metal going in and out of his arms and legs, but the irritation and stabbing feelings had stopped. All that remained was the pain. Pain he could handle.

Officer Raven hung his head and sighed. He slowly walked towards the door and opened it. He poked his head out and said something Smoke couldn't make out. Officer Raven soon brought his head back into the room and walked towards Smoke. A large muscular man walked through the door next. 'Officer Miller' was etched into his breastplate. In his left hand hung a young naked woman, he lifted her by the arm until she could only stand on the tips of her toes. This was her, this was Blue.

"Fuck you," Officer Raven said toward Smoke with disdain in his voice. "This could have been avoided had you submitted, but no, you had to remain strong. We always break people Mister Callahan, I broke, Miller broke, and even Portia broke! You are no exception."

Officer Miller continued to hold Blue while Officer Raven fetched a plain wooden chair. The look on Blue's face showed nothing but horror. She knew what they had planned, she'd been through the torture chamber before. She began to struggle against Officer Miller. Her feet came up in an attempted kick and to forcefully push herself away from her captors. Her struggling was all for naught however. Officer Miller never lost his grip on her arm and shoved his fist into her stomach. Smoke could hear the air being forced from her lungs as she hung limp in his arms gasping for breath.

Officer Raven placed the chair behind Blue. The Officer holding Blue placed her in the chair gently and cuffed her arms and legs to the chair. She pulled on the chains and screamed incomprehensibly at the officers. Smoke watched on as the frightened girl fought against her restraints. She even tried biting at Officer Raven when he came in close.

Officer Miller Walked to the table holding the mallets and hooks and pulled open a drawer Smoke hadn't noticed. He pulled out five pieces of cable with small metal jaws attached to both ends. He approached Blue carefully. Officer Raven held her head back as Officer Miller attached a metal jaw to her nipples.

Officer Raven soon moved around Blue and held her knees open. Officer Miller knelt down and began placing the metal jaws on both ends of her labia and one to her clitoris. Blue began breathing heavy as she eyed the men unspooling the wire towards the motor. She shot them a look of pure hatred as they attached the metal jaws on the opposite ends of the wires to small metal prongs protruding outward. Officer Raven soon went to work flicking switches, pulling levers and spinning dials.

"You're in luck Mister Callahan," Officer Miller said as Officer Raven worked. "You don't have to go through the needle chair again. Though there is some bad news in there. You don't get to go through stage four of the re-education phases. Instead you're bumped up to stage five. What is stage five you may ask; well, it's different for everyone. It's a forceful measure to break someone... There's an ancient book someone wrote a long time ago. I know I read it once but I can't remember what it's called. Some guy crosses his government and gets rats in a cage attached to his face until he submits. This is essentially the same thing. Only Blue here is your rat in a cage. Don't get me wrong though, the process always works much better when all the stages are met, but Portia must really want you to break quickly. Or, she wants you to suffer. It's always hard to tell with her."

Smoke glared at the officer. He could imagine the smug grin on his face as he explained everything. "Let me stop you there," Smoke said angrily, "If you harm one hair on that girl's body, I swear to whatever gods may be out there, I will tear this place down piece by piece. Do what you want with me, frankly I really don't care. I'll more than happily work for the engine. But, if you turn that machine on, I will kill you. I will kill Officer Raven. I will kill everyone in this engine and I will grin like a mad man doing so. You get me?"

Officer Miller stared at Smoke for a second. He couldn't see the man's eyes or any sort of facial expression. He desperately wanted to read his face. He doubted his words meant anything to the two officers in their armour, but Smoke wanted to know for sure. After a few moments of the only sound being Officer Raven working, Officer Miller stood straight and said, "It's not like we haven't done this before. You saw her struggle," he turned to Officer Raven. "Start on a low current. We'll up it shortly."

Officer Raven started the motor and waited the few second it took for the engine to stop chugging and begin running smoothly. He walked to the far side of the large motor and spun a small dial. Almost instantly Smoke saw Blue jump in her seat. "Right now," Officer Miller said, "We have a low current of electricity. Nothing more than a tingling feeling going through her body. Don't worry; we're not going to up the juice so much she'll die, unless you push us. She's even more important to us than you are. But it will hurt. She will scream. That much I can guarantee. And don't even think of saying you'll submit so early either. We know when a person is lying to us, and I actually want some fun with this. I'll allow you to submit after level three."

"You son of a whore!" Smoke screamed.

He didn't get a chance to say more. Officer Miller struck him across the face with his heavily armoured glove sending blood flying across the room and to the wall. His jaw ached as he could feel blood falling from his cheek. "Not another word Mister Callahan, otherwise she'll get the full dose. I don't care if she dies, we can find another one just like her eventually. The next words I want to hear out of your mouth are 'I submit'. And only once we hit level four. No sooner."

Smoke continued to glare at Officer Miller. Though he couldn't see the faces of either officer Smoke could tell Officer Raven took no pleasure in what was happening. He had seemed to hope Smoke would submit after the needle chair. That way this wouldn't have had to happen. It may have anyway, Blue was here for a reason, and it sure wasn't because she agreed with their methods or their ideas. She was resisting just as he was.

The look Blue gave Smoke seemed to be a look of apology mixed with sorrow, pain and pleading. She heard Officer Miller just as well as he had. She knew there was so much more she would go through with the chair. So much more pain and there would be nothing Smoke could do about it. She didn't look to be in any sort of pain at the moment, just mild discomfort.

Officer Miller nodded to Officer Raven. Officer Raven nodded back and spun the dial again. Blue shot back into her chair and gave a short scream. Her breathing became intense. Her eyes narrowed as she focused on Smoke. He pulled on the straps, as much tension as he could muster. Her eyes spoke to him. Her eyes told him to not give in and to keep his mouth shut. It didn't matter if they killed her or put her into a world of insurmountable pain. He wasn't to give in. She was going be disappointed in him - he had every intention of telling them he's submitting - in words in any case.

He slowed his breathing and did what he could to try and get his hands out from under the straps. A fool's errand, with his forearm tied down and ripped to shreds there'd be no way he could pull his arms free. Instead he tried breaking the arms and legs of the chair. After many years of being used, it would be possible the chair could have weaknesses. Smoke would have to find them.

Officer Miller nodded again to Officer Raven who in kind nodded back. He turned the dial again and Blue's eyes shot open and a shrill piercing scream came from BLue. Her pelvis raised and lowered and her chest swung from side to side in an attempt to shake the metal jaws off.

Smoke pressed his lips together and pulled on the straps. He could feel something in the metal arms give way. Over the sounds of Blue's screams the officers didn't hear the breaking of the chair's arms. Smoke began to pull with his legs and soon the legs came free as well.

He stood as several small pistons fell from the chair's arms. He looked at the jagged scrap of metal and slowly moved behind Officer Miller who had been watching Blue like a hawk. He lined up his blow as quietly as he could and brought the hollow jagged arm into the base of his neck. The way the big man went down he assumed he had severed the spine. He sure hoped he did anyway. Officer Raven saw what had happened and rushed in towards Smoke. He blocked several punches from the officer with the chair arms. As soon as he was sure he had a shot he drove the arm of the chair into the back of Officer Raven's leg. The Officer went down with a loud curse.

Smoke stood over the man and pulled off his mask. He was a handsome man with long blonde hair, a chiseled jaw line and high cheek bones. Officer Raven looked up and Smoke with his blue eyes and said, "I didn't want to do this."

Smoke snorted angrily, "I know, but you did anyway, and I'm a man of my word."

He drove the jagged ends of the chair arm and leg into the crown and jaw of the officer's head. He could feel the blood spatter against his face. He then turned to the motor and turned the dial to zero. Blue relaxed in her chair from muscular exhaustion. He searched Officer Miller's body until he found the keys to her shackles and let her free. She in turn released the straps and the arms and legs of the now useless chair fell to the floor. His arms hurt more than they had ever hurt before. He looked at the wounds and sighed. They'd heal, though he doubted he'd ever have much for feeling in them ever again, and that was if they didn't just turn to lumpy scar tissue.

They wasted no time. They dressed into the uniforms of Officer Miller and Officer Raven and left the torture room....

He wasn't going anywhere. No matter how hard Smoke pulled on the straps, the chair's arms or legs wouldn't give. He shook his mind from the fantasy and continued to pull. Blue had urinated. The warm blood he had felt on his face in his mind had been Blue's urine that had spattered in his direction from her flailing. Her screams persisted and Smoke could swear he could hear Officer Miller laughing through it. The rage within him grew as he kept his mouth shut. The moment Officer Raven turned that dial to the fourth level he would speak up. He would tell them he submits to the will of the engine.

Officer Miller stood and waited. Smoke could tell he wanted to see if Smoke would be stupid enough to disobey. Smoke continued to obey his order of silence, not out of obedience, but out of necessity. Once Officer Miller knew Smoke wouldn't say anything he continued to watch as Blue flung her naked self around in the chair. Smoke didn't know how long they had been sitting there watching the poor woman get tortured with the third level, but it had been much longer than the other two threefold.

Officer Miller eventually gave Officer Raven the nod to increase the current. Blue's body rose out of the chair as much as it could and proceeded to grip the arms. Her scream cut off into silence, leaving her mouth open, screaming silently. Smoke wasn't even sure she could breathe. "I submit!" Smoke said as loud as he could.

Officer Miller turned to look at Smoke, "What was that?"

Smoke took in a deep breath and exhaled loudly, "I give, I submit. I would have sooner but you wouldn't allow it. I submit my will to the engine and allow myself to be educated in the ways of the machine."

Tears began to fall from Smoke's eyes. Officer Miller looked to Officer Raven and waved his hand across his throat three times. Officer Raven nodded and turned the dial top zero. Blue's body relaxed and fell back into the chair. Smoke hoped she was breathing. Officer Raven seemed to have had the same idea and approached her. He removed his glove revealing a pale hand and placed two fingers on her jugular vein. He looked to be concentrating for a moment before taking his hand away and putting his glove on. "She's alive and breathing," Officer Raven said, "Her pulse is faint and her breathing is shallow, but she'll live. We probably shouldn't move her for a while though. Let her recover a bit."

Officer Miller looked to Smoke and back to Blue and finally to Officer Raven, "We'll leave him in here as well. Let him get an eye-full before he meets the real educator."

The two officers left the torture room. Smoke looked to Blue and felt a genuine tear fall down his cheek. He had allowed this to happen. He could have spoken up and allowed her to die. She'd have died a painful death maybe, but a death regardless. She would no longer be in a state of pain; she'd no longer have to suffer at the hands of those who worked the engine. She'd be free of her family and all they represented.

Blue's eyelids fluttered before she opened her eyes. She groaned and sat straight in the chair. "Who are you?" she asked in a weak voice.

"I'm detective Smoke Callahan," he said as softly as he could. "Are you alright?" When she straightened herself a little and nodded he continued, "Your parents sent me to find you and bring you home."

Blue nodded as she processed what Smoke had said, "You poor bastard, "she said. "Let me guess, it was Marla who sent you."

Smoke furrowed his brow. "Yeah," he said confused.

"They set you up. They sent you to find me with no real thought in their mind that you'd ever actually find me. They probably hoped you'd die along the way."

"Why would they do that?"

Blue showed a weak smile as she sunk back into her chair, "It's simple. Their daughter went missing. Their daughter who had figured out a way to make living in the underground much easier. I could have actually brought the first two underground levels to the surface. The eighth and ninth below would have become a distant memory. I was a prodigy. They couldn't let the public think I'd just disappear and have nobody come looking for me. They could check school records. They could check several legitimate means of my not being home. What they can't check is if I run away or if I'm kidnapped shortly after running away. Especially since knowing of this engine is the family secret.

"They would then hire a detective who they thought would get too close to the truth and die. An incompetent detective would just fail, he'd tell the story of the one he couldn't find and questions would be asked. If they got someone good - someone who knew who to ask the questions of, knew who to trust and was down on his luck enough that they'd be willing to go where they needed - that was the person they needed. He'd get too close, die and nobody would investigate because everyone would believe me dead in the underground. You got set up Mister Callahan. Though, I don't think my family expected this."

Smoke had known the case was strange. He had known the payment was too good to be true. He had tried to turn away, but had been threatened. He didn't expect to have dealt with his fourth below problem on his own.

"So did you run away or were you abducted?" Smoke asked.

"I left at first. I decided to get lost in the underground where I thought nobody would find me. I got as far as the seventh below when I was told I'd find a sanctuary on the ninth below. I decided to give it a look and was captured shortly after arriving at the ninth."

Smoke nodded as he thought about Blue's story. "I'm building a plan to get out of here," Smoke said. "I could have been out of here a while ago, but I came here for you. I needed to know where you were and that you were alive. Now you're right here. I don't think I'm going to get a better opportunity than this."

Blue gave Smoke a wicked grin, "I'm in. Let's get the fuck out of here."

17

The plan had a small chance of success, though it was their best odds of escaping. Smoke didn't know how long they had waited. The room lacked any sort of timepiece, but the plan hinged on the two of them appearing to be sleeping - make the officers believe they are in a state of weakness.

What seemed like several hours to Smoke had probably only been just over a single hour before Officer Raven returned to the torture room. This was a stroke of luck. There would be no real chance of a struggle if Smoke was unconscious.

Officer Raven spoke to a man outside the room before closing the door. Smoke raised his head slightly with half open eyes. He could see Officer Raven walk over to him and grab him by the head. He used his fingers to pull one of Smoke's eyelids open and took a look. Smoke did his best to continue the charade of weakness. He seemed to buy it. He let Smoke's head go and began removing the straps that held him down.

He let his head and arms fall free as the straps were removed one by one. Next, Officer Raven worked on freeing his legs. This would be the moment of truth. Once he was free it would only be a matter of time before he could make his move.

Officer Raven picked Smoke up from under his shoulder. "Alright, easy now. One step at a time," Officer Raven whispered to himself or to Smoke, it was unclear which.

Smoke watched as they continued to take small steps towards the exit. As they approached the door Smoke intentionally slipped causing himself to land on the tray of soft mallets and hooks. The force of his impact knocked the tray over and onto the floor scattering the contents across the room. Smoke picked himself up back onto his hands and knees, continuing to do his best at appearing weak. Under his body he gripped a soft mallet.

Officer Raven swore quietly and knelt down beside Smoke. He didn't see the mallet coming nor could he react when the mallet connected in the center of his face. Officer Raven fell backwards onto his back. Smoke could see blood gushing through the mask from what he could only assume to be a broken nose. Officer Raven gripped at his mask.

Smoke then stood and walked towards Officer Raven. "You tortured me," he said coldly. "I could forgive that. Unfortunately for you, I've been broken before. Many, many times in my youth, I've learned to stay strong. I've learned how to not give anything away, even myself.

But then you tortured Blue. I know you didn't take any pleasure in it. I know you didn't want to do it, but you did anyway. That said - I have to keep my word and kill you. Don't worry; it'll be a quick death. Blue, don't watch this."

Smoke knelt beside the fallen officer and raised the soft mallet. For a moment he wished it were actually made of metal and not hard rubber. He pulled the mask off the officer's face and saw the man looked very different than he had imagined. He had short red hair and a large amount of red scruff along his cheeks and chin. His nose had been crushed flat and sat sideways on his face. His two front teeth had been knocked out and possibly swallowed. Smoke looked over to Blue and saw she had obeyed. She had her eyes closed and her head turned away as far as she could.

Smoke brought the hammer down between Officer Raven's eyes. The sound of the Officer's skull crunching under the mallet was sickening. Nothing he hadn't heard before, but it'd be a new experience for Blue. He hoped she wouldn't vomit from it. The body twitched as the damaged brain desperately tried to send signals to the nerves and muscles.

It was the first chance Smoke had been given to check out his arms and legs. They felt worse than they were, not much in the way of deep tissue damage, but the skin on the surface was perforated to the point where it may as well have not been there at all. Movement would become more difficult once the adrenaline in his brain wore off.

Almost immediately after coming back to his senses, Smoke began removing the metal jaws from Blue. Once Smoke had pulled himself away she closed her legs and grimaced at the pain in her crotch. She looked up at him and said, "Thank you."

Smoke gave her a nod and then proceeded to undress the officer. He needed his uniform for the plan to work. Smoke thought of the plan and realized just how amazed he was that things had gone as smoothly as it had. He took in a pained breath as he pulled the clothing over his damaged arms and legs. Blood began to soak through - something he hoped wouldn't be too much of a giveaway as to who he was.

Smoke hoped their luck kept holding. In a matter of minutes he had changed into the officer's uniform. He picked up the mask that hid all facial features and placed it over his face. The mask was still wet from Officer Raven's blood. The smell was intense; he knew he wouldn't vomit, though he didn't care for it.

"Now we wait for Officer Miller to come get you," Smoke said with a hidden grin. He could image the look on his face when he pulled Officer Miller's mask off. Then the surprise as he smashed the officer's nose with the mallet. He could see himself tearing and rending the flesh from the officer's body with the hooks and blades. Perhaps he'd attach the officer to the electric chair, or the needle chair and leave him there until someone found him.

He shook the thoughts from his head. Officer Miller was a man who deserved to die a slow and painful death. He didn't know how much pain the man had inflicted on others; the fact that he took joy from it was on another level. It angered Smoke that vengeance for all the others would have to be put to the back burner and the officer would have to die quickly. It was the only way either of them would get out alive.

He didn't know what to do with the officer's body. The corpse had finally ceased its twitching, though now a pool of blood had formed around what had once been a perfectly constructed head. Now the front of the man's face, primarily his nose and eyes were somewhere in the mess of brain tissue and shattered bone. The best he could do was to leave the body there. Somehow they had missed that part of the plan. Once Officer Miller entered they'd have to improvise.

Smoke rolled the body of Officer Raven over so he was face down. He covered the officer's head with a large softcloth that he had found in the corner of the room. If Officer Miller didn't take any sort of time to inspect the body, they'd be fine. Smoke began working on a plan in the event he did decide to roll the body over to see the man's face.

Smoke soon got the idea to grab one of the knives and slash the fabric in in one of the arms where he had been bleeding. He then rubbed his blood all over the other arm and covered himself with as much as he could. If Miller asked, he could say he had been slashed with one of the small knives.

Blue pulled at her chains. "How long do you think we are going to have to wait until Officer Miller gets here?"

Smoke shrugged, "It's hard to say. If I were to make a guess he'd be waiting for Officer Miller to come through the door with me before he came in to grab you. He's probably wondering what's taking so long by now though."

Smoke began to scream. He knelt beside the body, removed the soft cloth and picked up the mallet and brought it down on the floor a couple times. Blue began to scream as well. The idea worked. Officer Miller opened the door just as Smoke pulled the soft cloth over the officer's head. Miller was currently maskless. He had tan skin with short black hair. "What's going on here?" he asked with haste.

Smoke gripped his nose from under the respirator; the blood down the front of the mask would be cause for concern. The best he could do would be to bring attention to it. "Fucker hit me in the face with one of the fucking mallets and then fucking slashed me. I got him with a mallet though," he said through his nose to simulate a broken nose. He hoped it would help excuse the voice change, "I can't believe he got the drop on me."

"It happens," Officer Miller said with a frown, "Did you have to kill him though?"

Smoke shook his head, "I didn't mean to kill him, I hit him back with another mallet and it crushed his skull."

"You know what you have to do now right?" Officer Miller asked without actually being a question.

Smoke nodded, "Yeah, I know. It's not something I want to do, I mean, it was an accident after all. Plus he did hit me first. But, I know we don't kill. We hurt, we maim and we scar, but we don't kill."

Officer Miller nodded, "That's right," he looked down to Blue and then back to Smoke, "She can wait here for another few minutes. Come with me, I am going to make sure you do what you have to do."

Smoke nodded, "I appreciate that," he said. "Though I think you should bring the girl with us. It'd be good for her to see what happens when someone fucks up."

Officer Miller grinned, "That is an excellent idea."

As he knelt down to unlock Blue he looked back to the body lying on the floor. "What is it?" Smoke asked as he maintained the charade of a broken nose.

"Something seems off about that body," Officer Miller said, "I'm going to take a quick look at it."

As Officer Miller approached the body Smoke slowly knelt down and picked up another soft mallet. Officer Miller knelt beside the body of Officer Raven. As he removed the softcloth he lifted his head, "Red hair, Callahan doesn't have red hair."

As Smoke approached with the soft mallet Officer Miller kicked out backwards. His boots connected with Smoke's shins and brought him down to the floor, his face connecting with the floor.

Officer Miller picked himself up and grinned, "I've got to say, I'm sad to see Officer Raven dead, but I am certainly glad you did this. I don't like you Callahan and even if you had come around to our side I can't imagine I'd have ever liked you." He pulled out a large blade from behind himself. "This blade is supposed to be used for torture, nothing serious, but enough to cause the right amount of pain to break someone. I'm glad it's going to be used for what I've always wanted to use it for, ending your pathetic life."

"I thought you don't kill down here," Smoke said as he removed the mask.

"We don't," Officer Miller agreed, "But there is an exception to the rule. It's written directly in our doctrine. We don't kill. That's to be sure we don't leave a trail of bodies to our engine. But, if you kill one of us, if you murder someone who works for the engine - well, your life is then forfeit. I am now within my full rights as an officer of the engine to kill you right here and now. I could throw you in the engine, that'd be a suiting death, but I don't wish to sully her parts with your taint. No, your blood is better suited for a common blade."

Blue made a small chirp before falling silent again. Officer Miller stood over Smoke and raised the blade. "Answer me one thig," Smoke said frantically, "before you kill me, I just have one question."

"Go ahead, I don't see a problem with giving you one last question. A bit of peace before I cut your throat wide open."

"What will be the engine's purpose if everyone from the underground is now living on the surface?"

"What do you mean?" Officer Miller asked.

"Everyone from the underground is evacuating, they're expecting the boomers to collapse the lower floors, and then they'd be placing one at the entrance of the first below so nobody can get out or back in. The engine produces water and air for those in the underground. It helps keep the people below the surface alive, that's good. I like that. But the technology is not affected by the electromagnetic pulse the engine is able to unleash. Essentially the engine will become useless. What would be the point in keeping it going?"

Officer Miller thought for a moment. That was before he produced a massive devil's grin and said, "I don't know. I don't care either."

He placed his foot on Smoke's ribs and lifted the blade. "How far in do you think the blade will go if I just let it drop? Where do you think it will land? Maybe it'll collapse a lung; or maybe it'll hit your heart. Maybe it will just bounce off the breastplate, I'll be sure not to let that happen, it'd ruin my fun way too quickly. Besides, these breastplates are really not high quality."

Smoke watched as Officer Miller raised the blade over his head with only two fingers. He could see the sweat on the officer's face roll down and around his grin. His eyes were crazed and uncaring for the man beneath his boot. Smoke almost wished he'd just go the easy way and cut his throat now.

Smoke heard an explosion go off and Officer Miller's face had disappeared. The blade fell from the dead officer's hand and clattered on the floor inches away from Smoke's face. The blade chipped at the tip as it hit the stone.

As Officer Miller's body fell to the floor Smoke saw Penelope holding a revolving pistol in her hand and two pairs of officer's uniforms across her shoulders. She wore an officer's uniform that fit snugly around her, "Do you have any idea how fucking long it took to find you?" she asked.

Smoke's eyes widened and stared at Penelope. "You're dead." He muttered.

"Well apparently not," she said in a rushed voice, "Let's go."

Smoke rose to his knees and began searching Officer Miller's body for the keys. He finally found them in a front pocket and began unlocking Blue's cuffs. Penelope threw the two of them clean officer's uniforms. "Do you see her too?" Smoke asked.

"Yeah," Blue said, confused, "Of course I do."

Smoke looked back to Penelope, "How are you alive? I watched your brains hit the fucking lift wall! Then that asshole said he threw your body into the machine. How? How are you here?"

"I'd also take a thank you," Penelope said as she turned towards the door. "Smoke, I'll explain everything once we are out of here. We need to go."

"Blue needs to get dressed first," Smoke said.

Penelope looked to Blue who had stepped out of the torture chair, "I didn't even recognize her. To be honest I hardly noticed her," Penelope said holding out her hand. "I'm Penelope; I'm a friend of Smoke's."

"Just Penelope?" Blue asked.

"I probably had a family name at one point, but I'll be damned if I can remember it. It's been a long time."

"I'm Blue Lang," she said with a faint smile.

The two women shook hands and Blue immediately began dressing. Smoke turned around as Blue dressed. Though he had already seen her naked he felt compelled to allow her some privacy while she clothed herself. Penelope rolled her eyes. He could tell she was pleased he had found Blue, though at the same time he could feel her sense of urgency. It was very likely someone had heard the shot and would be gathering reinforcements. Both Smoke and Blue were lacking weapons and he doubted the revolving pistol Penelope had held more than a few shots left. They'd be done before they had even been given a chance to begin escaping.

Once Blue had dressed she nodded to Penelope. "Lead the way," she said.

Penelope nodded back to Blue and exited the room. The two of them followed Penelope through the corridors and passageways. The place was like a maze, filled with twists and turns. Smoke never would have found his way out on his own. Even if he had been to the torture chamber enough times to memorize his way to and from his cage he'd have never made it out. He didn't know what stroke of luck had brought him Blue, and led Penelope back to him, but he was thankful for it.

Penelope turned a corner and immediately backtracked. "There are three guys over there," she whispered. "Come with me, I know what I have to do to get past them."

Smoke and Blue agreed and followed Penelope around the corner. "Hey," she said without any hint of fear in her voice, "I'm so sorry, but I'm new here. I'm supposed to take a couple new officers to the underground so they can get me to the surface safely."

The two officers looked at one another. Smoke looked to both the officers' breast plates which read 'Officer Tomlinson' and 'Officer Cherkasy'. Officer Tomlinson was a tall man with slender features while Officer Cherkasy was a short muscular woman. "You hear anything about this?" Officer Cherkasy asked.

"You kidding?" Officer Tomlinson said with amusement. "Those people don't tell me anything."

"Why are you down here to begin with?" Officer Cherkasy asked.

"I was visiting a friend of mine who had been recently captured. I wanted to see him before I left. He's in the process of being recruited. I just went down to tell him he would be wise to join us," Penelope spoke without missing a beat. The lines didn't sound rehearsed or made up from the top of her head. The way she spoke made it sound like the truth. "There was an officer before, I can't remember his name for the life of me, but he told us where to go to see him. But, on my way out I got turned around. These two are new and are having trouble finding their way out as well."

"Sound truthful to you?" Officer Cherkasy asked her partner.

"To be honest, I don't care," said Officer Tomlinson. "I don't get paid enough to give a rat's fart what the other people of the engine do. I'm just here for security and they're wearing uniforms. They look alright to me."

Officer Cherkasy shrugged as she pointed down the corridor. "Turn at your third right, then your second left. Go up the stairs straight ahead and turn at your first right. You'll find the engine ahead and from there you'll be able to find the lift that'll take you to the underground."

Penelope smiled at the two officers and thanked them. The three of them made their way forward not speaking a word until they turned down the third right. "That was incredible," Blue finally said, "even I believed it."

Smoke could see Penelope smile, "When you're as old as I am you learn to lie convincingly at a moment's notice. Those two were easy."

"How old are you?" Blue asked.

"I'll get into that once we've left this place," Penelope said as her smile disappeared.

The three continued on in silence as they followed the directions given by Officer Cherkasy. They walked with purpose and as if they had somewhere to be. Any officer they passed gave them a brief nod as they continued on their way. Smoke looked to Blue every once in a while to see how she was holding up. All in all she seemed to be dealing with the escape plan.

Blue was quite the trooper. She had been beaten, tortured, stripped naked and starved. Still she managed to find the strength to continue on. She didn't break despite all that had happened. Smoke didn't think he'd have had her strength at her age. Bringing her home was what gave him the strength he needed, even if it was for nothing more than to rub his survival in their faces as he claimed the reward.

Penelope perplexed him. He knew he had seen her die. He had felt her blood become sticky under his boots. He had smelt her blood and the gunpowder of the gun. He had heard Robert openly state to Portia that he had thrown her into the engine. How could she be alive? How could she have been there to help him escape? He didn't think any possible explanation she could give him would be enough.

The opening to the engine took Smoke's breath away. The expansive machine was still a wonder that would be a part of the earth for thousands of years to come. If the engine stopped at that moment the gears and pulleys and boilers and sprockets would remain as a forgotten machine that had the ability to end the world as well as it ran it.

The looks on Blue's face was one of amazement. She had

been feeling the same way Smoke felt. They both had seen the engine before. They had been given the speech on how it ran, why it ran and why it existed. It took some of the amazement away from the machine, though the view remained breathtaking.

The look on Penelope's face had been what Smoke imagined his face to be when he had first laid eyes on the engine. A look of sheer disbelief and wonder with an unwillingness to look away in case it was nothing more than an illusion that could disappear at any given moment. He slapped Penelope on the shoulder. "I know," was all he said.

Penelope sucked in her lips and pressed them together. "We got to get out of here," she said as she stepped on the grated path. The nervousness of being on the narrow grated path hadn't left Smoke. He could fall into the machine at any given moment and he'd never know anything again.

Blue and Penelope looked to be having no difficulty with the grated path. It put him at ease a little. The nervousness had remained, though he knew he'd be free from it at any given moment. As the path ended and Smoke stepped on flat earth he resisted the urge to drop to his knees. He turned to look at the engine one last time. He could see the people working on the boilers, making sure they ran properly.

Smoke almost felt bad for the men and women who ran the engine what runs the world. They weren't bad; they were not villains by any definition. They were folk who the people who governed the engine felt would be acceptable to do the dirty work. The majority of them were probably beaten and tortured before they submitted to the engine's will, or at least the engine's government. When the engine finally died, they all would die along with it. It was a sad thought that Smoke didn't like. He could try and save as many as he could, but that could mean his plan failing.

This time it was Penelope who put her hand on his shoulder. "Tell me about it when we're in the lift," she said calmly.

Smoke nodded and turned towards the doors to the lift. He saw a spin combination lock in the wall signifying a lift was there. He knew he had seen Robert spin the wheel, though through the discovery of the engine and the torture that quickly followed he couldn't remember the numbers. He looked to Blue and Penelope, Blue gave him a worried glance while Penelope smiled, "It's okay Smoke, I know the combination. I got a better view and trauma doesn't cause memory loss for me anymore."

She spun the spin combination lock and almost immediately the doors to the lift opened wide. Smoke breathed a sigh of relief and entered the lift. Blue quickly followed with Penelope in the rear. He pressed the button reading 'Close Door' and watched as the door closed. All three took in a deep breath and let the air out. Smoke pressed the button with the arrow pointing up and they felt the lift lurch. The sound of steam filling the hydraulics echoed around the lift before it began moving upward.

Smoke looked to the side of the lift and saw the red stain left over from Penelope's blood and brains. "Alright," Smoke said to Penelope, "tell me how you're alive. Tell me how you managed to survive a shot to the head as well as being chewed up by the engine. There is no possible way anything could survive that."

Penelope hung her head and leaned on the wall next to her blood stain, "It's the same reason I wasn't afraid when you pulled your revolving pistol out on me. I can't actually die. I'm a six thousand year old immortal. There have been other supposed immortals in the past, but one by one they all eventually die in a matter of speaking, typically from some accident or decision; gone from aliens, self-sacrifice, or banishment. Only I remain - the one true immortal."

"But how?" Smoke asked.

"I'm lost," Blue said as she gave both of them confused looks.

"When I was on my way down to the engine Penelope came with me. The guy who found us shot her in the head. That red spot over there, that's her blood. The guy then said he'd thrown her body into the machine. Now I'm trying to figure out just how she's able to stand here much less help us escape."

Blue nodded in acceptance. "So how are you immortal?" she asked.

"I don't remember what happened anymore. It was six thousand years ago. You can't reasonably expect me to remember everything that happened, shit two thousand years ago is pretty fuzzy these days. There's a lot I do remember, parts of history that stick out, but there's a lot I've forgotten over time."

Smoke thought for a moment and asked, "Were there really superhumans and supernatural creatures around two thousand years ago?"

Penelope hadn't expected such a question. She cocked her head to the side and soon gave Smoke an amused snort, "You're face to face with a six thousand year old immortal and the first question is about the superhumans?"

Smoke nodded.

Penelope sighed, her face giving the impression of amusement. "Yes, there were superhumans and supernatural creatures. Hell, I've dated a few of both. Well, vampires anyway. Vampires didn't like the taste of my blood; they'd always say it tasted wrong. Once I knew I wasn't prey to them I began dating a few vampires. They don't grow old and die, so it wasn't a big deal for me. Then the purge started and now - well, I'm sure you know."

"What about the superhuman?" Blue asked. "I bet that was exciting."

"I think it was," Penelope said. "I can't remember his name, heh, how sad is that. But I do remember he had some sort of darkness power."

"Night Child?" Smoke asked.

Penelope's face lit up and she grinned, "Yes! That was him. He went by a different name when we dated. Did we get married? I can't remember - anyway, we didn't date long, at least by my standards. He was one of the first immortals to disappear. I'm sure I'll eventually find out what happened to them, Writer willing."

"Again with your writer," Smoke said with an amused tone.

"Smoke, I know you don't believe in The Writer, but with everything I've seen, the leaps in logic and the broken chains of cause and effect. Sure, when broken down and thought about they sometimes make sense, but I can't help but think the world and history and our futures are all being designed around us. I can't help but believe there is a writer. Besides, I've been in so many adventures I wanted nothing to do with I know I am not a person as far as this world is concerned."

"Don't say that," Smoke said almost immediately, "of course you're a person."

"I'm human, sure," Penelope said, "but it's undeniable that I'm not a person, I'm a plot devise. I'm someone The Writer brings in if he doesn't know what to do or where to go with a story. Sure, my life has been long and there are dull gaps in between adventures, but since I can't die he can leave me out of many stories over the course of several thousand years and pick me back up as if nothing had happened. Gives me a bit of a dusting off and puts me back into the adventure."

"Would you want to die if you could?" Blue asked.

"If I could die, I'd kill myself right here and now. I want nothing more than to finally be at peace. It's rough watching everyone you've ever known grow up, grow old, die and still live long enough for them to fade from your memory. I remember Night Child and a few of my old vampire lovers because they're in history books. Most of the people I've ever cared about died before Judaism was even a thing. Judaism was a religion that died off in the late twenty second century. It was the longest lived religion of all time - even The Writer religion is only a couple thousand years old.

So yes, I want nothing more than to die, though I think I'm going to be alive to see my ten thousandth birthday before The Writer finally lets me die."

Smoke and Blue hung their heads. They were unsure what to say to Penelope on the subject. The rest of the lift ride was in silence. None of them wanted to break the silence and talk about what Penelope had said. Nobody wanted to be the one to bring it up. In a few short minutes the doors to the lift opened and the three of them stepped out into the ninth below.

18

"What do you mean the boomers didn't go off?" Cobble asked Homer, "How do the boomers that we have spent so many years getting ready and placing not go off?"

Homer put his hands in the air in surrender, "I don't know. I've checked the readings several times, they didn't go off. Maybe it was faulty wiring? Maybe somebody tampered with something. I don't fucking know!"

Constance watched as the two men argued about how the boomers had failed to bring down the underground. She had fought tooth and nail to get them to hold back the detonations until Smoke returned, but after a while even she had to agree they couldn't wait any longer. If Smoke was still down there he was more than likely dead. She had cried the night they determined his fate. She hadn't been sure as to why she spilled so many tears for him. He hadn't exactly been a close friend. There was no romantic interest towards him, not that he'd ever feel that way for her anyway. He had Glass waiting for him.

Not that any of it mattered, the boomers had failed, and if Smoke really was alive he'd have more than enough time to get back to the surface. If he really was alive he'd have figured to come to the surface by now, if he were alive he likely would be on the surface already. The last report she had gotten was from one of the lift drivers who had said he had gone down to the ninth below with one of the other lift drivers. That put her mind at ease for a little while. He'd have someone who could drive the lifts back to the surface.

The first few days back on the surface were cathartic for Constance. She met back with her former employer who agreed to give her job back once everything with the underground was done. He'd need her to keep the peace with everyone from the underground drinking and getting rowdy. She had met back with a good number of her friends and had slept in her own bed for a change.

She found she had gotten closer with Cobble than she'd originally thought she would. They had spent the majority of their time together, they drank together, they ate together and on a few occasions they slept together. When Constance had believed Smoke to be dead Cobble had been there for her in an attempt to comfort her. The next day she handed control of the Cartel to Cobble.

The attack on the tower had been fruitless. The soldiers of the tower prevented anyone from getting to the first below, and with the town of Tower's Shadow being in a danger zone, boomers couldn't be used to take them down. Many had tried to weaken the structure to force it to fall a certain way, though none had been able to make so much as a dent in the tower's outer wall.

The doors to the tower had been broken, though barricades around the tower's entrance prevented anyone from getting close. Constance could almost picture the people in the tower's faces. Some would be frightened at the prospect of people making it in the tower. Others would scoff at the struggles and try to throw more tower soldiers at the people. They'd have no fear;

they were too big to fail. It was seeming so to those from the underground as well. The only real advancement they had made in their lines had been brought on by those from the ninth below. They were all dead now, died in the line of duty.

Constance wanted nothing more than to bring the tower down. The information Blaze had given her had been helpful. He had told her not to kill the man who had killed her parents. He'd done nothing more than the job he had been payed to do; if he hadn't fulfilled his duty he'd have a difficult time finding more jobs and would ultimately starve to death, - if he hadn't been killed outright by the other assassins. Blaze had refused to give her the killer's name, though he was very forthcoming with the name of the family who hired him.

The Rocka family from the third above were supposedly the people who hired the killer. Constance knew the name, though she'd never met them before or had any idea as to why they'd want her family dead. The open accusation towards someone in the tower seemed suspicious. Though she didn't have any real reason to distrust what Blaze had told her, she couldn't find any reason to trust him either. He had been a slave trader. He had been a man of ill-repute, at least to anyone who disagreed with slavery. She knew she'd have to do some her own investigation to get to the bottom of it all.

One of the members of the Worms approached Homer and Cobble as Constance watched. "Sir," the boy said. "We've just got reports from the neighboring areas. Their boomers didn't explode either. Their plans were a failure and they are going to go back down soon to check it out."

Homer nodded, "We are going to have to do the same," he said as he ran his fingers through his hair and scratching his head. "We're probably going to have to leave someone down there to make sure things go right."

"Let's not base anything on assumptions just yet," Cobble

said with a wave of his hand. "It could be something to do with the wiring. Maybe we will have to boom the lower floors while a few floors up in the underground. Let's not jump to any conclusions until we've investigated. Has anyone else in the other areas investigated? That you know of?"

The messenger shook his head, "No sir. At least not as far as I know."

Cobble raised his chin and said, "Alright, You're dismissed. Keep me updated if anything new happens."

The messenger nodded and scampered away. Homer watched the messenger leave before turning back towards Cobble, "So, How would you like to proceed?"

Cobble scratched his chin, the stubble that had grown in the time since coming to the surface gave him a primal attractiveness that Constance liked. "Get three of your men ready. I'll bring three of my own and we'll go down and make sure things work properly."

"Not a bad idea," Homer said with a grin, "But how are we going to get down? The lift drivers made sure to use some mechanism to bring the lifts down slowly so Smoke could get back up. They don't have a mechanism to bring a lift back up."

"Fuck," Cobble said, "How much wire rope do we have?"

"Not near enough," Homer said with a worried look, "I'll talk to the towns folk to see if they have any ideas, but I think we're fucked. Someone from another area might have to come into our area."

"Fucking Smoke," Cobble said angrily. "Even while dead he's fucking things up. I'll think of something, just give me some time. We've got a lot of it now."

Homer placed his palm in the center of his forehead and

walked away. That had been a hand signal Constance came to know as a salute. It was rare for someone from the underground to salute another; they typically only did when an important mission was underway. Even then, they saluted only people who they felt to be in charge. If Homer saluted to Cobble it meant Cobble was the man in charge and he called the shots despite Blaze and Homer leading their own groups.

Constance looked to Cobble and watched as he approached and stood beside her. He shot her a smile and asked, "How are you doing?"

"I'm alright," Constance said absently. "I've been thinking though. I think it's about time I try and sneak into the tower. I might be able to get through a vent and make my way to the first above. I could then manually control the steam lift and bring everyone inside the tower. Once I'm in and on my way up the men can charge the front and take out all the tower soldiers. They're boxed in and we outnumber them exponentially."

"How would you get to the first above?" Cobble asked. "Unless the vents snake around at a slight incline there's no way you'll make it."

Constance nodded in agreement, "I know, but I have to at least try. None of the men here are small enough to fit inside. At least that's the assumption by the size of the vent opening. But, I could get in there. I wanted to run it past you first."

Cobble gave her an odd expression, "Why would you want to run it past me first?" he asked with genuine confusion. "You're fully capable of taking care of yourself."

"Mostly because it would be a great idea to let someone on the surface know what I'm doing. Hell, I could get up there, get access to the lift and bring our men up to the first above. If nobody knows what's going on I could be calling tower men back up."

Cobble nodded, "Good idea, let's do that. Anything you need? Did you manage to get the cover off at least?"

"Not yet," Constance admitted, "But it'll be off soon."

Cobble gave her a grunt in acceptance.

"I doubt I'll be able to bring much with me," Constance continued. "I can fit in the vents, but it would be a tight fit. Not that I'd get stuck along the way, though that is a very real possibility. The point being, you could lose one of your people for good, either through getting stuck, captured or shot. Granted, I haven't been able to take a look inside as of yet."

Cobble gave her a strange unreadable expression. She wasn't sure if it was annoyance or something not even close to it - all she could tell was he wasn't happy about it. "Do what you've got to do - get that vent cover off and don't waste any time after that. Also, make sure you bring a weapon and some food. If you are able to climb through the vents, you may be in there a while." he said before turning away from her.

It was all she needed to hear before she'd make her way through the vents. Once she had the grate open she'd gather some supplies and tie them to her ankle. She'd told Cobble she wouldn't be able to bring anything with her, but that had been a lie. She wanted to see his reaction. She wanted to see what he'd say. She felt disappointed when his reaction had been emotionless and cold. Although the insistence she bring a weapon and food was a good sign.

She however revelled in the knowledge that she could be one step closer to having her answers. All she'd need is a little patience and some hope the vent wouldn't narrow on her. She stopped for a moment to have a drink of water before making her way back to the tower. She'd need to get a look inside so she'd know what she could bring with her.

She approached the tower's base and took in a deep breath.

She had known the tower her entire life; the sheer size of it didn't impress her any more than grass would impress someone from the surface. When she had emerged to the surface with the leaders of the underground she had almost broken into fits of laughter when they first saw the tower - perfect white stone reaching over three and a half miles high and a quarter mile around. From a distance the towers appeared mystical, almost magic in origin. Once a person came closer it was only then they could feel the true intimidating effect the tower had on those from the surface.

Cobble had placed one of his guards at the base of the tower near the vent opening. Since the discovery, Constance had been working at removing the vent cover. She would have given up long ago if the vent had refused to move. Though she found the vent was quite firm in place within the wall, she had been able to budge the cover bit by bit. She was close to removing it, only a few more pulls.

Constance looked toward the guard. Having nobody on the surface willing to sacrifice themselves for the tower by compromising the missions, a guard was not needed around the vent. The placement was to be sure Constance was safe when she worked on her project. She grinned to herself, in the time of war he had to be stoic for his men to see him as the strong leader, but deep down he cared for her; at least enough to make sure she'd be able to get to the vent and forward safely. It gave her a warm and safe feeling.

She had fully prepared herself for the possibility the vents would go straight up and down. She had yet to even really look, something she probably should have done before bothering Cobble with her problems. But, hindsight was always clearer and she couldn't back out now. After all, she'd rather have a failed attempt at entering than have an option available and not take it.

She searched the long grass around the white tower and found the wrecking bar she had left the day before. She jammed the narrow end into the side of the vent and began to pry the cover off. The steel gave way enough to allow the end of the vent cover to show, but as she pulled she found the rest of the vent wouldn't budge. She pulled the bar out and moved it to the other end of the vent. She repeated the motions as before and the vent's corner gave way again. She could see a sizeable gap along the top of the vent, just the right size for the wrecking bar. She began to pry again, this time she could feel the vent budge slightly. She moved to the middle and the vent fell out of the wall and onto the grass with a heavy thud.

She rejoiced and placed the wrecking bar on the ground beside the vent opening. She crawled inside to her waist and looked forward. The vent had much more room than she had expected. Wide enough to fit her and some supplies with ease. The opening to the vent was much narrower than the interior. As she crawled inside, the more she found she'd be able to crawl through on her hands and knees. She felt more at ease knowing she'd actually have room to move around; the odds of becoming claustrophobia dwindled greatly. She leaned the vent back on the wall beside the vent opening. She didn't want to accidently trip over it or have anyone else injure themselves on her carelessness. The guard gave her a brief nod to acknowledge her action and proceeded to stare onward.

She left the tower in a hurry to get any supplies she felt she may need. She counted down the list in her head as she gathered the supplies: food, clothing, a weapon, knee pads, and a sack to put it all in, and rope. The underground army had been more than happy to give her everything she needed with the promise, or at least the hope that she'd be able to bring them all into the tower. She then relayed her plan to the soldiers. When they agreed to take out the tower army at the tower doors and hold the position until she could let them in, it left her with a smile.

Constance felt a twinge of pride as enough food to fill the small bag had been presented to her. The thought that she could be the lone person who turned the tide of the war filled her with an ambivalent feeling. On one hand, she'd be helping those she now considered brethren, including the people from the surface. If the wealth is spread around there'd be more for people to put through the system. On the other hand she'd be allowing the deaths of many innocent people. She didn't know if she'd be able to live with herself if everyone in the tower died.

She grabbed a revolving pistol from one of the soldiers and a few dozen shots to keep her safe. She let it sit in a clipped holster at her hip. Across her back she strapped the shortblade that Smoke had bought for her. Before strapping it to her back she looked at the shortblade's sheath, which had been decorated to resemble a walking stick. She remembered back to Smoke and all the lessons he had taught her during her time in the underground. She didn't really like the man, though she couldn't help but fight back a tear as she thought of him. She owed him a lot for what he had done for her. He had given her the opportunity to find the person who had killed her parents and the people who had supposedly hired him. Smoke, for all his faults was a good man - she felt sad for his death, but at least he wouldn't have to worry about the brewing war. That was something at least.

She grinned as she stepped to the base of the tower. The sheer size of the construct was impressive and intimidating. She couldn't imagine how long she'd be in the vents if they snaked around the tower at only a slight incline. The image was daunting. She closed her eyes and pushed the thoughts from her mind. She tied the rope around her ankle and the other end to the sack. If the vent did happen to narrow she'd be able to continue crawling and still be able to keep her stuff.

As she crawled into the ventilation shaft she couldn't help but feel as if she wouldn't be coming back to the ground. A silly thought that was caused from nerves, but she still couldn't shake it. It was unnerving.

The cool steel of the vents felt good on her hands and

through her trousers. She knew soon the steel would begin to hurt. As the thought entered her mind she removed the knee pads from the sack and strapped them into place. She tied the draw-strap until it was snug against her calf and thigh. She nodded to herself and began crawling through the vents.

Constance had been correct when she had thought the vents coiled around the tower. She assumed the coiling and the size of the vents were to accommodate the repair men who would come in and make repairs and maintain the airflow. She knew there'd be gear powered fans somewhere ahead that would suck air in, though she wouldn't be surprised if the majority of the air in the upper levels came from the artificial trees and from the steam that would be pumped through the copper pipes. These vents were more than likely for expelling the air from the tower.

The vents were tall but narrow. She could feel her shoulders rub against either side if she leaned too far one way. An annoyance that could eventually lead her to the closed-in feeling she dreaded; she'd have to do her best to fight away whatever fear came her way and continue onward.

Hours passed as Constance continued through the vents. Her hands began to hurt and the knee pads rubbed against her knees causing them to bleed slightly. She could feel her bladder fill and soon felt the urge to urinate. Constance fought the feeling as long as she could. Once the cramping began she knew it was inevitable.

Constance sighed as she stopped and brought herself down on her stomach. She rolled to her back. The sheath of the shortblade made the position uncomfortable. She pulled the sheath from her back, placed it on her stomach and pulled the sack of supplies she had been carrying towards her. She removed her trousers and undergarments down to her ankles, lifted her legs and let the stream flow. The feeling of relief washed over her as she heard the urine hit the vent and flow downwards. She let out a sigh and when she had finished she pulled her undergarments and trousers back to her waist. She dragged herself away from the urine stream and allowed herself to relax.

As she lay on the cool metal her mind drifted to the situation outside. The townspeople had been accepting of those from the underground coming to the surface, though they didn't know how long the food and drink would last with everyone there. Thankfully the majority of the underground people had agreed to help those on the surface in growing food and brewing ale. It'd be a bit of a different system for the underground people. The sunlight and rain would make things much easier for them, though Smoke had once told her darkplant grew at a much quicker rate than the surface plants. She worried the impatience of waiting for growing surface vegetables could cause unwanted tensions.

She opened her eyes suddenly. She didn't know when she had drifted to sleep or for how long. She rolled herself over, tied the shortblade sheath on her back and lifted herself up and continued along the ventilation shaft. The rope Constance had tied to her ankle had begun to cut off circulation leaving her foot tingling and numb. Constance stopped to loosen the rope and rub her foot until the feeling came back.

She let out a long breath and shook her head as she continued forward. She didn't know how far along she was or how much longer until she'd come across another vent. The feelings of anxiety from the enclosed vent began to take root in her head. She began to shuffle faster, she had to get out, she couldn't waste any more time. Her knees were bleeding, her hands hurt, her foot was going numb once again and her bladder had filled while she'd slept.

She pressed her lips together and let out a slow shallow breath. She wasn't going to stop, not this time, not in the dark. She couldn't afford to stop again, she had to make it to the first above and bring the soldiers from the underground. Once she managed that, she'd be safe to make her way to the third above and confront the Rocka family on the accusation.

She could feel the pain from her knees becoming intense. The wetness from the blood almost masked the warm wetness running from her behind and down her legs. She pressed forward hoping none of the blood or urine touched the sack holding a clean set of clothing.

She had to stifle a scream of joy when she had finally come across a vent in what appeared to be the first below. It was along the floor which was even better, she wouldn't have to try and fall correctly to avoid injury as she would have if the vent been near the roof. She quickly pulled the sack to her and pulled out the clean trousers she had stored away. She had hoped to wear these when she made it to the third below, that was no longer an option, she didn't care what the people of the underground or what the tower guards thought about her fighting and running around in urine and blood soaked trousers, she did care about the smell she'd have following her around and the uncomfortable moistness she'd be feeling until it finally dried.

Constance kicked off her trousers and undergarments and replaced them with the new trousers. She'd have to go without undergarments until she made it back to the surface, or if she happened to find a charitable family that'd give her some. Though the likelihood of charity happening at this time was next to none. She wiped the thought from her mind and continued.

Once she had dry clothes on she pushed on the small vent. She didn't have to push very hard for it to fall from the wall and onto the ground. She then pulled herself through the small opening and brought the sack through after her. She grinned to herself as she stood. She drew the shortblade from the sheath at her back and drew her revolving pistol.

The corridors were a maze of interconnecting hallways spanning in several directions only spaced between suites the size of large houses. Memories of her childhood came flooding back as she tried to recall where she needed to go. Many times she had run up and down the hallways with her friends, trying to find and catch each other and not be the 'it' person. Constance wiped a tear from her eye as she remembered; the innocence of her childhood was a fond and precious memory. Little did that child know that her entire life and everything she knew would be ripped from her in a matter of a few short years.

She passed a door she found familiar. She had remembered taking a feather pen to the door in her dawning years and her father being very upset with it. She looked to the symbol beside the door and sat the star constellation Orion where her families' feather pen and inkwell had once been. She found herself disgusted with the sign and slashed it with her shortblade. The shortblade entered the wall and slid through the drywall like butter. As the shortblade exited a small plume of white powder followed behind. Constance immediately regretted the decision, but there was nothing she could do about it now. The best she could do was to find the steam-hydraulic lift and bring as many people up as possible before she could make her way to the third above.

She left the door as quickly as she could and ran down the hallways until she finally found the lift. The doors were as perfectly white as the rest of the hallway making it difficult to see. She pressed the button to let the lift go down to the surface. She then removed the access panel and pulled out the control switch. She pressed several buttons giving her the lift's manual control over the typical automated control it usually ran with. She pressed the button to open the door and waited.

The sound of a revolving pistol erupted through the air and a shot flew past her head. Constance swore loudly and fired a single shot in the direction it came from. Several more shots were fired her way. She looked around to find nowhere to take cover. She fired the revolving pistol blindly at the corner the man had been hiding behind, hoping the shots would go through. At her fourth shot she heard a man swear and fall to the ground. She approached the soldier and kicked his revolving pistol away, "Go ahead," he gurgled through the blood in his throat, "Shoot me, I'm dead anyway."

"I'm only doing this because you shot at me first," Constance said disheartened.

She pulled the trigger and watched the man's head snap to the side as her shot entered through the temple. Blood began to pool around the man's head and the holes in his torso. Constance looked at the man's wounds and vomited all over the corpse. She hadn't seen a dead body since her parents and looking at the corpse brought the memories flooding back.

She picked herself back up and walked back to the lift control panel. She pressed the close door button and hoped the people in the underground had been given enough time to gather within. She then pressed the call lift to the first above and waited. She replaced the empty shot casings with new shots and placed the revolving pistol in her holster.

She drew her shortblade and waited for what she hoped would be enough men to guard the lift while she made her way to the third above. Victory hinged on their ability to guard the lift and conquer the first above while more men made their way upwards. They'd been given direct orders to not kill the families living within, though robbing and looting was completely permitted. The only time killing would be permitted would be against the soldiers and anyone who fought back, even then if crippling was an option, it would be the preferred method. Self-preservation was key though.

Constance watched as the lift doors opened and half dozen men in leather and iron armour emerged from the lift. The leader of the team, noticeable by his red armour and the medals on his breastplate looked down at her. "Glad to see you made it here alright," the guard said with cheer in his voice. "Sure took your time though," he finished with a laugh.

Constance gave him a nod and asked, "You have much trouble getting here?"

"No," the leader said. "The soldiers were easy enough to take down. It was the lift that scared us the most. I've never been this high in my life. I kept expecting the lift to fall back to the surface with us still inside. I don't know how people can stand living in this place."

"When it's all you know you don't think of it," Constance replied. "I need you guys to guard the lift and bring your men up. I got one dead guy over there, but there is no way those shots were not heard. There's bound to be people on the way. I've got other business to attend to. I'll be seeing you all back on the surface, and I better be seeing all of you."

The leader smiled and nodded his head, "Yes ma'am, I'll personally make sure all my men make it home safely."

Constance smiled and ran down the hall. Before she made it back to the vent she had one more stop to make. The Orion house. It wasn't their fault her family had been forced from the tower, but they were living in her childhood home - their goods were as good as hers. She wouldn't take much, only as many skins as she could carry and maybe a trinket or two. Either way, she was owed as much for her stolen childhood and for what had happened as a result.

She found the home easily; the slash through the family emblem was a dead giveaway at a distance. She fired at the door handle and the door opened without any effort. As she entered she was greeted by a swash of blues and forest greens. It was her childhood home exactly as she remembered. They hadn't even bothered to paint over the colours her parents had chosen for their home. She found it almost disgraceful. She knew she wasn't thinking straight, but her anger and mixture of several strong conflicting emotions didn't care. They wanted her to take vengeance and she would obey.

The family, stupidly, came running in response to the sound of the shot. They looked to be a likeable family. The man wore a grey button shirt with a black waistcoat. Constance could see the chain of his fob watch reach from his waistcoat pocket to his button line. He had a straight stance to him and a flat stomach.

His wife wore a long flowing scarlet dress filled with crinolines to add width to the waist of her dress. Her hair was done up in a way to add as much height as possible. The pendant around her neck looked to be made of gold with a large ruby in the center. She was a fit woman with perky breasts. She appeared as if she had yet to birth any children. Constance looked around the home and saw no evidence of children anywhere. This was a childless couple living the good life.

Constance pointed the revolving pistol at the woman, "Alright," Constance said, "I want two thousand skins, her necklace and your fob watch. I am not joking around here. I will shoot you both to get what I want, don't fucking test me."

Constance then shot at the roof and watched as the faces of the couple turned from confused annoyance to objective fear. Her rational side hated herself for what she was doing; her emotions tuned it out as best as they could. She'd be sick with guilt and grief later, for now she'd take what she could get.

The man handed his fob watch to Constance. She grinned in delight as she held the small piece of metal in her hand. She opened the watch and a picture of an old man sat within. "Who is this?" Constance asked.

The man looked to his feet, "It's my father. He gave me that watch before he died. It's not all I have from him, I still have the fortune he left me. It's just sentimental."

Constance had been ready to feel sorry for the wealthy man until she heard him say the fortune came from his father as well. After that her senses eased. A gift from a parent before their deaths are always the most treasured, but it seemed this man could go without a watch for a few hours before he left to get another.

She flipped the cover of the fob watch open and removed the picture and placed it on a shelf beside her. "It's just a trinket," she said to the man. "You can get another. It may have sentimental value, but it's not like it's the only thing he ever gave you before or after his death. You'll be fine."

The woman was slower to hand Constance the necklace. She fumbled with the gold chain before it finally fell loose from around her neck and in her hands. "Here," the woman said with tears in her eyes. "This is my best piece; I hope it goes to good use in your care."

"This will feed my men and I for over a month," Constance shot back. "Forgive me if I don't feel sorry for you. Now," she said looking at the man, "I believe I also demanded two thousand skins. Get to it!"

The man looked to the other room, to his wife and back to Constance. In a foolish attempt, he leapt forward towards Constance. It was an idiot's bravery, he had no idea what he was doing or that Constance would shoot. She fired a shot into his leg and he collapsed into a heap by her feet. "You cunt, you shot me!" he shouted.

Constance looked to the blood coming out of his leg at a slow but steady trickle. Nothing important had been hit; at least she didn't think anything important had been hit. She gave him an absurd look. "A person breaks into your home with a revolving pistol, threatens you and demands money and trinkets. What did you think would happen when you rushed me? That I'd just run away? Now," Constance said to the woman, "I'll be taking the two thousand skins."

The woman nodded and left the room. Constance expected the woman to grab a revolving pistol to fire at Constance. She knocked the man out before moving from the place she had been standing and hid around the corner from the next room. When the woman came through she'd know if the rich bitch had planned to get the drop on her or if she'd actually pay the two thousand to ensure the safety of herself and her husband. At worst the woman would call security, the same security that would be occupied with the growing army of underground soldiers. Constance felt she'd be safe.

The woman soon emerged with a small sack. She looked around only noticing Constance as she cocked the revolving pistol. "Here are your skins," The woman said with tears in her eyes. "Please leave us alone now. I beg of you."

Constance nodded, "Get a doctor for him as soon as you can. I don't think I hit anything important, but I'm not a professional so I couldn't tell you."

Constance then left the home and ran to where she had exited the vent. She wasn't keen on getting back into the tight space, but she had a job to do and questions that needed answering. The third above would be her next stop. It wasn't a long trip, but she suspected it would be the most important destination she'd reached as of yet.

19

The ninth below was just as empty and eerie as it had been when Smoke had first left. The dim light from the bulbs that hung from the ceiling barely illuminated the floor. Smoke, Blue and Penelope began to walk from the steam-powered lift in the direction of the lift to the eighth below. "How long do you think we've been down there?" Smoke asked. "I was unconscious a lot and lost track of the days."

Penelope shook her head, "I don't know. I hadn't even healed from the shot before they threw me into the engine. I had to reconstruct myself and it could have taken a long time, especially since I was a fine paste. Either way, I doubt we have a lot of time before the boomers go off."

"One of the officers told me they knew about the boomers," Smoke said with a contemplative voice. "There is a possibility he was lying, though I don't doubt there may be a few boomers they may have missed. I'm not willing to risk sticking around just in case."

"What are you talking about?" Blue asked.

"The underground decided to have a revolution against the

towers," Smoke explained. "They planned on using boomers to collapse the underground, making it uninhabitable for anyone. We need to get to the surface as quickly as we can."

"Can you run?" Penelope asked.

Smoke shook his head. His legs and arms had begun to scab over, but the pain still persisted. Running was out of the question. It was only a few miles between them and the lift, not a long walk, though he'd be thankful for when he'd get to sit and rest his limbs. Blood had begun to seep through the fabric of the body armour he had been wearing leaving it a disgusting purple colour. He looked to Blue who was also walking funny. He imagined she could still feel the effects of the metal jaws clamped to her groin. She probably would for quite a while.

Penelope was becoming noticeably agitated. "I understand your pain, I really do, but we have to get a move on. We're going too slowly and if the boomers are still in place - well, I really don't want to have to dig myself out of this much earth."

"We can't go any faster," Blue snapped. "Don't you think we understand the urgency? Smoke's legs are ruined and my groin just took more electricity than anyone should ever feel run through it. Forgive us if we can't move our legs a little faster."

Penelope scowled, "You two keep going to the lift, and I'll meet you there or on the way. I'm going to find something to make this go a little faster."

"See you at the lift then," Smoke said with a coy grin. "Bet you we beat you there."

He could see a semblance of a smile on Penelope's face before she ran from them. Smoke wished he could run as well. Penelope hadn't been wrong when she said time was running out. He was a little surprised the underground hadn't been collapsed already.

The pain in his arms and legs grew as he continued walking.

He silently cursed the engine and all those within. He especially cursed Portia Lincoln. Blue would be alright in a few days, maybe sooner. It would take several weeks for his arms and legs to heal enough for major use. Glass likely wouldn't like the scars.

He shook his head of the thoughts of Glass dismissing him for his new disfigurement. She'd seen him do horrific things in his past; she may laugh at the irony. He had disfigured many people in his childhood - now he got to feel what he had done to others. He had apologized for what he had done several times, as often as he could to the families that had been forced to deal with their scarred or missing family members. He had done what he could to atone for his past. This may be the poetic justice that had been needed to wash him of his discretions. He didn't think so, but it was a pleasant fleeting thought.

As Smoke and Blue passed the town he recalled the time they wasted looking through the homes in hopes of finding Blue. The eighth below was more of a waste, but at least he now had Blue in his presence.

Penelope rounded a corner with two chairs with wheels. Her grin was one of triumph and glee, "Look, I found something that should help," she said happily, "I'll push the both of you to the lift. You don't have to move at your snail pace anymore, plus you'll be able to rest your wounds."

Smoke had seen the wheeled chairs before. They were quite common on the lower levels of the underground. It wasn't uncommon for a person to hurt themselves bad enough to require alternative modes of transportation. The wheeled chairs were the best way to ensure someone could get around. Although, Smoke had been quite surprised Penelope had managed to find two in the ninth below. That sort of place didn't really allow for weakness and people who required a wheeled chair typically died shortly.

He sat in the chair and felt as his legs began to tingle and twitch as the tissue continued to try and stitch itself back together. The healing had been laboured by the walking; now his body could do what it needed to get better while they escaped the underground.

Once Blue had taken her seat Penelope began pushing the chairs. The smooth flatness of the floor allowed for easy rolling. Smoke continued to look around the ninth below in hopes it would be the last time he'd ever have the displeasure of seeing it.

They reached the lift quickly, much quicker than Smoke expected. Penelope rolled both wheeled chairs onto the platform and proceeded to turn the crank. Smoke watched as the chain the lift used as a safety mechanism tightened as the gears attached to the turn crank began to spin thus lifting the platform from the ground. Smoke had his doubts the lift from the eighth below would be there waiting. He had his hopes, but admittedly they were not very high. The lift driver who had been given the instructions seemed fairly dim and liable to forget to use the lowering mechanism.

He watched as Blue gazed at the spinning gears that permitted the lift to ascend through the vertical tunnel. Smoke always enjoyed watching the expressions surfacers tended to show when looking at the underground technology.

He didn't doubt the tower was a world more advanced, he'd only seen a few things during his brief visit to the Lang home; though the thought of having the area's best minds and brilliant inventors in the towers would bring on bigger and better technologies to improve the lives of the rich, only allowing the surface and the underground to partake only when the technologies had become old and outdated to them. It was all speculation, but if the evidence of such things had been presented to Smoke he wouldn't be surprised in the least.

The three had remained silent during the lift ride to the eighth below. Penelope continued to turn the crank while Smoke and Blue stared off into space. His legs didn't hurt as much as before, though the pain from the needles persisted.

He looked over to Blue who had avoided his gaze since

leaving the engine. He couldn't blame her; he had allowed her to go through the pain of electric torture. If he had been a bigger man he'd have screamed his submission over and over until they stopped. He had forgotten at the time that the people of the engine don't kill. They are forbidden to take lives. They wouldn't have killed either of them no matter how much he had screamed. He could have called their bluff and avoided her torture, but his selfish greed came through and she knew it. She also knew if he submitted they'd be in a totally different scenario by that point. There really was no winning.

As Penelope brought the lift platform to a stop on the eighth below she grabbed the two wheeled chairs and began to push them towards the next lift. Her demeanor was sullen and hurried. Smoke could understand why. If the people of the engine had missed a boomer and it went off they'd be buried alive. Smoke and Blue would die quickly under the falling rubble and would be buried for all eternity. Penelope would survive the blast, the falling debris and the lack of air. She'd spend the next century digging herself through several miles of dirt to get back to the surface. She wouldn't be able to eat, drink or breathe. She wouldn't need any of those things to survive, though he was sure she'd need them to feel any sort of comfort.

Smoke couldn't image what immortality would feel like. All the marvels and horrors she'd seen through her many years. She was old enough to have seen religions come into existence and then fade away into obscurity and soon die thereafter. Maybe there was something to her Writer religion. If anyone would have an idea on what happened in the afterlife, it was likely she would be the one to know. He couldn't bring himself to believe in an indifferent writer who cared for nothing but the story – a person who wrote on the few individuals all through the history of his world and their adventures and how they develop as people during their trials. It made everything seem like it didn't really matter.

Was he another one of The Writer's characters in an overarching storyline? Was he a person destined to change as a character through a period of time? He didn't feel any different. He could feel the same cynicism he felt towards the world he'd felt before. He still believed the tower should fall and the underground should be moved to the surface. His views hadn't changed. Maybe he wasn't the character The Writer had been following all this time. Maybe Blue was its main character and Smoke was the man who was to come in to save the day only to fail at the last minute. Was this just a series of random circumstances that Penelope happened to stumble into through a series of choices and this adventure would never be a story The Writer would ever write? The thoughts hurt his head.

The lift to the eighth below greeted them like a shining beacon of hope. No lights came from the contraption though Smoke could feel its light as if it had illuminated their way. He wondered if every lift from this point onward would have the same effect on him.

Penelope wasted no time putting Smoke and Blue on the lift and turning the crank to bring them to the seventh below. Smoke remembered his last time on the seventh below. It was the first time he had any sort of inclination that something was wrong. It was when he had found out about the plan that seemingly everyone else in the underground knew. Or at least everyone in the lower levels knew about. He didn't doubt the upper floors learned of it before he had left, but yet he had no idea.

His thoughts came back to Constance. She'd have been herded back to the surface with everyone in the underground. He wondered if she had still kept control of the fourth below despite not knowing what was going on. Smoke wouldn't have blamed her if she had chosen to give the reigns to Cobble and return to her regular job. He didn't think she'd get caught up with the fighting; she had no stakes in the quarrel or animosity towards those in the tower. The thought of her keeping his position worried him. The entire population of the underground on the surface was bad enough, but her trying to lead at the same time could be disastrous. He didn't think she'd have it in her.

"You going to be alright to take us all the way to the surface without rest?" Smoke asked. He had to say something to break the silence.

"I don't really have much of a choice," Penelope said angrily. "Having to push you two around as well won't help in any way. Remind me to go back to the engine and kick their asses."

"We'll try and walk as much as we can," Smoke said. "I know it'll be a little slower than you'd like, but it'll be even slower if your arms get too tired to move a lift crank. I'd turn the crank if I could, but my arms are just as fucked as my legs and Blue wouldn't know the right way to turn the crank. I can't say as I'm an expert, but I'd be able to figure it out just from years of seeing it. We need you at your peak Penelope, there's no way around it."

Penelope sneered, "Fine, just don't slow me down too much. I'm not going to leave you two down here, just try and go quickly."

The seventh below was exactly as Smoke remembered. The burned battered ruins of a world once fearful of slavery remained abandoned. This pleased Smoke; he would rejoice as soon as this place became crushed under the stones of the ceiling.

As Smoke stepped out of his wheeled chair his legs began to ache again. He took a step and when he didn't fall over or collapse from pain he nodded to Penelope and proceeded towards the next lift. It didn't take long before the pain in his legs returned. He'd be able to continue forward provided his legs didn't begin seeping.

"When we get to the first below I'm going to want to go to my home," Smoke said out of nowhere.

"Why?" Blue asked.

"I need a few things," Smoke said. "I need the contract your sister signed so I can get my reward for bringing you home. I am also going to want to grab some healing salve for my arms and legs."

"Isn't there healing salves on a few of the upper floors? I'm pretty sure we can find some in the next floor," Penelope said crossly. "I'm not going to want to take a detour just so you can feel better."

Smoke nodded, "Yes, there's healing salve on the next floor and up, but I don't know where exactly we'll find some. The shops will be boarded up and I wouldn't be surprised if people took their healing salves with them when they went to the surface. We may find something lying around, but that could take much longer than just stopping by my place. Besides, we have to stop at my place anyway. It'd make more sense to just get everything there all at once."

He could see the impatient anger rising inside Penelope. If he was going to continue having a lift driver he'd have to defuse the situation as best he could. He let his power flow through him - he doubted it would work perfectly, but it couldn't hurt. "If we do happen to come by some healing salve I will use that stuff and make the best of it. I just don't want my arms or legs to get infected. If we do find some along the way you can run to my place and grab the paper I need and we can be on our way much faster. Is that alright?"

Penelope narrowed her eyes at Smoke and soon nodded, "Yeah, that's fine," she said angrily, "But if you get us trapped down here I swear to The Writer I will find a way to resurrect you and I'll kill you again."

Smoke nodded, "Deal."

Smoke had impressed himself. He didn't think he'd be able to walk the several miles to the lift. He pushed his wheeled chair onto the platform. Blue followed behind and sat down immediately after. Smoke mimicked her action and watched as Penelope went to work on the lift.

The time it would take for the lift to reach the sixth below would not be enough to rest his legs. He could feel them seeping once again. He pressed the suit next to his legs in hopes of stopping the slow leaks between the scabs.

He looked to Blue to see her rubbing her crotch. He quickly looked away to avoid an awkward situation. "So," Blue said, "after all this you're still after a reward?"

"Kid," Smoke said, "after all I went through I'd better be getting the reward. Now, my reward comes as soon as you've crossed the threshold to your home. After that I couldn't give a fuck what you do. You can run away again and join the common folk for all I care. I can guarantee I will never work for your family again. Not that I'll have to with the reward in my pocket, or if Fulcrum gets to me."

"Fulcrum?" Penelope asked before Blue had been given a chance.

"I did something selfish and inadvertently fucked over a friend. He wants revenge and in some ways I deserve it. If he gets to me I won't put up a fight. He went through a lot because of me." Smoke's eyes shot open, "It was my fault he got caught, but was not my fault that my father tortured him afterwards."

"Do you know he was tortured?" Penelope asked. "If you escaped there's no way you could possibly know for sure."

"Yeah," Blue agreed. "This story does seem a little suspicious."

Smoke glared at the two women, "I know my father well enough to know he'd have tortured Fulcrum for trying to escape."

"I assume you've seen him recently," Blue said with an amused tone to her voice.

"Yeah," When I was on the second below.

"Did you see any scars on him?" Penelope asked. "Did you

see any real visible indicators that he had been tortured? I know if I were to torture someone I'd make sure scars were visible, even with clothing on - cheeks, necks, hands, forehead, anything that could show the others what would happen if they tried to leave. So, did you see any visible scars on him?"

Smoke thought back to the ale he'd had with Constance on the second below. He remembered Fulcrum remembering him and joining him at the table. He didn't recall any scars. Smoke shook his head. "Not as far as I can recall."

"I think Fulcrum and your father may be playing a fast one on you," Penelope said.

"I think I would have figured that one out long before," Smoke said defensively.

"No you wouldn't have," Blue said. "You were too close to both of them. By the time your brain would have allowed you to process any real logic in the matter you'd have already made up your mind on it. I don't know how long you've been holding onto that guilt, but it's been too long. You're only now figuring out you've done nothing wrong."

Smoke began to think. He knew his father to be the sort of person to play mental games on people when it wasn't worth the bloodshed. It was possible Penelope and Blue were correct in their assertion. He didn't want to admit it to himself, but the guilt he'd been harboring for the past decade may have been completely misplaced. "If what you're saying is true, then Fulcrum is a dead man. He'll likely kill me in the process, so that'll be two less bad men in the world."

Penelope and Blue exchanged glances. Smoke could see the lights of the sixth below above. He prepared himself for the empty floor. This would be a bit of a change, the seventh to ninth below had been empty when he had gone down, and they had left little impact on his way back up. This time the overcrowded sixth below would be empty. He didn't know how he would feel about it.

The moment Smoke saw the emptiness of the sixth below a feeling of finality swept over him. The knowledge of the underground going to the surface became all the more real to him. He could see the town just ahead with the vacated buildings and empty cages. He'd never seen the floor in such a state. He didn't think he ever would. As he stepped from the lift platform with his wheeled chair in his hands a tear fell from his eye. A small goodbye to the world he had known his entire life.

The empty cages made Smoke happy. The underground Nagara slave trade had ended. It was possible and likely the slave trade would continue on the surface, but having it out in the open instead of having it as nothing more than a dirty secret the rich allowed in the center of the underground could help end it once and for all.

Blue had begun walking straighter and didn't appear as if she still needed the chair. She'd be suffering from the electrical burns for quite some time, but she seemed to be ignoring the pain better than Smoke. "I can't believe I survived this place," Blue said suddenly.

Smoke gave her a concerned look, "What do you mean?"

"The whole time I was on this floor I half expected to get picked up by one of the slavers."

Smoke shook his head slightly, "You were safe here from the slavers. They'd never capture someone on their own level unless it's a person who had already escaped. The only place you were in any sort of danger from the Nagara was on the seventh below."

If anyone would get picked up it would be on the seventh below. All someone would have to do on the sixth would be to scream and a swarm of Nagara and spectators would be there in moments. Crime was pretty sparse in the sixth below. It wasn't safe by any means, but considering the floors surrounding it, it was one of the safest center levels.

The lift to the fifth below was a wondrous sight to Smoke. In one glimpse his previous question had been answered. Every lift would be a sight of magnificence and one step closer to the surface. They repeated their actions with the lift as they did with the platforms before it. Penelope began turning the crank and the platform began to rise.

"How are you holding up?" Smoke asked Penelope.

"Arms are getting a little tired," Penelope said as she made a pained face. "Don't worry, I'll be able to get us to the surface, though I am starting to think a quick stop at your place may not be the worst idea."

"What happened to wanting to get to the surface as quickly as possible?" Blue asked.

"I've been thinking about that," Penelope said. "My rush is obviously from not wanting to get buried. I'd have to dig myself out and that wouldn't be good for me. But, I'm starting to think something went wrong. I thought about the time Smoke and I spent searching the eighth and ninth bellows and then our time in the engine. It takes a lot of time for me to reassemble myself when I'm in that sort of state. It's not inconceivable that we missed the deadline. I think the people in the engine hadn't lied to you. I think there's a mole and they managed to get every boomer and dismantle them. The underground isn't going anywhere. Don't get me wrong, I don't think we should take any major chances and just wait. We should get to the surface as quickly as we can, but I think a quick break on the first below wouldn't hurt anything."

"Wonderful," Smoke said while rubbing his legs.

His arms still hurt but the pain had been dulled by the aching in his legs. They were going through the levels quicker than he had expected, that was good for everything but his legs. It had only been six hours since their escape from the engine and Smoke waited with bated breath for the surface. If they didn't stop before making the detour to his home they'd be on the surface early the next day, or at least what Smoke believed to be the next day. Without his fob watch or any visible timepieces it had been difficult to accurately determine the time of day.

The fifth below was as dark as ever. Smoke couldn't imagine what the floor would be like if the inhabitants had allowed for proper lighting. He believed it would look not much different than the first below. The lines of homes and the large center park convinced him of this. The level was dark and frightening - even more so now that nobody remained. "We need to get out of here as quickly as we can," Smoke said nervously. "I don't like this floor."

The women agreed and they walked as quickly as they could through the fifth below. Smoke thought back to the history of the level and the wars fought against the Nagara. Now the Worms and the Nagara were working together. He didn't know how all those years of hatred could be put aside. It was almost miraculous.

Smoke didn't feel the same wondrous feeling he had with the previous two lifts. He believed it to be from the darkness around him. The desire to be rid of the fifth below was overwhelming. Penelope waited for him and Blue to get settled on the platform and began to turn the crank. The three continued to make small talk on their way to the fourth below.

Upon emerging within the fourth below, Smoke's heart began to sink. This had been the place he had grown up. It was the place he'd known best of all and to see it as an empty shell of what it had been not long ago caused a shallow depression. He desperately wanted to go see his old home one last time, or to go to the gathering tavern or to see the old interrogation rooms. All of which he had to come to grips with never seeing again. They'd be abandoned forever now; a feeling of ambivalence came to him with that thought.

As he walked past the abandoned buildings he kept an eye out for anyone who had remained behind. A lot of inhabitants of the fourth below never wanted to leave their home. It wouldn't be shocking in the least if someone had stayed behind. On the other hand, Cobble was a man who made sure a job was done thoroughly. He wouldn't have left the fourth below unless he was sure everyone was safely on the next level.

They sped through the fourth below towards the next lift. Smoke gave a small wave goodbye to his past home and hung his head. He didn't realize how much he'd missed the fourth below. Even the last time he'd been there hadn't had as much of an effect. He'd maybe felt a slight sense of nostalgia, but for the most part he'd felt nothing for the place. The knowledge he'd never see this floor again brought all the good memories flooding back and he knew he'd miss the place more than he'd realized.

Once the fourth below had disappeared from view Smoke allowed himself to relax. He hadn't realized how tense he'd been until the last of the fourth had been hidden from view and he'd sunk into his chair. Penelope and Blue didn't say a word, they couldn't have understood why Smoke's emotions had been on high, nor did they ask. He was thankful for this.

The next stop wasn't going to be much easier.

The third below brought even more memories back to Smoke. While he wouldn't be sad to see it go, there was a lot of his history spent in this floor. There was a lot of history with Glass.

Glass.

The thought he'd see Glass on the surface pleased him. He'd be with his woman once again. It may not have been in the setting they'd imagined, but with the reward money he'd be able to get a home for the both of them and they'd be able to live together happily. Whatever the future had for them, if she was with him he'd be happy and he'd do his damndest to make sure she'd be happy as well.

"We're so close," one of the women said.

Smoke could hear the two of them talking though his head

was miles away on the surface. He could picture her face in his head. He'd been a horrible human at one point and not worthy of her affection. He still didn't think he'd done enough good to be worthy of her, but he'd try every day to do what he had to do to prove himself to himself. She didn't need convincing. She'd never needed convincing. She'd loved him for so many years and he'd just as soon leave her behind every time due to his own personal regret and arrogance.

"Never again," Smoke said aloud to himself.

"What was that?" Penelope asked.

"Nothing," Smoke said vacantly, "I was talking to myself."

Smoke hardly noticed when Penelope turned the lift's crank to bring them to the second below. The trip had been quick. It was the quickest Smoke had ever moved through the underground. He looked to Penelope and could see her beginning to tire out. Her breath became laboured and her arms shook. "Are you going to be alright to get us to the next floor?" Smoke asked. "If need be, we can stop for a bit on the second below. It's not like we'll be spending a whole lot of time at my place. If you need to rest, we will rest. It's fine with us."

Penelope smiled, it was not the reaction Smoke had expected, "I'll be fine for one more lift ride," she said happily. "I think I'm getting a second, or my sixth wind," she laughed. "The next lift may be a bit slower, but I'll be alright. So long as I feel I can get us there there's no need to worry."

Smoke nodded in agreement and kept silent. If she believed herself capable he'd trust her. She had as much to lose down here as both him and Blue, maybe more. At worst the two of them would die. He thought about her immortality and believed it came with some perks including a decent healing factor that would keep her muscles growing as she needed them. She may be going slower, but healing took time and energy. He couldn't imagine she'd had much to eat to keep up with the healing since she'd pulled herself together. That alone would have taken a lot of energy to accomplish.

He could feel himself getting hungry as well. "I'm going to insist we stop for a bit on the second below to eat," Smoke said assertively. "Penelope needs to keep up her strength and you and I should eat as well. It'll be good for healing our wounds."

Penelope nodded while Blue showed no reaction to his words.

As they reached the second below Smoke began to scan the area for anything to eat. He expected any surface vegetables to have rotted away. They'd have to look for darkplants to eat. They grew all year round and there'd easily be a plot of land still holding the darkplant - ready to eat.

Penelope told the two of them to wait by the lift while she scouted around and looked for anything to eat. Smoke agreed, considering she'd be able to get where she needed to be quicker alone than with the two of them.

Blue looked around the second below. "I don't remember being here," she said aloud.

Smoke didn't imagine she had intended to say it, but she did and he decided to engage. "It's not a very memorable place. You can get weapons here and some surface food, but that's about it."

"How about you?" Blue asked. "Do you remember your last time here?"

Smoke nodded. He remembered purchasing the shortblade for Constance. He remembered his bet with her as well. Most of all he remembered his deal with Fulcrum. The deal he now planned to break at his earliest convenience. "Yeah," he said softly, "I remember it very well."

"I guess that's not really surprising," Blue said with a straight face. "You've lived down here all your life. I bet you remember most of your times on each floor."

Smoke chuckled at that, "Kiddo, I have probably forgot more about the underground in my years than you'll ever know. Especially once the militia from the underground places the boomers again."

"Do you really think they'll be able to pull it off this time?"

Smoke nodded, "I really do. They're most likely going to be sending real killers to sacrifice their lives for what they believe to be the greater good. These men and women would die for the people of the underground. If not the underground as a whole, they'd happily die for those on their level. The people of the engine don't kill, there's no possible way for them to win."

"Funny you bring up that the engine people don't kill," Blue said with a smirk.

Smoke hung his head, "I know I should have stopped it when I could, or at the very least *tried* to stop it when I could. Instead I did nothing until they said so. For that, I am so sorry."

Blue surprised Smoke by giving him a hug. "It's alright. You had just been through a torture session. My first time I couldn't remember my own name. It's not surprising that you'd forget. You looked out for me as best you could down there, I appreciate that. And believe me, I'm sure not going to forget it either."

Smoke pressed his lips together and nodded. "Nothing will happen to you while I'm around. I won't allow the engine to have either of us again. Once we are on the surface we will get the underground collapsed and there will be no way back to the engine."

Penelope returned before Blue had been given a chance to respond. In her hands she held a small sack filled with darkplant and synthetic meat. "You know what the great thing is about the underground?" Penelope said with a grin. "Their food lasts so much longer than the surface food."

She passed both Smoke and Blue a raw darkplant and a sizeable slab of cooked synthetic meat. The three of them dug into their food and for a moment they had forgotten their troubles.

20

Smoke could imagine the hustle and bustle of the first below as Penelope parked the lift platform. With all the bodies gone from the first below the place looked to be a disheartening ghost town. The sixth below had been full of people and the other floors were busy as well, but the first below was the sort of place where people of the underground and surfacers could mingle and trade. To have experienced it without a soul in sight was not a sight Smoke ever thought he'd see.

"Alright, follow me to my place," Smoke said as he snapped out of the initial thoughts.

The first below was almost spooky. He could see the boarded up food carts and the empty produce stands. They soon passed the place him and Constance had eaten soup together. The memory seemed to be years old at this point. Had the first below been crawling with people, he didn't think the memory would have been so far away.

He could remember the look on her face the moment she had tasted darkplant for the first time, her enjoyment in having the second bowl and eating the soup the next morning. The memory caused Smoke to smile. He'd have tried explaining it to

Blue and Penelope, but he doubted they'd understand.

The path to Smoke's home was an easy one to navigate. Only two turns past the main road and there they stood. The place was a single story home made from synthetic wood. One single window was all that let in any of the light from the outside world. As Smoke looked on he could see a light was on inside. This worried him; he knew he had extinguished all his gaslights before leaving with Constance. He had checked several times to be sure. The fact that a light was on was a serious cause for concern. Someone was in his home, or had been inside recently.

He looked to Penelope and nodded his head. "Pull out your revolving pistol," he said quietly.

Penelope looked at Smoke and then back to the home. She repeated her actions twice before her eyes lit up and she nodded back. She pulled the revolving pistol from the holster she had stolen from the underground and readied it. He motioned for Blue to stay back and began approaching the home in a crouched position. His legs ached as he maintained his crouched walk. He waved his hand to bring Penelope to take point and watched as she moved in front of him and to the door. She took a deep breath and kicked the door open.

Penelope took one look inside before turning around and vomited. Smoke moved forward to the doorway. What could be so bad that out of everything the immortal had seen it would cause Penelope to vomit?

He looked inside and saw a heavily mutilated woman tied to a blood-soaked chair unmoving. Blood had pooled around the chair staining his floor and leaving a smell only bloodshed could carry. At first glance Smoke was not sure as to what he'd been looking at. But the human features along with the feminine features told him what he needed to know. Her jaw had been removed at the hinges. Her tongue lay uselessly down her blood-soaked throat. As Smoke entered further into the home he could make out all the damage that had been done to the woman. Primarily that her eyes had been removed. Smoke felt tears fall from his face, but as he looked over the macabre sight what his body was doing was less than an afterthought.

The woman's nipples had been removed as well as her sex. A thought crossed Smoke's mind and he had to know if his mental assertion was correct. He stepped down causing a floorboard to creak. The woman's head shot up. Smoke screamed and fell back. She was alive and capable of hearing what was going on around her.

"Who does this?" Penelope asked with horror.

Smoke swallowed a lump in his throat and said, "The engine. They don't kill. They will maim, mutilate and harm in any way they can. They don't kill though. If this is who I think it is, this would be their way of saying I shouldn't have left."

"How could they have got word this far up so quickly?" Penelope asked.

"They have communicators that work in the engine. Who's to say how far the connection reaches."

At the sound of Smoke's voice the woman in the chair began fighting the ropes and producing a dry gurgled whine as she whipped her head back and forth tried to pull herself from the chair. Smoke could see something on her head. He assumed it to be a third below tattoo. All the working women on the third below had a tattoo above her ear that gave them their ID number so customers didn't have to know a name. "It's okay, I'm not going to hurt you," he whispered to the woman.

She looked at him with her eyeless gaze - the look from her eyebrows and what was left in her face showed him that she recognized his voice. He placed his hand on the woman's head and moved her hair to one side. The number 432 became visible. He knew that number, it was the number he'd whisper to himself as a young man. It was Glass. Glass! The woman who had been there for him his whole life. The woman he loved more than any other human in existence. The woman he'd planned on leaving his world behind to be with. Here she sat, horribly mutilated without her eyes or bottom jaw. "Glass," Smoke whispered before a sob took his voice, "I'm so sorry. I can never make up for this. You didn't deserve this, I'm so, so sorry."

Glass made a sound between a gurgle and a scream. She tried to lift her right arm. Smoke saw this and ran to the kitchen to grab a knife. He cut the rope holding her right arm. It'd be the only rope he'd cut for her - she'd never survive out there and he needed her to remain still. Glass brought her hand up to Smoke. He took it and felt as she made a love symbol on his hand. He kissed her hand and placed it back down on the chair. "I'll be right back," he said softly.

He walked towards Penelope and soon brought her outside. "What's going on?" Penelope asked, "Why'd you let her hand go?"

Smoke frowned in the attempt to fight back the uncontrollable crying that would have to come out soon. He took a deep breath and said, "I need your revolving pistol."

"Putting her out of her misery?" Penelope asked.

"Performing the kindest thing I've done for her in a long time."

Penelope nodded and placed the revolving pistol in his hand. He made a mental note to thank her for not asking any questions. He re-entered the home and sighed heavily. "I'm back Glass. I don't think I can say I'm sorry for this enough. I think if I'd have stayed in the engine you'd have probably been okay. There's no real way I could know for sure, I didn't even know they had you captured, but it's the best guess I've got. I think if they'd have led with this, I'd have cracked immediately."

Glass hung her head without making any sort of sound. She looked to be taking in his words as best she could. He moved towards Glass and pulled back the hammer to the revolving pistol. He held the muzzle of the revolving pistol a few inches from her head. Tears began to fall from his eyes as the memories of Glass came flooding back. Their first kiss, the first time she sex'd with him without pay. When he'd come to her needing help. "I love you," he said quietly before pulling the trigger.

The side of Glass's head exploded into a fine red mist painting the side of the room. He couldn't hold it back anymore. He howled and fell to his knees letting the tears and the uncontrollable sobs flow. More memories of Glass poured through his head as he remembered the woman she used to be. He recalled their last encounter and the plans they had made. That she had asked him to remain in the third below with her. He wanted to do it. He'd have given anything to have that opportunity again. But he had to finish his job. He had to find Blue. He'd sacrificed the woman he loved dearly for a couple million skins. The trade didn't seem fair.

He soon picked himself from the floor and grabbed a blanket. He draped it over what was left of Glass and walked to his room. He pulled off the Engine Officer's uniform, washed his hands and face in the wash basin that had been filled with clean water before he'd arrived and dressed into a set of brown trousers, a burgundy buttoned shirt, a set of burgundy suspenders and a gold waist coat. He reached into his drawer and pulled out a copper fob watch and chain. He placed the watch into his waistcoat pocket and attached the chain to his button line. He grabbed a wide brimmed bowler hat from the top if his bed. It was a new hat that had yet to get much for dust on it.

He looked to the coatrack and grabbed a red longcoat he hadn't worn for several years. He grabbed a black faux leather belt and a brown holster. He walked to his wall and opened a loose board showing the spare revolving pistol he'd kept in case of emergencies. He then moved to his filing cabinet and pulled out the contract for his reward. He grabbed the book of the tower families and the history book of the 21st century.

As he stepped outside he could see Penelope and Blue talking. "I've got clothes inside," he said coldly. "You both should get out of the officer's uniforms and into some real clothes. You'll garner attention otherwise. I'll wait out here."

The women nodded and entered the home. He could hear Penelope tell Blue to not look under the blood soaked blanket. Smoke hadn't thought the blood would seep through the blanket, though now that his head was back on straight, or at least straighter than it had been he should have known it would. If Blue did as Penelope said she'd be able to live the rest of her life without the image of Glass's mutilation in her head. Penelope would live with it for a time, but in time would forget the experience ever happened. Smoke would see Glass's face in that horrible mangled visage for the rest of his life.

His tears had dried and all that remained was a fiery rage that needed direction. He knew exactly where to point that rage. Both targets wouldn't know what to do or how to survive his wrath. He knew this for a fact. One would be easier than the other, but his vengeance would be swift and merciless.

Blue and Penelope exited Smoke's home dressed in his clothes. The clothing was too big for the smaller women, but it looked less conspicuous than the form fitting suits adorned with metal armour. "We ready to go?" Penelope asked.

Smoke shook his head, "There's one more thing I need to do."

Smoke entered his home for the last time. He gathered his gaslights and poured the fuel over Glass. If she wouldn't get the proper burial she deserved she'd get the next best thing. He didn't have time to dig the hole for her and give her the funeral. The fire would burn her body away and scatter her ashes along the underground. That was the best he could hope for. If he was lucky the fire would consume the majority of the first below. It'd be a fitting end to such a place.

He made a trail of fuel to the doorway and grabbed a box of matches. He frowned heavily as he exited his home. "Glass, I Smoke Callahan set your spirit free and lay your soul to rest. May you rest in peace and find your way to the great beyond you so greatly deserve."

Smoke lit the match and threw it at the fuel. It immediately caught fire and made its way to the shrouded body. Smoke closed the door before the fire had been given a chance to burn the blanket away and reveal Glass to Blue. She didn't need to see it.

"You alright?" Penelope asked placing her hand on his shoulder.

Smoke shook his head, "No, not in the least. I'm sad and I'm angry and I'm confused and I... I feel lost. I have all this rage that needs to be directed mixed with the desire to walk away from it all."

"What are you going to do?" Blue asked.

"I'm going to see it through. I've come too far and lost too much to not finish the job. You go to the lift and I'll meet you there. I'm just going to stand here for a while."

Penelope nodded her head knowingly and took Blue to the lift. Smoke watched as his home began to fill with smoke. Dark plumes came from the window as it shattered from the heat. He watched as the place became a roaring inferno and as soon as he knew nothing would be left of Glass, he left.

Smoke no longer felt the pain in his arms and legs. He was numb all over as he remembered Glass as best he could. The engine would die for what they had done. They would die for all those who had been hurt by their obsession; all those who had died from their wounds. They would pay and Smoke would be the one to deliver the bill.

Smoke reached into the pocket of his longcoat and found a small knife he had stored there years before. He brought out the knife and unfolded the blade from the hilt. He pressed the point of the blade into his palm and watched as the blood began to slowly pool. He pulled the blade away and closed his hand. As the blood poured from his closed fist to the ground he said, "I vow, in the name of Glass that I will... I will avenge you. I will not rest until my dying day until all those who brought this on are punished."

He took in a deep breath and put the knife back into his pocket. He thought of Glass being alone in Smoke's home while the people who had done that to her roamed around free. That was unacceptable. He stepped into the center of the town and shouted, "Take me back to the engine. I'll go without a fight. Just don't let her sacrifice mean nothing."

Smoke then dropped to his knees and placed his hands behind his head. He stopped everything and waited, the only sound around him was his breathing. After several minutes of waiting he heard a set of footsteps. An elderly man with long grey hair stepped from behind a food cart. "Mister Callahan," he said with a smile. "I'm glad to see you. I'm also pleased to see you've reconsidered our proposal. It disheartened us greatly when you chose to leave us so forcefully. Please stand, we will take you to the lift to the second below promptly."

Smoke obeyed and waited as three more men stepped into view. "Why did you do that to her? Why her?"

"We didn't want to, Mister Callahan. We captured her not long after she came to the first below. We would have then held her until we had confirmation that you had been turned. We'd have set her loose and she'd have been free to go where she wished. There was a lift here waiting for her to let her back up to the surface. Instead you had to escape and kill two of our officers in the process. That sort of behaviour is unacceptable and you needed to be punished.

We've had eyes on you for many years Mister Callahan. We knew your every move before you made it. When the Lang family hired you to find Blue, well that was a bit of a godsend for us. We'd have both Smoke Callahan and Blue Lang. All we had to do was wait. But then Robert had to fuck it all up by killing your friend and you began fighting back. I don't doubt you'd have been more pliable had that not happened."

"So you did that to her because I refused to be abducted?" Smoke asked trying to choke down his rage.

"I wouldn't put it that way, but if that's how you choose to see it."

"Is this everyone down here?" Smoke asked.

"Yes, we are the only four that are on the first below. All our other agents are on the surface."

The four men didn't have time to react as Smoke pulled out his revolving pistol and fired at the men. Blood spattered everywhere as the shots erupted from the revolving pistol. Everything seemed to move slower as Smoke aimed and fired in one fluid motion. Once the last man had dropped he put the revolving pistol back in the holster and made his way to the lift.

He found Penelope and Blue at the lift ready to go. Blue asked, "We heard shots, is everything okay?"

"Things will not be okay for a while," Smoke said dryly, "though I did find the people who had carved Glass to pieces."

"That explains the shots then," Penelope said with a tone that said she didn't blame him.

Smoke nodded and sat in the wheeled chair Blue had brought to the platform. Penelope began to turn the crank. "Who was she?" Blue asked.

"A woman I loved very dearly," Smoke said bluntly. "She deserved so much better."

"Nobody deserves that," Penelope said with narrow eyes.

"I meant me," Smoke said. "She deserved better than me."

"You're not that bad," Blue said in an attempt at comforting him.

Smoke took in a deep breath through his nose and let the air out through his mouth. "I wasn't always," Smoke said as if nobody else were present. "I wasn't always a good man. The two of you wouldn't know this but I grew up in the fourth below. A man gets tough or dies really quickly in a place like that. I was one of the hardest of my generation. I had no problem carving a person up like a darkplant to get answers. I never did what those dead men from the engine did though; I always made sure they died. I was a monster, but I wasn't inhuman.

"After a while I was permitted to take deliveries to the other floors. Plain and simple, I was a narc - a person who delivered drugs to suppliers on other floors. I was good at what I did as well. I had movement permissions from the Worms as well as an open invite to the sixth below. I even befriended a few of the Nagara. After a while though I wanted to sample what I was delivering to everyone and most were more than willing to share at least a little of their shipment. It was a steady decline from there. I wanted to use all the time. It wasn't until I made my way to the third below on a high that I found her. I still remember how she looked that day - her red hair flowing behind her as she ran to me, the voice of an angel telling me to get through it, and her skin. It was the softest I'd ever touched.

I was a mess; anyone with any sense would have walked away and allowed me to die. Instead she brought me in. She took care of me as I fought the addiction, through the sickness, mood swings and cold sweats, nights when I didn't sleep - even through the violent outbursts. She stuck by me. Once I was clean she invited me to stay with her and I accepted. I don't know what she saw in me, but from then on, I dedicated myself to her.

I stayed with her for a long time before my father came for me and dragged me back to the fourth below. I couldn't have been more than eighteen when I met Glass. She was beautiful. The most beautiful angel I'd ever seen in my life. I've still yet to see someone who strikes me in the same way. I owe my life to that woman. Through the years we've entertained the ideas of her coming to the fourth below or my staying in the third below.

She didn't want to leave her job and by the time I left the fourth below I wanted to put as much distance between my father and myself as possible. Last time I saw her I made the plan to stay with her for good. I wouldn't need to work after the reward so I left to find you and here we are."

Blue placed her hand on Smoke's arm, "I'm so sorry Smoke."

Smoke looked to Blue. She had tears in her eyes. "It's not your fault," Smoke said reassuringly, "It's the people from the engine who did this. It's them who I'll be hunting for the rest of my life. I will be doing everything in my power to bring them down. So don't you worry, this is not your fault. Had I chose to stay in the third below I have no doubt in my mind they would have abducted me all the same and captured her. The outcome would have been the same no matter what choice I had made."

Blue nodded as tears welled in her eyes. "How are you going to do it?" she asked after a moment of silence.

"I don't know," Smoke said, "But I have a very good idea as to where to start."

21

Constance had been gone for twelve hours before the soldiers had begun filling the steam-powered lift and entering the tower. Cobble couldn't have been more proud of her. During her time in the underground and as a part of the rebellion against the towers he found himself feeling an attraction towards her. He could tell she was beginning to feel the same way. The feelings had to remain in the back of his mind until the end of the rebellion however.

He had spoken with Homer and Blaze a couple times since Constance had left in hopes they'd find a way to get the boomers down to the ninth below. They had decided that they'd send a handful of men to make the ultimate sacrifice for the greater good. It would be strictly voluntary. Cobble even agreed to volunteer if they didn't find enough people provided Homer and Blaze accompanied him. No leader would be left behind. Before leaving he had planned on leaving Constance in charge again.

The biggest problem in their way was finding enough rope to find their way back down to the first below. The lift drivers had sent the lifts down so Smoke and his lift driver friend could make it back to the surface. By this time it had been entirely obvious that Smoke was dead. That was a pity. He had liked Smoke in his younger days. Though being a man full of ambition he knew Smoke would be a great leader and have Cobble as his second in command.

Once Smoke left, he had lost all the respect he had garnered for his friend over the years. He wanted nothing more than to see Smoke dead. He harboured that hatred for over a decade. Then Smoke returned, not as an attempt to reclaim his throne, but to pass through. If Cobble could have had his way he'd have let Smoke go and that would have been the end of it. Smoke wanted nothing to do with the fourth below. But Thomas had to go and fuck everything up. He had to capture Smoke and try to reconnect. He had to give Smoke a job and try to bring him back into the fold. Metal Jaw would have done his damndest to obey, but Cobble would have had to do something about it. Had Smoke teamed back up with his father he'd have convinced Smoke to leave and remind him as to why he left in the first place. Not optimal, but manageable.

Cobble never expected Smoke to stab his own father and claim the throne for himself. It really was nothing more than a get-out-of-the-fourth-below tactic. A clever one, but a move that could have very well gotten himself and Constance killed. Instead he became the leader and soon left again. Now that Smoke was surely dead Cobble couldn't help but hate the man again. His job had cut the rebellion off from where they needed to go.

"Sir!" the messenger boy said. Cobble believed his name to be Tide.

"Yes?" Cobble said as kindly as he could. The boy was nothing more than a messenger, no reason to be nasty to him.

"I was sent by Homer, he says he's got something you really need to see."

Cobble cocked his head to the side, "What is it?"

Tide shook his head, "I don't know sir, all Homer said was that you had to come see. You wouldn't believe it otherwise."

"Where is he?" Cobble asked.

"He's by the lift sir," Tide said before walking away.

Cobble shrugged and began walking towards the lift. People avoided the lift as best they could. It reminded them of their oppression and the days without sunlight. He thought to when they had first emerged from the underground. Everyone became afraid of the openness and began running for whatever shelter they could find. The openness of the surface didn't bother Cobble, what he had difficulty with was how high the sky was. He looked all the way up and he still couldn't see a ceiling. A few white puffy clouds hung in the air that could have been the remnant of what had once been a ceiling. A thought he had kept to himself. A thought he'd soon learned was very wrong.

Homer had been standing by the lift as Tide had said. The Worm leader stood with a massive grin on his face. "What's going on," Cobble asked.

"Look," Homer said with excitement, "The lift is coming up. Someone was still down there and they are making their way back."

"Do you think it's...?"

"It could very well be Callahan," Homer said with less amusement. "Honestly, I hope it is. We could ask what took him so long. I don't think he'd have wanted to stick around too long once he found the seventh below and lower had all been evacuated."

"We gave him a lot of time to search as much as he could. If the girl he's looking for is down there he'd have found her long before now. I don't know what took him so long, but we will certainly find out."

"Do you think he'll talk?"

"I know he will," Cobble said with a grin.

He looked down the hole and to his surprise he could see Smoke, a lift driver and a young girl siting on the platform. "Callahan!" he called down.

He could see Smoke look up, "Cobble? Is that you?"

"Goddamn right it is!" he called back. "Get your ass up here, what took you so long?"

"I'll explain once I've gotten a good meal and a drink for myself and my friends here."

Cobble nodded, "Sounds fair to me." As Smoke emerged he saw the two women he'd traveled with. The lift driver was a muscular woman with long curled black hair and dark skin. The young girl had been the girl from Smoke's photo. Blue, if he recalled correctly.

"You have no idea how good it is to feel fresh air right now," Smoke said with a grin.

Smoke began to walk away from Cobble towards the town. He was walking funny; in fact all his movements seemed to be off. "You alright?" Cobble asked.

"I have one hell of a story to tell you. I just need to eat first. So does Blue and Penelope. Take us to the town and we will regale you with our stories. They need to be heard."

Something in Smoke's voice caused Cobble to shudder. It was cold and unfeeling, the voice of a man who had taken a walk through Hell and lived to see the other side. He followed behind Smoke along with Homer.

He'd have tried to bring Blaze along as well, but truth be told he didn't know where the Nagara had gone. Not long after emerging, the Nagara had done what they needed before disappearing completely. Cobble believed them to be at the borders taking messages and sending some back, Cobble didn't have the time, the resources or the caring to find out. The Nagara had a desire for power and to be seen as superior, provided there was no real danger for them. They took in slaves and sold what they could. They had no interest in being a part of a collective; they wanted to be important. Receiving and sending messages was an important job. That is, if they were doing that at all.

The town was filled with people from the underground. Many were busy building shelters from baked clay to hide away from the weather that plagued them every night. People helped each other in the building and in a short time the town had grown to triple the size. Several shops had been built, a church had been erected as well as another blacksmith and other gardening projects that would exponentially grow the amount of food the town could produce.

When Cobble opened the doors to the tavern everyone stopped and cleared a table for him and placed enough chairs for those following him. The barkeep immediately began pouring ale into large mugs. "You've certainly made a name for yourself," Smoke said.

He wasn't sure if it had been intended as a compliment or an offhanded remark. He chose to take it as a compliment. "People appreciate a person willing to take charge and tear down the tower that has repressed them for so long. Imagine what we could do with the skins."

"Yeah about that," Smoke said angrily. "Why was I left in the dark about the revolution?"

"Because I know you," Cobble said nervously. "Your reaction literally could have gone either way, especially with the job you have and the number of skins you had to lose if we succeeded. You may have wanted to preserve the tower, considering you'd be eligible to live in the towers. Plus with your abilities you'd have the means of doing just that."

"I only wanted one thing with my reward money," Smoke said. "I wanted to get a small plot of land for Glass and me to live. We could have lived in peace and done as we wished."

"Where is Glass?" Cobble asked. "I haven't seen her since the first below."

Smoke hung his head. Cobble could see the pain in his face and he didn't need to say another word.

The barmaid placed the mugs of ale in front of everyone and walked away. Cobble, Homer, Smoke and the lift driver all took a drink. The young girl didn't seem to be interested in the drink until the lift driver nodded to give her the go ahead. Blue took a drink, made an odd face and took another sip. She'd get used to the taste in time. When Smoke brought the mug down he said, "Alright, so you two know what happened after I left the fifth below, probably even the sixth below. That said, I'll start my story at the seventh and go from there."

The tale Smoke began to tell seemed standard, him looking for the young girl Blue. It was once he got to the part with him and the lift driver, who he learned was named Penelope, found a man in the ninth below - that was when the story got interesting. Cobble listened on and soaked in every word.

22

Smoke awoke in the same inn he had slept the last time he had been to the surface. The room was different; the placements of the washbasin, wash tub and desk gave it away.

He sat up and felt the scabs that coated his arms and legs pull with each movement. He grimaced with the pain and made his way out of the bed. He filled the tub with the hot running water and lowered himself in. The heat felt great on his wounds as the scabs became moist and more pliable. He sank into the tub until the water covered his face. As he re-emerged from the water he could feel his face without the caked-on dirt and blood from the four engine men. He pulled more water to his face and scrubbed until he was sure his face had become perfectly clean of the dirt and blood that had coated him.

As he exited the tub he looked at the dark brown water and pulled the plug. Those days were officially behind him. He needed no more reminders. He then moved to the mirror and took a long look at his face. He didn't recognize the grizzled man looking back at him. Smoke had often been the sort of man who preferred to be clean shaven. Odd times he'd grow a bit of facial hair, but those days were few and far between.

He picked up a straight razor from the desk and began running it along his cheek. The hair from his face fell off in small clumps into the small bowl filled with water. He enjoyed shaving. It made him feel like a new man every time he put the razor down.

As he looked at the man in the mirror, now without the beard he could see the pain that hid at the corners of his eyes and mouth. He didn't think there'd be any chance of hiding it, nor did he want to. The pain was what would keep him alive. The pain would be what forced him to see it through. He'd made a vow and he had every intention of following through with it. First, he had a reward to cash in.

He exited his room and walked down the long hallway to the tavern. The barmaid came and took his order and left shortly after. He and Blue had made the agreement that she would meet with him after a long sleep. She needed a comfortable sleep for once and Smoke was willing to wait, at least for a little while. However, he didn't trust that she wouldn't leave in the middle of the night, despite the plan they had made on the lift, so he had posted a guard at her door. Once he'd eaten he'd go check on her. If she were still sleeping he'd wait outside her door and they'd leave for the tower.

Cobble entered the tavern and grinned as he saw Smoke. He moved and sat on the opposite end of the table, "Good morning," he said cheerfully. "I trust you slept well. You're certainly looking better now that you've slept and shaved."

"I feel better too," Smoke said. "Where's Constance?" he asked without skipping a beat, "I haven't seen her since I got back."

"She's storming the tower. I'll be honest; I thought that woman would get eaten alive by the fourth below when you left her in charge. I was pleasantly surprised. She's quite the exemplary leader. She helped bring us up to the surface and took charge as a surface representative. She wanted to be sure nobody on the surface would be hurt. At least those who chose to stay out of the combat."

"I knew she'd be alright," Smoke lied. "She'd shown me she had what it took. I wouldn't have left her there if I had any doubt she'd be harmed. Although, I figured it'd be you taking care of her."

"She didn't really need me," Cobble said with a grin, "but, since we are on the subject of leadership."

Smoke nodded his head knowing exactly what Cobble wanted to hear. The barmaid returned with Smoke's meal of synthetic eggs and real sausage with two pieces of bread. "Quite simply, I am going to remain the leader until everything is done here," Smoke said. "I know it seems unfair and in all honesty I don't want the title. But, it's the one thing protecting me from Fulcrum right now. Once I know Fulcrum has been taken care of I will happily hand the reigns over and you can run the Cartel any way you wish. You can go legit or keep living a life of crime, I really don't care. I have my own fish to fry. So, if you want the title you can get your people to start hunting Fulcrum down. He'll be on the surface; he probably has been for quite a while."

Cobble stared at Smoke, "So you want to be sure that you're going to live past this?"

"That's exactly it," Smoke said. "I do have a question for you though."

"Go ahead," Cobble said. "My leader."

"What happened to Fulcrum when I left the fourth below?"

"What do you mean what happened?" Cobble asked with his head cocked to the right.

"Fulcrum and I had planned to leave the fourth below together. I made it out and he got captured. We were supposed to meet at the lift. When he didn't make it I knew he'd been captured."

Cobble shook his head, "Fulcrum was never captured. He never tried to escape, he didn't want to. He knew you'd had a change of heart and I'm assuming decided to use it against you. He certainly harboured a lot of hatred for you for leaving. We all were angry, but I think he took it personally."

"Well," Smoke said before taking a bit out of one of the sausages, "I want him found and brought to me alive. I have some questions."

"Did you seriously think he tried to escape and had been captured?" Cobble asked.

Smoke didn't respond; he didn't need to. He continued to eat his meal while Cobble waited for his own meal. The two sat in contemplative silence. Cobble had been used to being the leader and Smoke's return would throw a serious wrench into his plans. What he didn't seem to know was that he had no intentions of getting in the way of the siege or stopping people from living on the surface. This was a better life for them.

He stood and thanked Cobble for his time and left for the inn again. The guard on duty was dressed in a set of thick leather armour. Nothing that could stop a revolving pistol shot, but it could stop most blades and blunt attacks. The guard gave Smoke a nod and allowed him to knock on the door. There was a brief moment of silence before Smoke heard Blue's voice, "Yeah?"

Smoke silently let out a sigh of relief, "We should get going."

"I'll be right out," Blue shouted through the door.

He only had to wait a few moments before Blue walked through the door. She looked Smoke up and down, taking in his new image. "Wow, I hardly recognized you," she said with a grin.

They passed Cobble in the tavern again. "We reached the second above this morning. I let my people know to let you into the second above when you get there. I gave strict instructions to leave the Lang family alone so you can finish your job."

"I appreciate that Cobble," Smoke said with a smile before leaving the tavern.

Penelope had been up all night wandering the surface. She couldn't remember the last time she had seen the sun or the moon. The light warmed her face and kissed her skin. She had wandered away from everyone at one point and stripped naked to bask in the sun's rays. Once she had finished she dressed herself and made her way back to the army of people by the tower.

The army was a rag-tag group of people in varying types of armour, some ranging from thick cloth armour to thick metal. All of whom seemed kind in passing though she had no doubt in her mind that many had a mean streak she had no intention of getting to know.

She could hear raised voices coming from inside a war tent. As she approached she could make out that the voices were the two men she had met the night before, Cobble and Homer. "No volunteers means it's just the two of us," Homer said impatiently.

"We'll find some. I know we have to get this plan in motion as quickly as we can, but there is no way we can get this done with just the two of us."

Penelope didn't know what they were talking about. She leaned in close to the tent, she wanted to know and maybe help if possible. "Have you seen or heard from Blaze at all?" Homer asked.

"Not a word," Cobble said. "I'm actually kind of pissed about that. The guy was supposed to help us. Shit, his Nagara were supposed to help in storming the tower. I think they're relaying messages back and forth, at least that's what a few of our messengers have said. I haven't the resources or the time to check it out anyway. But still, we don't need that many Nagara along the walls."

"I agree, we could use whatever Nagara they can give us. I'll send a messenger out to the walls. If we are lucky we will get some Nagara as help, maybe that will encourage some of our own men to come down to the underground and blow the place up."

Penelope's eyes widened with intrigue. Cobble had told them the boomers hadn't gone off and Smoke explained why. Cobble didn't seem to believe him at first until Smoke showed him the wounds caused by the needle chair. Cobble had listened more intensely after that point. Thankfully, during the story Smoke had said she had stayed behind and hadn't taken part in their escape. She appreciated that greatly. She may be an immortal but she had intended to keep that sort of thing under wraps as long as she could.

"So why am I here?" Cobble asked angrily. "I should be going over battle plans with Smoke."

"The alchemists brought us a boomer last night," Homer said nervously.

"Why would the alchemists bring us a boomer?" Cobble asked. "It's not like they have much in the way of stakes in this war. They do what they do and we do what we do. Nobody's bothered them in a long time."

"They didn't tell me why they wanted us to have it, they just told me they're not surprised the boomers didn't go off and they know why. They gave us this new boomer to take out the culprit once and for all. I asked if they gave one of these to every area and they said just to ours... They said I'd find out why and that we would find the person to deliver it soon enough. What do you think that means?"

Cobble shrugged, "I don't really know. What makes this boomer so powerful?"

"Something about splitting Adams."

Penelope's eyes grew wide with fear. She knew exactly what the alchemists had brought and it wasn't going to be pretty. Immediately she burst into the tent. "I volunteer to do what needs to be done!" she said loud and too quickly to stop herself.

Cobble and Homer both turned to look at her, "You're Smoke's lift driver," Homer said as he gazed at her. "What could you possibly do that we can't?"

The look on Penelope's face must have given them cause for concern since they stepped back a few steps. "I know that if you don't take great care of that boomer then you may as well kiss this whole war goodbye. You'll lose; the tower will lose, as will several of the areas around us. I know what you have in your possession. I know what it can do and I know what you have to do. I also know how to get this boomer to the proper place, the place where it can do the most damage; I can get it to the engine. After that, all you'll have to do is close the lift to the first below."

"How can we trust you?" Homer asked.

A fair question and one Penelope had been anticipating, "You can't really know for sure, but Smoke trusted me so you will have to as well."

"Alright," Cobble began. "Let's say we trust you. How do you plan to get the mega-boomer to... where it needs to go?"

Penelope stopped herself from chuckling at the name 'mega-boomer'. "Just put it inside me," Penelope said without thinking.

The two men gave her a strange look. "It's umm... it's a little big to fit in your..." Homer stammered.

Penelope rolled her eyes, "Fuck sake no, not there! Cut me open and put it in my body."

"Have you seen the boomer? It'd kill you," Homer said with a concerned voice.

Penelope looked around for a quick second, "Hand me a

blade."

Homer and Cobble looked to one another before looking back at Penelope. "Why do you need a blade?" Cobble asked confused.

"Holy shit," Penelope said as she began to lose her patience, "I'm not going to use it on either of you; I'm going to show you something."

Cobble reached into his pocket and pulled out a small blade. He handed the small blade to Penelope. She looked it over and tested the edge as well as the point. It wasn't as sharp as she'd have preferred, but it would get her point across all the same. She removed her shirt and threw it at the men. "Hold on to that, I don't want to get blood all over it."

The two men gave her confused looks and grinned at her naked chest. She rolled her eyes again and plunged the knife into her stomach just below the rib cage. Pain flooded her mind as she pulled the blade down. She could feel her intestines begin to fall from the cavity. Tears of pain began to stream from her eyes as she pulled the blade away. She threw it to the side and began pulling her intestines back into her body. As soon as she had them all placed back inside the wound began to close. She then pulled her hands away revealing the lack of a wound or scar.

Cobble and Homer stared at her blankly, unsure as to what they should think or say. She grabbed her shirt from them and pulled it back over her body. "Do you see? I can't die. The wound you make will heal as soon as you put the boomer inside me. Don't worry about my organs either, they don't need to be in any particular place, they're really just for show at this point anyway."

"Why would you want to do this? This could actually kill you," Cobble said with a look of genuine concern.

Penelope nodded, "It won't kill me. The last one didn't and I was damn near standing on the drop zone. I've been vaporized before, it hurts like a bitch and it will take a long time to pull myself back together, but I'll pull through. Since this one is inside me I probably won't even feel it at all. You two, I only want you to seal the first below. I'll find my way out in time, but I don't want you to keep this open waiting for me. It could take a very long time to reassemble myself after that, could take years. So, seal it up enough that nobody can go down, but when I make it back to the first below, I am going to want to be able to get back. I'm sure as shit not digging my way to the surface for the next fucking century. You got that? Do we have a deal?"

Cobble nodded, "We will board up the access to the first below, not that anybody would be able to get down with the lift at the bottom. I'll give you a key to the lock we will use and when you come back up you can unlock the trap door and get back out. Put it in a place you will be able to find again, but in a place where someone won't be able to find it if they are also on the first below. I don't think I'll let anyone live who comes back up if it's not you."

"I know where I'll put it," Penelope said feeling the gravity of the situation. What she had agreed to had just hit her and she wasn't looking forward to it. She looked to the table beside the two men and the devices on display, "Put the boomer on a switch that I will have to arm manually in order to detonate it, that one there," She said as if she were the one in command. "Also put a failsafe on my heart, if my heart stops for a certain amount of time it'll detonate. That way if they take the detonator from me I'll still be able to make it go boom."

Homer grabbed her hands gently, "We will not forget this sacrifice Miss."

"Penelope," she said with a faint smile, "Also, it's not a sacrifice. I'm not dying... well, not permanently anyway so you don't have to worry about it. At worst I'll be uncomfortable for a while, that's it. As I said before, I don't think the explosion will even hurt; I'd be gone too quickly for it to hurt." She let out a quick sigh, "Anyway, let's get going. I don't have all day and neither do any of you. I'll talk you through the whole thing."

She'd hoped neither of the men present had been the engine's informant. Even if Homer or Cobble were working for the other side it wouldn't be possible to stop her and with a manual switch she'd be able to detonate it at will. Not that they'd be able to get any messages from the surface to the engine anyway. The signals wouldn't go so far down and the lack of frequencies down in the engine would make it impossible for them to know anything about the atomic boomer that would be in her chest.

She scratched the back of her neck and followed Homer and Cobble towards another tent, the one she assumed housed the weapon that would change the world for everyone, the boomer that would end the oppression and set the world free. She didn't want to be any part of it, but The Writer put her in that place for a reason, and she wasn't going to ignore her calling when presented.

Smoke and Blue were greeted by soldiers from the underground as they approached the tower. Smoke had to look at the armoured men a few times to convince himself they were not the same men from the engine. One of the men removed his helmet and gave the two of them a grin. "Mister Callahan, Miss Lang, I am pleased to see the two of you. Cobble has already relayed our orders to allow the two of you into the second above," the soldier said, "I can honestly say that what you're doing is foolish considering you'll be walking into a battlefield. But, that's not my call to make. I'll be sending four men to keep you safe as you go through the second above to the Lang residence."

Smoke slapped the man in the shoulder. "I appreciate what you are doing for Blue and myself. Your men will be well compensated for their time."

The soldier gave Smoke a grave look and nodded, "Very well then," he said before turning to the rest of the soldiers, "Sanchez! Hardy! Politchuk! Leon! You four are to escort Mister Callahan here and Miss Lang to the Lang residence. These two know the way and will guide you. It is your job to be sure the two of them make it there and back safely. You got that?"

The soldiers stood straight and saluted, "Yes sir!" they all yelled in unison.

Four soldiers from the crowd stepped forward and guided the way to the steam-powered hydraulic lift. As the doors closed one of the soldiers pressed some buttons on the side of the lift and in a matter of moments the lift began to ascend. "Alright Mister Callahan," one of the soldiers said, "Once we get to the second below the four of us will exit first to test the area. If there are any shots fired I want you two to get as low as you can. Once we are convinced it is safe we will motion for the two of you to move forward and you can give us directions. I know you have a little combat experience Mister Callahan, I've read your file, but it would be best to leave it to us."

Smoke raised his hands, "No arguments form me. I have my revolving pistol, but I'm not wearing any protective gear. I agree with your plan."

"Do any of you have a communicator?" Blue asked.

The soldiers nodded, "All suits of armour are outfitted with communicators as standard issue. It's so we can stay in contact with each other."

"Are your communicators capable of making outgoing calls to anyone outside your army?"

The soldier leaning on the wall spoke up, "Why do you ask?"

Blue shot the soldier an idiot's glare, "If my parents see a squadron of soldiers approaching their home there is no way in hell they will answer the door. We will just get to stand outside and nobody will get anywhere. If I can call them and warn them in advance there is a better chance they will let us in."

The soldiers all looked at one another before the one Smoke assumed to be Leon handed her a communicator. She pressed the code to contact her home and waited for an answer. "Do you think this will work?" Leon asked Smoke.

Smoke shrugged before Blue began talking, "Hello? Mom? It's me Blue. Yes, Blue, I'm coming home. I'm a little sore from the trip, but I'll be alright…. I'm in the lift right now on my way. I've even got my own military escorts…. Yes, Mister Callahan is right here with me. Would you like to talk to him?"

Blue then handed Smoke the communicator, "My mother would like to speak with you."

Smoke took the communicator with a confused look before bringing the device to his ear, "Hello?"

"Mister Callahan," I'm glad to hear you're alright. And that you have my charming baby girl. I know what Marla offered you, but it's not enough. When you get here we will discuss your reward."

"That's wonderful ma'am," Smoke said hiding a grin. "Does this mean you will let us in when we get here? Despite the soldier escorts?"

"If they're just escorts as you say then I don't see a problem. I know there's a lot of shooting going around out there, but it's my child come home. I can't not let you in. She may get hurt."

"I'm glad you think that Mrs. Lang," Smoke said, this time not hiding his grin at all. "We will be seeing you shortly."

He pressed the button to end communication and handed it back to Leon. "We still are going forward with our plan?" Blue asked.

"Yes," was all Smoke said as he continued to look forward.

As the lift approached the second above the only sounds to be heard were the sounds of steam in the hydraulics and the sounds of revolving pistols being cocked and loaded. Smoke could feel his heartbeat in his chest as he prepared to hit the ground as soon as the doors opened. He didn't think he'd need to, but he'd prepared himself just in case. He looked to Blue whose face had been drained of all colour. The fear in her eyes told him she didn't want to die, especially being so close to home after coming all this way. He wished the war had held off until after his task had finished and he'd been safely away from the tower and everything within it.

The doors opened and the four soldiers poured into the hallway. They pointed their revolving pistols around and when no signs of movement had presented themselves the soldiers waved Smoke and Blue forward. They quickly moved through the gap and Blue proceeded to give the soldiers directions to the Lang residence.

The white walls Smoke remembered so distinctly were spattered with blood and littered with the dead bodies of the underground and tower soldiers. As Smoke walked by each of them he found it more and more difficult to distinguish one from the other. Blue had been trying her best to keep her head pointed ahead and to not look at the bodies of the fallen men and women who fought for what they believed. Neither side was really right or really wrong.

Smoke exhaled out his nose as the soldiers stopped in front of the quarter-moons in a circle. Blue pushed herself forward and pressed the ringer. The sound of the chime that rang through the home was prevalent in the hallway. After a minute of chiming the sound stopped and the door opened. The servant boy looked as if he had recently taken a beating. His eye had been blackened and several spots on his skin were bruised. His livery uniform had been speckled with blood from his nose.

Mulholland Lang soon walked from the side room to the front room to greet them. "Mister Callahan," she said with obvious false sincerity. "I'm so glad you could make it. Please, come in. I'm afraid your escorts will have to wait outside. I hope you understand."

"We assumed as such madam," Leon said with a blank face.

The expression on Mulholland's face was a cross between offence and amusement. "I'm sorry," she said with a snarky tone, "Did I say you could speak?"

"Mother," Blue snapped as she stepped forward, "these men are not your servants, or anyone's servants. You are not to speak to them in such a manner."

Mullholland blinked several times before smiling devilishly, "Of course, please forgive me."

Smoke nodded to Leon and the door closed in front of the soldiers. Mulholland then crossed the room and took Blue in an embrace intended to seem loving. Smoke watched her movements with careful caution. "It's always a great feeling to see family back together."

Mulholland stood and gestured for Smoke and Blue to follow, "Come, your father and sister are waiting for you in the study."

"Excellent," Blue said with a smile more fake but less forced than her mother's.

The home of the Lang's was the exact same as Smoke remembered. Every bust and every book never seemed to have moved an inch in the time he was gone. "I'm glad to see you're able to keep yourselves safe under all this fire," Smoke said as he looked around.

"We left a gift and a note asking for the soldiers to leave us be," Mulholland said with her chirpy voice.

The study was exactly as Smoke recalled with the exception of the levels of the liquor in the decanters, some were much lower while some seemed to have risen. Row and Marla stood around the green inverted table and smiled softly with forced glee as Smoke and Blue stepped into the room. Smoke and Blue stopped several paces before her parents. Mulholland turned and scowled at Smoke and Blue. "Alright, now that I know nobody is listening we can cut the shit. Blue, how are you here? And Mister Callahan, how are you alive?"

Smoke and Blue looked at each other and grinned, "Wow," Blue said, "I thought it would take a lot longer to get a confession out of them."

"What are you talking about?" Row asked as he pulled out a revolving pistol.

"Father," Blue said with a smirk, "in all my years I've never seen you use a revolving pistol. I don't think I've ever seen you hold one. You know who this man is, he's a quick draw and accurate with his weapon. You know he'd put holes through all three of you before you'd ever have the courage to pull that trigger. Let's face it, when I went for pistol training you said I was wasting my time."

Smoke knew Blue was bluffing. Smoke was a great shot, but he wasn't the best by any means, nor was he especially quick. Regardless he pulled out his revolving pistol and fired at Row Lang. He screamed in pain as his hand erupted into a spray of blood and fingers as the revolving pistol fell to the ground. Row clutched what remained of his hand and remaining fingers. "Alright," Smoke said. "Sit."

Marla, Mulholland and Row obeyed. "What are you going to do to us?" Marla asked.

"First off, there's the issue of my reward," Smoke said with a grin. He handed Blue the magic pouch he'd attached to his belt, "Blue, would you go pick up the revolving pistol and escort Marla to collect my reward? I'll wait here and keep your dear parents company until you get back."

Blue moved to the revolving pistol and picked it up. She grabbed a cloth from across the room and threw it to her father who wrapped it around his damaged hand. "Looks like my training has some uses after all," she said with malice. She pointed the pistol to Marla, "Up, let's get moving."

Marla obeyed and Blue followed her out of the room. "What's the point of all of this?" Row asked. "We were going to pay you anyway."

"Oh I assumed as much," Smoke said, "But it's best to be sure. Anyway, this is not about the skins. This about who you are, what you know, and what you've taken from me."

"You know we know about the engine," Mulholland said angrily. "Blue would have told you about that."

"It's true she did, she also explained that you set me up to die."

"So that's what this is about?" Row asked. "Because we tried to get you killed?"

Smoke chuckled, "Oh hell no," he said with amusement. "I couldn't give two shits about that. Do you have any idea how many people want me dead? Of course you do, you've done your research on me. Trying to kill me doesn't faze me at all. I don't even care about the torture, it hurts and will hurt for a long time, but I already killed the men who did that. What I do care about is what you know about a certain company still strong in Red City and the person that I lost because you sent me on this hunt."

"What are you talking about?" Mulholland asked.

"First off," Smoke said as he sat in an easy chair across from Mulholland and Row. He threw the book of tower families between them. "You two are not native to this level. You're from much higher in this tower; you're from the tenth above. Felt like slumming it for a while? Doesn't matter, what you do need to know is that I'm a bit of a history fanatic. I love learning about the past and the secrets it holds. I know you are a part of the engine, which means you are privy to the Ares Corporation and their dealings."

"What are you talking about?" Row asked.

His eyes gave away everything Smoke needed to know. He knew about the Ares Corporation and everything they did. "The Ares Corporation began in the late nineteenth century as a part of the Legion of Twelve. The Ares Corporation was the head of law enforcement and military funding. They kept their part up while several companies in the legion went under. Eventually the Ares Corporation began its own superhuman law enforcement unit. Need I continue on the history of Ares Corp? No? Alright." He took a pause to move to the liquor stand and poured himself a drink, all the while keeping a keen eye on Row and Mulholland.

"Anyway," Smoke continued, "while I was in the engine their leader of this area tried to recruit me. She told me the history of the engine in the vaguest way possible. I don't think she really knew who she was talking to. I put things together, sometimes it's a leap of faith, but many times it's nothing more than putting the pieces together, even if they seem unrelated. In this case I have to go back to the origin of the engine. People dug down into the ground to end a war. It's not a far cry to realize it was the Ares Corporation that funded the engine and what it's used for. It wouldn't surprise me if the Ares Corp building had been built to withstand electromagnetic pulses. They're setting themselves up to rule the world with their technology that's safe from the pulses."

"You're going to try to take on the Ares Corporation?" Row asked while laughing.

"Not at all. I don't need to. There's nothing they can do or else they'd have done it already. They may be looking to take over the world, but the technology they'd spread could be a benefit to everyone. I would actually encourage everyone to accept it," Smoke said as he watched Blue and Marla return with the magic sack. "Though my plans are not yours to hear - I just wanted you to know I know your actual family secret. You're a part of the Ares Corp. Nothing too bad, I'm not even sure why that's your big secret. But, if word got out that your secrets had been found you'd be labelled soft. A title and claim that could get you extradited from both the towers, and the knowledge of the engine could get you removed from the surface and the underground. You'd be pariahs everywhere you go. I'm not going to do anything with this information, because as I said before, I don't have to."

"Then what's the point of all this?" Mulholland screamed.

"Because of Glass," he said with a cold and angry voice. "You sent me to the engine, I escaped and they carved her up for me to find. I made a vow to her to kill all those who were a part of this, including all those in the engine. In the end, I'll have to end myself as well considering it was my escape that caused it, but I think I have a lot of time before that happens. Any last words?"

The Lang family stared at Smoke and Blue with their mouths agape. Smoke and Blue looked at each other and open fire. The bodies of the Lang family jumped with each shot; and with each shot fired Smoke felt a little weight lift from his heart. Glass would be avenged, one body at a time.

The look on Blue's face was one of retribution and horror. She had just killed her family, though it was a suiting vengeance for the life they'd pushed upon her. He'd have to make sure this didn't become a habit for her, but there was more to take care of before then.

23

The third above was bare. No signs of anyone on the floor remained; no civilian or soldier occupied the hallways. Constance looked around but she didn't know the Rocka family emblem. She'd seen a wide variety of symbols as she wandered. Stars of varying styles, a rain drop, a dog's head and several other symbols greeted her.

It wasn't long before she realized she was lost. The white walls, white doors and white floors made direction hard to pinpoint. There were little to no distinguishing features to the tower halls to the point where Constance realized she could have been going in circles and not known it. The only indicators that she wasn't spinning around were the door symbols.

She didn't think the soldiers had made it to this floor as of yet. It was possible the majority, if not all the tower soldiers had been sent to the second above to make their final stand against the underground army. They wouldn't want the underground people to make it any higher; it would betray those who had paid for their safety.

After several hours of wandering and guessing as to which door held the Rocka family she decided to press a random bell.

The sound chimed through the home for over five minutes before someone finally turned the bell off and slightly opened the door. "Please don't hurt us."

She was a small mousey woman looking to be in her last legs of life. Long strands of grey wispy hair fell down her face and swayed side to side as she moved. "I won't hurt you," Constance said, "I'm looking for a family; I don't know their symbol so I don't know which bell to press."

"I heard about the fighting downstairs. I knew this day would come someday. I knew the underground would come to reclaim what they believe is theirs."

The old woman seemed to be ignoring Constance. "Can you tell me where I can find the Rocka family?" she asked impatiently.

The old woman stopped in her steps and gave her a look of deep suspicion, "What do you want with the Rocka family?"

"I have some questions to ask them," Constance said assertively. "Do you know where I can find them?"

The old woman nodded her head, "I'm their door servant, "I will fetch them right away. I hope you don't mind if I place you in a small waiting room. It's just to prevent people from wandering where they shouldn't go."

Constance nodded, "Yeah, that's alright."

The old woman took her by the hand and led her through the room. The old woman's hands were soft and frail. Constance believed if she pressed too hard she'd shatter every bone the woman had in her hand. She soon brought her to a small empty room, not much bigger than a closet or a pantry. Constance agreed to play along and entered the small room.

Constance hoped she had at last found the people who had hired her parent's killer, though a part of her hoped she hadn't. The last thing she wanted was to have to shed any blood she didn't have to, but if the Rocka family had been responsible for her parent's deaths she'd finally be able to let that part of her past go. She doubted she'd ever find the hitman, that wasn't a thought that bode well with her, but it was a reality she'd have to live with. If the Rocka family had been the people who had contracted a killer, she'd be getting answers first.

She stood in the small room for hours before the small mousey woman opened the door, "I apologize for the wait miss, things have been hectic here with the war going on below. My masters will see you now."

Constance exited the room and followed the old woman, "Are you happy here?" Constance asked.

The old woman looked up at her with sorrowful eyes and said, "Of course I am. They took me in a long time ago; I've lived my whole life here and will likely die here."

She chose to drop the subject. The old woman probably viewed her as a woman from the tower and didn't want to be caught talking harsh words against her employers. The chamber the Rocka family had been sitting was larger than most rooms Constance had ever seen. A young man sat in a chair with a revolving pistol pointed at Constance. A young woman sat beside him dressed in similar attire as the woman she'd robbed from the first above had worn. She gave Constance a dirty look before looking to the man with the gun. An aged man and woman sat on a sofa comfortably. Both were dressed lavishly to show off their posh lifestyle.

"You have five seconds to explain what you're doing here before I fill you with shots," the younger man said angrily.

Constance held her hands up in surrender, "My name is Constance Ibot and I have some questions for you. Your family has been accused of hiring a hitman to murder a family who had lived on the surface."

The aged man sat straighter in his seat before waving to the young man, "Clarence, put that thing away before you hurt yourself." Clarence looked at the aged man, who Constance assumed to be his father, with careful consideration and carefully placed the revolving pistol on the table in front of him. Constance made a mental note that the revolving pistol was within arm's reach and could be quickly picked up in the event of trouble.

"You said your name was Ibot?" the aged man asked.

"That's right," Constance said as she stood straight.

"That's a name I haven't heard in many, many years; a dozen at least. What do you want with our family Miss Ibot?"

"I've been trying to find the killers of my family," Constance said quickly, "and your family was accused of hiring the hand that pulled the trigger. I'm here because I want to know if it's true. I want to know who wanted my parents dead."

"And what do you plan to do with this knowledge?" the aged woman asked as she looked at the shortblade at Constance's back, the old woman had forgotten to take it from her before entering. "Would you kill them?"

Constance shook her head, "No, the knowledge would be closure enough for me. There's been too much bloodshed this past day. I've seen more than enough of it. Besides, I don't have the stomach for killing."

"I'm sorry," the young woman said with a sour scowl. "We can't help you."

"Shut up Dorothy," the aged man said before turning to Constance. "Please, take a seat. I have to explain everything before I get into the event of your parent's death."

Constance sat on a small stool and stared at the aged man, "Alright," she said, "tell your story."

The aged man took in a deep breath and let it out loudly through his nose, "My name is Harvey Rock., I hadn't gone through proper introductions yet. I apologize for that. This is my wife Francine and my two children Clarence and Dorothy.

"I knew your family. Your father was a great man who was soon to figure out a way to bring many of the underground inhabitants to the surface. He was a brilliant doctor and botanist who specialized in mixing plants genes together. I don't understand much of it so I couldn't really tell you exactly what he had been doing. What I do know is he created a plant that grew quickly and could fill a stomach with little food. The underground would have been able to come to the surface and grow much more of the population we in the tower had fought so hard to keep small.

Your father was a humanitarian you see; he believed that all man should be equal and living on the surface. He was the first and probably the only man in the tower I'd ever seen who believed the towers and the underground should be abandoned and have every civilian living harmoniously together."

"A philosophy that didn't sit well with the people of the tower," Constance said knowingly.

Harvey nodded his head, "Precisely. It wasn't just my family that banished your family from the tower - everyone wanted them out. But then on the surface they began doing all these great things that would have similar results as when they were in the tower. They made life better for the people on the surface, this brought people from the underground to the surface. Tower's Shadow was almost a ghost town before they arrived. Now, we wouldn't have allowed the town to go into ruins, but it was at a manageable number. We had people to maintain the agriculture, people to serve food and drink to those who worked the forge or the fields. It was a small but functioning ecosystem. Then your parents came and brought them education and medicine. They brought them a better way of life that knocked our ecosystem that we had fought so hard to create and maintain off center. We had to do something.

It's not uncommon for someone from the tower to get one

of the dregs from the underground to do the dirty work for us. If they pointed a finger nobody would believe them. Or at least that's what I thought. I mean, here you are."

"I never found the hitman," Constance said grumpily.

"Dear, what was the hitman's name?" Harvey asked his wife.

She shook her head, "I don't remember. It was a long time ago. It was an odd underground name. Not the sort that rolls off the tongue, but when you say it you want to wash your mouth."

Constance figured she'd take a shot in the dark and name the only hitman she'd known, "Fulcrum?"

Francine's eyes opened wide and she smiled, "Yeah, that's the name."

Constance's brow furrowed. He had been right next to her in the second below and she'd had no idea. She could have made an attempt at killing him, she may have even succeeded. She'd go searching for him - that was for sure. "So you killed my parents because they were helping people?"

Harvey nodded his head, "I did, and I'm not sorry. The world has a balance to it; the rich, the poor and those in the middle. It is important to keep all levels happy to maintain the balance."

"Based on the war going on downstairs I'd say you've done a hell of a job," Constance said with angry amusement. "Why did you want to keep the population small, you've captured my curiosity?"

"Simply put, small numbers are easier to manage. If you get too many people in one area, they all start to want more, typically because there isn't enough to go around. Eventually an eager mind will begin to stir the masses with their ideas of equality or supremacy. All it takes after that is a single spark before the landscape becomes an inferno of emotions, shots and blood. Much like what we have going on here now. Hence why we did our best to keep the underground population as spread out as possible. We implemented crime syndicates, gangs and the whore houses to keep people on their toes and to discourage them from venturing."

"You didn't think they'd ever all work together."

"There had been a lot of fighting between the center floors for a long time. Old wounds heal the slowest, if they ever heal at all. Someone was clever and brought all the right players together. I am certainly surprised at the outcome."

"And you thought the system to be so perfect that you didn't expect a revolution?"

"Revolutions happen, but do you know the reality of it?" Harvey asked with a crazed grin, "No matter the revolution or why it's fought, there will always be those who are wealthy and there will always be those who are not. History shows this. History is constantly repeating itself and this revolution will not change a single thing in the long run. My family may or may not survive this attack. The distribution of the tower's wealth my get spread out to everyone, but in a matter of time a small amount of people will once again own the majority of the skins and a large amount will have very little."

Rage filled every part of Constance with every word Harvey spoke. His arrogance and the belief that the revolution would soon amount to nothing made things even worse. She could feel herself beginning to lose control.

"That doesn't mean this revolution isn't worth anything," Constance said as she pulled her revolving pistol from the back of her trousers. She pressed the button that took the safety mechanism off and shot at the other revolving pistol. It shattered into several pieces which skittered across the small table and onto the floor. Dorothy screamed and Clarence swore loudly as his hands and knees were shredded with shrapnel. "After meeting a couple families here on the tower I have to say I'm glad my parents had been exiled from the tower. It helped me grow into the woman I am now and that says a lot. I am so glad I didn't turn out like any of you. I'm glad I didn't grow to have your ideals about other people. You make me sick. And then you killed my parents, for what? For trying to make other peoples' lives better? That's deplorable. You deserve this."

Constance fired two shots, hitting Harvey in the chest and head. Constance could hear screaming though she wasn't sure if it had come from Francine or Dorothy or herself. She took a breath as she shot Clarence once and Dorothy twice. She took another breath as she pointed the pistol at Francine. "I'm sorry I had to kill your children. You're too powerful to allow any witnesses to live. You know my name, you know my face. I'd never have a day or night of peace with you people looking down at me from your tower. This is for my safety and for those I love."

Francine nodded, "I hope you never have a peaceful night for as long as you live."

"I expect I will sleep like a baby after this. You have no idea how much I've wanted this."

She pulled the trigger and Francine's head snapped backward with a spray of blood and brain spattering across the room. She had lied through her teeth when she had said she'd be sleeping well after this, she knew quite well she'd be having nightmares for years. It didn't change what had to be done or her reasoning for it, although, she wasn't quite done with her vengeance as of yet. She had to track down Fulcrum and take him out.

He didn't strike Constance as the sort who would still be down in the underground. He'd have come up with the mass exodus of the underground. If Smoke were still alive, Fulcrum would have been keeping tabs on him. It would have been a matter of finding Smoke and waiting. That not being the case Fulcrum could be anywhere. It was even possible he'd left the area somehow and was miles away. Constance would then never have her full vengeance. The thought aggravated her, though she knew in time she may be able to live with it. After all, nothing said

Fulcrum had actually left and if he had, there was a possibility he'd return someday.

She left the home slowly and languidly. The images of the Rocka families death poses haunted her thoughts. As her anger subsided she found tears rolling down her face. She wiped one away before bracing herself against a wall and crying. She had just killed four people in cold blood and it was not sitting well inside her. She'd told herself several times it was vengeance for her parents, and retribution for the surface and the underground. Those people had to die for their part. She stopped herself from going any further in the thought process, not that it had helped anyway. Where would it have ended? With the complete destruction of the tower and everyone within? She wouldn't have been able to live with herself if that ever came to pass.

She approached the lift and pressed the down button. She didn't have any means of going up nor did she have any desire to ascend farther in the tower. The doors to the lift opened and she stepped inside. The steam pressed the hydraulics to close the door. The boilers then let the steam loose to bring the lift downward.

The lift stopped at the second above. As the doors opened she was greeted by six revolving pistols aimed directly at her face. She screamed and fell to the floor. Finally one of the armed men said, "Arms down, that's Miss Ibot. Cobble would be some pissed if he found out we'd killed her."

The revolving pistols disappeared from her view and she returned to a standing position. Constance took in a deep breath and regained her composure. "Why have I stopped on the second above?" she asked inquisitively.

"That's our orders ma'am," one of the soldiers said. "We are to stop any and all lifts going to the bottom because they are likely filled with enemy soldiers. When this lift went to the third above we assumed that's what you were. I apologize for the scare we caused, but we can't be too careful."

"I understand," Constance said with a voice of authority. "Now, could you let me get to the surface? I have a hunt to continue."

The soldier shook his head, "I can't do that right now," he said apologetically. "We've got more soldiers coming from the first above with new orders. I'm afraid that takes priority over your trip to the surface. Once they are up here and have given the new orders we will escort you to the surface. Until then you'll just have to sit tight."

Constance nodded. "Alright," she said hiding her anger.

Four shots were heard in the distance. Constance drew her revolving pistol and told the soldiers to sit tight. It'd be easier and stealthier for one person to go alone. She would whistle in the event she'd need help. The soldiers agreed, not a difficult thing for Constance to achieve considering they all wanted to stay and wait for their orders.

Smoke left the Lang's home with Blue behind him. The four soldiers gave the two of them grave looks. "Things go as expected?" Leon asked.

"They did," Smoke said with a grin.

In his arms he held the sack containing the two million skins he'd been promised. Killing the Lang family was dirty business and he didn't expect he'd get a detective job ever again because of it. That was fine by him; he was done with looking for people. He had his new purpose. That was enough for him.

Four shots rang through the halls and the four soldiers dropped dead. Smoke spun on the balls of his feet to see a masked soldier approaching them. "I almost didn't think you survived. There have been a lot of rumours about your death. I'm glad to see you're actually alive."

"Who are you?" Smoke asked.

"Oh right," the soldier said before removing his mask and helmet.

Fulcrum's face grinned at them as the headwear hit the floor. Smoke had guessed the soldier had been Fulcrum. Smoke raised his hands and motioned for Blue to do the same. "I wish I could say the warm feelings are mutual Fulcrum."

"Oh come now Smoke," Fulcrum said. "I know our deal was that I kill you and take the skins, but I'm willing to make a deal, one where you walk out of here alive. You leave the skins and I shoot the girl and you and I are square. Deal?"

"Tell me one thing first," Smoke said with narrowed eyes.

"Alright," Fulcrum said with hesitation.

"You're pissed at me because I left and you got captured right?" Smoke asked.

Fulcrum nodded, "Yeah, still mad about that."

"I assume my father put you through quite a bit of torture to teach you a lesson."

"Still have the nightmares. Thanks for bringing that up by the way, what's your question?"

Smoke gave a slight smile, "Why would my father let you go without any visible scars? He'd have at least given you a cheek scar or some way of making an example of you. I've even spoken to people from the fourth below; apparently you didn't even try to leave. So, tell me again why you've got a fucking revolving pistol aimed at me!"

Fulcrum scowled, "Because you left. You left the fourth below and I can't forgive you for that. I tried playing on your humanity and your knowledge of what your father would do to a deserter. I don't expect you to understand my point, but we were close. When you left you took a piece of me with you, I didn't want to leave. I had a great job and was starting to garner some power. I learned to live without you being around, I had to figure some things out for myself, but seeing you again brought that piece back so now I have to kill it. I loved you as a brother, but now you're nothing to me. Just another life I have to extinguish."

"Wow," Smoke said shocked, "Fulcrum, I'm so sorry. I am so sorry you're such a little bitch that you have to resort to killing me because I decided I didn't want to be a fucking criminal anymore. Seriously, I'm embarrassed you even got this far. I should have shot you back in the second below; at least I would have been safe to do what I have to do."

"Here we are though," Fulcrum said as Smoke watched his mood go from calm to a rising anger. "Your newfound sense of honour stabbing you in the back again."

"You don't have to do this," Smoke pleaded.

"Who are you?" Blue asked.

"Nobody you're ever going to know," Fulcrum said, "After all, I don't leave witnesses."

Fulcrum raised his revolving pistol a little higher. Smoke closed his eyes and heard the shot go off, matched with the thud of a body falling to the ground. Smoke opened his eyes slightly to see Constance standing before him and Fulcrum lying in a pool of his own blood. "You're alive?" she said softly.

Smoke looked at the woman as she approached him slowly. She seemed to want to be sure he wasn't a ghost or some evil specter sent to haunt her. She placed her hand softly against his face. "Hi Constance," he said softly.

Her face immediately went from soft amazement to harsh anger. She slapped him across the face snapping his head to the side. "You left me in the fourth below!" she screamed, "You left me! Why?"

Smoke hung his head, "You know why," he said quietly. "Also, be glad you stayed behind. You wouldn't have survived the trip. I almost didn't make it."

"I didn't think you had survived. But why do you think I wouldn't have?"

"Trust him," Blue interjected, "Where we've been... It's not the sort of place you're ever supposed to escape from."

"Well, we've got some time," Constance said angrily. "Tell me the story."

"Later," Smoke said. "Right now we need to get back to the surface and find Cobble. With Fulcrum dead, I have a promise to keep."

Constance gave him a look before following behind him. As they approached the lift the soldiers saw Smoke and stood at attention. "Mister Callahan, we have some new orders. We want you to confirm them. You are the leader of this group now and we need you to let us know which direction to take."

"Alright," Smoke said confused. "What could you possibly need me for?"

"We just recently got orders to blow the tower up. We'll be placing boomers along the first above and detonating them tonight once Tower's Shadow has been evacuated."

"No!" Constance yelled, "You can't do that!"

"We can though," the soldier said.

"There are innocent people here in the tower. Not everyone is an evil bastard who deserves to die. If you blow this tower everyone here will die."

"What's it going to be Mister Callahan?" the soldier asked.

"Smoke thought for a second, "We'll blow the tower

tomorrow afternoon. Send soldiers to each home in the tower and inform them of the plan and that they can't stop it from happening. Those who wish to leave the tower will be escorted out to safety. They will be given opportunities to make their fortunes again, if they can. Those who choose to stay behind... well, they will die with their tower."

"Smoke!" Constance said angrily.

"That's my decision," he shot back at Constance, "I'm giving them a fair chance to leave. No harm will come to them when they come down and they'll have as much opportunity as the rest of us. The tower needs to come down; it's a symbol of the oppression to those in the underground and the surface, we've suffered for generations. After that, I have a bigger job to do." Smoke turned back to the soldiers, "Spread the word. Those who don't answer their doors will have their doors broken down; those who wish not to leave will not be forced to leave. We don't have time to fight with people who don't want to be with us."

The soldiers bowed and saluted, "Yes sir," they shouted in unison.

"Now, Let us down to the surface," Smoke said with authority.

The soldiers nodded, "We have our orders now. We can let you back down. We apologize for the inconvenience Miss Ibot."

"No need to apologize," she said with a forced smile. "Staying here worked better than I imagined it would."

"Writer be praised then," a soldier said happily before closing the door to the lift.

Constance gave Smoke an odd look at the mention of The Writer. "Did he really say Writer be praised?"

"He did," Smoke said rubbing his eyebrows with his thumb and middle finger, "It looks as if Penelope has been talking with the locals. She'll likely be setting up a church soon."

"Who's Penelope?" Constance asked with a hint of amusement. "You sure seem to have a way with women don't you."

"She's an im-" Blue began before Smoke stopped her.

"She's the woman who brought me to the lower floors and brought me back up through the underground," Smoke said as he listened to the steam being released from the lift's pipes and ignoring Constance's bad joke. "She also saved the two of us from the engine."

"The engine?" Constance asked.

"Oh right," Smoke remembered.

Smoke proceeded to tell Constance the story of what happened starting from the point he left her in the fourth below. He told her about the encounters with Homer and Blaze, she then told him of her encounters with the two men. Smoke listened when she spoke and when she had finished he told her of the emptiness of the seventh, eighth and ninth belows.

The doors to the lift opened and the three exited only for the lift to be refilled by soldiers. Smoke could see a large crowd gathering in the direction of the lift to the underground, "I wonder what's going on over there?" Blue said.

Smoke shrugged, "I don't know, but I'm sure Cobble will be there."

Constance and Blue nodded as they began walking in the direction of the crowd. As they walked he told her about the engine and the tortures him and Blue had gone through, even going so far as to show her the heavily scabbed backs of his arms and legs. He told her about the escape and the mad dash to get to the surface.

Once Smoke had finished his story Constance began telling

her story. She told him about her time on the fourth below and as the liaison for the surface during the talks. She told him about how she had pushed back the date of the boomers to give him more time to find Blue and make it back out, only for him to be late anyway. She told him about the climb up the tower's vents and the claustrophobia she had felt as she climbed. She told him about how well people from the underground had integrated into Tower's Shadow and become a functioning large community.

"Why were you on the third above?" Smoke asked.

"Dealing with some unfinished business," she said in a dismissive tone. "I'm sorry; it's just not something I want to talk about. All I'll say is that things are alright with me now."

Smoke chose to accept her decision and continued toward the crowd. It seemed everyone from the underground and the surface had gathered around the lift. "What's going on?" Smoke asked one of the men.

"Someone is going down to blow up the underground," the man said. "From what I've heard there's no coming back for her, the boomer will explode and that will be all. We'll be safe from the underground forever."

Smoke's eyes scanned the crowd. He couldn't find the center. He pushed himself into the crowd and through people as they pushed back against him. As he got closer to where people were gathering around he could make out three distinct faces: Cobble, Homer and Penelope. Why was Penelope with the two of them? Also, why did she look so uncomfortable?

"Penelope!" Smoke called out.

The immortal woman looked at Smoke and gave him a soft smile. "Let him through," she said loudly.

The crowd obeyed and Smoke made his way to the lift entrance. He wasn't sure when he'd lost Constance and Blue, but he believed it to be before he shoved himself into the crowd.

"What are you doing?" Smoke asked. "What's this I hear about you sacrificing yourself?"

Penelope smiled, "Smoke, you know as well as I do that I'm not going to die. It might take me a few years to pull myself back together, I mean after this boom there will be nothing left of me to reassemble so my essence will have to take elements from the surrounding area to come back. That will take a long, long time. I have my way back to the surface, so you don't have to worry about that. I'm just doing something that I really don't want to do for all the right reasons. I'll be around long after the engine is gone no matter if it decomposes on its own or if I blow it up. But you people, you need to be able to advance again. You need to be able to survive in comfort. It may not be in your generation or your kid's generation that will find that comfort. But you will all live freely."

Smoke placed both his hands on Penelope's ears; she mirrored the motion and closed her eyes. "You come back," he said with a smile. "I'll buy you whatever you need when you get back. I can afford that now."

Penelope smiled, "I'd like that," she said softly. "I have to go now."

She pulled away from Smoke and he watched her step on the lift platform. She gripped the crank and allowed the lift to descend into the first below. Smoke watched as she disappeared from view with a heavy heart. Five men approached the lift hole with a wooden cover and placed it over top. Penelope would not be getting any light until she reached the first below. "What's that for?" Smoke asked.

Cobble approached Smoke, "We are trying to prevent anyone else from surfacing from the underground. We can't trust that any of them would be from that engine you escaped from. Until I have a metal cover I'm going to have guards posted here at all hours. Nobody is getting out without us knowing."

Smoke smiled, "That's a good plan. On that note, as

promised, I Smoke Callahan hereby revoke my claim as the leader of the Cartel and the fourth below and hereby give the responsibility and perks to Cobble Raw. May you use this power wisely and without corruption."

"Of course," Cobble said. "Is there anything I should know before we part ways?"

"What makes you think we'll be parting ways?" Smoke asked.

"You've got a vow to fulfill," Cobble said, "You're going to be very busy taking down all who had something to do with that engine. That said, once you've gone I am not going to be able to know if you've given any orders in that time. I will respect any and all choices you've made."

Smoke placed his hand on Cobble's shoulder, "I'm pleased to hear that. The only order I've given was to hold off until tomorrow afternoon to blow the tower and to give the residence a chance to exit the tower. They will then live among us and adhere to our laws."

"Seems fair to me," Cobble said. "Now, if you'll excuse me, I have a lot of work to do."

24

The lift was a steady stream of people leaving the tower for hours. People dressed in lavish suits and dresses and servants dressed in livery suits. Many looked lost and confused as they stepped from the artificial life of the tower into the fresh air of the outside. Cobble had known many of the inhabitants would choose to remain within the tower, their skins were much more important than their lives and they would die rich rather than live poor. He also knew many would leave the tower if their lives were in danger, this showed him they viewed their lives more important than their posh lifestyles.

"Excuse me?" one of the men from the tower said as he stepped out of the line. "Where are we going to go? You've effectively kicked us out of our homes. Now what?"

Cobble frowned, "Follow the line sir, we will be gathering everyone together and explaining what we will be doing after the tower's exploded. Nobody will be left guessing. Until then, I ask you stay patient and feel grateful we let you know what was going on and allowed you to leave. I wouldn't have been so generous."

The man stepped back in line and kept his mouth shut. This

was for the best; Cobble knew someone would eventually start asking questions just as well as he knew this man would not be the last to demand answers. So long as they felt their lives were gifted by generosity there was a better chance of them being more workable than if they were greeted with pure hostility or glee. This was a game of will and brains and Cobble intended to win.

He'd always thought the power of officially having the means to command the army of the fourth below would feel great in his hands. Instead all he felt was the same old feeling he'd felt since Smoke left the second time. Duty, responsibility and the knowledge that the lives of everyone he commanded were in his hands. It was everything he'd wanted, and now that he had it through legitimate channels the feelings of responsibility seemed worth it. Before he'd tried to show he was capable, now he could say his efforts had been reciprocated.

The soldiers closed the doors to the steam-powered hydraulic lift and sent it back up the tower. Once the soldiers had taken complete control over the lift there wasn't a floor they couldn't reach. Many of the soldiers had expressed discomfort and a feeling of gratitude at a lack of windows on the fourteenth above, the highest point of the tower. Cobble couldn't imagine being so high in the air. Just looking at the sky was intimidating enough; he didn't need to imagine seeing the ground from such a height.

"Looks like everything is going accordingly to plan," Homer said as he entered the tower.

"It does," Cobble agreed. "I can't seem to shake this feeling that it was a little too easy. It's possible that the tower's defenses were meant to take out small skirmishes or enough to kill enough people from a single floor; thus making it easy to kill their army and bring them all down with the force of a full army."

Homer leaned against a wall, "Makes sense to me, they probably relied on the fact that none of our men could get into the lift. That would have prevented us from ever getting up there.

THE ENGINE WHAT RUNS THE WORLD

They didn't even have to send soldiers to protect the surface lift. If Constance hadn't have crawled through that vent I don't think we will have ever gotten in."

"That's what I mean though," Cobble said. "You don't think that vent being there and being the right size was just a little too convenient?"

Homer shrugged, "I don't know, nor do I really care. Odds are the vents were forgotten about, or maybe nobody actually thought the opening at the outer layer of the tower was big enough to fit a person. It's best not to dwell on these things Cobble, We've won. That's what matters."

Cobble hung his head. Something was not sitting right with him. "I just can't seem to shake this feeling that it was too easy. We won with minimal casualties, the people of the tower were more than willing to leave to save their own lives, I think only a few families refused to go anywhere. It could just be nothing. It's probably nothing."

"Exactly," Homer said with a smile, "Our men have the boomers in place and are in complete control of the lift. There's no possible way that will go wrong. Those who chose to stay made their choice. Once the boomers go off it won't make a difference anymore. You're paranoid because you just learned about the engine, to be honest; I'm a little on edge as well. We don't know who the agents are or who we can trust. Supposedly we have a mole in our midst. I know it's not you; you've done nothing but try and win for the underground. That's a relief. It's probably Blaze. That would explain his disappearance and why Penelope was able to get down as easily as she did."

"I hope she makes it," Cobble said with a glimmer of hope.

"I don't suspect we'll know for sure if she succeeded or failed until she resurfaces."

"Yeah," Cobble said, not wanting to leave the comment open.

"Come on, the boomers are about to go off," Homer said with a grin, "Let's go find a seat and we'll drink a big mug of ale in celebration. Then it's all you from there, you'll officially be running the show here."

"Let's just see if this part goes off," Cobble said looking into the distance, "then we can make plans for the future."

Smoke sat on the grass with Constance and Blue in anticipation of the explosion that would take down the tower. The only people who knew the exact time of detonation were the soldiers who had placed the boomers; and they weren't saying a word on the subject.

Constance continued to wear her look of disgust at the situation. She strongly believed the tower shouldn't be demolished while any living person was still inside. But, a forceful eviction which would take days of soldiers time to bring down people who would have done anything to disrupt the ways of the surface would be nothing more than a waste of time for the soldiers; the law enforcers the town would have to elect the people who would have to deal with the consequences of their actions. It wasn't a perfect plan, but time was of the essence and nobody wanted to lose the war due to a few bleeding hearts.

Blue watched the tower with anticipation and fear. The tower was the only real home she'd ever known. Though she'd left to escape her family, she would have always known that she could have returned at any time if things had been too difficult. Had the engine missed her or had taken no interest Smoke believed she would have inevitably returned within a few months.

Smoke wasn't sure how to think or feel about the situation. He believed he had done his best to do right by both the people of the tower and the people of the surface. He wanted to save as many lives as he could while not inhibiting the progress of the revolution. There was no real way to win in his situation, but if he had the choice to do it again, he'd have made the same choice. Bring down those who wanted to live and hope the rest find peace in whatever afterlife they wind up in.

It was still weird for him to think of the people from the underground as surfacers now, though he could see it in the majority of their faces, they loved the surface and wouldn't go back to the underground under any circumstances. Those from the tower would have a longer transition time; it was harsher on the surface than the lavish luxury of the tower. Now they'd have to work to survive. They wouldn't have servants to kick around or slaves to force to do their biddings. This was a world for the individual now, the individual as a part of a community. A world where one got what they worked for and received enough in kind.

An old mousy looking woman walked past the three of them and gave Constance a smile. Constance smiled back and watched as the old woman continued on her way. Smoke didn't understand the exchange, nor was it for him to understand.

Constance took in a deep breath. "I did something awful," she said quietly.

Smoke turned his head and gave Constance a look of friendship. "By whose standards?" he asked.

The question was intended to make her smile. That no matter what she did Smoke had done worse. Instead she broke down crying. "I killed a family up there," she said as she tried to control her sobs. "The old man and his wife put the hit out on my parents and I killed them. I then killed their son and daughter just to prevent anyone from coming to kill me. I can still see their faces.... Smoke?"

Smoke placed his hand on her shoulder. "Yeah?" he said softly.

"Do the images ever go away?" she asked as she looked at him with her tear-soaked eyes.

Smoke pressed his lips together. "No," he said apologetically. "They never do. You'll see them always. After a time their images will get moved into the back of your mind, but they will always be there. It's like losing someone you loved. They're always there; you just learn to live with it after a time."

"I don't want to learn to live with it," she said angrily. "I want it to go away. I want to be okay again."

"That's the price of vengeance," Smoke said, "You have to live with the knowledge that you are no better than the people you killed. It's a tough lesson and I wish I'd have known the quest you were on. I'd have talked you out of it."

Constance sniffled, "I know you would have. I don't think there would have ever been a way that I would have been okay. If you'd have talked me out of it I'd have never known who or why. But now? I'm not sure which fate is worse."

"You never will," Smoke replied, "The best you can do is try and move forward and always keep in the back of your mind that you are not those people. You are not their kind and you did what you had to in order to avenge your family."

Constance looked down at her feet, "I don't know if that helped or not."

The sound of the boomers detonating took Smoke's and Constance's attention from their conversation and brought it to the flying rubble being forcibly ejected from the tower. The crowd had sat at a safe distance away from the tower, but even now Smoke wondered if anyone would get pelted by a rogue stone.

They could hear the sound of the heavily weakened stones shattering under the weight of the rest of the tower. The tower began to lean in the opposite direction of the town and soon fell over. The sound of the tower hitting the earth made a boom bigger than Smoke had ever heard. The bricks from the tower fell apart upon impact leaving a line of white bricks and home interior wreckage in a long linear mound.

Smoke didn't want to think about how many people had lost their lives in the tower as it fell. How many stood stoically as they faced their death or how many prayed to their gods or how many people broke down and begged to be let out only moments after the boomers had gone off. He tried his best to not think of it. They were at war, and in war people die.

"Well," Blue said with boredom, "that was a little more anticlimactic than I expected."

"What did you expect?" Constance asked.

Blue shrugged, "I guess I thought the explosion from the boomers would be bigger."

"Oh I'm sure those explosions were pretty big," Smoke said. "We just didn't get to see them because they were inside. The point wasn't to make a spectacle. It was to bring the tower down. We've succeeded in that. We've won the war. Officially."

The destruction of the tower seemed to have truly sunk in as Smoke spoke the words. He could hear people begin to cheer and applaud over what had happened. They were free from those who resided in the tower and the oppression they held over them. This was a great day for the surface world.

Once the cheering had died down Cobble walked to the head of the crowd and spoke. "I had originally planned to have a meeting with everyone in the town, or what would be left of it. I'm glad to see the tower didn't fall on the town nor did any of the debris wreck anything. But, since everyone is here already I think we will have our discussion now and get it all over with. Is everyone in agreement?"

The crowd cheered in agreement. Smoke smiled as he watched Cobble use his natural charisma to hype the crowd into excitement over the meeting. This place was in good hands. "What's the first order of business?" a man from the crowd asked.

"First I want to say that the majority of these points have been made by the people who have lived both on the surface and in the underground. Every concern will be addressed here and we can make decisions as a group.

Now, to address those from the tower," Cobble said with a grin. "Welcome to our town. It's not very big and with the recent boom of settlers it's not going to seem very big for a while. But, with some hard work and cooperation we can make our town into a living, thriving and growing community. Now, I know you're all used to a relaxed lifestyle where you don't have to do any hard work, or at least hard work with your hands. That's okay; our people will show you the same patience we would expect in return. Some of us come from backgrounds harder than you could imagine. We are all in this together now.

Second order of business," Cobble continued, "we will be having elections for leader of the town in two weeks' time. We will give a week for any who wish to be leader to step forward and from there we will give a week for them to explain why they should lead this town."

The crowd gave a cheer of approval and Cobble continued, "The third order of business. We need a new name for the town. With the tower gone, Tower's Shadow no longer makes any sense. Does anyone have any suggestions?"

People immediately began shouting out random words and names they thought the town should be named. Smoke could hardly hear anything over the unbearable cacophony. "One at a time alright?" Cobble said as the crowd began to quiet down. "Now, you." He said pointing at a woman in the crowd.

"What was the name of that lady that went back into the underground? I don't know what she was doing, I doubt many of us do, but I can tell she was going back down to do something important and that she may not come back up in the end. What was her name?"

Cobble's eyes grew wide. "Penelope," he said loudly.

"I vote we name the town Penelope," she said with a grin. "I believe what she's doing will make the biggest difference toward our freedom. Why else would you, Homer and Mister Callahan, all be there to see her go. Why else would she go alone?"

Smoke had been taken aback at the mention of his name. He didn't think anyone outside Cobble's military knew who he was. Apparently he was more well-known and respected than he had expected.

"All in favour of naming the town Penelope?" Cobble asked.

Almost every fist entered the sky simultaneously. Smoke couldn't believe the people would name the town after Penelope. He agreed that it was a great idea and he supported it fully. It was just surprising.

Smoke smiled and stood. He grabbed his bag of skins and turned the opposite direction in hopes of not being noticed. He walked through the crowd quickly and without much difficulty before a hand grabbed his sleeve. Smoke turned and saw Blue clutching his arm.

"Where are you going?" she asked.

"My vengeance isn't done," he said slowly.

"What about all that stuff you said to Constance about the price of vengeance?"

Smoke gently pulled his sleeve free from Blue's grasp. "There is always a price for vengeance. Some are not able to pay it fully. Constance is one of those people. I however am fully capable of paying the price, even the one I know I'll have to pay at the end."

"Let me come with you," Blue said a little louder than Smoke would have liked. Not that anyone had paid any attention to either of them anyway. "You saw me at my parents place; I am able to pay that price."

Smoke nodded. "Yes you are. But, I don't want you to have to pay that price. I want you to grow to become the woman you need to be. You have a future here; you can have a pretty decent life here."

"I'm not okay with that!" Blue shouted as tears filled her eyes.

Smoke sighed. They hadn't known each other long. A few days at most but she seemed to have grown on him as much as he seemed to have grown on her. "I'll be back," Smoke said as reassuringly as he could. "I promise you that. I'll tell you what, if you're leading some organization or the town when I get back, I will take you wherever you want to go. I do mean anywhere. But first I need you to be what you should be, the city builder."

Blue sniffled and nodded her head. She placed both hands over Smoke's ears and he did the same. "I won't let you down," she said with the makings of the beginning of a smile.

Smoke nodded again, turned around and walked away. He had every intention of returning to the town that would soon be called Penelope. He smiled as he heard the crowd get quieter and quieter in the distance. Before long he'd hit the wall, pay to cross it and he'd be on his way to Red City.

25

The underground was a frightening place for a woman by herself. Penelope thought about all the near misses she'd had in the past by crazed people wanting her body or to kill her in a fit of rage. Sometimes she'd been able to fight them off, other times she'd lose the fight and fall victim to the urges of others. In the end what happened to her didn't matter. She'd always know it happened, but the memories of the attacks would fade over time until nothing remained.

Once she had managed to become a lift driver she'd found the attacks came much less frequently. She'd been free to do as she wished and live in the underground in peace. Food and drink came to her more often and life became much more bearable. Still, she'd watch her back. Lift drivers were few and far between and it was difficult to train others how to turn the crank the right way to prevent gears from jamming or to build the necessary strength to bring groups of people up the lift at a consistent pace. Nonetheless, it didn't stop crazed psychopaths from attacking lift drivers. Those people were usually killed quickly or sent to the ninth below and the mad dash would begin to find another lift driver.

Now alone, Penelope found the underground to be even

more of a frightening place than before. While full of people Penelope knew what to expect from the underground. She knew to keep her guard up and be aware of her surroundings at all times. With the underground being devoid of all life she found herself on guard more than she thought necessary. She knew some people had chosen to stay behind and die with the underground. That was their choice. However, nothing would stop those people from killing one another. If someone came across her they'd likely attack.

On the way up there had been three of them. That would have been an effective enough deterrent for many attackers. Most didn't want to die and three against one was a fool's battle; especially when one had a revolving pistol on display. She still carried her revolving pistol; she refused to come down unarmed, especially with a destination as dangerous as the engine.

She turned the crank to the ninth below quickly. The trip down had been much quicker than she had anticipated. It seemed like no time at all. Although, she didn't have to escort two people who had been tortured to the point where walking was painful, that alone made her trip much quicker.

The ninth below was just as dark and grim as she'd remembered. It hadn't been long ago, but it seemed as if ages had gone by. So much had happened in the course of a few days and the fact that she had never intended to come back to the underground made the memory seem farther away than it actually was.

She walked past the small settlement and towards the barns. She remembered exactly where the lift was hidden and intended to walk directly toward it. She could easily spin the lock to the right combination and make her way downward, but that could lead to her capture and she wanted to be able to walk into the center of the works before detonating the atomic boomer. Before she broke into the engine she'd try and get their attention. "Hey engine people!" she shouted, "I want to talk to you!"

She waited for a response before continuing forward. As she

walked she continued to shout at random points.

"Hey engine people! How would you like to have the person who allowed Smoke Callahan and Blue Lang to escape?"

"Hey engine people! I'm immortal; you're going to want me!"

"Hey engine people! Don't pass this up; I'm not going to wait here forever!"

Once she reached the lift she sat and waited. She was done shouting and announcing herself. She closed her eyes and relaxed. If she hadn't been taken to the engine or at the very least greeted by engine personnel soon, she'd break in.

After several hours of waiting and a short nap Penelope knew she'd have to break in after all. She stood and cracked her back. The bones popped with her every move as she stepped to the combination lock in the wall. She spun the dial until the two doors opened. As she stepped in she could feel the boomer shift inside her and crush her lungs. Breathing wasn't something she needed, but it made things comfortable for her. She shook herself and leaned forward to allow air to fill her lungs. She scowled at the pain in her chest and watched as the doors closed and sealed her in the metal box propelled by nothing more than steam.

The thought occurred to her that someone would notice the lift coming downward and suspicions would be aroused. That was not something Penelope wanted, her plan would work best if she were either escorted to the center or managed to make it in and around the engine without being noticed. But, that was a problem that couldn't be avoided. There was one way in and out and nobody was coming to bring her down. Perhaps they smelled a trap, maybe they didn't hear her and had no idea she was even there. It was hard to say and she wouldn't know until she got there.

A thought did occur to her. When Robert had taken her and Smoke to the engine it was said there hadn't been anybody waiting at the bottom for them. Even going back up nobody even looked at them twice. With all the people who consistently go up and down from the engine there was the possibility there would be nobody there to greet her, she'd be able to go about her task unimpeded. There was no real way to know for sure until the doors opened.

    The lift ride was longer than she thought. The anticipation was the worst part of her situation. She was walking around the underground on her way to the engine that had enslaved the world with an atomic boomer hidden away in her abdomen. Once the boomer went off she'd cease to exist for a time. The thought of truly dying was a wonderful thought, but she knew her curse was a permanent affliction. The only being that could remove it was The Writer and it didn't seem to have any interest in helping her out. However, there was still the possibility The Writer would allow her to die after this act. Maybe this was what she had been intended for. Maybe everything she had endured through her six thousand years of life all would lead to this point. Where she saves the world. She smiled and hoped her death would be the thanks she'd get, considering the fact that if she survived and by the time she made it to the surface nobody would remember her. She wouldn't get as much as a thank you from the people.

    The doors of the lift opened and she stepped out to the Engine What Runs the World. As she looked around she saw the workers maintaining the engine. They all wore the same white work shirts and brown trousers. Many of them were stained with the oil and burned from steam from the boilers. She hated the thought that the innocent people would be dying along with the engine. Many didn't have a choice and were subjected to several tortures and brainwashing to become complaisant and willing to work the engine. They didn't deserve to die. Although, she didn't imagine any of them would leave willingly, even with the threat of death.

    Many of the workers outside the blast zone would die a horrid death. The radiation from the atomic boomer would cause their skin to fall off and for them to vomit blood among other horrible symptoms. The workers that would be close to her wouldn't know what had happened. She doubted they'd even hear the boomer detonate, while many within the blast zone would have time to react before the inferno ripped them to pieces. Still, the thought of innocent people who did not deserve death bothered her. It wasn't the first time she'd killed innocent people and if she survived she'd likely be the cause of many more innocent deaths.

She took in a deep breath and continued toward the center of the engine. The place was even more expansive than she had realized. She remembered her first look and how it had taken her breath away. She had never seen a contraption so great and intimidating. Even now she had to keep her mind from getting lost within the moving parts. It would be too easy to watch the cogs spin all day and see where they go and find the function and purpose of each piece both large and small.

"You look new here," a woman's voice said from behind her.

Penelope spun and faced the woman. She had a plain face with black hair and brown eyes. She gave Penelope a smile. "What gave me away?" Penelope asked with a forced smile.

"The way you look at the engine," the woman said. "It takes a few weeks for the mind to become immune to the engine's hypnotic ways. It's really easy to fall under its spell and walk off the platform."

"I wouldn't have walked off the platform," Penelope said with less of a smile, but maintaining a semblance of friendliness.

"A lot of people say that before walking off the ledge, or at least trying to," the woman said.

Penelope nodded, "Well thank you then. I don't think I'd walk into the gears, but I don't doubt people do it on the regular."

"Yeah," the woman replied. "They need to do better training

in that matter. So how'd they break you?" she asked out of nowhere.

It was a personal question. Penelope considered telling the woman off, but then she thought it was possible the question may have been commonplace with the locals. "I wasn't broken," Penelope said with surety, "I came in voluntarily."

"Oh good," The woman said. "I always enjoy hearing that people are willing to embrace the engine and what it does for the poor souls in the underground."

"What do you mean by poor souls?" Penelope asked.

The woman gave Penelope a strange look. "You obviously haven't gone through the orientation yet then. I can't believe they are allowing people in the engine without orientation now."

"Yeah," Penelope said. "Officer what's her face said we would do it tomorrow and let me loose in here. There has to be a better way about this."

The woman gave Penelope a smile. "Go easy on the officers. I didn't know it was an officer that was piloting you. They've been out of sorts and a little understaffed since the breakout."

"Breakout?" Penelope asked knowing exactly what she was talking about.

"Yeah, a man and a young girl managed to kill two officers and escape the engine. It's only a matter of time before the surface or even the tower comes down with their boomers and revolving pistols. I'll be honest, I'm actually quite frightened over what will happen."

"What makes you think I'm not one of them?" Penelope asked. "You've never met me, I could be anyone."

It wouldn't hurt if Penelope told someone who she was. She wouldn't waste time with details, but if the woman guessed who she was it would be nothing to start running down the path, or even to detonate the atomic boomer. She was too far in to fail now. "You aren't shooting anyone nor are you blowing anything up," the woman said. "I grew up in the fifth below. I know how the people from the underground work."

"I was a lift driver," Penelope said. The look on the woman's face said everything she needed to know. "It's true; I ran the lift between the seventh and eighth below."

"Wow," was all the woman said.

"Step away from our worker!" another woman's voice shouted.

Penelope turned and looked upon a woman with two male officers behind her. From Smoke's descriptions this had to be Portia Lincoln. "You must be Portia," Penelope said with a grin.

"I am," Portia admitted, "Who are you? Why are you here? How did you get here?"

"You remember Smoke right?" Penelope asked.

"Sure," Portia said with a sneer. "I also know what we did to his whore of a woman."

"Oh good, that was going to be my next question," Penelope said as she grabbed her thumb and readied the trigger to the atomic boomer that had been carefully implanted in her hand. "There are a lot of things I will allow to go. After all, I can't fix the world nor can I do anything to change the nature of people. But, I can't allow for the horrific mutilation of innocent people nor can I stand by and allow people to torture and brainwash other people to maintain their own ends. It's not right, Smoke will bear the scars from the needle chair for the rest of his life and I don't think Blue will ever be able to be touched in her woman parts without grimacing. This is for them and all those who have been brainwashed and killed for your engine."

Penelope pressed hard on her thumb and bit her lip as she

bent it backwards until the joint fell out of the socket. She screamed in agony before grinning. The countdown had begun. "What was that about?" Portia asked.

Penelope gripped her hand, "I don't think anyone has said this in almost two thousand years, but, boom motherfucker."

One of the officers pointed his revolving pistols at her and fired. The shot entered and exited her head moments before the boomer detonated. She never felt the explosion; neither did Portia, the officers or the kind woman she had been talking to. Had she been alive to feel the boomer rip her apart she may have smiled.

26

Dear Penelope,

It's been two years since you left for the engine. Cobble says that you should be coming back any day now so I decided to write you this little letter just so you know what you're getting into when you get back up here. A lot has changed and I figured it'd be nice to avoid any shocks.

First off, we destroyed the tower. We allowed for whoever lived in the tower to come down to the surface to live with us. There were a few families and individuals who chose to die with the tower. I'm not surprised but I'm still not pleased with this choice, I do understand the necessity of tearing the tower down as quickly as we could. If we had waited for the people to change their minds or forced them out they would have been a nuisance on our society. They could have gathered the people who used to live in the tower and recreate the class system. Or they could have found the boomers and our plan would have failed. The deaths weigh heavily on my head, but Cobble and everyone in the town is helping.

The town is getting really big. It wouldn't surprise me if this place became a city in the near future. I should let you know that everyone appreciates what you've done for us. I know there no real way to know for sure if the engine was destroyed, but in honour of your sacrifice the town decided to change its name (considering Tower's Shadow was no longer a relevant title). By a landslide majority we decided to name the town Penelope, after you. There really is no way we can repay you fully for what you've done for us and what you had to do to yourself to make it happen. People will remember you Penelope. Stories and songs will be recited for all time. So again, thank you for everything you've done for Smoke, Blue, the town and the world.

You only really knew Cobble for a short time, but he is now the elected law keeper. It's a bit of a far cry from what he used to do, but as he puts it, "This is a new world. New world for us means a new start. The Cartel is done. It was done as soon as the plans to come to the surface had become a reality. We're a community now and our main focus should be making sure everyone has what they need and being sure that everyone works for their share."

I really love that man and what he's standing for. We have a jail house now, although we don't use it for much these days. A great thing if you ask me.

Another one of the bigger changes was our anti-slavery laws. The Nagara were angry with the decision and many left the area. Blaze and a good number of his Nagara tried to overthrow the town but were quickly defeated. They were tried with treason against the town of Penelope and were executed. It wasn't a job anybody wanted, but it's the way it went.

Nobody has seen Smoke for quite some time. After the tower exploded he disappeared. Blue was the last to see him before he left. She says he's off to Red City to deal with the organization that first created the engine. Nobody knows if he's alive or dead. I'm hoping he's alive and on his way back. I think if anyone deserves a time to relax and enjoy life, even if it's only for a minute, it's him. But, I don't know how long that would last. Blue told me of his vow to Glass (who I was very upset to hear what had happened. She was an amazing woman and I very much liked her). I think he'll be searching his whole life to fulfill that vow.

Blue is doing well. She's been seeing this young man she said was once her families' servant. I've met him a few times, he's a nice boy. Nothing too exceptional, but nice and he's been very good to Blue. She's been doing some great things for the town. She's adapted the technology she wanted to use for the underground and made it work for the surface. We've been able to get our electricity back from the use of wind power. I don't know how exactly it all works. Blue tried explaining it to me at one point, but I just don't get it. I can see why the engine wanted her, if she had brought her wind machines to the surface or water machines to the underground it could have made the engine obsolete.

In fact, many of the scientists from the tower have been working nonstop to create technologies for our town. They've built bigger and better weapons to defend ourselves; they've built devices to help plant larger crops to prepare for the winter. Things are getting better and better every day. You really have to see it for yourself.

We never did find out who the informant for the engine was. We all assume it was Blaze and I think we will continue with that, but there are parts that don't quite add up. Like why did he help me by letting me know who killed my parents if he didn't want me breaking in? I don't know, It doesn't make sense for the informant to be Cobble or Homer either. There's a clue I'm missing, but I think I'm going to give it a rest regardless. The engine is gone, the tower is gone and life is good. Whoever it was, they're working for the town or dead.

There's not really much more to fill you in on. I hope you come back soon. You are well missed around here and we all eagerly await your return.

All the best wishes,

Constance Ibot

Constance placed the letter down on the table and folded it into a third of the size. She stuffed the onionskin paper into an envelope and sealed it with a dab of wax. She sighed as she removed the cork from the bottle of mulch liquor and took a long drink. The alcohol burned her throat as she took several more large drinks. She looked at the letter and smiled, the town she had described in the letter was a very real town. The outside world was bright and buzzing with industry and comradery. It was a shame she did what she could to lock herself away from it all.

Constance had never forgotten the faces of the family she had killed. The twisted faces of fear, the smell of the blood and the woman hoping she never slept again plagued her. She'd grown to hate herself and everything she'd done. She hated the tower, the bricks of the tower that now made up several buildings within the town. She hated Smoke for leaving and she hated Blue for living a great life. She believed if Smoke had never left she may have been alright, or at least better than she was now. She'd have had that person who understood and had been in her shoes more times than she dared to guess. But he had his own mission, one he may never return from.

She had promised Cobble that she wouldn't take her own life. A promise she wished she hadn't made. She loved Cobble with all her heart; he had made things easier on her. He'd been there during the nights she'd wake up and vomit because it was the only reaction her body had at the time. She'd woken in cold sweats and become a night thrasher. All the while Cobble had been there to help.

She stood from her desk and took a step outside. She eyed a couple children playing in the street before stepping out onto the street and toward what used to be the lift to the first below. The gears and chains had been maintained from the surface as best as the people could, but Constance wouldn't trust the lift to bring her down or back up. If the lift had broken while Penelope made her way back up she would have no way of letting anyone know what was going on. Constance and Blue had tried to come up with a way for Penelope to let them know she was on her way up. The problem was the distance between the first below and the surface. Shaking a string or a chain wasn't the best way to go about it. The movement would end well before it got to the surface. There was nothing they could do about it. Penelope would have to dig herself out if worse came to worse.

Constance looked at the steel covering Cobble had placed over the hole. A small slit large enough for a letter was all the space given to allow air into the underground. If the engine was destroyed no more air would be pumped into the underground. Though it was unlikely the fresh air would flow all the way to the ninth below or even so far as the sixth below. Once Penelope made it to the third below she'd be able to breathe easier and as soon as she made it to the first below she'd be able to breathe properly.

She dropped the letter into the opening and hoped it managed to make it to the bottom. If it got caught in a gear or on the wall it could get ground up as Penelope made her way upward. She wanted Penelope to know what she was getting into on the surface. What happened to the letter next was out of her hands. She took in a deep breath and sighed loudly. Whatever was to happen next was not for her to know, but she hoped it got better, because with the images within her head, things couldn't get much worse.

The sun began to set as Constance made her way back to the town of Penelope. Cobble would be waiting for her at the tavern with a dish of sausage and potatoes and a large mug of ale. What went on in her mind was horrific, but the knowledge Cobble was there for her and would be there for her the whole way set her at ease. Things would have been easier if Smoke had stayed, but she believed she would be better in time with Cobble than she ever would have been with the ex-detective.

She managed a smile as she looked at the setting sun. She stopped for a second to take in the colours before returning to town.

THE END

The Engine What Runs the World

Author's Note

Wait, that can't be the end. Can it? There are so many questions!

What happens with Smoke in Red City? What was The Apocalypse War all about? How did Penelope become immortal? What happened to the superhumans and supernatural creatures? Who the hell is Alex Cooper?

All those questions, and so many more will be answered. Every book I write will be in the same world, just at different points of history. Trust me when I say, this world has one hell of an interesting history.

Naturally, I'm not going to be writing anything in order. It's more of a matter of which ideas tickle my fancy at any given moment. It should help keep things as interesting for you as the reader as well me as The Writer.

Acknowledgements

There are so many people to thank for making this novel; a reality. First and foremost, I have to thank my Mum. She was my beta reader, she let me bounce ideas off her and she helped me get an editor. Not to mention everything else she's helped me out with in getting this book published. Seriously, I wouldn't be anywhere close to having this book out without her help.

I would like to thank my other beta readers, Kim Webber, Anastasia Shewchuk and Keri Daly. Your notes let me know where I needed work.

I would like to thank my editor Christine Dixon for doing an incredible job with my book.

I also want to thank my friends and family for their undying support and excitement for this book.

Made in the USA
Lexington, KY
02 July 2018